JOURNEY BEYOND INNOCENCE

By the same author

Flaming Janet
Shadow of Palaces
Marjorie of Scotland
Here Lies Margot
Maddalena
Forget Not Ariadne
Julia
The Devil of Aske
The Malvie Inheritance
The Incumbent
Whitton's Folly
Norah Stroyan
The Green Salamander
Tsar's Woman
Homage to a Rose
Stranger's Forest
Daneclere
Daughter of Midnight
Fire Opal
Knock At a Star
A Place of Ravens
This Rough Beginning
The House of Cray
The Fairest One of All
Duchess Cain
Bride of Ae
The Copper-Haired
  Marshal

Still Blooms the Rose
The Governess
Children of Lucifer
Sable for the Count
My Lady Glamis
Venables
The Sisters
Digby
Fenfallow
The Sutburys
Jeannie Urquhart
The Woman in the Cloak
Artemia
Trevithick
The Loves of Ginevra
Vollands
A Dark Star Passing
The Brocken
The Sword and the Flame
Mercer
The Silver Runaways
Angell & Sons
Aunt Lucy
O Madcap Duchess
The Parson's Children
The Man from the North

Journey Beyond Innocence

PAMELA HILL

ROBERT HALE · LONDON

© Pamela Hill 1994
First published in Great Britain 1994

ISBN 0 7090 5431 9

Robert Hale Limited
Clerkenwell House
Clerkenwell Green
London EC1R 0HT

The right of Pamela Hill to be identified as
author of this work has been asserted by her
in accordance with the Copyright, Designs and
Patents Act 1988.

Photoset in North Wales by
Derek Doyle & Associates, Mold, Clwyd.
Printed in Great Britain by
St Edmundsbury Press Ltd, Bury St Edmunds, Suffolk.
Bound by WBC Ltd, Bridgend, Mid-Glamorgan.

Part One

I

The late Lord Croom, who disliked both his heirs, had accordingly caused to be inserted in his will the most sadistic provision he could think of on behalf of either, to wit that neither twin should succeed to the fortune he himself had acquired in devious association with Old Q until a certain condition had been fulfilled. (He closely resembled that unsavoury nobleman and their tastes had been similar). The house of Fortune's Field itself was left equally to both brothers, which as the twins loathed each other would irritate everyone concerned while making it impossible, until the fortune was won, for either to reside anywhere else. Gilbert, despite his prowess at Waterloo and his acceptable marriage into the county, was an unabated lecher; Tobias, who had a philosophical turn of mind, had ruined his prospects by marrying an actress. Gilbert had produced a puling heir whose health gave cause for concern: Tobias had none. The title, for lack of proof one way or the other, would go to Gilbert and after him, to his young son Anstey if the latter survived, which was doubtful.

As was obvious to everyone who set eyes on them, the twins themselves were far from identical in appearance any more than in habit. Tobias was probably the younger. The whole thing had happened prematurely in the summer-house or, as the late Lady Croom (who after all had been closely involved) preferred to call it, the folly, with no witnesses. Tobias, sly as boots, with the mind of a

lawyer or even a diplomat, which he could have become
except for his marriage, the only rash act of his life,
resented the situation extremely but did not, as Gilbert
would have done if left to himself, give open battle. By
now Tobias's spouse, who had of course been the
notorious Tilly Loftus, lived separately in an upper part of
the west wing. Gilbert and his wife, with their wailing
infant and its nurse, inhabited the east. The Field was
large and sprawling enough to ensure that the two
households could remain fairly separate. This was as well,
as Beatrice, Gilbert's excessively well-bred wife, had
refused to receive Tilly from the beginning and, after
Gilbert himself was promoted to general's rank after
Waterloo, had not only put on airs but had got herself
pregnant by him after fifteen years of marriage. Return
from the war had of course called for a certain extra
celebration. It was a pity poor Anstey was such a miserable
result.

Altogether the prospects roused by the terms of the will
were diverting: old Lord Croom lay enjoyably in bed
after his first seizure, thinking of possible ways to make the
situation even worse. However a second attack carried him
off on a rainy evening in September of 1816. In the
unlikely event of his and Old Q's meeting peaceably in the
hereafter, the rapscallion pair would be able to compare
notes and watch, with detached enjoyment, what was
happening next. The Croom fortune would, in fact, go to
the first of the brothers proved, without doubt and before
witnesses, to have seduced the schoolmistress at Fortune's
End, the village four miles off. She was a lady of
thirty-seven named Miss Ellen Shearwater. There had
been a time when the old lord, then a mere sprig of
forty-eight, had tried to seduce her himself, but as her
virtue was impregnable had not succeeded. His failure had
festered in his mind as few things did, and the thought
that not one but both of his sons would without doubt
attempt to retrieve his honour in the whole matter pleased
him remarkably.

Miss Shearwater had red hair. This, apart from her
impregnability and a cultivated taste for botany, was her
only notable feature. She had held her appointment now

for many years without a breath of scandal, as the latter would have meant that the former was instantly terminated by her employer, the board of governors. In appearance Miss Shearwater was, these days, unexciting, by this time had porcelain teeth accordingly, and wore metal-rimmed spectacles by habit. It was in fact a formidable assignment, only spurred on by a certain smugness of expression adopted by Miss Shearwater herself as she sat each Sunday, upright and corseted, in her pew in church beside her mountainous old mother. It was as though, above the sound of hymns, prayers and the sermon, she still recalled the time the old lord had thought it worth his while to raise his quizzing-glass when she had first arrived, to have a good look; and congratulated herself that she had resisted all improper attempts that followed.

Gilbert and Tobias, the will having been read after their sire's moderately attended funeral, promptly evolved their separate plans of campaign. Both were in debt.

The General's plan – it was some time before anybody got used to calling him Lord Croom – was simple. It resembled that used by custom on the housemaids, whom he bowled over with experimental ease in a kind of *droit de seigneur* before marrying them off, if necessary, to the local tenantry with a small reduction of rent as a *pourboire* and wedding present. He was a fine upstanding, if stocky, man of military appearance, his handsome countenance embellished with pepper-and-salt whiskers which would early turn white: he considered himself, with some reason, irresistible to women. All he had to do, he told himself, was to slip Miss Shearwater a small glass of brandy to render her a trifle more amenable, as well as one to himself to blur his own perceptions. All of that would have to happen after he got her inside the house. How to do this without arousing the good lady's suspicions – or, more to the point, those of Beatrice – took him some time to evolve, like any other campaign: one could not suddenly say to a woman who'd taught in the village for God knew how long to come to take tea at the Field, let alone brandy. If Beatrice could have been induced to co-operate about the tea, that would have been one thing, but her principles wouldn't allow: at least, Gilbert Croom supposed not.

Luck however favoured the General in that, on an ensuing Sunday, Miss Shearwater's mother was absent from church: the thin upright figure sat in its pew alone, bonnet-strings neatly tied over a cap which concealed the still beguiling red hair. Afterwards, at the lych-gate where as usual everyone assembled to watch the squire's party emerge, General Lord Croom approached the schoolmistress and raised his tall hat – he was out of uniform by now – respectfully.

'I trust, ma'am, that your mother it well? One missed seein' her today as is the rule.' It was in fact impossible not to notice the old lady, who resembled a vast black tent about to subside. Miss Shearwater having replied respectfully that dearest Mama was confined to bed with nothing more serious than a cold "but at her age one has to be careful" prepared to withdraw, but the General, as briefly at Hougoumont and the night he had at last dosed Beatrice with enough champagne after Waterloo, seized his advantage.

'I've been wonderin' for some time about a certain book in my library. Might be a first edition or somethin', never know. Care to come and have a look at it, hey? Schoolmarms are bound to be full of book-learnin' or they wouldn't be where they are.' He finished, despite himself, with a broad wink, which caused Miss Shearwater, a lady whom her profession had long since taught never under any circumstances to quail, to bridle slightly. The General meantime barked out a time when it would be suitable for her to come, and Ellen Shearwater declined primly.

'It is most kind, Lord Croom, and I should be interested to see your edition; but it so happens that on Saturday I am taking the children on a botanical expedition to the Near Wood to examine the turning leaves, and shall not return before having to hasten home to Mama. Perhaps on some other occasion it will be convenient for us both.'

This fired the General: the woman had spirit, after all. He finally arranged to send the carriage for her on the following Sunday afternoon, at half past three. An enquiry as to whether Mama was to accompany her daughter was firmly quashed. 'Come, come, my dear, you're well past chaperonage.' He did not intend this to be ungallant, rather in fact to reassure. Beatrice came up at this point from where she had been enquiring about the health of some of the tenantry, and firmly took his arm. She bowed pleasantly to Miss Shearwater, of whose identity (but nothing else regarding the matter) she was aware, and they departed to the waiting carriage. It had already occurred to the General that in the matter of his wife's mild acquaintance with the schoolmistress perhaps danger lay: but danger, after all, was his chosen profession. It was as well Beatrice hadn't been present at the readin' of the will; little Anstey had had croup as usual, and she had preferred to be in attendance in the nursery. In any case, with the fortune garnered by way of Old Q at stake, Beatrice could be put in her place in the event, as had happened before.

Beatrice Croom, *née* Delahaye, came of so ancient a family that her blood was rather thin. She was a faded blonde with a long nose which constantly needed polite blowing, and was given to jabbing gestures like those of a nervous stork. Her passion, if so colourful a term could be applied to her by now, was correctness in all things. If some matter happened to be incorrect, one ignored it until it went away. This had happened frequently in the instances of the housemaids; and the regrettable Tilly, unmet with back at the house, was another such instance. One simply ignored her existence, as by now so did Tobias, who had been known to dine with them lately on occasion. One understood that his wife – unfortunately, the marriage had taken place without doubt and Tobias at the time had been infatuated – had become addicted to strong liquor. That situation was one Beatrice likewise preferred to ignore; the same criterion applied to her husband's infidelities, many of which had without doubt taken place while he was away at the war in the Peninsula. That accounted for the fact, of course, that after so many years of marriage there was only dear little Anstey, whose conception Beatrice preferred not to remember. It was true that, besides recurrent croup, the dear little fellow had a constant rash, which the doctors said would go away when he grew older. The whole thing however made Gilbert rather impatient; he expected everyone to enjoy health as rude as his own. Lady Croom's pallid eye – there seemed nothing about her that had not faded with time – sought her husband's solid figure as it clambered into the carriage after handing her in, but avoided his grey gimlet gaze; it had the uncomfortable property of making one feel quite naked.

The coachman jangled the reins and the lordly carriage bowled on its way home to Fortune's Field, with a final salute by its occupants to the vicar, who had come out just too late. The Honourable Tobias Croom had not attended church: he seldom did.

The following Sunday came, and on emerging from the carriage at the east door of Fortune's Field – how impressive a place, built, or rather rebuilt, in the classical style, with a portico, wings, offices, stables and the enchanting little folly! – Miss Shearwater looked as usual, unperturbed in her plain dark gown, frilled cap beneath the bonnet, and formidable black umbrella. On being asked by the footman to divest herself of the latter item she refused. 'I shall only be staying for a matter of moments,' she stated firmly.

The General, emerging from his study, overheard these words and was depressed, and still more so by the schoolmistress's appearance, not that he need have expected it to be different. He nevertheless attempted to usher Miss Shearwater into the smaller drawing-room to partake of a small glass of something to warm her. 'Revives the spirits,' he said curtly; he felt as if he were about to order a regiment to charge, and could certainly do with a drink himself.

'I thank you, Lord Croom, but I never, under any circumstances, touch strong liquor, and certainly not at this hour of the day.' This qualifying statement contained much disapproval, expressed also from behind Miss Shearwater's spectacles. He noted that her eyes were pale green. Having asked her permission to fortify himself, they both became seated briefly; Gilbert found that he had no idea what to say to her. It was different with little girls one could chuck under the chin. For the first time in his life, and it included campaigns in India, Spain, Portugal and, more recently, Belgium, the General was feeling nervous. The sensation almost diverted him. To be scared of a middle-aged spinster! She ought, in a way, to consider herself lucky. The General finished his brandy and said rather helplessly, 'Well, ma'am, we'd best go up to the library.'

As they neared the first landing, where the library was situated, Gilbert tried to reassert his authority by giving Miss Shearwater, under pretence of helping her upstairs, the premonitory squeeze of the upper arm indulged in by hopeful males in general. Miss Shearwater twitched away like a bullet shot from a gun.

'I can contrive the stairs quite easily, thank you, Lord Croom. Where is this possible first edition?'

He led her into the library, which was lined with titles, and at first she expressed animation and interest at their richness, even becoming enthusiastic enough to try to remove a volume which particularly interested her from the shelves, to take a look at it. The lot came away from the wall and the General guffawed. 'You've spotted it,' he remarked. 'M'father wasn't a reader by any means, but in those days it was fashionable to have a library, or at any rate to look like havin' it. He got some feller in London to gild and print titles and put 'em all in at once as a false wall or two. Looks well, don't you think?' He then advanced and gave a further squeeze not only to Miss Shearwater's arm, but to such other parts of her anatomy as he could reach despite the corsets. 'Come, let's not waste time, m'dear,' he said, with his arm about her. 'Now I've got you here, let me say how greatly I have always admired your looks in church. Fine woman, wasted on schoolteachin'; expect you lead drab lives. Let me liven it up a bit, hey? What about a kiss and cuddle up here? Nobody will see.' This was of course a lie; he had servants ready posted to give the necessary evidence in the event, but it appeared, most lamentably, that there was to be no such thing. Miss Shearwater bridled and backed like a recalcitrant mare, wielding her umbrella and raising her considerable voice.

'You are a most unprincipled man, like your father. He tried exactly the same thing. I am not one of your servants, Lord Croom, and I must ask you to unhand me immediately, and to let me return at once in your carriage; I can hardly be expected to walk home after this outrage. You should be ashamed of yourself, and I can only assume that your advancing years are causing you to behave as disgracefully as you have just attempted to do. Fortunately, as a woman of principle, I am armed against such assaults. I can assure you that I will not permit you to advance one foot further. First edition, indeed! Kindly direct me to your equipage, in which I was misguided enough to come. This incident will not be referred to by me again, and I assume that what shreds of honour you have left will induce a similar silence in yourself.'

The umbrella was poised, and could quite easily jab him in an awkward place: besides, the game was lost, and if Beatrice should overhear it would be particularly unfortunate; there had been signs – only signs, mind you, no more – that there might perhaps be a successor to Anstey who didn't have constant croup. As for the listening servants, he'd been made ridiculous by this shrilling virago; best get rid of her with such dignity as remained. One wouldn't have thought she would make a threat to jab one in quite that place: most improper of her, surprisin'.

Miss Shearwater having turned her back and marched out of the library, the General followed, not too abject. He probably couldn't have gone on with it; and there were, after all, the rents, and Beatrice had brought along a little something on their marriage which wasn't yet quite spent. Altogether the whole thing was perhaps a relief. He would not, however, tell Tobias himself, although that feller would certainly hear in his usual prescient way, never movin' from his armchair at the other end of the house. One would deny him the satisfaction of knowin' it was his turn to win the money, that is if he could; the end would be that it would probably sit in the bank till everyone about the place was dead except Anstey. He, Gilbert Croom, had been particularly stung by the remark about his advancing years, as if he was finishin' the course when he was nothin' of the kind. Tobias, after all, was the same age as oneself. Let him try what he could do. It would be entertainin' to hear about it in due course, if anyone ever did; Tobias was damned mysterious, had always been from a boy.

Tobias had of course heard about Gilbert's failure immediately, as Gilbert had guessed he would. He himself attached less importance to the spinster's initial refusal of persuasive brandy than to the General's expected crass approach. Anyone but a military man – Tobias himself had never had ambitions in this direction – would have known in advance that a bookish and independent female of mature years was a different proposition from any little housemaid or, for that matter, tasty young peasants behind the lines of Torres Vedras. He himself had never shared his brother's indiscriminate tastes and could easily resist most women unless they threw themselves at his head, which however tended to happen. His marriage to Tilly, which mistake still caused Tobias unrevealed pain, was long over in all but name. At times he recalled the rash young man he had then been with some incredulity; by now, he was quite different; it had been a year's madness: for once, he had been deceived.

He surveyed himself in his pier-glass now with a certain satisfaction. Less openly handsome than the General, and lacking the title – this accolade he did grudge Gilbert, the decision had been arbitrary and unfair, no doubt influenced by his own disgrace over Tilly and the fact that Beatrice was, after all, a Delahaye – he could still make heads turn in any dressing-room. The understandable confusion of dear Mama – one hardly remembered her – at the birth had caused him and his brother somewhat to resemble the tale of Jacob and Esau; the hairy twin and the smooth, who in the beginning had grasped the other's leg and in the end, his birthright. Miss Shearwater, perhaps, could be regarded as the mess of pottage; after all Gilbert had had his chance.

Tobias made no open declaration to her until well into the new year, allowing time for the General's earthy approaches to fade in her memory if such things ever could: no doubt she had a retentive mind. Then Tobias made discreet enquiries, by way of the servants, as to where and when the next botanical expedition with the village school, probable by spring, would take place. Being informed, he set out on the day in question on a well-groomed bay. He himself, as usual having paid great regard to his toilet, was spick-and-span, buck-skin breeches snowy as his linen, coat well-cut by his London tailor, boots polished to a degree although, as his valet knew, there was not the slightest need to waste champagne. Tobias's thick grey hair – it had turned that colour early – was brushed to high fashion, a low-crowned hat perched on top. His slim person contrasted with the stockiness of his brother's, which was unfair to Gilbert as Tobias took much less exercise. However what he did, he did well or, like Louis XIV, not at all. His suave charm flattered women whoever they were, and of whatever age: and a telling look from under his hooded eyelids proved to watchers, if they had been in any doubt, that Tobias Croom knew his world better than most. He also had beautiful hands: women liked him to touch them.

It was Saturday, of course. Miss Shearwater was discovered in a wood full of new-sprung bluebells, early because of the clement weather. She had plucked a long limp leaf and was explaining to her assembled horde – they were not very bright, the best girls having been kept at home by their mothers to help with the ironing for tomorrow, and the boys preferring to play football on the village green – that monocotyledonous plants had parallel veins, whereas those which came out at a more competitive time of year had others of different varieties, created at a later stage during the third day mentioned in the Book of Genesis, when God had no doubt had time to diversify His plans. The children stood and picked their noses or sucked juicy bluebell stems to see what they tasted like, then threw them away surreptitiously. It was pleasant enough in the wood, with the pale sun slanting down between the grey beech trunks, and birds' eggs to steal afterwards. They'd brought their bread and margarine with them and were prepared to make a day of it; might as well. The advent of a gentleman on the satin-smooth horse diverted them and one, a boy who was there for some reason, darted across to hold its head and hope for sixpence. Miss Shearwater, frowning a little at the signs of increased inattention, turned her head. Tobias slid down from the saddle, advancing and extending one fine well-kept hand.

'My dear Miss Shearwater, I had no idea of this unexpected pleasure: I have but lately returned from London.' The last part of the statement was true. He led her aside a little. 'I have been meaning,' he said in a low voice, 'to apologise to you for the disgraceful treatment accorded you by my brother, of which I only learned recently. He has these lapses, I fear.' He raised his eyelids and looked at her with the look that proved he knew the world and that, of course, so did she. 'Had I known at the time,' he added, 'I myself would have made a point of being present to protect you. Alas that one only hears these things too late!' He noticed that she was not looking at all pleased, was doubtless wondering if the matter had become one of general gossip, and changed the subject deftly. 'I see,' he said, 'that you are greatly interested in botany, as I am myself. I too cherish monocotyledons for their courage, likewise fungi. Are you interested in the mysteries of those? There is one which can, if cooked in milk, taste like chicken stew, they say, but I never myself essayed it; such a pastime is somewhat dangerous unless one knows precisely which variety is which.'

Miss Shearwater, flattered despite herself – any appeal to her knowledge always gratified her, although she had been somewhat taken aback to learn that her expedition to Fortune's Field, and its disgraceful conclusion, should have become common property – made the little bob she normally did to her betters, and had in fact done at the outset to General Lord Croom, though certainly not on parting. She then replied, expertly and at length, on the subjects of *Amanita muscaria* and *Hyphonoma fasciculare*. 'It is true that even the wild mushroom itself is something of a risk,' she admitted. 'So many varieties of toadstool resemble it that I myself have never dared to cook any, although I have found them frequently in the fields.' The reference to cooking was, perhaps, vulgar; she blushed a trifle, which became her.

Tobias however merely agreed that it was best to be prudent on such matters. Neither of them had referred again to the General's lapse. Tobias himself was wily enough not to obtrude his presence further on that occasion, but said he trusted that they might meet again on some similar expedition with her little party of followers, when he would show her what he suspected might be a dictyophol. 'I am, however,' he said, reverting to low-voiced confidence, 'somewhat unwilling to reveal its whereabouts to these young people. It is very beautiful and they might, with the best of intentions, pick it and spoil it. As you will know, it has a phalange somewhat resembling a bridal veil of lace, and is seldom found.'

Miss Shearwater was greatly tempted by the sound of the dictyophol, and discounted any flutter which might have arisen in her breast at the mention of a bridal veil, it having been assumed from the beginning that she would never wear one. She blurted out, with an impulse especially foreign to her since the episodes of both Lords Croom, father and son, 'If perhaps we might bring Mama instead of the children –' then faltered; it had perhaps been a forward suggestion to make. But Mr Croom was smiling, as if she had said exactly the right thing; what an attractive smile he had, almost puckish!

'Let us bring your mother indeed, and make a picnic of it,' he said gallantly. 'That need put neither of you to any trouble at all; my fellows will see to everything.'

Miss Shearwater felt her internal flutterings increase quite notably; it would be delightful, she told herself, to see a dictyophol, and if dearest Mama was present there could be no question of impropriety. As it was, the dear children were *not* the most stimulating of company, and she had very little other; and this was a perfect gentleman, quite different in manner from his lamentable father and brother. There could be no ulterior motive in his suggestion, which had after all, come to think of it, been her own. A picnic! She hadn't had one since she was a child. She would look forward to the event immensely; if only Mr Croom didn't forget!

Mr Croom remembered. A polite note of invitation, despatched by hand, arrived shortly at the schoolhouse, asking if it would suit the convenience of Mrs and Miss Shearwater to join him and a few friends on a certain day (it had, of course, to be a Saturday) either on the following week or the one after? After that he feared the dictyophyl might not be at is best, but the main thing, after all, was the pleasure of the two ladies' company. A carriage would of course be at their disposal at the door, at the time and on the date arranged.

Miss Shearwater, acting on behalf of her mother who was in fact a good deal past answering letters or anything else, wrote a happy reply to accept the earlier date. How different from the crude, inconsiderate ways of General Lord Croom! *He* hadn't even given her a choice.

The day in question arrived, and thankfully was fine. Miss Shearwater's chief anxiety, overcoming her even while she corrected the children's three R's during the week, had been lest it rain. The carriage arrived, and she was glad to see that Mr Tobias himself had not accompanied it; he was always tactful, mindful of one's reputation, and would arrive quite separately on horseback; that went without saying. The grandeur of the equipage itself overawed Miss Shearwater no little. It was not the usual carriage employed by the family for church, but in fact the very coach in which the first lord's father, not himself a peer, had long ago attended the coronation of George III. It reposed as a rule in the coach-house at Fortune's Field and had never been dispensed with, being used now and again for attendances at funerals. Tobias had forseen that it might conveniently house the old lady. Moreover, it contained two sizeable hampers and an ice-bucket.

Two footmen – they wore the wine-coloured livery familiar from outside church – sprang down from front and rear to assist Miss Shearwater and her ponderous old mother up the step, the last-named operation being the equivalent of using ropes and pulleys. Both ladies wore black, the elder in a broad mushroom hat to shade her from the rays of the sun. She had long been past speech, expression or the realisation of wherever she happened to be or why. The coach drove off.

Trundling on – it was certainly safer not to go too fast –

they took the direction of what, come to think of it, Miss Shearwater, whose perceptions were acute and who in course of time had explored every aspect of the surrounding countryside she could reach on foot, recognised as the Nether Wood. She had been there often, knew it thoroughly, and in any existing recollection of plant and animal life contained in it had none of anything whatever resembling a dictyophol. A moment's unworthy suspicion that this might be, as it were, another wall of false books was almost instantly dispelled. That true gentleman, Mr Tobias Croom, had after all no reason (that she knew of) to play elaborate tricks on her; as his brother had ungallantly remarked, she was past the need of a chaperone; but, in any case, Mama was present. It was also possible that a dictyophol was only a briefly appearing phenomenon. She must enquire more particularly about its habits: she preferred to verify all facts before reflection.

They reached a spot where Mr Croom himself, accompanied by a bland middle-aged gentleman introduced as Mr Lyons, were already walking their horses. The sight of so respectable a companion caused Miss Shearwater's doubts, if any remained, to fade. She had no means of knowing that Mr Lyons was the Croom family lawyer, fetched by prior arrangement from Norwich. The two ladies having been assisted tenderly out, the horses were then taken care of; and the *al fresco* contents of the two hampers revealed and spread out with astonishing speed by the two footmen on the spring grass. Miss Shearwater forbore to suggest that they might go first of all to look at the dictyophol; she was really most anxious to see it, but this luncheon looked delicious; in fact the whole thing had a magnificence worthy of Versailles before the Revolution. A snowy linen cloth, already spread, bore equally snowy laundered napkins, likewise elegant glasses in a Greek key pattern (she herself must of course decline any intoxicating liquor and would ask for a glass of water at once) which sparkled invitingly in the sun. The bucket of ice contained narrow-necked bottles which were regarded with equal narrowness by Miss Shearwater, but dearest Mama suddenly remarked, from the provided stool on which she had been thoughtfully placed, 'Heh,

heh'. This put rather a different complexion on the matter; perhaps she herself would after all indulge in a very little, and Mama could of course have as much as she liked.

The feast was by now fully apparent; hothouse grapes from the Field conservatories; freshly baked bread rolls and small curls of butter on a fluted plate. Silver gleamed everywhere; a subtle cheese appeared, whose blue veins, as Tobias assured the ladies, had been injected at careful intervals with port during its year's maturing process in the Field dairy. This statement for some reason banished Miss Shearwater's lingering hesitations. It would be churlish to refuse anything at all. She suddenly decided not to. This was a most particular and delightful occasion, one she would remember for the rest of her life, and she would give herself to it fully, without let.

She began to listen with pleasure to the informed conversation of Mr Lyons, whom she found very agreeable and who appeared interested in her work. At some time, she watched with admiration the deft way in which Mr Croom's fine-boned hands – truly, the hands of a gentleman born – carved the cold fowl, with suitably sharpened silver accoutrements. Did he ever do anything badly? Miss Shearwater almost asked him, but desisted out of natural diffidence; she was, after all, a favoured guest, and must on no account presume. She glanced at Mama, a black amorphous heap on her stool among cushions, and asked if she were quite comfortable. There was no reply, which meant that things were again as usual. Meantime the footman, one of them, was decanting a bubbling golden liquid into the key-pattern glasses. 'Pray, dear Mr Croom, a little water instead, please, if that is convenient. I am *not* in the habit of drinking intoxicating liquor.' It was, she admitted, a different way of saying what she had already said to his lordship; but then the situation was hardly similar.

'Dear lady, everyone knows that this beverage is quite innocuous if a little water is added, especially when taken with food,' replied Tobias smoothly. 'I anticipated your request, in fact, and have brought a water-bottle with me for the purpose. I respect your position, and greatly admire your prudence.'

She watched, gratified and lulled, while he poured a clear fluid from a small bottle into her glass, having previously put in a lump of sugar. He then topped the whole thing up himself with champagne. Mama meantime was slurping away at her already twice-filled glass; there was no doubt that she was enjoying herself. Mr Croom, also meantime, pointed out that the lemon ices, prepared from their own ice-house at Fortune's Field, would melt soon in the sun, and that it was advisable to eat and drink fairly quickly if they wanted to enjoy them at their best before the cheese. All the time Mr Lyons continued with his informed talk. Miss Shearwater could not afterwards remember what it had been about. She was already giving over to a strange and creeping delight. At first, it was true that the addition of water had made what she was drinking taste a little odd, perhaps, but that was her own fault, and the sugar helped. Recalling history, Queen Elizabeth had been used to mingle her wine with water; there was a comparison one should be proud of. Miss Shearwater would by now have raised her glass in an unintentional toast, but found it being done already by Mr Tobias.

'To the ladies!' And they all drank, even Mama, which on reflection Miss Shearwater realised should not have happened; one stayed quite still, she had read somewhere, while one's health was drunk. She was in fact beginning to feel rather reckless. It was true, as somebody or other had said lately, that her life had been drab; she was unused to such manners, such experiences, such delightful and interesting people. It wasn't any good to look back. Tears started in her eyes by the advent of the cheese; she found she couldn't remember tasting it. Mr Tobias came presently and pressed grapes upon her and Mama, then filled her own glass with more of the wine and water and sugar. The water was almost finished, and so was the wine. The ices had been delicious, melting in one's mouth. Miss Shearwater put her tongue under her false teeth to loosen them a little; cold, cold ice, cold champagne, and a fire lit nevertheless somewhere inside her; she would remember this day always, always.

'The dictyophol, before the sun leaves it,' murmured the Honourable Tobias Croom. He gave a broad wink to Mr

Lyons which Miss Shearwater naturally did not see, and that gentleman began to move cautiously in the direction of the wood, but quite separately.

Miss Shearwater found herself crossing the grass towards the woods on Mr Tobias' arm. A faint memory of compunction came for dear Mama, left behind without much more champagne in her glass. Somebody ought to stay with her, she was unfit to walk, and if anything happened ... oneself also was unfit to walk, it was as if she were being half carried, half leaning on Mr Tobias, which was however very agreeable, such a gentleman ... the bluebells would be past their best ... dictyophol, a veil like lace ...

'Only a little further now,' breathed Tobias gently.

He guided Miss Shearwater's lurching form to where a large grey beech tree reared, its leaves unfurled enough by now to disguise the watching forms of one lawyer and two footmen. While Mr Lyons took down his deposition, Tobias took down Miss Shearwater's drawers, aware of mild surprise that these were still made of flannel for protection despite the clement weather. He had by then, naturally, laid her with care in a horizontal position. She had made no resistance at all. What followed was not entirely silent; the quiet of the woods was presently also broken by certain agreeable cooing noises on the part of Miss Shearwater, which not only disguised the sound of the notary's scribbling pencil but would certainly give the lie to any attempt of Gilbert's (or for that matter of Miss Shearwater's later on) to try to prove coercion in the matter. Tobias permitted himself to celebrate a little; everything had gone strictly according to plan. The prospect of the fortune acquired by way of Old Q shimmered, and would enable him to be generous as to any untoward event. It was also advisable to obtain as much proof positive of this one as could be acquired, by every means in one's power.

Afterwards, when he and a flushed but amenable (she would remember nothing immediately of what had happened) Miss Shearwater emerged from the wood, it

was to find the coachman, who had stayed meantime with
the old lady, perturbed. 'I think, sir, she's either out cold
or else no longer with us,' he observed truly. The latter
assumption proved to be the case; old Mrs Shearwater, in
the middle of having the time of her life, had chosen to die
the happiest of deaths, swilling the last of the champagne
round her antique tongue and palate. Tobias thoughtfully
laid Miss Shearwater down again much, but not
altogether, as she had recently lain beneath the beech tree,
and was able to tell her, when at last she came to herself,
that she had fainted at news of the demise of her mother
and could doubtless recall nothing for the shock. As for
the rest, it was possible there might after all be nothing
more to it; surely, at thirty-seven last birthday – he knew
he had however, for some moments, laid aside a prudence
he now habitually resumed.

  'Go to the vicarage,' he said to one returned footman,
'and tell the clergyman, his wife, and her maid, to expect
Miss Shearwater very shortly, as her mother is dead and
she requires sympathetic attention.' The man rode off on
Tobias' horse; Miss Shearwater herself was bundled into
the coach by himself and the lawyer; the other footman
was left meantime to guard the corpse and clear away the
picnic débris; and everything was, with certain mild
deviations, according to plan. Tobias himself rode the
other horse home, Mr Lyons having accompanied the still
swooning schoolmistress to the vicarage in the funeral
coach. Appearances had been preserved at all costs. The
whole thing was highly satisfactory, perhaps to all parties.
Miss Shearwater's spectacles had remained, despite
everything, as usual on her nose.

Miss Shearwater came to herself at last to find a stone hot
water bottle at her feet, and herself unlaced and in bed in
the vicarage; she knew where she was because the vicar's
wife, Mrs Evitt, a kindly soul, was quietly seated beside her
sewing a summer petticoat. On seeing Miss Shearwater
blink herself awake she set the sewing aside, came to the
bed, took the schoolmistress's hand, and gently told her
her mother had died quite suddenly on the picnic. 'My
husband will see to everything,' she said. 'Do not trouble

yourself, my poor dear.' The old lady's vast corpse lay, in fact, already on the kitchen table downstairs, the doctor having been, and the undertakers sent for. Mr Lyons, who had brought this poor soul here in the Croom coach, had been most kind and practical, going back afterwards to do what he could.

Miss Shearwater knew that she ought to manifest some kind of grief, and did her best, not that poor Mama had been anything but a burden for a very long time; also, warring in her own mind was a memory that would never be permitted entirely to rise to the surface, so alien was it from anything she had ever known. Memories of lemon ice cream, port in the cheese, and so on were neither here nor there; or, had she known, was ninety per cent clear aqua vitae, which still made her head ache after mixing it repeatedly with champagne. It almost shut out the other, unaccountable inner pain which wasn't, by now, pain at all, but a pleasure to which she must never admit even within herself; whatever had happened, one must of course forget it immediately. She said aloud 'Poor Mama has been with me for a very long time,' which on the face of it was a foolish statement; then closed her eyes and thought how after all, without Mama, oneself was free; free perhaps to think of greater things than remaining merely the village schoolmistress at Fortune's End, though what she was otherwise to become would take a little more time to formulate than was available at present. Certainly she hadn't – now she remembered, it was usually found in foreign parts – managed to encounter the dictyophol with its lace veil: at least, she couldn't remember seeing any, but it might have been one more thing she'd forgotten; one more thing.

II

Gilbert and Tobias, for once in relative amity, travelled together to Norwich to ratify the clauses in the old lord's will. Gilbert was not only prepared to admit, from the evidence, that the best man had won, but hoped as a result to touch his brother for a *quid pro quo*, which was however smoothly refused to ensure that things went on as they had begun. Thereafter conditions worsened again, especially after a letter came to say that Beatrice had suffered a miscarriage, that the doctor had said there ought to be no more of that kind of thing for the present, or the future, and that poor little Anstey almost certainly had worms as well. The General went dolefully home, and Tobias, having completed the business to his satisfaction, travelled on to stay at his St James's club and consider his future.

He intended bringing lawyer Lyons to the capital from Norwich, setting the man up as his own agent in a vacancy which had occurred at Middle Temple. Lyons was able, trustworthy, and married; it remained to persuade his wife that selling the provincial legal practice and moving to the capital was wise and desirable. Tobias however had several projects in mind now that he had the money to embark on them. Meantime, he paid his outstanding debts but would by no means be responsible for Gilbert's.

He also arranged to rent a small flat in Half Moon Street; although everyone was in the country at this season or else about to go there, it was useful to maintain a base in town. Tobias chose servants, and having done so left them to see to such matters as concerned his general comfort. He bought a few articles, knowledgeably, which it would be a pleasure to look at; an interesting Louis XV gilt mirror, a small buhl desk, a great four-poster which had to be reliably assembled and then hung with curtains fashioned from material of his choice. Lying in the bed at last, he felt lonely.

Over the next few days he was to be seen walking about the half-empty capital with his lean elegant stride, showing for once the nervous energy which consumed him even while he sat at Fortune's Field in his armchair. He was never devoid of plans. He could have visited, at their country houses, great hostesses he knew; old Betsy Melbourne, her daughter Emily Cowper at Panshanger, the Hollands God knew where. He recalled how one day some time before, while visiting Lord Egremont at Petworth – it must after all have been some years back – he had encountered there an uncommunicative painter whose very surliness had intrigued him; the man had talent, which was interesting also, and worked mostly in London down at the wharves. They had had one thing in common which had emerged in course of such talk as he had contrived to elicit from the man, who was named Turner; they had been born in the same year. Turner had then vouchsafed the information that he was generally to be found at the Ship and Bladebone in Limehouse Reach. It might, now one was in a position to do so, be possible to buy one or two paintings if the painter would sell; he showed a curious unwillingness to do so as a rule, hoarding what he wanted to keep and attempting to charge an extortionate price in order to drive hopeful buyers away. At the same time, perhaps for this reason, he was personally mean to a degree. It was a combination that diverted Tobias, himself inclined to be close-fisted except when spending money brought him more, as had happened by means of the memorable picnic. He recalled the episode now with detached amusement. At worst, the schoolmistress had been educated better than she knew.

In search of diversion, he at last called a hackney and instructed the driver to follow the Thames. He himself lay back comfortably enough in the vehicle, smelling the acrid floor-straw and idly watching the horse's moving rump, the occasional flick of the driver's whip to dispel the flies that were already beginning to be troublesome, and now

and again turning his head to survey the grey eternal
river. Its presence always reminded him of early days, of
Ranelagh, of his marriage: and he wanted to forget his
marriage. It should never have taken place.

The Thames was thronged as usual with coal-boats,
wherries, barges, the passenger-ferry plying to and from
World's End. The tide was going out, and hopeful
mudlarks were wading out already into the shallow water,
their bodies black from constant immersion in the cast-up
silt. They would grub there while they could for whatever
passing vessels might have thrown out overboard or let
escape from the scuppers; perhaps a button, a cork,
sixpence by accident, enough to buy gin, enough to live
another day. Tobias, as was not his habit, cast down a few
coins more out of curiosity than pity: he saw the mudlarks
scrabble for them eagerly, and one, a woman, empty black
dugs hanging naked, called out some kind of blessing, her
voice hoarse with the damp forever eating at lungs and
bones. Tobias had forgotten her as soon as the cab passed
on beyond the turn of the bank, forgotten also the thin
dark apes of stunted children bending forever at work in
the immemorial mud. He was keeping an eye out for the
man Turner, who might be painting out of doors as was
sometimes his habit; from a boy, he said, he had haunted
these places.

   The driver of the cab chewed tobacco contentedly. His
client was evidently mad, like many of the quality. It was
however a good fare, though he would have to keep an eye
on his horse while they waited, unless he was paid and sent
away at once. He didn't want to be hit on the head,
awaking to find himself robbed like a fool; nor did he want
to lose sight of his customer. Gentlemen had reasons of
their own, no doubt, for coming down the likes of here;
himself, he preferred Piccadilly.

   He was instructed to wait beneath the inn with its odd
incomprehensible sign; Tobias got down and went in. The
landlord was polishing glasses at the bar counter, and
when asked if the painter was in residence jerked his head
upwards, not graciously. ''E's busy,' he vouchsafed. Tobias
shrugged, absently turned the knuckle-duster he wore on

his finger for protection, and went up.

Opening the rickety door of the room Turner evidently chose to inhabit for the time, Tobias became aware of a curious musk-like odour which he found attractive. It came from an ivory-skinned woman, thin as a bone. She lay on a stand at the end of the small room, perhaps one that had once held a four-poster in the grand days here. The light fell on her sparse naked figure. Turner was drawing her, and did not turn his head. The easel he used for painting was stacked against the wall; his work in that way was mostly done out of doors. The room was bare of anything but necessities, on which the sunlight slanted dustily. It picked out the woman's skinny shape and her great dark eyes, which moved in her head from the stillness of her pose to fix themselves on Tobias. She had black hair, straight and drawn back into a Grecian knot. It was evident that she was not an Englishwoman. Her face was plain, with high cheekbones and nothing notable except the eyes. She held the pose passively.

Tobias was not looking at the drawing, which was oddly one of those which would fail to be destroyed, half eaten by mice, a lifetime later by a prudish personage named Ruskin, acting on the instructions of his dominant father. This one would survive. Still regarding the model, Tobias murmured that he would buy the completed drawing. As usual, Turner grunted that it was not for sale. His intensely blue eyes, whose observant brightness gave life to his whole face and whose colour would not have been believed if it had been described unseen to anyone, surveyed the visitor with irony.

'You can buy Paola instead,' he muttered. 'I have finished.' To the model he called 'You can get down and dress. You can go with this gentleman if you want. She speaks very little English,' he added without lowering his voice. Then he rose, laid aside his pencil carefully, set the drawing by him, and despite what he had said counted out a few pence to pay the model. Tobias stared at the woman's limbs as they moved stiffly; she had held the pose for an hour.

'She will not need the money,' he told Turner. He then addressed Paola in French. He had taken the trouble to learn that tongue from an *émigré* tutor in boyhood, knowing that at some time, when the wars were over, it would come in as useful as it always had. Few English now spoke it; it had for long been a despised language among them, representing the long shadow of the nation's unforgotten enemy. Tobias was unaware how he knew that Paola would be able to reply in it. As it was, she answered him in a Gallic torrent. 'Get out of here,' said Turner. 'I have to work.' He might have been addressing one or both.

As they walked back to the cab and travelled home, Tobias learned her history. She had been married during the Italian campaign to a French soldier who had been killed at Quatre Bras. Later she had become the mistress of a British one in Belgium 'because I needed food.' He had brought her to England only to be claimed by his legal wife. 'I have starved now and again since then,' Paola said. 'I have take what I could find; as a model to that man, other things. He is *avaro*, mean. His money does not matter.'

'I will give you money,' Tobias promised. He had known from the beginning that he had to have the woman, that he and she had a bond that could not be explained or, God knew, regularised; not that that would have been thought of; she was a peasant, most certainly. He would have taken her with him whether she would or not, but she seemed willing enough. It would do very well. He would no longer be lonely in the bed with the selected curtains.

The intensely bright-blue eyes of Joseph Mallord Turner had watched them go, and then had turned to survey his finished drawing. There were plenty of women; but the drawing itself he knew he would not part with. It represented something he elicited out of the depths of himself, an essence, a precision; meticulous, erotic, unique, to be taken out and savoured as and when he felt like it. Figures, however – women were figures, never personal in the sense that they might be different from one another – did not interest him so much as the rolling of waves, the movement of water, the looming of great ships out of fog. One day he would paint those, having served his own apprenticeship to himself meantime with lesser things. He must also see Italy, and had almost saved up the means on which to travel there. The woman Paola had told him certain things he remembered, but he wouldn't have taken her back with him; it cost money, and once on Italian soil she would have left him, in any case, to go back to her village, wherever it was: she'd told him, but he had forgotten. He forgot, in the end, everything but his work: that was usual with him.

Tobias took Paola back with him to Half Moon Street, had the servants bring food, any food that was in the house, and watched her eat ravenously, contenting himself with a glass of wine they later shared. He then took her to bed and they made love. By the end she had begun to kiss him passionately; this for her was different from the rough embraces of the soldiers, the necessity of earning a living in such ways since, the times of hunger and despair there had been. She would cling to this protector, later on protecting him herself as though he were her child. All this she had begun to know as he stood at the inn-room door on first entry; there was no explaining such a happening, and Paola, who was a realist, did not try. She even put aside her aching desire, which usually assailed her when she was not feeling hungry, to go back home to Italy, to the long sunlit days, her father and mother, the grape harvests. This –
Over the days that followed, he bought her clothes, in the bright colours that suited her; shoes, a comb. 'Nevertheless you are better without clothes,' he told her. It pleased him to nuzzle in her armpits, imbibe the curious musklike smell they emitted; to caress her ivory flesh, filling out now a trifle with proper feeding, but she would always remain thin. Her flat stomach and high-set breasts had intrigued Turner briefly, and did so now with himself, but the mystery remained: in ways, and with her deep harsh voice, she was like a boy about to become a young man. He still had no idea why she had attracted him, only that it had happened. Presently, he would take her down to Fortune's Field; town was becoming uncomfortably hot, being by now mid-August.

* * *

In the nature of things it was some time before he made a late call in at his club for any forwarded mail. The porter handed him three or four letters on a salver, and Tobias opened them absently. He had left Paola drowsy and naked on the four-poster, eating fruit. His blood still surged agreeably at the memory as he slit open the envelopes. One letter was from Lyons in Norwich to say that everything was arranged, he had overcome his wife's objections to a removal to London and would be at Mr Croom's disposal by the autumn. Tobias smiled at the thought of any man's being so subject to a wife's whims, opened the other letters, which were bills he could pay: and last of all one which, to his surprise and not much pleasure, had been sent on from Fortune's Field some time before. It occurred to him that he had not sent anyone the Half Moon Street address, and would be unlikely to do so: it must remain private.

Opening the final letter, it would be too much to say that his heart stopped; that organ continued to beat coolly as usual. However he had certainly, with late events, forgotten about Miss Shearwater. It was evidently time to remember.

> *The Schoolhouse, Fortune's End, the twenty-fifth of June 1817.*
> *Dear Mr Croom,*
> *I am directing this to you at Fortune's Field altho' I am informed that you are not at this time in residence. I trust that my missive will reach you in due course, and that you will forgive me the liberty of having written. I have nobody else to whom to turn, as I dare not relate this extremely private happening to anyone except the person who, I fear, must be responsible. I may add that I myself recall nothing whatever of what took place in the Nether Wood when propriety – a faculty on which I generally pride myself – should have prevented me from entering it with you at all.*
>
> *In short, I am in a Certain Situation, and it will no longer be possible to keep my Appointment here once the thing is known. I fear that this will become the case before the winter.*
>
> *I trust in your Better Nature to accord me Assistance in some way, or perhaps even a Reference subsequently. I have always done my duty, and will continue in it as long as I can; but Events are overcoming me and I will soon be undone. I greatly hope to hear from you, as nothing else will save me from a Fate I had never thought myself as at all likely to have to Contemplate.*

I am, Sir, yours most respectfully,
Ellen Shearwater.

Tobias was duly remorseful. He tried to persuade himself that he had not intended to inconvenience the unfortunate schoolmistress, only to obtain his father's fortune, as was natural. However, he admitted to himself that the first premise was not strictly true; he had certainly made assurance doubly sure. The first thing to do, however, was to write a letter to the poor woman, who must be convinced by now that he had abandoned her: he trusted she had not drowned herself in the village pond, as had once happened to one of Gilbert's housemaids. He sat down, therefore, and wrote a letter on the club paper, assuring Miss Shearwater that he had only today heard, that she might rest in the deserved assurance that he would atone in every possible way, and that he trusted she was well. The letter was phrased carefully enough to have been shown to any lawyer to whom she might meantime have gone, but this was unlikely; schoolteachers did not have enough money for such enterprises.

Secondly, having sent that off by special messenger, Tobias wrote to Lyons for God's sake to come at once, and not to wait for his wife. After that he ordered himself brandy, sat in a leather armchair and drank it; there was nobody else in town. Under the influence of the spirits he mellowed, and reflected that he had never before fathered a child. If it proved a boy, he would bring it up himself.

Returning to Half Moon Street, he poured out the whole tale to Paola; she would have to know in any case. She was still lying on the bed, but got up, threw a wrapper round herself and came and kissed him. She was not jealous of this poor unknown woman; he had done it for money, it was understandable.

'You, you are *vigoroso*,' she said mostly in English, which he was rapidly teaching her. Then she placed his hand on her body under the robe. '*Vous m'avez fait la même chose*,' she told him. 'Feel it already.' She then said none of the others had managed it, even Fernand in the years of their marriage.

He was pleased. He should have noticed, perhaps had

done so but had put it down to better feeding, that her belly was no longer almost concave, not even any longer flat. He kissed it, then the rest of her. That would, he thought, make two children; the village would talk; let them. The boys – he hoped for boys – could grow up together. Meantime, he had had an idea, which he wanted to discuss with the lawyer Lyons, about what to do with Miss Shearwater. He had no particular desire to see her again, but had no wish to be unjust.

Matters thereafter, not to date having precisely stood still, began to rearrange themselves with the rapidity of coloured shapes disturbed at the further end of a kaleidoscope. In London, as society began to return, Tobias took his mistress for gentle walks in the Park at other than the polite hour, visited his club daily, saw old acquaintances, talked with them well into the night, and would return to find Paola diligently letting out her dresses. She was never bored and always placid, although she could use her tongue on the servants in whatever language came to mind. As time passed she began to assume the shape of a ripening pear, which intrigued Tobias; when he thought of it, he supposed the same thing would be happening to Miss Shearwater. That lady was now in a guilty refuge found for her at Scarborough, duly provided with a wedding ring and being looked after meantime by Lyons' wife: all of it had taken a little arranging, and a replacement had also been found to take over the school at Fortune's End, without undue gossip. When the days of Miss Shearwater's tribulation should be accomplished – Lyons' wife had written in some amusement about the so-called widow's outrage when the doctor described her as an Elderly Prim – a suitable house had been purchased in the Midlands, remote from anyone who had formerly known her, to be turned by her own efforts, and Tobias's money, into a young ladies' academy. Tobias himself would retain shares in the venture. The project had also enabled the poor lady to give in her notice respectably at the end of term as she could say with truth that she had been offered a headmistressship. She had no desire, evidently, to do anything but return to teaching, which was undoubtedly just as well. Being already a trifle worried about her laces – children were observant – she had declined the offer of a farewell tea-party, but had nevertheless received, privately, a small pewter tea-service towards the cost of which the pupils' parents had unenthusiastically subscribed. On receiving it Miss Shearwater had been observed to shed a few tears behind her spectacles. Nobody had asked where she was going next and the waters, as it were, closed over her head; she was soon forgotten despite her long service, a tragedy which overtakes many such.

In Scarborough, attired in a bonnet with blinds behind which concealment she remained tight-lipped with mortification at what was happening to her, she then awaited her time. The solicitor's wife, who had left a hopeful brood at home in charge of her eldest daughter, wished the event would take place soon. Although very well paid by Tobias, it was not a particularly grateful assignment, Miss Shearwater becoming increasingly aware of how subtly, and inevitably, she had been betrayed; dictyophyls were rarely to be found in the British Isles: in fact, Mr Croom had been quite as bad as his brother if not worse. She would be thankful to shed the whole responsibility (to put the matter in a distasteful way).

The time arrived. 'Ease up, dear, if you can,' said the lawyer's wife knowledgeably. 'It comes easier if you could learn not to stiffen.' Miss Shearwater regarded this as an affront; many women in her opinion did not stiffen nearly enough, and she nearly said so; but, instead, gave vent presently to a series of birdlike squawks. These in some manner retained their gentility until the last, which was a loud yell such as any other woman would have given; and resulted in the timely emergence of a handsome baby boy, with red hair. Miss Shearwater, on being informed, gave a moan, and said somebody was bound to find out sooner or later; and the things that had to happen after that were an even greater indignity than the birth. However she survived, and when recovered departed at last for the Midlands, while Mrs Lyons thankfully went back home to see the furniture packed for the move to London and her husband, now installed in Middle Temple.

Some weeks later, Paola gave birth, with the ease of a viviparous insect, to a second handsome boy, this time with black hair. The first was by then ensconced with his wet-nurse at Fortune's Field. Remembering his own pangs at being excluded from the title, Tobias acted fairly and gave the elder of the two his name; the other was, for no particular reason, christened Claud.

The General had watched these goings-on with amazed indifference, but was adamant about one thing; Paola must be kept out of his end of the house. 'Can't stand the smell,' he said roundly. Tobias continued to like it. Also, it was comforting to know that at least one woman was safe from his predatory elder brother, whose habits in such ways appeared rather to have increased than otherwise.

As for Beatrice, she said nothing. There was after all nothing to say. The two illegitimate boys could most certainly not be permitted to play with Anstey in due course. It would be no proper company for the heir, which Anstey still was despite everything. In fact, he was only now learning to walk. The whole situation was most incorrect, and anybody could see that young Toby was the son of that schoolmistress who had understandably been sent away.

III

Tobias had from the beginning carefully considered the education of his two sons, which he intended to undertake for himself when they were old enough. He was well aware, having himself lived through them, of the conditions pertaining at the average public school; canings, sodomy, starvation, and rats in the dormitory. Moreover the nature of their birth would be a handicap to preferment. He himself would prefer – Toby especially would benefit from it, having a kindly nature, while Claud, probably resembling his Italian ancestors, was as hard as nails – both boys to have the full benefits of travel abroad, available again at last to Britons. All Tobias's own breadth of mind and experience of the world could give them would prepare them for such an outcome; and money, thanks to his own effort some years ago now, was not lacking. Later, they should of course marry well on the strength of that last; it had been done before in such cases.

He had already selected progressive reading for them, having acquired, over the years, a small private library of his own. It was from this, in fact, that he had culled enough knowledge of fungi initially to ensnare Miss Shearwater; any other subject could have been read up in a similar manner for the occasion. From time to time, Tobias learned by way of Lyons, who had by now taken silk, of the progress of the young ladies' school in the north, and noted that the best families were beginning to send their daughters there; he received satisfactory dividends twice a year. The mansion he had bought had been cheap at the price, having belonged to a bankrupt aristocrat. The salons had made imposing classrooms, he understood, and the long-neglected gardens had been taken in hand, with paths cleared for the young ladies' daily crocodile. Miss Shearwater could teach botany to her heart's content if remembrance did not prove too much for her; and she had lately employed a second-in-command, a widow named Jemima Ludd. According to Lyons, this lady was formidable and adept.

Meantime, the fact that the cat sat on the mat was taught to young Toby and young Claud, also their multiplication tables. The governess was a hook-nosed lady of thirty named Miss Beavis whom even Gilbert (who in any case only saw her in the distance) would never dare essay. He, Tobias, was contented with Paola and had ceased to look at other women. At the east end of the house, however, he understood things were different; Anstey's nurse having long since been taken advantage of, two governesses were likewise observed to depart in tears; and it was known that Anstey himself could not yet read or write. Tobias's own sons, wrestling together on the lawn like rutting stags, were dimly aware of the pale-faced little boy who was to be seen now and again on fine days at the other end of the garden, but he always disappeared sooner or later, wheezing with asthma. He did not interest them greatly.

It was this situation which at last brought about the capitulation of Beatrice Croom. She appeared one day while the boys were at lessons, leading poor Anstey by the hand. Tobias, from his usual armchair which had a foot-rest he enjoyed, rose courteously to greet her.

'My dear Beatrice, this is a pleasant surprise.' He could not in fact recall when they had last addressed one another. Beatrice looked down her long nose.

'My son,' she said, 'is an ignoramus.'

It was settled between them that Anstey should share lessons with his cousins and the incorruptible Miss Beavis, but Tobias was not the man to let a bargain slip. He surveyed Beatrice with his worldly gaze; she wasn't getting any younger. 'If,' he suggested, 'they are acquainted in such a way, and I'm glad of it, might I suggest that we all take luncheon together on Friday? It would repair an unnecessary breach, as you will no doubt agree.'

'Gilbert —' began Lady Croom, at a loss to know how to

explain without being unmannerly; it would be a relief to have Anstey reliably taught at last, but the odour of that Italian woman at one's table was not to be thought of; the General would go stumping off, probably accompanied by language he had learnt in the army. She tried to murmur as much; but Tobias, who for his own part would rather take luncheon where he was, showed understanding in the matter.

'The boys alone, then,' he said gently. 'Their manners are sufficiently advanced for them to attend without Miss Beavis.' Miss Beavis had, as it happened, no sense of smell.

'My dear Tobias, I shall be delighted,' replied his sister-in-law with real gratitude. Had she known what she was building up for herself, her delight would have been mitigated.

Anstey said nothing. He never in any case said very much. From then on his days became a purgatory, both by reason of the fact that he was far behind his cousins in the three R's and everything else, and that his cousins knew it and, when they could, let him know that they knew.

So things continued, time passed, the two younger boys progressed under their father's tutelage, and Miss Beavis was kept on mostly for the benefit of poor Anstey. She was to be one of the few women to escape with an intact virginity from Fortune's Field, but that was in the future. Meantime, Paola settled down into being a kind of housekeeper at the west end only; she was generally to be met with seeing to the linen. Tobias himself, while retaining his figure, became increasingly lethargic as he grew older; the flat in Half Moon Street was given up, as his sons were not yet ready to occupy it. He had decided that it would be best to place them in separate merchant banks; that was after the Grand Tour had made men of them. They were handsomer than ever, quite different from one another, and he was proud of them. He did not permit himself a favourite, though oddly, of the two, he inwardly preferred Toby, whose kind heart might however lead him into trouble one day, as had happened to oneself. Tilly, the reminder of that, still lived on upstairs: for good reasons she never showed herself at the window. No doubt she was ageing as well as diseased. He had made himself forget the horror of it. *Salud, pesetas, y amor,* as Gilbert and his fellow-officers had come home boasting from the Peninsula: he himself, without either wars or honour, had achieved them all. The enterprise long ago amid the bluebells had atoned for his ruined youth. He, Tobias Croom, was content these days; except that he still lacked the title.

Anstey both feared and worshipped his father. He was also aware that to the latter, he was a disappointment. As a child Gilbert had taught him to ride and to shoot; Anstey, who was afraid of his pony, also lacked a sense of direction and an eye for a target, was slow at both. Nevertheless his greatest ambition was to resemble the General in every way, perhaps by entering the army later on. This was made unlikely by Anstey's uncertain health and spindly physique, also his asthma which, as the General himself barked at him, would be bound to come on at the moment of orderin' a charge. As time passed it became increasingly uncertain what, if anything, was to be done with the heir. The church was briefly considered, as Beatrice, after her ultimate miscarriage, had taken to spiritual consolation and used to carry Anstey off with her to attend a church, further off than that at Fortune's End, where they actually swung censers. The smell of incense however brought on Anstey's asthma unfailingly, and the notion of a sportin' parson enjoyin' a livin', which the General might just have tolerated, was abandoned in its turn.

An earlier memory had contributed to the unhappy young man's disbelief in himself and, in fact, encouraged a delight in being bullied which found ample opportunity both in the company of his father and his cousins, slightly younger though both were. It had concerned a young governess named Mary Tregown, who had come as the second holder of the position to Fortune's Field when Anstey was a small boy. Anstey had thought Miss Tregown looked like an angel. She was always kind to him, never made fun of his inadequacies or his asthma – in fact attacks of the latter were rare in her presence – and encouraged him gently to learn what he could. Anstey

adored her, used despite their lethal pollen to pick
bunches of wild flowers to put in her white hands, and
sought out her company whenever he could, even to the
extent now and again of visiting her in the attic upstairs
where she slept and which contained an iron-framed pallet
bed such as servants used, a chest of drawers, and a
looking-glass in which Miss Tregown could look at her
pretty face each morning and comb out her fair mermaid's
hair. She was, he thought, like one of the figures carved in
church; pure, good, and flawless. So, at that time, was he.
He had never been as happy or as secure.

This pleasant state of affairs came to an end in summer,
because at that time of year Anstey suffered from
recurrent diarrhoea and was forced frequently to hurry
upstairs, where lately plumbing had been installed to
allow, as was already explained to him, the pressure of
water to build up. Hastening past Miss Tregown's door
one midnight accordingly, he saw a light underneath. On
the way back it was still there, and, able to pause this time,
he found that odd sounds were coming from within.
Somebody was hurting Miss Tregown, but she sounded,
strangely, as though she liked it. Anstey stood outside the
door uncertainly in his nightshirt and bare feet; his
distress at the whole matter made him start to wheeze. He
endured the cramping agony of asthma, aware of the
sudden opening of the door. His father stood there, large
and wrathful; and behind him, in the room, Miss Tregown
could be glimpsed, sprawled on the bed with her
nightgown pulled up; she no longer looked like an angel.
Anstey, shocked at the first sight of female parts, felt his
heart break in two: the General bawled at him angrily.

'Get back downstairs, you snivellin' spyin' little rat. Go
on down.'

He shut the door. Anstey didn't wait to hear if the
sounds started again. He found himself blundering along
the upstairs passages, lost, foolish and betrayed, aware
already that he had taken a strange direction into the
western part where his uncle and cousins lived downstairs;
in fact, he had never ventured here before. He was
however afraid of going back, and passing the bedroom
door again; it might be still going on, or else his father

might again come out. There must be a way down from this end, but Anstey didn't know any longer where he was, or how to find it.

He came to a second door, also lit. It might belong to one of the servants; Anstey scratched on it timidly. A strange voice, a woman's, called out to ask who was there. 'It's Anstey,' quavered the little boy uncertainly; his feet were cold, he wished he'd taken time to put on his slippers, but that was the least of it; misery claimed him. He'd have to go back again to the lavatory, after all. He stood there shivering, a wretched little animal on thin legs. The door opened and a woman was revealed there, with a lamp in her hand. She had a white bloated face. Anstey didn't know who she was; not a servant, she had different manners.

He heard words begin to come from her, coarse blasphemous words such as he had never been allowed to hear before, even from the General in his rages; this was different; this woman – Anstey knew it already – was a damned soul. He turned and stumbled off, feeling the liquid shit spurt out again and stain his nightshirt. She still called obscenities after him. Sobbing, he ran back past the other dreadful door, into the lavatory – it was anyway too late – and presently crept downstairs, writhing at last into his own bed and lying there on his stomach, unable to sleep. For the first time in his life he saw the dawn come, his mind a turmoil of wretchedness, his body filthy. He didn't know which was worse, the strange white-faced woman or the earlier deep betrayal.

Next day, he refused to go to lessons. Nothing and no one would persuade him; his mother came at last, and asked if he were ill. Wretchedly, Anstey poured out the whole story: he had to tell somebody. His mother didn't say much, or not to him: he heard her having high words later with his father.

That had been the beginning of Anstey's distrust of women. He never saw Miss Tregown again; she was sent away, and shortly after that he had been allowed to begin lessons with his cousins. Miss Beavis was safe, and didn't look like an angel. Much later he was told, probably by Claud, that the General had set up Miss Tregown in one of the cottages, and visited her there instead. Later on she died of pneumonia and was buried outside the churchyard wall. As for the other woman in the west attic, she was Uncle Tobias's wife. Nobody every saw her except the servant who carried up her food. Anstey ventured to ask why, but Claud, who knew most things, didn't know that. It appeared that it wasn't spoken of.

Later on, by the time his cousins were under the instruction of Tobias and Miss Beavis had been sent on her upward professional way, a young German tutor was found for Anstey, Gilbert having stated that he was damned if his brother was goin' to put any ideas of his into one's only son's head. Moreover, German could come in useful. Herr Schlesinger, from Munich, was a kindly and reliable soul in metal-rimmed spectacles, who plodded on patiently enough to be allowed, in the end, to take Anstey with him on a prolonged visit home. The Italian tour on which his cousins were by then about to engage was considered inadvisable for the sickly heir; Beatrice was afraid her son would catch some infection with the foreign water, and Claud and Toby, who intended to enjoy themselves in various ways prescribed in worldly fashion by Tobias, did not want his company anyway. The house, emptied shortly of all its young men, remained quiet, or at least quiescent, although neither the General nor his brother could be entirely described as inactive. They were, at this time, almost on speaking terms and had even been known to pass the time of day.

Anstey and the German tutor meantime journeyed gently towards the snow-covered Alps, rising abruptly as they did beyond the fantasies of the ancient city. Thereafter Anstey's dutiful letters home were almost enthusiastic. He wrote about the art galleries, the Glockenspiel with its painted dancing figures in the Marienplatz, which had intrigued him greatly: the palaces and the churches. Finally he asked permission to stay on for the Oktoberfest. 'Doesn't sound like the feller,' the General remarked to his wife, with whom he was at the moment also on terms. 'Somethin' in the air there, maybe; good for his asthma.'

Whatever the Oktoberfest did for Anstey, his letters

thereafter changed their tone. First of all he announced
that he would prefer to become a monk, and would like to
take instruction in the Catholic Church. At this the General
angrily demanded his instant return home; what could
Schlesinger be thinkin' of? He ought to be well aware by
now, even if Anstey wasn't, that the young man's duty was to
marry and beget an heir in the Church of England.

However it appeared that Schlesinger, whatever had
happened, was no longer with his charge. When the latter
at last returned, abject, less at his father's command than
at the cutting off of money, it proved to be in the
company, instead, of a young valet whose name was Franz.
One look at Franz alerted the General's suspicions; Franz
was lithe as a snake, with curly hair and long eyelashes.
Having, in literal terms, uncovered the situation soon,
Anstey's father sent the young German packing. Anstey
himself, despite his age having never had one before – his
health in boyhood had been deemed too delicate, but the
present situation was untenable – received what the
General described as a damned good hidin'. He retired,
howling, to his room, lay once again on his stomach, ached
for Franz, and was by no means reconciled to the means
thought expedient by Gilbert for curing all alien
tendencies; a speedy marriage to an eligible young woman.
It would be better if she had some money.

Gilbert had in fact very little idea of how to set about
finding such a bride for his son. It was pointless to expect
Anstey to stay the course of a London season and look
about for himself; he wouldn't, though any eligible young
female worth her salt was to be found there at the balls and
assemblies. Swallowing his pride, the General crossed the
grass beyond the folly. Tobias, whatever his limitations,
would be bound to have practical advice, in which Beatrice
– it had of course been impossible to explain the whole
state of affairs to her, and the notion of an early marriage
for Anstey had made her hostile again – had failed him.
Being master in his own house, or at least one end of it,
Lord Croom intended to proceed in any case. He took a
deep breath, recalling the pending presence of that
damned smelly Italian woman: and went in.

* * *

'Leave the assemblies alone,' said Tobias, turning his wineglass; Gilbert had declined to drink. 'Ambitious mamas with a daughter worth selling will net the best prizes in the market.' He added, in what the General could not but reflect was vulgar parlance, that it would be necessary to undercut. He himself knew of a girls' school in the north which produced finished young ladies. Although Norman blood might not be available, a bank balance might be. The times were coming when some discreet association or other with trade might cease to be frowned on; money after all was money. Tobias then finished the wine.

'You've got somethin' in mind,' remarked the General. 'You were always a damned slippery proposition; look at the way you took down that schoolteacher's drawers.' A thought struck him; young Toby, everyone knew, had emerged from that encounter somehow, one only had to look at the hair and remember the date. Schoolteachers had to end up somewhere; he himself wasn't a fool.

Tobias smiled. 'I can put you in touch with this young ladies' academy in the Midlands,' he said. 'It is becoming celebrated for turning out correctly disposed fiancées. There are several heiresses, who in the ordinary way would go on to be presented and launched, with hope briefly, on the marriage market. I have, perhaps, a little influence. I am happy to use it on your behalf now that you accept my sons at your table, Gilbert. I am anxious for them to enjoy the widest possible advantages, and can understand your similar ambition for poor Anstey. It is better, I think, if I were to write rather than yourself, remembering certain circumstances.' His smile widened. The General slapped his thigh.

'By God, you're a cool customer,' he said. 'Get me a good little bitch with breedin', not a pauper; somethin' in between.'

After he had stumped off, Tobias wrote not to Miss Shearwater – he had never maintained direct dealing with her, rightly deeming it tactless – but to the second-in-command, Mrs Ludd. That lady managed the girls, would know which one to select, and would hardly refuse him when, after all, he could close the whole institution down if at any time he so decided. As it was showing a reasonable yearly profit, Tobias knew he would do no such thing.

Having sent the letter to the tray, he then began to reflect equally on the superior prospects of his own two sons; they were at least not compelled to marry and breed until they chose. He had arranged, on their expected return – they had been away now two years – one place at Coutts's for Toby, and one at Crowbetter's for Claud. A slight air of arrivism pervaded the latter bank, and Claud was better equipped to deal with its hazards than Toby, who should sink gently into tradition for the time being, having without doubt polished himself to the required degree in Florence and Rome.

Paola appeared at his elbow with coffee, and Tobias accepted it gratefully, caressing her arm with his fine fingers. She always made everything of the kind exactly as he liked it. The thought of life without her would, by now, be impossible.

It was on his return from the Grand Tour that young Toby Croom asked his father a question which put him out of favour for the time. It was of course known to everybody in Fortune's Field that his father's wife inhabited rooms upstairs and never under any circumstances came down. Toby had seen her once long ago at the window, a pale blur against the glass, but never since. Before his travels he would not have had the confidence to ask such a question, as his father's unspoken authority had always overawed him; but by now he considered himself, for good reasons, a man of the world. It was surely in order to ask what had happened so long ago. However his father frowned on hearing the query, and dismissed him coldly.

'You should have learned by now, in the course of your instruction from myself and your recent acquaintance with the world, that one does not ask such questions. I put the *gaffe* down to your youth. Youth in fact was my own undoing, and its results will never be discussed by me with anyone. I forbid you to mention the matter again.'

After the young man had retired, crestfallen, Tobias dismissed Paola and sat alone. He might as well make himself remember; the affair had no power to hurt him now. How he had loved her, with a young man's inexplicable passion! How he had deemed it a favour to be allowed to receive her embraces, when she had already slept with half the town! To him, she had been a goddess, the perfection of beauty; he had begged her, as soon as he was of age, to marry him, risking his father's wrath, the world's censure; he had told himself he cared nothing for the world. For three weeks after the marriage he had remained in halcyon bliss; he had showered presents on her he could not afford, furs, jewels, bibelots, French novels bound in gilt leather. Her bed to him was heaven; then, one day, coming in unexpectedly, he had found another man in it. Tilly had screamed, and Tobias himself, with the grip of steel that lay in his fine fingers, had seized the man by the throat and forced the truth out of him; he wasn't the only one, they came daily. In the end two of them, not himself, had fought a duel over Tilly, one killing the other; at the same time he, Tobias, had found a chancre on her arm. By then, she was afraid of him; and he had faced her with the truth.

'You have syphilis. Fortunately you have not given it to me, and I will never touch you again. In time, being in your blood, it will reach your brain, which will rot and you will die raving. I have married you, and for the memory of what has been between us I will continue to maintain you; once it is known you have the pox your trade, in which you indulge by habit, will be closed even to you. You will remain where I will place you; you will receive enough food to keep you alive. I myself will take nothing more to do with you, will have no further speech with you, and expect you to remain unseen.'

She had flung herself at his feet, sobbed and howled, begged him to have pity on her; but she knew well enough that her days as a whore were numbered, and her career – she had after all been an actress – gone. She had agreed, therefore, to do as he ordained in the matter; his father at the time had agreed to house her; and as he himself allowed her unlimited liquor by now might drink herself to death before madness overtook her. It was preferable, no doubt, to happen so; but Tilly Croom still lived.

Tobias regarded his hands. There was no need, here in the country, to wear the knuckle-duster he slid on as a rule for protection in town. It enabled him to walk unmolested in places otherwise dangerous, like Ranelagh, where he had met her. Of late years he had however grown contented here; at Fortune's Field with his sons, and Paola, and his armchair. It no longer mattered that Tilly was upstairs.

Within a few days a reply arrived for Tobias from Mrs Ludd. He sent it round to his brother without further comment. The matter was no longer any business of his

at The Shearwater Academy for Young Ladies,

20th May 1836

Dear Mr Croom,

Miss Shearwater has asked me to reply to your letter and to say that the reputation of the School continues in all ways to progress.

You state that you require a suitable wife, or your brother does, for his son, who is unable to proceed in the customary way because of asthma. It is assumed that in due course, he will succeed to the Title and to half the existing estate.

As a rule we would have nobody available. Our young ladies not only emerge very greatly in demand because of their Superior Education in Manners and Accomplishments, but are frequently earmarked, if one may use such a term, for the Marriage Market before they have embarked on their first Season. Alliances with the Nobility are not uncommon. (she here quoted four instances, over which Gilbert skipped).

It so happens, however, that owing to an Unfortunate Circumstance, which I will relate to you in full, a Single Young Lady of considerable Fortune and some looks remains available; in fact, it is time she was married. I can assure you that we have done our best in Amy Killigrew's somewhat unfortunate Circumstances from the beginning; her Grandfather has Immense Wealth altho' he is, I fear, a Common Person. He entrusted Amy to us to be brought up, as her widowed Mother – his Son is dead – is quite Unsuitable for the Purpose of rearing her child as a Lady. Mr Killigrew is anxious that his Young Granddaughter – Amy is now seventeen – shall shine in Society. He has spared no Expense to that end. She had been instructed in all the Extras including the

*Use of Water-Colour, but what she Excels in is Dancing, of which
she is very fond. As to her Character, we have tried to steady it by
every Means including, occasionally, Suitable Chastisement. This
became necessary recently again owing to a Regrettable Episode
(which however did not go too far) with the Drawing-master. I
have no doubt that Amy led him on. A suitable marriage would I
believe steady her; I need perhaps say no more except that it might
be Expedient for your Brother and Lady Croom to Visit here by
arrangement and inspect the Young Person for themselves.
Otherwise it will be necessary to find some Lady of Title to
undertake Amy's Presentation in the Autumn. I await your
Instructions, and remain, dear Sir,*
Jemima Ludd, Mrs
To the Honourable Tobias Croom, at Fortune's Field.

By God, the General thought, that's old Killigrew the army
contractor, who made his pile sendin' cardboard boots out
to the Peninsula; he's tried it again in time for the
Waterloo campaign, which might well have been lost if he,
Croom, hadn't taken a sample pair along to the Duke
himself after a single route-march, and the latter had
remarked that the army was infamous enough already
without having to charge on the soles of its feet. Killigrew
had been circumvented that time, and lucky to escape
trouble because more urgent matters had of course
intervened; but one had some hold over him, in
retrospect. The man must undoubtedly have made his
pile; if the granddaughter was to be the sole recipient of
his ill-gotten gains, that was somethin'. Oneself – with
Beatrice, of course – must go up and inspect the filly. The
less delay the better, *pace* the drawin'-master.

Beatrice was disturbed at the order to pack herself a few
things and get ready to travel north; she seldom left home
nowadays, and was in any case not feeling very well. Also,
she considered it unnecessary to marry off poor Anstey
quite so soon; his health was by no means robust enough.
However she had no choice but to obey, and instructed her
new maid, Lizzie, to pack night-gear and hairbrushes – no
more would be required, they would of course be
returning at once – in a small valise. Lizzie obeyed,
wordlessly as was her way; she was a respectable young

woman acquired from a village further off, and had the advantage of being saved: the Wesleys had preached within living memory among her immediate forebears, although unfortunately they had not penetrated as far as Fortune's End. Lady Croom had been permitted – things had got to that stage by now, Gilbert's reputation having spread well beyond the Croom feudal limits – to take Lizzie into her employment on the strict understanding that she never once let her out of her sight. This was in any case convenient, as the girl was willing and neat-handed, also ugly enough not to have interested Gilbert unduly in the first place.

They set out, therefore, all three in the carriage, Lizzie with her back to the horses and the General beside his wife. As there was nothin' worth lookin' at, he closed his eyes and meantime thought less about the possible bride to be inspected for Anstey than of a memory he still held remarkably dear; that of lovely little Mary Tregown, dead all these years outside the churchyard wall because that damned Evitt wouldn't put her inside. He himself had taken some pains to point out that Mary, despite everythin', had been a good young woman, had said her prayers regularly to the end, and had been greatly troubled at no longer bein' permitted to receive communion after the whole thing became known. However it had been a waste of breath, all these fellers were cut to pattern, old women in cassocks. Mary, good devoted girl, would get to heaven wherever her pretty bones lay. He thought of her still with pleasure; she'd been innocent as a child when he'd started with her, that time she was teachin' young Anstey his three R's; he himself, he dared say, had taught Mary a thing or two else before long. Movin' her down to the cottages later on, after Beatrice had cut up rough, had been convenient: he could stroll down there and take his pleasure any time it suited him. A great pity Mary had died after a year or two: while she lived he'd been contented enough, in fact – the recollection surprised him – entirely faithful. It had taken him a good two weeks after the funeral to begin to think again of other women, but a man had his needs: and Beatrice, on doctor's orders, was no use for anythin' of the kind nowadays.

He looked at Beatrice, opening his eyes again in order to do so; she seemed to have turned a curious hyacinth colour. 'Feelin' all right and tight, m'dear?' the General asked affectionately. They'd left Anstey at home, wheezin'. It was better to inspect the young woman first. He –

'I am not feeling at all well,' replied Beatrice resentfully. 'I shall be glad when we reach an inn.'

He duly left her at The Feathers, which was further away than he'd anticipated from the school; it meant seein' the young person alone, which he didn't mind for himself, but these damned women might object: never mind. He'd have brought the maid along, for the look of the thing, but Beatrice wouldn't part with her; nobody after all could say anythin' was his fault. He watched the driver turn at last into the long drive; it was lined with laurel bushes. Presently they drew up before a gravelled front, beyond which the great house reared, not as large as Fortune's but well on the way; they'd added a wing, one could see the new stone. A posse of young ladies was paradin' up and down, with none other than Miss Shearwater herself, grown old and grey, presidin'. The General left the carriage, and removed his hat.

'Good-day, Lord Croom,' remarked Miss Shearwater very coldly indeed. 'I trust Lady Croom is not unwell? Her letter stated that *both* of you were to be expected. I hardly think –'

The General listened with half an ear only; it was no more than he'd foreseen would happen, and meantime the sight of the young ladies in crocodile was, not to put too fine a point on it, enough to make a man's cock sit up. Pretty bosoms – he'd always had an eye for a good one, and those skimpy dresses had gone out of fashion long ago elsewhere, a pity, the new furbelows disguised everythin' – and shapely limbs, although one or two of the young ladies were still too fat, it was their age, they'd shape up – the older girls walked in front, no doubt, havin' been almost finished; the unfinished ones were, Gilbert supposed, behind. He wondered which was Amy. His attention returned briefly to Miss Shearwater; the other woman, formidable in maroon and with a turban on her head, was approachin'. Anyone would think the sight of a man among this little covey was dangerous. One or two of the young ladies, passin' by, showed a shy interest; at his age, he, Gilbert Croom, knew he still didn't look too badly, considerin'. He spoke up, without apology or explanation.

'Show me the filly,' he said. 'Get her out of line.'

She wasn't, he decided at once, too bad; not the best of the bunch, certainly; not the little takin' creature with honey-coloured curls, or the tall dark one with the come-hither eye, or even the redhead he'd briefly noticed; best to leave redheads out of it. Altogether what young Amy seemed might suit poor Anstey well enough, if anythin' could. She was small, with, as Gilbert perceived without delay, a good frontage; that was hopeful. Her arms and legs – these skirts were too short, they'd been the fashion in 1812, showed a good deal, stoppin' at mid-calf, however – were agreeable, not too thin, with a quality somehow like milk; he'd like to stroke them. Her hair was pallid, and hung out of curl; in fact, everythin' about her seemed slightly discouraged, in especial her little wet pink mouth, which almost looked, with its spiritless droop, as if she'd spent its formative years suckin' in the lower lip with her front teeth, the way girls did to try to look as if they were sorry when they weren't. Gilbert almost demanded to inspect Amy's teeth, then remembered that after all he wasn't buyin' a mare. It was probable that the turbanned matron, in the way of her kind, had been hard on the girl. Miss Shearwater had meantime excused herself, marchin' off bristlin' to remove the rest of the little troupe (and, by God, she'd aged). The General barked out an enquiry, regardless of tact; after all, the rest had gone; there was nobody left in the garden except himself, young Amy and the presiding dragon.

'What's this about a drawin'-master, hey? Out with it, miss. What happened? Did the feller lift your skirts, or not?'

Amy shrank; such open frankness was worse than Grandfather. She had been much impressed by the sight of the handsome General, fine and upstanding in his topcoat and half-boots for travelling, with magnificent whiskers, by now white as snow, pricked up amiably on either side his weatherbeaten countenance. Now, however, the grey gimlet eye which had helped to win Waterloo was fixed full on her, and her own glance wavered as usual. It was worse than anything that Mrs Ludd should be present. She, Amy, wouldn't be allowed to say any more for herself than she'd ever been since being taken away from Ma in the first place. She therefore hung her head, muttered shamefacedly to the effect that he'd only kissed her – this much Mrs Ludd knew already, having witnessed the crime – and heard that lady interrupt immediately. It might have been foreseen that she herself wouldn't ever be allowed to finish a sentence to the end. At the beginning, when she'd first arrived here, they'd said she spoke in a vulgar fashion, like her mother. Amy had then been induced by hallowed means to stop. Since then it had hardly been worth while saying anything at all, as what she said was always wrong and what she did, if anything, usually punished. It wasn't as if she got away from here even in the holidays, like the rest. Grandfather had said, evidently, that she wasn't to be allowed to go home lest her mother again influence her (he had in fact used a stronger word). Amy was allowed to receive letters from Ma and write them once a month, provided everything was supervised. Ma herself was given a suitable allowance provided she behaved herself and didn't try to see Amy. It was to be understood that Amy was to be turned into a lady, but she didn't feel like one quite yet.

Mr Timothy the drawing master had been the one excitement. In the holidays, Amy and the single other girl who remained, and whose parents were in India, had been allowed to have extra water-colour lessons to pass the time. Mr Timothy had kissed Dorothea as well, more than once, during these, but of course it had to be herself, Amy Killigrew, who was caught out. Mr Timothy had been admonished and told that if it happened again, he would be dismissed without a character; so since then things had become very dull. Now, here was this handsome old boy glaring at her. He made her feel, somehow, like a small, scared rabbit. In its way it was exciting.

'Nothing of the kind, Lord Croom, I assure you,' replied Mrs Ludd about the lifted skirts. 'The mildest impropriety, however, shows a certain disposition. I should advise keeping a strict eye, or that Lady Croom should keep one –' She began to flounder, which was unlike her usual behaviour; in fact, they had expected to entertain husband and wife to tea, to produce Amy under full supervision and in her other gown, but Lord Croom had arrived by himself a little early. Mrs Ludd, however, had not been informed either of the General's propensities or, naturally, of Miss Shearwater's past; dear Ellen had always been reticent. Also, Mrs Ludd had herself been married, and understood that gentlemen were often a little coarse in their speech. She hoped dear Amy would perhaps not understand the reference about skirts. In fact the girls' walking-dresses, those they also wore for lessons, were deliberately cut to save laundry; for special occasions it was different. One way and another, Mrs Ludd was feeling a trifle flustered, or she would never have agreed to the General's taking Amy away more or less as she was, quite unaccompanied by any other female. It was most unfortunate that Lady Croom was said to be unwell. At first Jemima Ludd demurred; it was impossible, she said to allow Amy to go anywhere without a chaperone, and she herself had duties at this hour; so had the maids, including the non-existent laundry-maid whose payments were regularly inserted in Shearwater's accounts, deceiving even so astute a personage as Mr Tobias Croom. The thought flitted across Jemina's mind that that unknown gentleman did, after all, own the school. Ellen was out of sight; and would moreover agree fully with oneself that the opportunity of a Title for the unlikely Amy should not be lost by unnecessary prevarication.

'My wife is at the nearest inn, ma'am,' barked the General. 'I will take this young lady straight there, she will be interviewed by us both and, if unsuitable, returned to you without further trouble.' He glared at Amy as if the whole thing was her fault. Mrs Ludd hastily instructed the girl to fetch her light travelling-cloak and her bonnet, and to make haste: this irascible peer might well change his mind if there was any unreasonable delay. She saw them off, at last, without trepidation; there was a respectable driver in wine-coloured livery on the box, and the horses were very well-groomed. It would only, after all, be a short journey: nothing could go amiss.

Gilbert had wasted very little time in further thought about the drawin'-master; in the event, or quite possibly other events, and if that schoolmistress hadn't come in in time, there might be some question of a little bastard inheritin' the title, and that would never do. He had already decided, in his swift military fashion, that for Anstey's sake it was his own plain duty to find out whether young Amy had, or had not, retained her maidenhead. If she hadn't, she could go straight back to school.

He set himself to the matter in hand at once, almost before the carriage had drawn out of the school gates. Amy made no resistance, being in her way as innocent as poor Mary Tregown had once been; besides, remembering the brief experience with Mr Timothy, it was at first easy to assume that this was what men always did, that was if one was left alone with them. However the smacking and bewhiskered kisses Lord Croom was showering now on her little pink mouth – Mr Timothy had told her it was a rosebud drooping with dew – aroused sensations Amy had never before felt; her mouth fell open. After that, if she had wanted to cry out, and she wasn't sure she wanted to, she couldn't have: nobody could, in the circumstances. There was nobody in any case to hear, except the coachman on his box: and he didn't seem to take any notice. Never having been warned of the existence of the god Priapus, Amy could hardly have been expected to know that he was almost certainly with her here in the carriage. What followed bewildered rather than hurt her, because of all the men left alive in England Gilbert Croom was probably better at painless provings than any; then, then Amy began to understand at last, but was somehow incredulous; Mrs Ludd had said that if she behaved properly, she might be married to his lordship's son. This wasn't – at least, one didn't suppose so – behaving – oh – it – oh, it must be – oh, oh, oh, oh – the reason why they never left girls alone with man. She didn't suppose she minded.

The horses jogged on, other sounds remaining unheard.

Smithers the coachman, who had been in Lord Croom's employment long enough to know when not to drive too fast, drove fairly slowly. The old devil was at it again; that was to be expected, no young girl was safe for as long as it took to unfasten his lordship's fly. If the school had let her come with him alone, that was their fault. Smithers flicked imaginary gnats away from the horses' rumps with his long-handled whip and thought of other things, in especial Lizzie, back at the inn with poor Lady Croom. Lizzie might be ugly, but she was safe. Smithers had for some time now considered embarking on the courtship. Being a cautious person, he liked to think things out beforehand. He'd found out already, by way of Lizzie's aunt who was married to the blacksmith at Fortune's End, that Liz had a light hand with pastry, and was thrifty. Nobody would have guessed, from the way her ladyship kept hold of her always, that Liz was fit to go out on her own; one day soon, however, he, Smithers, would suggest that on her day off, when she had one, they begin to walk out, that was if it suited her. There was a comfortable flat above the stables at Fortune's Field for later on, with a pump nearby in the yard. Lizzie could stay on with her ladyship as long as it was prudent. The poor soul had seemed a bit better today, before they left; but Gawd knew how she'd put up with this latest. At any rate, he himself might hope for a word or two with Liz while this young hussy – you could see, or rather hear, that she was one, there hadn't been much struggle from the sound of it – was sent in to be inspected as a wife for the unhappy heir. It wasn't his, Smithers's business, though he knew everything that went on; always had, in fifteen years' service. That pretty little governess, betrayed and then kept down at the cottages where everyone treated her as a loose woman and knew every time his lordship called, he, Smithers, had been sorry for; he'd seen her sometimes in evenings, out picking marigolds in the front garden, only the size of a handkerchief that had been. He'd known then he needn't expect anyone of that kind; like an angel, she'd seemed, Miss Mary. She was dead; had died of shame, to his way of thinking. It couldn't be helped. Lizzie, at any rate, he told himself once more, was safe.

*   *   *

'Tie up your tapes again, my dear; we're approachin' the inn. Get your cloak back on. Pull down that skirt; it's too short, told'em so at the time. Don't mind Beatrice; she looks down her nose anyway. Come along.'

It was all right, he'd discovered, for Anstey; short skirt or not, Amy had had a maidenhead, only now, of course, she'd lost it. He himself hadn't meant to go as far, but there it was; or rather was no longer; and the journey had been exactly the right length. After all, come to think, it didn't matter one way or the other now; Anstey wouldn't know the difference, and the whole thing was kept neatly in the family. Damaged goods would have been out of the question. He'd write tonight to old Killigrew, puttin' it to him that a handsome dowry for his granddaughter might lead to certain investigations bein' dropped; no need to say there hadn't been any yet, the War Office was slow in any case. Meantime, one hoped poor Beatrice was feelin' recovered after restin' for the time.

Gilbert and the coachman then assisted a flushed, bemused and crumpled Amy down from the carriage and into the Feathers Inn to confront her future mother-in-law, who was in fact slightly better.

Back at Shearwater's Academy, Miss Ellen had raised her hands and eyes predictably to heaven when informed that Amy Killigrew had been permitted to go off quite alone with Lord Croom. 'I thought you would have had more *sense*, Jemima!'

She said very little else; after all it was probably too late. She did however remark somewhat tartly that at that rate, it would be unsuitable to take Amy back again, and that her things might as well be packed at once and sent after her. 'You may fetch her yellow trunk,' she finished faintly, adding that if Mr Killigrew made enquiries, he was to be referred direct to Lord Croom at Fortune's Field; she herself abandoned responsibility.

Mrs Ludd, normally the dominant partner, pursed her lips. She had frequently told young Amy with some conviction that she would come to a bad end, and perhaps it had happened. It remained to be seen whether or not the betrothal announcement would appear in the gazettes. On the whole, it was better for Shearwater's not to be mentioned in the matter. A veil would be suitably drawn in one's mind without delay.

It was shortly after that that Claud and Toby, by now in positions in separate banks and going their separate ways although, for the time, they shared a lodging, happened to see the announcement in the papers of Anstey's recent nuptials. Toby raised his arched red eyebrows, remarking that there had been no previous word of any betrothal: since starting at Coutts's, his mind had begun to run on lines somewhat more conventional than formerly.

Claud, as he seldom did, guffawed openly. Toby then – he had the more comfortable nature of the two by far – said that it might be the making of poor Anstey; nobody had ever given him a chance.

'He won't manage anything,' remarked Claud with coarse confidence. He had taken, out of office hours when both young men wore black coats, high stocks and pale grey peg-topped trousers, to wearing a loose Byronic collar and allowing a lock of black hair to fall nonchalantly over one eye. The eye itself glittered shrewdly. Claud was extremely handsome, knew it, and turned the heads of lady customers at Crowbetter's with mathematical precision. Toby himself turned fewer at Coutts's; for one thing ladies were not commonly seen there, only their husbands; also, his heart was softer than Claud's, and women enjoy being ill-treated. This reflection itself made Toby remember the mysterious woman upstairs at Fortune's Field who was his father's wife, and Tobias's snub at the time he had ventured to ask about it. He dared now to tell Claud the whole thing in confidence, and Claud shrugged.

'You should have asked me at the time instead of our father,' he said, and told him the story with dry accuracy. Toby flushed beneath his fashionably *en brosse* flame of notable hair; anyone would think Claud, not he, was the elder, merely because Claud knew who his own mother was. He, Toby, would not now dare to ask Tobias that as well; perhaps it didn't matter, but he never had been told.

Claud always seemed to ferret out things he didn't, although Toby himself was certain their father was just, and certainly made no favourites. However Claud needn't be so damned uppish in any case; everyone knew Crowbetter's was an inferior and somewhat racketty bank, only begun early this century by that man of parts, old Nick Crowbetter, who lived in Hyde Park Gardens under circumstances which were not considered respectable. Oneself had a steadier background and had begun to meet the socially élite, like Letty Pembridge, who had her own handsome bank account and cashed her own cheques on occasion. With regard to Anstey, Toby supposed he ought to go down soon to Fortune's on a Friday to Monday, meet the bride and see how things sped there in general. Also, he wanted to make it up with his father. He mentioned some of this, but not all, to Claud, who suggested that they might share a carriage down later on after the shooting had started; meantime, there was enough to do in town.

IV

Amy was unhappy. She had been married now for almost two and a half weeks. Anstey didn't like her. Neither did her mother-in-law, who as Lord Croom had predicted looked down her long nose from the beginning, and seldom spoke. As for the General, he was busy at the coverts. It was not even made clear by anyone what she was supposed to do with herself during the day, except for the orchard.

She had, in fact, been left with her own company long enough by now to be able to reflect on what had taken place following her first acquaintance with the General, after which events had seemed to follow one another with notable speed. She had been informed brusquely by him, after a slightly unsatisfactory interview with Lady Croom at the Feathers (Beatrice had been still in bed after what had, in fact, been a mild attack of angina) that she would not be returned to Shearwater's Academy for Young Ladies but would, on the contrary, be comin' straight back with them to Fortune's Field, Smithers having been sent at once to collect a light valise and night-things from the school authorities and to order Amy's trunk to be sent on by carrier. That this virtual kidnapping of an heiress happened to coincide with Miss Shearwater's already expressed opinion on the subject was as well, as it secured a peaceful solution to all parties. In Lord Croom's view, it was no longer safe to let the young woman return because, known' what she now did, she would only want to do the same thing with the drawin'-master. This would take the whole business out of the family. He himself could handle Killigrew by letter, and saw no additional need to handle (God forbid) either Miss Shearwater or Mrs Ludd.

He behaved with unnatural propriety on the journey down, which had to be taken in slower stages because of Beatrice's health. At nights Amy slept uncomfortably with the latter lady, Lizzie the maid lying meantime on a pallet in the room at two consecutive inns. Talk was kept to a minimum, Beatrice had in fact, while having long since abandoned open suspicion of any young woman left alone even for moments in Gilbert's company – it was a waste of emotion – knew, with the prescience of those indubitably born into the top drawer, that the bride destined irrevocably for poor Anstey was either out of the third or even the fourth, with a mild veneer of finishing. One would of course keep an eye for Anstey's sake. Croom said there was a good deal of money involved, which was of course vulgar, but becoming increasingly necessary; their end of the Field wasn't as well kept up as that of Tobias, and she herself had worn nothing new for years. Finding herself back at Fortune's Field (she had never expected to see it again, that mysterious pain in the arm had been most unpleasant and one hoped would not recur), Beatrice went to lie down at once, and did not therefore see the first meeting between her son and his (by now, one supposed) betrothed.

Amy found the sight of Anstey's thin colourless presence uninteresting, but not having met many young men in her short life she supposed he would do. Anstey himself was unenthusiastic about the prospect of regular marriage, but assumed that it was his duty although he knew he didn't care for young women. The memory of the lost Franz assailed him and then was suppressed, alongside the cheerful monk on the coat of arms to be seen everywhere at Munich, which had induced a desire for peaceful cloisters in some way resembling the orchard at Fortune's Field, this being almost the only place to which Anstey could retire by himself, though not in the pollen season. Otherwise, he continued rather unsuccessfully to try to imitate his father, having adopted a military stride although the army was long since out of the question, and taken to raising his voice loudly when not interrupted by asthma and if he happened to have anything to say. However he loathed shooting because the sight of blood

made him feel sick, a fact he attempted valiantly to
disguise and which the General, panting with enthusiasm
like one of his own retrieving springers bringing back the
birds, had unaccountably failed to notice on such
expeditions.

At any rate, Anstey contrived to greet his future bride
with politeness if without enthusiasm, and as Amy had
already had whispered to her, in hasty sibilants while in
process of fetching her light summer cloak, by Mrs Ludd
that she was lucky to have the chance of a future lord if she
behaved herself, she behaved. What had happened on the
ensuing carriage-journey, while startling and pleasant,
had not been repeated, and Amy supposed – among the
extras paid for by Grandfather had, of course, been
riding-lessons – that it must perhaps have been some kind
of preliminary marital canter. She also had a vague
recollection from a geography lesson, in which subject Mrs
Ludd was progressive, that they had certain initiation
ceremonies in darkest Africa, but these had not been
described in recognisable detail.

The wedding itself was held up briefly by two factors.
One was that Amy's trunk was lost on the way and never
did arrive. It added to her depression that she still had to
wear her skimpy school dress, even, in the end, being
married in it in the drawing-room, because the General
had sworn that he wasn't spendin' a penny on anythin' but
the licence, both parties being under age, until Killigrew
stumped up the dowry in hard cash. Grandfather himself,
evidently after an exchange of letters, stormed furiously
down to Fortune's Field from Liverpool, where he was
being cautiously successful in the cotton business, and
remained closeted alone with Lord Croom for some time
in the library. Angry roars were heard issuing therefrom
by Amy, who happened to creep past; through the door,
she was able to hear that there hadn't been nothing wrong
with them boots, they'd got the bloody army through
Spain and Portugal, hadn't they? and would have got them
on to Paris after the battle, wouldn't they, if some damned
interference hadn't been set about at headquarters by
whoever thought he could do better at the price? Evidently
some answer must have been forthcoming, because

Grandfather, who had a red face and grey whiskers, emerged from the library looking redder still, signed cheques thereafter without trouble, and even remained in person to give Amy away. There weren't any guests at the wedding because of Anstey's health, except for old Mr Tobias Croom, who arrived as usual looking elegant, was evidently rather amused at the whole business, and made Amy feel foolish and badly dressed in her wretched tight calf-length gown. It wasn't that Mr Croom said anything, it was the way he lowered his expressive eyelids.

Anstey had, at any rate, survived the ceremony without further asthma, and after the vicar had departed and healths were drunk, it was still only afternoon. The General suggested, as he did daily, that she and Anstey should take a turn in the orchard before dinner, as it was settin' fruit. The General winked at Amy as he said it, but it wouldn't have been ladylike to wink back.

In any case, nothing happened in the orchard. They simply walked, as usual – it had been an enforced habit since her arrival – across the garden at the east end, in which Beatrice took a mild interest because it would be incorrect not to, and Amy turned her head towards the giant oaks, far older than the house, which stood in the park where deer grazed, but they weren't tame; then in the other direction towards the hothouses, where a few grapes ripened half-heartedly. The orchard was beyond, where it was sheltered; and as usual Anstey pointed out which were apples and which were pears, which it was difficult to be certain of meantime because all one could see among the leafy branches were tiny green fruit. 'You will have to come by yourself in the blossom season,' said Anstey dispiritedly, adding that it was very pretty but that he himself could only look at it from inside the house, upstairs, at that time of year.

Nothing else took place, certainly nothing as exciting as the carriage-journey encounter. However Amy decided that she didn't mind being married, even though, from what Anstey let drop, it was evident that he preferred to be by himself in the orchard as a rule. They then returned to the house, in time for tea.

*   *   *

The wedding night later on was not a success. First of all Amy was chilled by the sight of the immense cold bed, in which various members of the Croom family had, it would appear, been born, wedded and had died since the late Middle Ages. It was even claimed that the room in which it stood had been part of an original Saxon residence, exemplified now by a depressing piece of pinkish plaster and some old wood struts on one wall, the others having collapsed at the time the first lord made his extensive classical alterations to the front following the lucrative association with Old Q. Saxons having known nothing about chimneys, one had of course subsequently been built, but the large grate contained no fire at all at this season. Amy regarded the Croom coat of arms embroidered on the tester and bedspread with equal depression; a large crane rampant with a long beak was portrayed, which reminded her of her mother-in-law. It had in fact been explained to her that the bird itself was the Delahaye device, which was thought more delicate in the circumstances than the clenched fist proper which pertained to the Croom escutcheon.

Amy was in a state of not unnatural interest rather than one of bridal qualms of any kind, as she rather hoped for some repetition of what had happened in the carriage. However Anstey, by no means as fine a figure in his nightshirt as the General in anything at all, proved somewhat inept although he did not, as Claud's unheard gibe put it next day in London, fail to manage. He got up presently, however, and left Amy abruptly, standing with his back turned and staring at the empty fireplace.

'Somebody has done this with you already,' he said stiffly. 'Who was it?'

Amy, disappointed about the whole proceeding, replied somewhat tartly that of course it had been his father: what else did he expect? The effect of this announcement on Anstey surprised and scared her; he advanced, slapped her face, then burst into tears and retreated to his dressing-room. Amy lay on alone in the cold bed and decided that she would have liked to send for a stone hot water bottle, but that perhaps in the circumstances it would appear unfeeling.

*   *   *

Anstey slept in his dressing-room on ensuing nights, and this fact was duly elicited by the General on enquiry at last of the valet who served them both: he himself had noted the estrangement of the pair by day and hoped that everythin' by night was as it ought to be, but nobody gave any indication one way or the other. Beatrice, whom he consulted, replied coldly that she had had nothing to say to Amy on that subject or, in fact, on any other; the young woman spent her mornings mooning about the house, while Anstey read a book by himself. 'You ought to have a word, perhaps, Croom.'

Gilbert had a word, which took the form of asking Anstey in private why the devil he felt he had to sleep in his dressin'-room. The bridegroom then vouchsafed, with dignity, the fact that his bride had been tampered with and had when asked blamed no other than the General: he himself had said nothing on the matter till now.

'Thought you seemed mumpish,' remarked Gilbert. 'No need to trouble y'self, my boy; did it on purpose, for your own sake.' He then illustrated his point by referring to an uncorked wine bottle. If you left it open, it either went wild or someone else came along and drank it. This parable having failed to impress his son, Lord Croom then related briefly the story of the drawin'-master and how it had been necessary, for the sake of the family honour, to ensure that no bride brought down to the Field had had her own such perquisite tarnished in any respect. The whole thing had been perfectly in order, a tight little virgin, take his word for it; the word, after all, of an officer. It was, the General added, safe to charge ahead. Anstey wondered dismally if he was thinking of Waterloo.

A walk in the orchard being out of the question because it was raining, Anstey did not resume these for the time, but instead began again to have relations with his bride in silence on the nights that followed. He had given her no explanation of this resumption and Amy felt hurt, even turning slightly sulky; after all, he'd slapped her face and then, without apology, come back to bed after taking no notice of her at all for the past week or so. In any case what happened was nothing like the carriage encounter. She began to make her lack of enthusiasm evident, and Anstey himself began to adopt a bullying manner to her, which made everything worse. It wasn't as if he was even getting better at what this was supposed to be all about.

The depressed pair were duly sent off for their orchard walk on the first fine day, which did not occur for some weeks; it was by then well into the season, and the popping sounds of the guns could be heard not far off, nearer the coverts. Amy asked Anstey politely if he wouldn't like to go off and shoot; he replied that what he did was his own business, and to mind hers. They walked on in silence while the guns ceased; then, from the opposite direction, two godlike young men made their unexpected appearance at the further end of the orchard. They had merely been rabbit-shooting together, and Claud held a brace by their feet, blood already congealing on the soft dead noses. Amy turned her head away; she didn't like the sight of blood any more than Anstey, it was one of the few things, if she had known, that they had in common. Toby and Claud nevertheless came up, bowed, and were presented: then made their way back to their own end of Fortune's Field.

Claud was the first to utter. 'Drab little thing,' he said, adding once again that he hoped Anstey could manage.

'They can use the money,' said Tobias kindly. He had personally thought Amy was like a soft little rabbit herself, with scared eyes. He didn't envy any girl married to Anstey: Anstey not only wheezed, but gave himself airs as though he were his own father. Anyone could see the poor girl was bullied by everyone.

Amy and Anstey walked on as far as usual, and then, still without words – they had long ago run out of much there might have been to say – turned and went back to the house. Amy was aware by now that sharing a bed with Anstey would never, or it didn't seem likely, produce the delicious excitement the previous experience with the General in the carriage had done. She hoped she would see the two handsome young men again. Perhaps they would come round to dinner, but one didn't like to ask.

* * *

The General, at that point, received a letter from Mr Killigrew's solicitor to say that his client had expired of a seizure minutes after signing the document which transferred a handsome sum in dowry to Amy, and had moreover some years previously made a will leaving her all his worldly goods on condition of her suitable marriage. It was evident that that to Lord Croom's heir came firmly under this heading, and he therefore had the pleasure of informing his lordship of the encouraging and relevant details. Amy was therefore, as hoped, an heiress, with the sole provision in the will that she must continue to provide for her mother on condition that the latter did not approach her daughter in any way. Nobody had ever thought of inviting Ma to the wedding.

The realisation that his wife was, even meantime, of more importance than himself caused Anstey to succumb to the most violent attack of asthma he had ever had, and Beatrice at this point intervened and insisted that for his health, her son must certainly occupy a separate room. If Amy wasn't yet in a hopeful situation, all of that could be seen to later. By this time a fire had been lit in the grate of the Saxon chamber, as it was autumn and growing colder; that and Anstey's absence in a room along the passage – he continued now and again to visit her – afforded Amy considerable relief. Otherwise, it had been almost as bad as being back at school. She continued to dream of the two young men. The one with red hair, despite his pleasant smile, reminded her of – it was extraordinary as well as being unlikely – of all people, Miss Shearwater.

V

Toby Croom was watching his father Tobias, who was asleep, or at least pretending to be so, in his favourite armchair with its hallowed footrest. The hooded eyelids were at any rate closed over the worldly, amused eyes with their lack of illusion or, by now, surprise about anything. Toby therefore felt a measure of confidence increased by his experience of the world and Coutts's, although he had come to his father, being now again on affectionate terms, to ask for advice about a situation which should probably never have occurred. Toby was an increasingly correct young man, but had remained by nature kind-hearted, as he himself was only too well aware.

On a previous visit – both he and Claud had begun to acquire the habit of them again, finding matters at Fortune's Field improved in the way of hospitality since Amy's money had opened doors at the west end by buying, among other things, new curtains and enabling the General to replenish his cellar – he had happened to find Amy sobbing by herself in the folly. This edifice was almost a place of sentimental pilgrimage since the concurrent, and unwitnessed, births of Gilbert and Tobias, and had been lined by the first lord with mirrors for separate reasons of his own. Amy's sobbing figure, therefore, had been reflected many times like that of Niobe, and Toby, who only knew one way of comforting young women, had duly comforted her.

The results had surprised him; as Claud would undoubtedly have put it, little rabbits have hot tails. Amy's response had so enchanted Toby that the matter had progressed beyond mere comfort to something far more mutual and interfused. They had made love several times then, and often since; asked why she had been found sobbing at the time, Amy replied that Anstey was unkind to her. 'Well, you have my heart instead,' replied Toby gallantly, and by now it was true. He had been sorry for her; Anstey continued to behave to her like a Prussian officer; and, by now, Toby himself was most urgently in love.

They had taken, or rather Amy had as Toby himself was mostly too prudent to put much in writing owing to rigorous training at Coutts's, to leaving little notes of assignation in a certain hollow oak in the grounds. When Amy said that she would be alone at a certain place, or a certain time, Toby would do his utmost to be there; it had, naturally, to be out of banking hours and preferably at the end of the week, although he'd once ridden down very early in the morning and back to town, feeling jaded, in time for opening hours. That mustn't happen often; he was not so deeply in love as to want to compromise his position, as it was uncertain to which of his sons Tobias would in the end leave his money if he didn't decide to leave it to both; one could not borrow on expectations of such a kind, and the alternative – Toby had looked at the matter rather coolly from other angles – would be a rich marriage of his own. Incredibly, Letty Pembridge was interested in him; and Letty had declined half the offers in town. However, for the present, Amy's plight alone filled Toby's mind. It was necessary to have worldly advice, and there was nobody better equipped to give this than his father.

Matters had come to a head today. She had arranged to meet him without fail at the folly, where nobody else was likely to interrupt them at this time of year. Toby had accordingly been surprised, and somewhat put about, to see, among the thinning trees, her delectable little figure come running towards him. There was no doubt that, as the General had once remarked to himself, Amy had a good frontage; she also ran very gracefully, like one does who loves to dance. She had on a new gown made for the winter by a local seamstress, who had unfortunately followed the pattern of the last; Beatrice had said she hadn't time to take her into town for more, and the General – she had told Toby this earlier – had said she should have new gowns when she'd done something to deserve them, which evidently wasn't quite yet. 'What does he mean?' Amy had asked Toby piteously, adding that she always looked like a fright.

Now, however, she had flung her arms round him, an action which alarmed Toby slightly; they might, after all, still be witnessed from the house. However he had no chance to reprove her, as she began to babble heedlessly against him, and clung. 'Toby, Toby, Lizzie Smithers says I'm going to have a baby. It isn't Anstey's. I'm sure it's yours. Of course I didn't tell her or anyone about us. Oh, Toby, Toby, what shall I do? It means I shall have to sleep with Anstey again, for the look of the thing. Nobody knows yet that I haven't lately, he hasn't been back. I don't want to.' Amy bit her lip; it was evident that Lizzie, by now a wife in truth, must have instructed her in certain facts and dates. 'Don't tell, don't tell; only, help me.'

She started to cry, and Toby was reminded of the distasteful evening some days back, which as it had been the General's birthday and hospitality was the theme, they had all, Tobias bestirring himself for once, except of course for Paola, foregathered at the festive board at the further end of Fortune's. The General had become slightly drunk, and ended the meal not by standing before the port while the ladies withdrew, but had instead taken Amy in her skimpy new gown on his knee and had handled her in an intimate fashion which reduced her to blushing confusion and Toby to plain rage. It was, the General had roared, to let Anstey see what he ought to begin to do with a fine young woman, instead of mopin' as he did. Old Tobias had lowered his gaze and played with the stem of his wineglass; Claud had followed suit. Beatrice, who was still present, had stared icily. Toby had begun to blush as hotly as Amy, only with difficulty restraining himself from getting up and punching his host on the avuncular nose. Anstey had, as usual, maintained a stiff upper lip and had somehow in the end been thrust into the small drawing-room with Amy, where there was a sofa, under barked orders from the General to get on with it. It hadn't, from what she was saying now, been got on with to any appreciable extent after the door had been resolutely slammed on the pair. Toby was indignant for Amy, then and now; and now, here outside the folly, he became aware, as did Amy likewise, of the square-set figure of the General himself, standing irrevocably between them and it.

'Madam.'

The single, snapped word caused Amy's limbs to quaver beneath her, very nearly giving way: he must have followed her out. 'You been meetin' often, the pair of yer?' he demanded now. Toby, lying valiantly, said no, it was merely a chance meeting. Amy's mouth drooped and she said nothing at all. Toby wished at times that she would show a little more spirit. He watched while the General led her off by the wrist, like a straying whippet, if such a term applied. In the nature of things they moved towards the folly, but Toby, from where he was uncertainly standing – ought he to have protected her? – did not see them go beyond it. For Amy's sake he decided in any case to take himself off. The small pillared edifice where they so often made love together would of course be empty; the usual path led past it to the house, and he could not, without showing an undue interest he had just denied, step out to remark whether or not they had yet reached the east door further beyond.

Nevertheless, once he had returned to his own place, the suspicion increased that they had not gone beyond the folly. It was too late now to go back and look. One's imagination ran riot instead, and Toby found himself afflicted with unbecoming thoughts about the whole situation. He had decided, as already stated, to seek his father's advice.

It proved impossible to ask Tobias, as Paola had appeared in the way she usually did. Although she was not, for olfactory reasons, a welcome guest at the other end of the Field she was by now pre-eminent in this. She practically, the young man thought with resentment, ruled his father.

'You will not wake him,' she said firmly to Toby.

'He probably isn't asleep.'

Tobias remained firmly out of the picture, and Paola said 'You must not remain. He is tired. He is an old man, and needs his rest.'

Old men appeared, Toby had decided, to have their

secret proclivities. The whole business was fairly disgusting. However he himself was not the kind of young man who pitted himself against the inevitable. He therefore bowed, took himself out of the room, and was not in time to see Tobias open first one eye, then the other.

Toby's suspicions had been correct; the General and Amy had indeed not passed beyond the folly. Her limbs being by now already turned to water, the episode of the carriage was repeated with added vigour and with the help of genuine rage on the part of Lord Croom, who was damned if Tobias's bastard was goin' to complicate the inheritance further; he himself would take a hand again, and took it. The mirrors reflected this energetic activity and Amy watched in a kind of mesmerised trance; it must be happening to someone else. She had already forgotten about Toby.

She heard Lord Croom speak presently. 'If you've let that cub cuckold Anstey, by God, madam, you'll smart. In the meantime –'

Amy heard herself scream. In the doorway of the folly, like a statue of matronly Roman endurance, stood Beatrice. It was uncertain how long she had been there. Neither of them had heard her approach. Amy pulled down her inadequate skirts and fled wordlessly, on limbs which by now really would hardly support her. The General was left to face his wife.

'Gilbert, I am leaving you.'

He flushed an unbecoming puce: this statement was ridiculous.

'Nonsense, m'dear,' he said. He was fond of Beatrice, and relied on her; but that little bitch was strayin' and Anstey couldn't be expected to deal with her in heat. The General made some such explanation, which sounded lame even to his own ears. Beatrice, as usual, looked down her nose. For some reason Gilbert thought of Lot's wife, turned to a pillar of salt for lookin' back. Damn it, Lot had slept with his daughters to make sure of the inheritance; granted he had been drunk at the time. Beatrice, in any case, was perhaps less made of salt than of stone, or even ice these days. For once the General felt unable to deal with the situation; in its way, it was worse than Waterloo. Women –

'You are my wife,' he said majestically. 'Can't leave like that. It's only the second time, when all's said: had to find out, then teach her a lesson just now. Good reasons for everythin'. We need an heir as you know, to carry on the name.' He began to flounder. 'If you'd managed anythin' but Anstey in the end, there'd be no need for all of this,' he finished triumphantly. It was always possible, given time and diplomacy, to put oneself in the right, remaining master of one's house as usual.

His wife remained unimpressed. 'I have endured much in the way of unfaithfulness from you all these years,' she said, as if she were talking to a stranger. 'The governesses were bad enough; this latest disgraceful business with your son's wife I will not endure. I have had to watch your disgusting behaviour lately at my own dinner-table in the company of guests; that was almost enough. Now –' She turned away, and he began to realise that he had lost her. 'I am going to my sister at Tunbridge Wells,' she remarked coldly. 'I am going at once, with Smithers and Lizzie; they will return to you in proper course. My personal belongings can be sent later. I shall not return to catalogue them.'

'Beatrice –' The cold word catalogue had convinced him; she was really going. Turning her narrow back, she marched off; Gilbert watched her go with a kind of stupefaction. It was true he'd married her long ago chiefly because of her breedin', but they'd got used to one another. She'd always been at home, waitin'; that had been the case while he was out in India with old Arthur, out in Spain and Portugal later with the same remarkable feller for years; then there had been the champagne celebration after Waterloo, and Anstey born at last as a result. Poor Anstey wasn't what he ought to be; an upstandin' heir would no doubt have managed for himself in the first place. If only he and Beatrice could have been like other couples, together always at the beginnin', there wouldn't have been this end. That it really was the end Gilbert Croom could not bring himself to accept quite yet; the present silence of the garden both defeated and reassured him; Beatrice was always workin' in it as a rule, with her old gloves on. She couldn't leave. She must come back. He would persuade her. It might take some doin', but meantime he would leave that little Amy to her husband, or to the devil. That feller Toby was neither here nor there. Who was goin' to see to the housekeepin'? He wouldn't have that Italian at his end of the house for all the wine in Portugal.

Toby meantime, hurt and cautious, found it was some days before he could bring himself to travel down to Fortune's Field and visit the hollow oak. There was, as usual, a letter.

> *Dearest beloved T.,*
> *Lord C. has gone to Tunbridge Wells to try to persuade Lady C. to return. I hope he will be away some time. Meantime, what I told you is true, but A. will take nothing to do with me just now, and I am at a loss, and fryted.* (This spelling melted Toby's heart.) *Come to me in my room before Lord C.'s return; you know the way. I long to hold you in my arms, you do not know the half of it. My love for ever and ever, A.*

He twisted the letter in his hands; it would be revealing if anyone else had found it: she must, he feared, have been waiting in vain for longer than she had perhaps expected. It was difficult not to go to her at once; Toby reproached himself for his late suspicions. It was clear that she loved him with all her heart. What had happened was, after all, his fault. The child was his; the thought intrigued him. For its own sake, there must be some way found of inducing Anstey to believe that he was the father, distasteful as the prospect was; also, scandal must not on any account reach Coutts's. Toby began, for both reasons, to regard his ineffectual cousin with deep resentment. Had Anstey treated Amy kindly in the first place, she would not have been found crying in the folly; and if not, nothing would thereafter have happened that had. That was the simplest way of looking at it, and Toby began to feel himself a knight rescuing a damsel from her asthmatic dragon. He would certainly, at any rate, make his way along the passages tonight; she would know, having no doubt heard the sounds of his arrival, that he had come home. He pondered the possible effects of a draught of brandy on Anstey; certainly something or other would have to be done.

Night came, and as it happened to be the dark of the moon Toby had some difficulty in finding his way; stealing upstairs, he could hear the besotted murmurings of poor Tilly behind her shut door. What must it be like to be ostracised by everyone? It mustn't happen to Amy. He found her door at last, knocked, and heard her call out to him to come in. She was waiting in bed, with the curtains left open and the lamp still lit. His appearance however did not seem to enchant her as much as Toby had expected.

'O God, Anstey's coming. He sent word that he would be here tonight. It's the first time since – I daren't let you stay –'

He had already begun to kiss her tenderly, trying to explain that he had been delayed in going to the oak; but her heart beneath his hand beat so fast in alarm that at last he took in her words. 'Amy, Amy –'

There came a knocking on the door, which he had already closed. Amy thrust him away, her face white.

'Quick, here he is; get behind the curtain, there's no time to leave. Don't move or let him guess; hide yourself, please, please.'

He had no choice but to obey, and betook himself round the bed's bulk to where the further curtains would conceal him. He heard Anstey come in, climb into the bed and begin at once to exercise his marital duties. They hadn't spoken to each other. Toby found leisure to feel some surprise that Anstey's breathing appeared to be, for once, like that of other men. A suspicion that flitted across his mind was quickly stilled; the General was certainly away in Tunbridge Wells. Anstey's transports sounded satisfactory. Amy began to make small ecstatic noises herself, which caused Toby's bosom to swell with a certain understandable indignation; things didn't seem to be nearly as bad as she had made out.

The process continued for a little while, with the rejected lover standing stiffly against the wall, his presence unsuspected and duly closeted by curtains; he stared without enthusiasm at the remaining fragment of pinkish Saxon plaster. Suddenly there came a second knocking at the door, peremptory and loud. He heard Amy gasp; there was a scuffle in the bed, the door was heard to burst open, and Amy screamed. Toby, unable to contain himself any longer, erupted out from behind the curtains to perceive his half-brother Claud, whom he had no longer seen for some time as they no longer shared lodgings in London, rising in disarray from the bedclothes, Anstey standing in open-mouthed stupefaction at the door in his nightshirt, then hurling himself across to the bed and pummelling Amy with his fists before succumbing, naturally, to an attack of asthma. Amy was howling by now so much that nobody had heard a third arrival; within what seemed like moments, a stocky figure in travelling-clothes appeared at the door, a lit sconce in its hand seized suddenly from the hall.

'What the devil's goin' on?' roared the General, returned disconsolate from Tunbridge Wells without his wife. 'What are you two bastards doin' in here? By God, if I leave this house for a day, madam, this is what to expect, it would appear; get out of here, all of you: yes, even you, Anstey, m'boy; take your accursed wheezin' back to bed. I warned you, madam, what would happen if this occurred once more, and it's happenin' twice, that's evident. I'll thrash your tripes.'

Toby and Claud had meantime been standing stiff as grenadiers, not looking at one another. The almost deliquescent young woman on the bed was sobbing against the pillows. Toby spoke. The General looked as if about to begin flogging her like a recruit with everyone watching. That must not happen.

'You will not lay a finger on Amy, or I will take her away,' he said angrily. 'You have the use of her money, and Anstey does not treat her well. She is due some consideration from you both, and if any harm befalls her you will answer to me.' He was aware that his voice faltered slightly on the last note; what would they say at Coutts's?

'Toby, Toby – I didn't mean – I thought you weren't coming, it's been so long, and I –'

'Be silent,' said the General, but appeared to be staying his hand. Claud remained offended; he considered that he had been made to look ridiculous, a state of affairs he found particularly intolerable and which seldom happened.

'I should call you out for this,' he remarked to Toby. 'but the cause is unworthy.' He then stalked out of the room, having rectified his clothing. Anstey and the General followed, the former still wheezing disastrously. Toby took one last look, a stern one, at the figure on the bed. The sight of Amy was particularly depressing by now.

'You must bear your child safely,' he said. 'Its paternity is now, however, in question. I will neither visit the oak tree again, nor yourself. I have no more to say except that I am leaving this house, and am unlikely to return.' This resulted in a final wail from the bed, and Toby turned without more words and left. Claud was waiting as he gained the further corridor. The latter had lit his own candle and the light flared on his set humourless face.

'It started with the pair of you in the folly, I dare say,' he said. 'I had my suspicions, but I found the wretched little creature cowering in the linen-cupboard, saying she had seen old Tilly at the end of the passage and was frightened. I took it as an open invitation, and there have been others since. The fact is that Anstey can't hold her or any woman down. It is no longer my affair.' He made no further reference to a duel.

'I suggest we consult our father,' Toby ventured weakly. He did not add that old Tobias seemed to be the only male in the household who had not enjoyed the favours of Anstey's bride. Peace was however desirable, and his bruised heart was already mending. There were, after all, compensations waiting in London.

Thereafter Amy was kept under lock and key in apartments in the north tower, in much the same way as Tilly was kept, with somewhat more freedom nowadays, in the south one. The difference was also that Anstey, drilled by the General, continued to visit his wife as he had intended to do on the famous night when everybody else had revealed the same intention. As for the General, he took Amy routinely for an occasional turn in the grounds for the benefit of her health. He had after all no wish to be unjust. The fact that Beatrice had proved obdurate despite all pleadin' and housemaids were getting difficult to come by, as no respectable mother would now permit her daughter to enter employment at Fortune's Field, meant that one had to make do with what one might. The situation was no longer anybody else's concern.

Time passed, and on one occasion in Amy's bed in the tower the General happened to notice that her stomach was swellin' notably. He questioned her severely on the matter, but Amy, predictably, burst into floods of tears, swearing the baby was either Anstey's or the General's and that Claud had been visiting her for the very first time, on the occasion in question. She forgot to mention Toby at all. It was impossible to beat the truth out of her in her condition, rememberin' how Beatrice had been prone to miscarriages if anythin' adverse happened in any way. Missing Beatrice badly – her advice now would have been invaluable – the General tried, with a fair degree of knowledge, to assess the state of the pregnancy for himself: it might be three or four months, or maybe five. He wasn't sure and, evidently, neither was the wretched Amy. His handling of her in such a way made her sob and cry with outrage; they'd all used her exactly as it suited them, she didn't want a baby anyway, and Toby didn't come here any more. She gave vent at last to an atavistic wail which made the General start back, perturbed and, for once, considering the possibility outlined by Amy herself.

'I want my Ma! I want my Ma!'

In the meantime, there was no sign of either Tobias's sons at Fortune's Field, that personage having, as might have been expected, advised them to make themselves scarce for a very long time. This was no real hardship to either young man as they had plenty of relaxation in London, usually, but not always, in separate strata of society. They heard, and drily compared notes on the matter when they met, of the arrival at Fortune's Field of Amy's mother, who appeared incomprehensibly to have been sent for according to an elegantly scribbled note to each son from Tobias himself. It appeared to be a matter of no great interest, and they forgot about it in the light of ensuing events concerning their broadening futures.

Amy was by now hopelessly in love with the General. Her dreary situation, the fact that she otherwise saw nobody at all except for the occasional lugubrious visits of Anstey (who was becoming singularly odd) and the servant who carried away her slops, caused her to rely increasingly on the single exciting masculine presence still available. At first she had wept for Toby, it is true, but not for long; the stocky presence of a man with magnificent whiskers, who had even threatened to beat her and still might, and whose occasional undoubted possession of her for a brisk quarter-hour involved very little talk, enlivened Amy's situation remarkably: and so when the General informed her that her mother had been sent for as she herself had requested, Amy was not too pleased. However, Ma came, bringing with her a great deal of baggage. She hadn't changed from what one vaguely remembered, except to have grown comfortably plump, and she had also adopted a false front of brown curls. She took Amy's part at once.

'Men. They leave you so's you don't know whether you're lying or standing, dear. All the same, we couldn't do without them, could we?'

She then took charge, including the housekeeping; that was a relief. Fortune's Field, or one end of it, had since Beatrice's departure grown extremely neglected, particularly the garden; the furniture was dusty and the linen untended. The General couldn't seem to find a housekeeper. It was a blessing to have Ma in that way; also, she would know what to do at the birth, which was a comfort. As for the money, the General said there was no need to worry; he'd continue the allowance; they could call it a housekeepin' payment if anyone asked.

Bets were meantime being taken in the village as to the true paternity of the coming heir, as the bride seemed unusually large. When it was known at last that labour had begun, healths were drunk in advance in the local taproom. It was decided that that there Anstey couldn't possibly be the father; he had taken, by now, to shivering alone in the orchard in a monk's robe and cowl, and talking to himself. The coming heir was probably, like half the village if you faced up to it, the old General's. Many admired Gilbert and even had an affection for him, as it was said had happened with Henry VIII, still re-membered in folk tales from the time he'd made a progress through the village and stopped overnight, with some queen or other, perhaps at the Field and perhaps not.

The labour started earlier than expected, and poor Amy, having given a sharp cry that brought the remaining servants running – Lizzie and Smithers had not, after all, returned from Tunbridge Wells and there was a new coachman – strained piteously for nine or ten hours, helped by her mother as far as it could be done; there was finally extracted from her a fine handsome boy, who was said at once to resemble greatly the late first lord before he grew as dilapidated as he had in the company of Old Q. The news was relayed to the anxiously awaiting General, and brushing aside the past he hastened upstairs to kiss Amy warmly on the cheek. 'Well done, well done, m'dear,' he said, his whiskers joyfully pricking her exhausted cheek. He beheld the baby with pride; didn't matter whether it was his or Anstey's, it was a Croom, and healthy and that was that. Anstey himself had never yelled as loudly in all of his life, let alone on the first occasion. Gilbert dandled the fine little fellow, who was by that time sound asleep; and was mildly irritated by the subsequent appearance at his side of the midwife, with whom he had previous acquaintance.

'She's not comfortable yet, my lord; there's another to come.'

They had remarked, he'd heard, in church that Amy was lookin' big for her time, though nobody includin' herself had seemed to know exactly what the time might be. It didn't matter; here was the heir; twins no doubt ran in families. It might, after all, have been a cross-birth with the size she'd been by the end, and wasn't; a good thing. Gilbert retired to the library to drink port, and reflected on his improvin' fortunes. He had banished Toby and Claud from his mind; the whole thing had been started much sooner, and wasn't their concern.

The midwife – Amy's mother was busy attending to her – came down presently with a second baby. 'My lord, it's a beautiful little girl. You've never seen such a beauty. She'll turn heads, to be sure.'

She showed him the newborn beauty. It had red hair.

Tobias Croom was disturbed for once, not in his armchair but in bed; it was by then two in the morning. He was confronted by his brother Gilbert, carrying, somewhat in the manner in which one carries a kitten for drowning, a very small red-haired new girl baby.

'Take it,' said the General. 'Do as you like with it. Won't have it at the west end; advise you to get rid of it somewhere, don't want talk. Hares can conceive two litters at once, but I never knew a woman who could, even Amy. Young Toby can either provide for it or smother it; not my affair which. The whole thing will have to be done again from the beginnin'. No doubt next time, never fear; we'll keep the little bitch locked up: as for the boy, he'll stay with me, better than nothin'. By God, Anstey can make another on her next time, or else I will. Nobody else will get at her.'

He thrust the bundle, which writhed slightly, towards its undoubted grandfather, who took it gingerly; there was very little to be said in the circumstances. Tobias then handed the burden to Paola, smiling a little.

'It would be amusing, would it not, my brother, if my blood were to inherit after all?' he remarked evenly.

After the General had stormed off – it was beginning to rain outside, and he would get wet in addition to everything else – Paola quietly got a clean cloth, diluted some cow's milk in a jug with water, waited till the baby awoke and then gave it a dipped corner of the linen to suck. 'We will have to find a *balia*, a wet-nurse,' she said. 'It is one way in which I myself can no longer oblige you.'

'We will find one on our way north,' said Tobias with firmness. He had no intention of having a troublesome little girl about the house: Boys were different. When morning broke, still dismal with rain, he gave orders for the carriage to be got ready and then, taking Paola and the baby wrapped in a shawl, caused the whole party to journey leisurely northwards once they had won their way clear of gossip or detention. At one stopping-inn he took leisure to write two letters. One was to Miss Shearwater to say that he would shortly be presenting, with his compliments, her grandchild to her to be educated. The second letter was to Toby in London. Would he care to think of a name for his daughter? It was unlikely that her existence would otherwise hamper his career.

VI

Toby and Claud had meantime continued on their predestined ways, meeting occasionally, but always by accident, at the houses of mutual acquaintances they made in and beyond London. Their natures had never been similar, and were by now growing increasingly divergent. The episode of Amy rankled in both their minds, though it was never spoken of. Continuing mutually polite but distant, they would take part as requested in shooting arrangements, card games, walks with the ladies in the host's garden, or politics in the evening over port. Neither of the young men were Tobias's sons for nothing, each having an undoubted eye to the main chance; but Toby's was perhaps the less firmly fixed of the two. He was still cautious about marrying Letty Pembridge, whereas Claud, given the like opportunity, would long since have snapped such an heiress up.

Officially both young men were handsome and unattached. It was known that they were the sons of irregular unions, which were beginning to be frowned on in this prosaic age which had succeeded the Regency and old King William only last year. Also, although it was known there would be a large fortune at their father's death, it was by no means certain how this would be divided. Mothers of eligible daughters, therefore, saw to it that while the two young men were certainly to be invited as dancing-partners, there must be no lingering behind the potted palms on any occasion.

This state of affairs had suited both Toby and Claud perfectly well up to date. Both had assured careers in their disparate banks, and were by now reasonably certain of promotion, Toby's *gaffe* with regard to prudent conduct

by clerks having been concealed by the timely intervention
of his father in removing the evidence. Neither, therefore,
need be content with a citizen bride or, worse, one whose
father had engaged in trade: both young men already
looked higher. Toby knew he need look no higher in fact
than Letty, who was well-born as well as rich, but he still
had misgivings; he knew she would manage him, even
possibly launch him on a political career whether he liked
it or not; and he was at peace behind Coutts's counters,
where the late tempests of Reform troubled nobody
except the Duke of Wellington, its most famous client.

As for Claud, things changed for him when one day, he
took out a hack to ride in Hyde Park, where he had been
staying by invitation with old Nicholas Crowbetter, long
since a widower, and his mysterious and unpresentable
Maud. It was very early in the morning; there were few
riders about as yet, and in the distance Claud saw an
unprecedented sight approach at full gallop; a young lady.

Claud, like his half-brother, was a correct young man,
and one did not gallop in Hyde Park. He would have
distanced himself immediately from the erring female,
except that, as she approached, he could not but admire
her horsemanship; secondly, he already knew who she
was. Her father was an exceedingly rich retired nabob of
the East India Company, who had shaken the pagoda tree
to his own extreme satisfaction, and now collected
paintings which he hung, one understood, all over his tall
and exclusive house in Piccadilly. Claud had not seen the
pictures, and had only once in fact seen the nabob;
generally the latter sent his footman for money. However
on the one occasion he had visited the bank in person and
limping with gout, he had had his young daughter on his
arm; and this now was the daughter. One understood that
the mother lived abroad. Possibly that was the reason why
no eye was kept on Miss Flora Whittinghame's early
morning behaviour: she was seldom to be met with later in
the day.

Claud cantered up, therefore, raising his hat elegantly;
he knew he looked his best in riding-clothes, even better
than he did in the pearl-grey inexpressibles demanded by
Crowbetter's during banking hours. He made no bones

about the social inferiority of a bank clerk; this young woman needed a preceptor. 'Miss Whittinghame, you will lose your reputation if you gallop,' Claud told her firmly. 'Allow me to escort you at a canter instead.'

'I don't care if I do lose it,' replied Flora Whittinghame, who was accustomed to having her own way except when Papa grew difficult, as often happened. She then observed that the interfering young man, whom she remembered seeing somewhere or other, was extremely handsome; such broad shoulders above a narrow waist, and such black hair and shining well-kept whiskers! He would look magnificent in a uniform coat; a pity civilian gentlemen had to wear dull colours. Flora had been, for some months last year, passionately in love with a colonel of dragoons, but Papa had found out in time that the gallant colonel was a fortune-hunter. Flora tossed her brown-gold curls, revealing a long white throat above the riding-habit. She didn't wear veils, as she despised them.

'We've met one another before,' she said, 'but I can't remember where.'

'Perhaps not. It was at the bank.' There was no point in concealing his profession; it was a question of win or lose. How beautiful she was, with her long blue eyes and delicious mouth! For one of his naturally cautious temperament a singular thing had happened; Claud Croom had fallen instantly in love.

The end of it was that Flora impulsively invited him to take tea with her in Piccadilly, during the following week. He knew he could just contrive it after the bank closed, if he took a hackney. At the same time, he wondered if it might not be a little imprudent of an unmarried young lady to issue her own invitations. It was evident that Miss Flora needed a guiding hand, lacking, as he already knew she did, her mother.

After such reflections it was illogical that Claud felt annoyed when, on being ushered up to the first floor of the Piccadilly house by a footman – priceless primitives, not yet generally fashionable, hung tastefully on the ascending walls of the grand staircase – he discovered that there was, after all, a third party present to drink tea.

Another young woman – not after all so young; several years older than Flora, by the look of her – was seated, much at her ease, turquoise faille skirts spread out becomingly and with intention, on the striped sofa. She was handsome rather than beautiful, with a strong jutting nose. The gown she wore was expensive and in the very latest mode, and on her head, of which the dark hair was profusely curled by tongs, reposed not a bonnet but, instead, a beribboned veil in eye-catching colours, the bunches of ribbon disposed on either side the young lady's ears, in which diamonds swung. She was, Claud decided at once, overdressed, with the evident intent of attracting notice in general. Flora introduced her warmly, having greeted him on arrival.

'Letty, darling, this is Mr Croom. Mr Croom, this is my very dearest friend, Letty Pembridge. She agrees with you that it is incorrect to gallop in Hyde Park.' Flora laughed good-naturedly, showing pretty teeth, the sunlight from the curtained windows shining on her bright hair. She, Claud assured himself, didn't need curlpapers; the fact was worth noting.

He watched in fascination as Flora moved to the bell-pull to order tea. She was wearing a plain dress of a lilac colour. When they were married, he had again decided, he would dress her up a little to outshine Miss Letty, but certainly in quieter taste.

Meantime Letty Pembridge, who had not risen – she seemed to regard herself as greatly at home here – had caught at his name with eageress, smiling in somewhat predatory fashion to display, in her own turn, excellent teeth which would, Claud thought, tear some unfortunate man to pieces when Miss Pembridge should elect to make him her victim at the altar. 'Mr Croom,' she said, in a metallic voice which had a slight Welsh ring to it, 'I think that I have met a relative of yours, Mr Toby Croom; is that correct? The name is not usual.'

Claud replied with equal correctness that Toby was his half-brother, but he was unwilling to discuss the latter subject in Flora's presence. He and his half-brother had already shared a mistress in Amy; this in itself made Toby unfit for close acquaintance with the young woman who would become, Claud had already assured himself without knowing yet quite how it was to be done, his own dearly beloved wife. Meantime, the sight of Flora pouring tea from a heavy George III silver pot into fluted cups delighted him; her bare arms and hands were a pleasure to watch, milk-white and graceful; she had a fine young bosom whose prospects delighted him. There was a pianoforte in the room, and he asked if she played it. 'Yes, Flora plays very well,' put in Miss Pembridge, 'and sings also; don't you, my pet?' It was as though Flora could not be permitted to answer for herself; Claud resolved to change this situation, if possible at once.

He announced firmly that he likewise sang. 'Let us attempt a duet later on,' he said winningly to Flora. He hoped devoutly that Miss Letty would not endeavour to make it a trio; her speaking voice was harsh, but some Welsh people overcame this disability when they melted into song. Claud himself had a good tenor note, got no doubt from his Italian ancestry. He reflected with satisfaction that as for Toby, he couldn't sing a bar without going out of tune.

During tea, they conversed equably about mutual acquaintances, life in the bank – Letty put in idly that old Nicholas Crowbetter's private life was a scandal and always had been, there had been an Austrian mistress before he became a widower, and now again Maud – and other matters hardly suitable, Claud decreed inwardly, for the ears of an innocent young woman like Flora Whittinghame. Miss Pembridge, while careful of her own reputation in most ways, was obviously a denizen familiar with the great world; she title-dropped a little, mentioning dear Lord John and the new under-secretary for the colonies, a young man whom personally she found sanctimonious; Mr Gladstone's father, as everyone knew, was himself concerned in the ownership of slaves abroad, whatever his son said in public. Flora, Claud noticed, hung on Letty's every word, and some of the words could not yet be overset; so, for the time, he said little, as was in fact his nature.

Tea over, and the china and silver taken away, he asked

again if Flora would play for him; he wanted to watch her hands on the keys. Letty luckily stayed where she was, and Flora went to the piano and began to play, very competently indeed, an air by Mrs Bogan of Bogan, a mysterious lady dwelling in Scotland who had tried among other activities to purify the poems of Burns. The melody, however, was pleasant, if the words themselves by now a trifle banal. Claud heard his tenor voice soar in unison with Flora's sweet low soprano. This was the way it would be, he thought, in the evenings after they were married: and, by then, they would be alone: he would see to that.

The idyll was interrupted by a figure which suddenly manifested itself in the opened doorway. Flora's white fingers faltered on the keys; the singing died away.

'What's all this caterwaulin'?' demanded the nabob, leaning on his stick. His eyes, the long and rather prominent blue of Flora's own but unredeemed by youth, regarded Claud with disfavour. 'Who the devil are you? Didn't know you was here. Heard a man's voice. Young men don't come to this house except at my invitation. Get out.'

'Papa –' put in Flora uselessly; she was trembling. Letty Pembridge stood up.

'Mr Croom arrived with me,' she announced mendaciously. 'We were about to leave together.' She smiled, showing the tigress teeth. Claud disliked her more than ever; he would write to Flora's father later, with an apology and an explanation: all of this was not to be endured. Meantime he bowed, feeling almost as much of a fool as that time with Amy, and allowed himself to follow Letty out. Her carriage, it was evident, waited below.

Inside, on turquoise velvet cushions – did she always have her upholstery changed to match her gowns? Or was it the other way round? – he heard Letty justify some of it. 'He is a little difficult at present,' she explained about the nabob. 'Flora is impulsive, and has been involved in several flirtations with young men, the last of them an utter scoundrel who would have made off with her for the sake of her fortune. Since then her father has kept her closer than at any time; and you will be aware that she is never, in any instance, to be met with at assemblies. The fact that you were able to encounter her in Hyde Park at all means merely that she slipped out without first asking Mr Whittinghame's permission.' She had evidently been told all.

Claud's despair overcame his dislike for moments, and he said 'How in the world, then, am I to meet her again?' He had, of course, given himself away by this query and immediately knew it. Letty smiled confidently on.

'You may leave it to me; but give it time, to allow his alarm to settle itself,' she replied. 'I am in a position to take Flora for little carriage-drives. In return, tell me about your half-brother; that is who he is, as you say, is it not? You see I know a certain amount.' She plied him with further questions about Toby, and Claud felt an access of spite dictate his answer.

'I would not ask too much about my brother,' he said, staring out of the window at the passing carriages and the fading trees in the Park. 'I could not say this in front of Miss Flora because of her youth, but you yourself are clearly a woman of the world. My brother is, I fear, a womaniser. He has one illegitimate child at the least.' It was perhaps not politic to mention the boy twin as well; Claud's innate caution told him one mention would do, at least for the present: his mother Paola had told him everything, including the fact that Lord Croom showed continuing interest in the boy baby and had had him christened Delahaye. 'Toby turns many heads,' he told Letty Pembridge, adding deliberately 'I do not think he will turn yours.'

He turned his own gaze; the two pairs of hard eyes met. Claud, not being a woman, had however failed in intuition, however swiftly he had seized his advantage. He had in fact said the very thing to convince Laetitia Pembridge, heiress in her own right and sought after by aspirants far more elevated than Toby Croom, that Toby must be rescued by her, placed on the straight and narrow path as her husband, made to love her later if not sooner, taken out from behind the counter at Coutts's and placed firmly at the next safe by-election, all of the above for his own good.

She smiled, made some diplomatic reply, they parted at Claud's destination, and Claud permitted himself to hope that they would not meet again other than was necessary. Despite Letty's bribe about the carriage-drives, he would advance his suit for Flora, in some way, for himself.

> *at Brick Street, the 8th of September 1837.*
> *Dear Mr Whittinghame,*
>
> *I must convey my deepest apologies for having appeared to take advantage of your hospitality without first asking you permission. I did not like to contradict Miss Pembridge openly for her attempted championship of me, but in truth I arrived alone, at Miss Flora's invitation, which I felt I could not refuse although it seemed at the time a little imprudent.*
>
> *In fact, despite this trait in her character which I think, knowing myself, that I could venture to correct, I should greatly like to ask your permission to pay my addresses to her. I am not entirely devoid either of fortune or prospects; the details of the latter would be available from my employer, Mr Nicholas Crowbetter, who I know will gladly give them to you as a valued client.* (Here Claud paused with quill poised; old Nick hadn't actually confirmed the promotion, but hadn't denied it either; he had been sympathetic when consulted and would certainly do his best). *I believe that I could make Miss Flora happy, and steady her; I myself am a man of considered decisions and cool temper. If I may at least further her acquaintance I am convinced that both you, and she, would come to my own way of thinking as concerns so desirable an outcome.*
>
> *I am aware that you are a connoisseur of pictures; I greatly admired the Italian primitives on the staircase on the occasion when — so unfortunately, alas — I ventured to call at Piccadilly. I have private information about a possible Masaccio which has just come on the market. If this news interests you, and I think that it may, I can give you the direction at once. The painting is to be found at Van Hakluyt's gallery in Vine Street, but I doubt if it will remain there very long; I have asked the dealer meantime to reserve it behind scenes in case of your interest, but the decision in this matter, as well as the one I have raised above, is, of course, your own. Not all of us appreciate the value of these early works.*
>
> *I remain, Sir, your very obedient servant,*
> *Claud Croom.*

It had, of course, been old Nick who told him in the first place of the Masaccio, having already, with his foreseeing eye, had it reserved for himself. Claud had no idea why he should have agreed to relinquish it so easily. If he had known, Nicholas Crowbetter in his inmost soul still reproached himself for his own conduct, long ago, in the matter of separating his young niece Sal, dead now after a most unhappy marriage, and his almost as young clerk Hugo Loriot, whom Crowbetter had sent deliberately to Hamburg. Love – Crowbetter himself had had certain experiences of it, but never, as it happened, legally – would do no harm to long-headed young Croom, whom in any case he was thinking of promoting for his agate-hard sense of good business. Old Nick had listened to the whole story in his office with patience and mild amusement, and had sacrificed the Masaccio (if it was one) gladly enough.

The nabob was so pleased with the information about the picture, which he rushed down despite the purgatory of gout and bought at once, that he allowed himself to overcome the sensation of faint dislike the smugness of the young man's letter had aroused in him, as well as the impertinence of a mere bank clerk in aspiring to the hand of his only daughter. However Gerald Whittinghame admitted that he himself had been a clerk once, in India. The plain fact also was that Flora had spoiled her own market a little with one flirtation after another, and damned nearly an elopement last year with that dragoon. Gerald himself didn't want her to take to the ways of her mother, whom he had for many years now paid to stay away from him and to reside in Italy. It would be better if Flora were married soon to some steady young fellow. He therefore replied graciously to Claud's letter and invited him to be present at the hanging of the Masaccio, which portrayed a large serene-browed Madonna and Child and was brought to Piccadilly by the dealer in person, an earnest young man in half-spectacles with a thick Flemish accent. Mr Van Hakluyt departed shortly as was proper, while young Croom stayed on for madeira.

Flora herself was however understandably furious on being told of Claud's letter of apology, with its remarks about her character and how it might be controlled by himself. 'What a pretentious prude! Who does he think he is?' she burst out to Letty, visiting as usual in course of her

own whirl of desirable social activities. Letty, still with an
eye to the capture of Toby Croom in her net, replied
soothingly as was her wont.

'Let things take their course; don't anger your father
any more, Flora. If you appear, at the least, to be
considering the matter, he will no doubt permit you to
attend rather more events than has been the case lately,
and I will be at them also; it is worth it, is it not, my dear,
for a little more freedom than you have had all year?'

Flora agreed that it was worth it for that, and contrived
to be polite, if somewhat distant, to Claud Croom on the
present and subsequent visits he made. The fact that she
was being difficult stimulated Claud's desire even further;
it would be charming to master her in the end, quite
different from the ready Amy. He persevered in his suit
despite continued mild discouragement; shortly, as he was
after all very handsome indeed, Flora forgave him in her
good-natured and unthinking way. In the meantime, they
all four, including Letty and Toby, happened to attend the
same subscription ball.

The two half-brothers now took less than ever to do with
one another, and Claud was coldly angry at perceiving,
almost at once, Toby's red head among the dancers on
first arrival. He was evidently alone. The two young ladies
were to be conveyed here together, Letty being of an age,
and independent enough – she was an orphan, officially
supervised by a nervous great-aunt who had long and for
good reasons become a recluse – to act as chaperone to
Flora, he himself having avoided escorting them here out
of a continuing sense of what was proper and approved.
Likewise, propriety would not admit of his refusing
tonight to introduce Toby to the girl who was not yet his
own betrothed. In fact, Miss Letty's predilection being
known, it would be impossible to avoid such an encounter:
she would certainly demand to include Toby in the
evening's programme and would no doubt expect them all
to go in together for ices. It was damned annoying, and
would ruin the evening if one were not very careful
indeed.

Nevertheless Claud listened to the strains of a waltz with

reassurance; it had become respectable since the time of
Queen Adelaide, who had herself waltzed very well, as did
the new Queen. Propriety would not however permit that
Claud yet be seen to dance it more than twice with Flora,
but he would certainly ensure that he claimed those two;
the prospect of encircling her waist, of holding her little
gloved hand, enchanted him.

Unfortunately, when they arrived – Flora was looking
her best in a white gown, and happy at the nabob's
permission to show herself again in public a little, it had
grown very dull last year – Toby, eagerness on his flushed
and innocent face, made his way at once towards the
group, and having been made known to Flora claimed her
at once for the waltz, filling in her card himself with a
flourish in several places. Claud, furious, found himself
landed instead with Letty. They circled round for some'
time, without mutual attraction, then retreated by Letty's
request to a secluded corner, Claud furiously realising that
he would no doubt be put down by everyone as Miss
Pembridge's latest flirt. He was meantime aware that Flora
and Toby were waltzing together very well indeed; in fact,
moving together as one. Toby was laughing down in his
pleasant, instantly attractive way, and on whirling Flora
about to the violins at one point the jealous half-brother
saw her face as he had never yet seen it; entranced and
gloriously, unthinkingly happy. He hoped it was merely
with her unwonted freedom; he himself had never yet
aroused any such expression of joy in her. He listened
lugubriously to Letty's customary well-informed talk; she
herself kept an eye on Toby Croom. She would see to that
quite evident development later on; she already knew
exactly what to do to scotch it.

Her chance came when the ladies retired to tidy
themselves after a cotillion, following which there would
be refreshments. 'Be a little careful, Flora, of that young
brother of Claud Croom's,' Letty said in a low voice. 'He is
notorious with women; he has one illegitimate child at the
least.' Claud's lack of complete information had allowed
Letty's invention full play without realising that she told
the truth. Flora's crestfallen face – the little goose was

never apt at hiding her feelings – told Letty that the shaft
had struck home. Over ices, which they all ate together,
Flora's attention was evidently taken up again entirely by
Claud. Later, going in on Toby's arm, Letty remarked to
him that he must have noticed the attraction of the pair to
one another. 'They are in fact about to become engaged,'
she said, smiling. 'Nothing has yet been said openly, of
course; do not spread the news until you see it in the
papers.'

Toby, who had been in process of falling in love with
Flora – she was, he thought, the most natural and
charming girl he had ever met, rather a relief in fact after
Letty – was downcast, but like a man did not show it. He
gallantly asked Miss Pembridge for the next waltz
although the sight of her deep bosom, and the possible
prospect of having to lay his head on it one day if her
evident passion for him persisted as far, daunted him a
trifle. If he tore his eyes away from this sight, however, it
would be to observe the one instead of Flora dancing with
Claud and displaying the sudden docility she had shown
during the refreshment interval. As he himself did not
greatly like Claud quite apart from the episode with Amy,
depression settled on Toby rather visibly.

'Come,' cried Miss Pembridge, 'dance with me in the
schottische. It will make you more cheerful.' Her bright
and masterful face sparkled with determination. At the
end of the schottische, she asked him to marry her.

It was not the first time. He had formerly never been
certain whether or not it was merely the flirtatious habit
Letty Pembridge assumed, having no doubt done so with
many men before him; she was a known coquette. He
himself was vulnerable, and knew it; illegitimate, unaware
who his mother had been, without solid prospects unless
he married well; and that, in the present instance, would
make him forever the tool of his wife. It would no doubt
be a trouble-free existence, and a comfortable one; but
some lingering remnant of independence in Toby still
rebelled. He wasn't sure he could marry a woman unless
he loved her; but love had betrayed him in Amy, and again
tonight, very briefly, with Flora herself; he had thought
he'd attracted her, but she'd evidently been in love with

Claud all the time. As for Letty, he was fond enough of her; he mightn't after all mind being managed in the end: it saved trouble. He murmured something of the kind, and saw a sudden flash of panic, of defeat, in her eyes, perhaps fear of never, after all, being married, her money forever like a wall between her and any love for herself; never the security of knowing that a man had after all married her and would have done so had she been poor. The knowledge of what he guessed instantly that she felt aroused pity in Toby; it seemed easier to think of the prospect of marriage with her. He would consider it. He stared at her handsome face. He supposed he was fortunate: most men would envy him.

'I will send you word,' he said in a low voice, as they waltzed on following the energetic schottische. 'I will write to you without fail tomorrow.'

Claud and Flora were waltzing yet again; the last waltz, to tired violins. With her hand clasped in his, her waist protected by his arm, Claud asked Flora outright if she could trust him enough to marry him. 'It would give me great pleasure to protect you always,' he said, not loudly; the other couples wouldn't hear. 'You know that I have loved you since that day we met in the Row; perhaps even earlier, when I saw you with your father that day at the bank. They are going to promote me there: Mr Crowbetter told me this morning.'

It sounded dull, but it was time, Flora knew, that she had an establishment: otherwise, with one thing and another, she'd soon be an old maid. Papa approved of Claud. She herself had thought, tonight, that she liked Toby Croom better; he'd seemed boyish and frank, without the intent determined gleam in his eyes that she saw now at the back of Claud's and which always made her slightly uncomfortable; it was as though she herself were some prize he hoped to win, or else some bird or other he's stalked with intent, like a cat; that wasn't perhaps quite fair; he certainly loved her. No doubt she would contrive to love him in return, once they were married. If Toby was a womaniser, it was best to forget him. She said yes to Claud. His hand in hers, and the one about her waist, tightened.

'I will make you very happy, Flora,' he said. He was coldly aware of triumph. He'd bested Toby at, no doubt, his accustomed game, nipped the affair in the bud before it started; or rather, he suspected Letty had. Nevertheless the friendship between Flora and Letty must cease. It was probable that tonight had ensured it. If she married Toby, Flora would resent it; at least, for a little while. After that he himself would fill his wife's mind completely.

The announcement of the engagement of Claud Croom to Flora Whittinghame appeared two days later in the *Morning Post*. A day later still, that of Toby Croom and Laetitia Pembridge was announced. On reading the paper, Flora fled to the nabob, her cheeks red with betrayal. Gerald was still in bed, his nightcap over one eye, the clean bones on his demolished breakfast chops beside him on their tray; despite the gout, he liked a good sound breakfast, port along with mutton.

'Papa, Letty told me things about Toby Croom, and now she's going to marry him herself. I think it's sly of her. I shall never forgive her. I don't even want her at my wedding.' She began to cry.

'Well, well, m'dear, women are that way inclined. Never liked that young lady greatly m'self; too consequential by half. I hope her husband beats her; she's taken long enough to get one. Marriage ain't all jam, y'know; I had trouble with your mother. I'm glad to see you settled, Flora, and that's the truth of it. You're like her in ways, but not all, thank God.' He then suggested that the ceremony should take place as soon as possible, in the drawing-room here, privately because of his gout.

Flora agreed somewhat miserably. She couldn't get over Letty's betrayal. Thinking of the night of the ball, she began to wonder if she had been actually tricked into accepting Claud: but it was too late now to undo it all, Papa would be angry; she'd given him enough trouble already, though not as much as Mama in her time had evidently done, and in her way was probably still doing; one never heard from her at all. Letty had, in a way, for four years now, taken the place almost of a mother, or at least an older sister; but all of that was certainly over.

'Claud seems a steady young feller. He'll look after you,' said Gerald Whittinghame. Presently, when he'd risen and been shaved, he'd limp down again to take a look at the Masaccio. It was worth all of it to get that. Flora, as he'd said, would be looked after, and off his hands. That serene Madonna he'd just bought wouldn't try to run away with a colonel of dragoons or anyone else. It was better to be on one's own, with a collection of fine paintings. The young couple could live by themselves upstairs.

After some weeks spent in calling the banns and fussing about with dressmakers for the ceremony and the honeymoon trip, the wedding of Toby Croom and Letty Pembridge, a tremendous affair in the presence of half London, took place in St James's Church in Piccadilly. Royalty itself was not present, but everybody else worth mention was, including a certain hook-nosed martinet from Apsley House, given over by now to politics rather than the army. The Duke of Wellington in his tall hat, laconic and erect as ever, was affable to everyone; particularly so to that old crony from the Peninsular campaigns, General Lord Croom, who had come up from the country without his wife. It was understood that he was the bridegroom's uncle, which proved a point in favour of the young man who had unaccountably carried off the rich and influential Pembridge heiress at last. It was decided that with young Croom's looks and charm, and the acceptable speech he made at the reception, he had a future; Letty would see to that. It was understood he had already been taken up at Woburn by Lord John.

Otherwise attention focussed on the bride, the famous Letty, captured by love at last despite her fortune and her connections. Everybody had assumed that she would marry into the peerage. She wore one of the new narrow crinolines of flounced Brussels lace, and looked radiant with happiness, diamond earrings – she always wore them – swinging, hair curled triumphantly beneath a white bonnet trimmed with silver-and-white ribbons in grand style. She was given away by a cousin who was a marquis. The polite world sparkled at the reception afterwards, drank healths in champagne, and finally saw the newlyweds off to united cheers, thrown shoes and shouted good wishes. It was understood that the honeymoon would be spent in Wales.

One pair of invited guests who had not been present were Claud Croom and his young wife, who had been married quietly in her father's drawing-room a few days previously. Flora had not wanted Letty at her wedding and also now said she didn't want to go to Letty's either. Claud was agreeable: it was better for Flora not to see Letty or Toby again at least for the present. Instead, as usual in evenings now, they sang together to the pianoforte, while Flora played. Their young voices floated out over the Piccadilly scene as the carriages of the great lumbered home.

They were in fact very happy, a surprised Flora deliriously so. It was wonderful to be so cherished, her every wish met. Also, as she was too innocent to know, a prudent lover is a charming cure for impulsiveness in young females. As Claud had hoped – and it happened even more quickly than his hopes – she now saw nothing beyond himself. With Flora a submissive and dutiful wife, and his promotion at the bank a wedding present from old Crowbetter – Nick himself had come to the quiet ceremony – Claud's life had become one of supreme contentment. He was already working hard and ambitiously to promote himself still further. Meantime, it was certainly much better if dearest Flora did not encounter Toby and his wife on their return. The circles in which they moved would in any case be quite separate.

Toby meantime, in the honeymoon carriage opposite his wife, recalled the fact that his father Tobias had not exerted himself to come to the wedding any more than he had troubled to attend Claud's. He said he seldom now left Fortune's Field, but had sent a letter with good wishes and advice, also certain information. *It is time, now that you have launched your future in the world, to tell you that your mother was a schoolmistress, profoundly interested in botany,* the old man wrote drily. *She is at present in charge of your daughter Amanda, who will receive a thorough education in lieu, no doubt, of a favourable marriage, which is unlikely. At some time when you have leisure to bring your bride down to Fortune's Field, you should make a private visit to inspect your son. My brother dotes on him at least meantime, but as another is on the way it may be politic later on to make alternative provision. Meantime, for what it is worth, I give you my blessing and send my felicitations to you and to your wife. At some time I look forward to having the pleasure of making her acquaintance. I am, my dear Toby, ever your affectionate father,*

Tobias Croom.

VII

Amy lay with her feet up on a sofa in the room upstairs, discontentedly regarding her body, swollen a second time with pregnancy. What discontented her chiefly by now was that the coming child was certainly Anstey's, because it couldn't be anyone else's. The General hadn't visited her at all except to play with young Delahaye, whom he'd called after his departed crane, that old Beatrice.

However, Ma was in charge now, and had made no bones about what she felt about everything. 'Be kind to poor Anstey, dearie,' she'd said. 'He's your husband, after all; they're none of 'em perfect. Gus Killigrew, that was your father, had his faults and used to drink like a fish, but Gawd knows I made as good a wife to him as I could, as long as his old father let me.'

Her lips had tightened ominously; old Killigrew had made her a good enough allowance, to be sure, after Gus died young of the bottle, but it had involved dull and respectable living, she hadn't been allowed to go back to the boards then, and now it was too late; and, worse, she hadn't been allowed to see poor little Amy all these years, not even to come to her wedding. Looking at Amy now, it was difficult to remember the taking little thing she'd been before they sent her to that school to be turned into a lady. Now, she didn't look like anything much, but it couldn't be expected at such a time; nobody did when they couldn't see their own feet for what was in between.

Amy in her turn noticed that Ma herself had put on a good deal of flesh, and this was a warning of what might happen to herself in time; there seemed nothing to be done about it at present. However Ma's ponderous figure, with its tiny feet which had once kicked her height beguilingly and done the splits while Gus Killigrew happened for some reason to be in the hired hall in Leighton Buzzard, where the company were on tour, teetered now resolutely about such parts of Fortune's Field as Clara Killigrew was allowed to penetrate. Paola, of course, was still in charge at the west end, and as might have been foreseen the two women did not get on.

'Stinks like a civet; how that old Tobias can put up with it I'm sure I don't know,' had remarked Clara, fluttering her still considerable eyelashes beneath the curled brown front showing coyly beneath her cap. She was still what is described as a comely woman, but the prospect of resembling her was somewhat unwelcome to her daughter; after all, having been reared at the Shearwater Academy, though in itself not pleasant to recall in many ways, had no doubt turned one into a lady, which Ma most emphatically was not.

Amy turned her head aside now to where her hopeful heir, Augustus Delahaye Croom (Gus Killigrew had been remembered at the christening) was meantime trundling a hobby-horse's head about on wheels, having been allowed down from the nursery as usual to visit his mother after tea. He was a healthy, beautiful and energetic child who resembled, everyone still said, the first lord in his handsome heyday. Del enchanted everybody including the General, who knew damned well he was that Toby's son though in default of any other heir, one said little for the time bein'. Amy had not seen the red-haired twin girl to whom she had at about the same time evidently given birth and who was her only remaining memory of Toby; he was married, that was all she knew. As for Claud, they said his young wife was expecting her first at some time soon; he'd been handsome as well. Those days were over. She, Amy, had nobody left now except for Anstey's cold and disdainful couplings, which had only been contrived in order to achieve this pending result; after it was certain he'd done what he called his duty, he'd left her alone. Everyone left her alone, except for Del with his everlasting horse on wheels. The wheels creaked.

'Stop that,' said Amy sharply. Delahaye took no notice, seeing no reason to do so. This fact, coupled with the one that nobody else took any notice of her now either, even Anstey having gone back long ago to his monk's robe and the orchard – he had had a small cell built there recently – caused Amy to lose her temper.

'Stop, I said,' she repeated, and Del looked up cherubically and said 'Won't,' thereafter going on dragging and creaking. The sound got on Amy's taut nerves; she heaved herself up from the sofa, swung her heavy weight to its unwitnessed feet and went and slapped Delahaye's face. Del burst out into indignant crying, and the sound, coming from his strong young lungs, ought to have brought the nurse running now they'd unlocked the room and one could come and go instead of living in prison until everything was certain. Nobody came, of course; they used her as a brood mare, that was all; she was tired of everything and everyone. She went listlessly to the window, to perceive the General, far below on the shaved grass, courteously handing Ma's stout form into the folly.

This was the last straw. Amy began to scream, then shortly to feel herself go into labour. It was a month too soon. 'Go back to the nursery,' she gasped at Delahaye; and whether he went or not she didn't notice, because the pains were certainly coming strongly. It had been the shock; to think of it! The child's head was already here, and there was nobody about: what was she to do?

When anyone came at all, it was to find a pallid and premature baby lying on the carpet. It was a boy, would perhaps live, and resembled Anstey. The early birth ensured that Stephen, as he was called for no particular reason, would always be undersized and prone to colds, though fortunately not to asthma.

By all accepted standards Amy ought to have died in childbirth or to have succumbed to fever, or perhaps even a broken heart. However she did not, but her mouth acquired a permanent droop of disappointment. This, all things considered, was hardly surprising.

Part Two

I

Toby Croom was working in his wife's garden at her house of Aberaniog in Powys. They had lived here now for five years, during which time their daughter Victoria had been born. Toby was vaguely aware that Letty was disappointed in him, though she had said nothing. It was not as a lover – that aspect seemed satisfactory, though little Victoria, a placid but plain child, seemed so far the only result – but in his own failure, despite Letty's constant urging of influential persons by letter, to obtain a position in Parliament. Anti-reform, the Corn Laws, the rivalry of Melbourne and Peel and the general election that followed should have given Toby his chance; but he was still without a seat despite favourable impressions on selection committees and a near-victory in an obscure constituency in Montgomeryshire.

In other words, having given up the Coutts's position on his marriage, he was nothing now except Letty's husband and, possibly, her gardener. The latter occupation interested Toby greatly; it was said Prince Albert also was devoted to the study of botany. Toby compared his own position briefly with that of the Queen's German husband: the influence of the latter was however said to be subtly in the ascendant, proved by the fact that he was able to discourage dancing at Court as frivolous. Toby however did not feel himself competent to discourage any inclination at all in his own wife. However they got on well enough.

He resumed his clipping of the ancient box hedge – it had been in a state of overgrown neglect when they came, but like everything else Toby had kept it in fair order since – and thought again how he was fascinated by the great variety of trees, the shrubs that had survived, some from the time of Letty's grandparents and earlier; and, of course, the plants he himself had selected for the parterres now he had finally cleared them. The house itself reared, old, plastered and timbered, many parts dating at least from the seventeenth century, behind him. There was – he smiled – a reputed giant underneath, who according to legend was supposed to be coming up at any minute, like the return of King Arthur. Letty, two years ago now, had whimsically ordered a great stone hand to be installed across the bridge, beyond the stream where they by custom fished for trout. It could be assumed from the hand that the rest of the giant would follow.

He became aware that one of the Welsh servants was standing there respectfully, a letter in his hand. 'It has just come by Jones the post,' the man said. The superscription was in Tobias's hand and Toby set down his shears and tore open the envelope at once. It contained news of a forgotten woman; Tilly Croom was dead, having died raving, a prey to general paralysis of the insane. He himself could not recall ever having clearly seen her face.

I myself will not attend the funeral, the old man wrote. *I would be grateful if this letter arrives in time for you to represent me. Claud cannot be expected to attend; his own tragedy is fairly recent, and I understand he intends shortly to go abroad. The funeral will be on Tuesday first, at eleven o'clock.* That was all. Toby went thoughtfully into the house, where Letty was at her desk, quill in hand as usual. She would no doubt not accompany him, having engagements locally. He told her of the death at once, and went to order the carriage. It was still light enough to make good speed on the journey; he should arrive at Fortune's Field after a single inn-stop, and should be well in time for the funeral: also, the thought stirred in him that he would like to see his son, Delahaye.

He arrived, in time to see Tilly's sad coffin lowered into the grave. Ironically, being a wife, she was buried inside the churchyard, while poor Mary Tregown's stone lay, lichened now, beyond the wall. Toby, in his tall hat and blacks, found himself wondering if his father would now trouble to marry Paola. That might mean – it mattered less now that he himself was married to enough money – that Claud might end by being the favoured, almost the legitimate son. There was no sign of widowed Claud here, mourning as he must be alone in London; but the General had presented himself, no doubt out of some burst of family feeling. As he stumped down the churchyard path along with the rest he barked at Toby, whom he seldom encountered if he could help it, 'Ought to come and take a look at your boy; he's growin'.'

Toby was not only taken aback because the old fellow hadn't lowered his voice; it was also the first time Lord Croom had openly admitted to the fact of alternative paternity for Delahaye. In other words, now there was Stephen, young Del was of less importance than formerly. The whole thing would have to be explained to Letty at some time or other, but one could hardly discuss the matter further at present. Toby shared a mourning-carriage home with his uncle afterwards in silence; there had otherwise been only a smattering of villagers present, more out of curiosity than grief at the disposal of the ashes of long-ago lust. He would discuss the whole business more fully once he was left alone with his father.

He found Tobias in his armchair, not notably affected by the death. He asked idly how many had been present at the funeral, then remarked without emotion 'Once, half London would have been at her obsequies. *Sic transit gloria mundi* is perhaps a trite observation in the circumstances. How are your wife and daughter?'

The hooded lids, as usual, lay half over his eyes; it occurred to Toby that it was difficult to be certain of their colour. He mentioned that the General had said aloud that he ought to visit his own son, and Tobias smiled.

'The difference between my brother and myself is that he is concerned with appearances,' he said. 'Our father no doubt appreciated this difference when he left his will as he did.' He eyed Toby lazily. 'There is no doubt that money is extremely useful,' he went on, 'in enabling one to

acquire confidence. Now that you have married your
heiress, you can beat her with impunity and spend her
money.'

The thought of beating the considerable Letty
unmanned Toby so much that he said nothing at all, and
his father went on talking. 'I have no doubt that your
interest in gardening, which you have told me of, stems
from your mother,' he said. 'However it is hardly a career
in itself, except possibly for employed persons. I am glad
that you have made a suitable marriage and I wish you
good fortune in politics. Had I myself acted as you have so
far done, I might have made some mark in the world: as it
is, watching from the wings is a diverting enough
occupation.'

Paola entered the room then, skirts brushing stiffly
beneath a linen apron. 'You must go now,' she said as
usual. 'He is tired.'

It occurred to Toby that she seemed to regard his father
more as a child now than a lover; she had never displayed
the same fierce affection for Claud. The latter had merely
happened to arrive at the time. Paola had not attended
Claud's wedding or, probably, been invited to it; nor had
she gone up to town for poor Flora's funeral. She never
left Fortune's Field for any reason; her entire life centred
round his father.

Before leaving – he was anxious to get back to the
Aberaniog garden at this season – Toby ventured to the
opposite end of the house to see his son. It would interest
him to have a look at the boy, at least. He watched him – it
could be none other – happen to ride across the near field,
on a pony; behind him was the smaller Stephen, still led by
a groom. Delahaye was a fine little fellow; Toby was proud
of him. Perhaps, if Letty bore no son, Del's adoption might
be considered; but, again, perhaps not. It was after all
unbecoming to assert oneself without having succeeded in
any other way except by trimming a box hedge in Wales.

There proved to be one more way he had forgotten about.
As he was about to turn and make his journey back to the
prescribed end, Amy came running suddenly out of a side
door and flung herself at him. Her arms were about him

in the old way; it might have been no more than days since he had left her. She was kissing him repeatedly, her pink mouth on his, saying his name over and over as though it were a litany.

'Toby, Toby, Toby. It has been so long. I thought you would never come back. I have loved you always, always; don't you remember? Love me now, before you go away. Nobody has loved me for years. Anstey's in his cell and the General sleeps with Ma, did you know? How do you suppose I feel? I didn't want to have Stephen, but they made me. They kept me locked up until – oh, love me again, love me again, Toby, Toby.'

She broke down into sobbing, and her dreary appearance aroused pity in him, a quality which he found rather too easy to achieve. He asked no more of himself or her; he allowed her to lead him into the house, to a small room, and lay with her there on the sofa. It was as simple as that; as before, he genuinely wanted to comfort her. Later on, after leaving, he reproached himself; he'd been unfaithful to Letty. He mustn't come again, without her, to Fortune's Field; matters here had again become compromising. Amy had clung to him, at the end, as if she would never let him go.

'Promise that you will come again soon,' she begged. 'Promise, Toby. You have seen our son. I saw you stand watching by the field fence; that's how I knew you were here; nobody told me. Don't leave me alone again for so long. Nobody else here cares for me now I've given them Stephen.' Her body still writhed against him, hungry as a cat's. He was sorry for her; Anstey wouldn't satisfy any woman.

'Look after Delahaye,' he said uselessly. The fact that Del might as well be the General's son, as far as anyone knew, seemed to have escaped Amy by this time; her mind evidently only remembered what it wanted to. He kissed her, made a promise to return for what that was worth, and left, travelling for the time being back to town. He ought perhaps to pay a visit of condolence to Claud. There was no need to prolong the feud between them indefinitely.

* * *

The General was in a quandary, a state of mind which irritated him; wouldn't have done at Quatre Bras, let alone Waterloo. In fact, he was getting too damned fond, if one faced it, of young Delahaye, a fine little fellow who liked to canter his pony and showed signs of becomin' a true Englishman. Stephen, on the other hand, was a weak-kneed snivellin' child who picked his nose furtively, was afraid of horses, and wouldn't speak up for himself without burstin' into tears. He, however, was the true heir and Del, when it came to all that, nowhere at all. It was certain, knowin' of the existence of the red-haired girl twin, that Del could only be Toby's son and therefore bore the blood of loathed Tobias: but the child's resemblance to the old lord, of whom the General had himself been unaccountably fond, warmed one to Delahaye when one considered his other attributes. The only thing was to give both boys a good tutor and schoolin', and hope for the best; but there was perhaps one other way. The General made this plan to himself on horseback while inspectin' the coverts, away from the influence of all women.

The result was a furtive visit or two to Amy, not tellin' Clara. Anstey was neither here nor there in the matter; if all he could do was to produce somethin' like Stephen, he was better left out of it and told to stay in his cell. A son of one's own was the thing, and Amy had shown that she could, in vulgar parlance, rattle them out with greater ease than poor Beatrice, who at any rate was playin' cribbage at Tunbridge Wells and past it long ago. The General took renewed possession of Amy without enthusiasm; she was a wretched little creature compared to her mother; but one's duty prevailed, and it only took four or five visits upstairs. Shortly it appeared that Amy was again pregnant. The General was satisfied, and returned, as formerly to Clara.

Clara herself was very satisfactory indeed, in fact a damned fine woman. She looked after his house to perfection; she had made him roar with laughter once or twice by dancin' on the table-top when they were alone, with Amy safely upstairs; she returned his embraces in their shared bed with enthusiasm, havin' had a damned dull widowhood because of old Killigrew's allowance: and she kept the maids in order. Now that there was plenty of prospect, one way or another, regardin' heirs in general, Lord Croom allowed himself to drift into a happy and belated honeymoon state comparable to nothin' but certain aspects of life long ago behind the lines of Torres Vedras.

'You know Turner's work, hey? Rum devil; that's what he says about painting, a rum thing, he calls it. You've seen his latest, *The Fighting Téméraire*? Not everyone likes it, can't understand it, no doubt, but they will, they will.'

Claud, roused for once from long grief, murmured that his parents had known the painter slightly. The nabob, who sought his company oftener since Flora's death, regarded him with faint interest. He was coming to dislike his son-in-law less than when poor Flora had been alive; great pity about her, and the child too. It meant that he himself might as well never have married; better perhaps if he hadn't. Peg hadn't sent any word at all from Italy, never having cared for Flora one way or the other, let alone for himself. Perhaps he, Gerald, hadn't cared enough for either his wife or his child: he missed Flora now she was gone, the sound of her laughter, the sound of the pianoforte and the voices upstairs. Croom kept the instrument always open, with the music his wife had been playing when she went into labour still on the rack as she'd left it. He wouldn't have anything in the room moved, evidently, though it was some years now since Flora's death; how many? Four or five; he, Gerald Whittinghame, was himself getting old.

He went on talking about Turner as they dined together: one had to talk about somethin'. The painter fellow was so mean he hadn't paid his engravers enough, and they hadn't finished one series; a pity. A great many things were a pity. When he, Gerald, was dead, he supposed he'd leave the art collection to Croom to sell; the fellow was knowledgeable about markets, and he had dealin's often these days with Van Hakluyt the art wallah, who'd brought the Masaccio to Piccadilly. Croom was talking, morever, of going himself to Hamburg, where Nick Crowbetter had offered him still further promotion in the foreign branch. Van Hakluyt lived there when he

wasn't in London; married, he'd said once, with a young
family. Other men had families; he himself, Gerald
Whittinghame, had nobody left. It no longer mattered.
He'd soon join Flora and the child, in the vault in Kensal
Green. Till then, the house would be empty, no doubt,
after Claud left, except for himself and the pictures.

Claud, fingering the walnuts at last, hardly listened to his
father-in-law; the old boy talked on, as a change from
talking to nobody. Claud himself was thinking of
Crowbetter's offer, which he had decided to accept; might
as well begin some kind of new life, in another country.
That was in another country, and the wench is dead. He knew
that love itself, which had come to him so suddenly, so
irrevocably, would never come again: for some time now
he had begun to take casual women, had even kept a
temporary mistress in Brick Street in the former lodgings
he had had before marriage. That had been a matter of
physical need only: that persisted, naturally. Perhaps he'd
marry again, when a suitable opportunity offered itself.
Meantime, Nick Crowbetter had told him, with the curious
golden eyes fixed on his face, that there were related
subtleties concerning the Hamburg branch which he,
Claud, was now expert enough to handle; and Hugo
Loriot, for some time manager in the branch out there,
would make him at home till Claud found his own
residence. It meant leaving the old nabob alone, but that
couldn't be helped; and, more, it meant leaving the rooms
where he and Flora had known great happiness. They
were empty, however, even of her ghost; servants dusted
the piano nobody ever played. He might as well go abroad.
Toby had come the other day a second time to visit: they
got on rather better these days. One's life was separate,
after all, from events past and done with; he himself was
alive, had his knowledge and his contacts in the business
world, and that passed the days and years. He must write
to his father to tell him about Hamburg. Old Tobias would
be interested.

II

In Wales, Letty was striding up and down the room with rustling skirts, for once not occupied with letter-writing; nobody would do anything about Toby's career unless they were actually confronted; it was beginning to seem pointless, they themselves ought to be in London, at the heart of things. Matters such as equal suffrage, the removal or otherwise of Habeas Corpus from the Irish, the rearrangement of boroughs, and similar subjects occupied Letty's mind to a far greater extent than the hanging of new curtains here at Aberaniog or even, though she did not neglect the dear good child, the welfare of placid Victoria, at present vaguely occupied with a doll. Victoria was all very well, but she made the third generation of female inheritance if there were to be no sons of one's marriage: and whatever Toby might have achieved in his time with other women (Letty reminded herself that she had known all about this from Claud before she married his half-brother) he had so far failed to provide this necessity for Letty herself. It was, perhaps, one more instance of his general ineptitude. One had to begin, at least to oneself, to employ this harsh term, though dear Toby was certainly a considerate and affectionate husband and father. At the moment he was outside, putting, the servants had already told her, mulch round the paeonies. Griffin, the housekeeper's husband, could have done this under instruction perfectly well; the couple had been here all of Letty's life, also part of that of her late mother before the latter's marriage. Such retainers could be trusted. They themselves must certainly leave here, much as Toby loved the place – so, of course, did she – and return to London soon if Toby was to be induced to make anything at all of his life. Fishing for trout under the bridge in the evenings, when flies rose, and walking below the great old trees which lined the upper walk were all very well as a pastime now and again: but they had shaken the giant's stone hand in passing many times now, and so had Victoria. They had told Victoria the old legend and she had listened without great interest; she was a child without much imagination, and too fat. Altogether Letty needed other outlets for her energy.

She went, nevertheless, to join Toby on their habitual walk afterwards round the grounds, having meantime returned Victoria to her nurse to be put to bed; later she would go up to bid the child goodnight and hear her prayers. While they walked, Letty thought she heard the sound of coach-wheels stopping beyond the gate; the post passed that way, but there wouldn't be anyone visiting: those who did rode or drove up in their own light carriages earlier in the day. It was unexpected, therefore, on their return to be met by Mrs Griffin, bobbing respectfully as usual in her apron, to say a young lady had come, and had said she must wait but that she hadn't been expected. 'One way and another, Mrs Letty *bach*, I let her in.' The young lady hadn't given any name, as they would see for themselves.

Letty, puzzled – who could it be, out here? – went into the smaller drawing-room, closely followed by her husband. A young woman of depressed appearance, pallid with recent childbirth, sat there, breast-feeding a small boy with red hair. The sight so pulverised Letty that at first she heard herself ask politely if the child were a girl or a boy.

'It's a boy,' said Amy. 'I'm calling him Henry, whatever anyone says.' She hitched together her bodice and began to cry. 'They turned me out,' she said. 'The General said I could go where I liked, but that I wasn't staying at Fortune's Field any more. I can't say I mind much. He – the baby – looks like you this time, Toby, I think.' Her voice sounded aimless and hardly very interested. She turned Henry's head, his mouth still dribbling with thin milk, towards her erstwhile lover and his wife. The baby resembled his father. Letty felt a slow surge of outrage assail her. This was beyond everything. It must have happened at the time Toby went home for his father's wife's funeral: otherwise, he'd been constantly under her eye.

Such a situation might have been expected to end in melodrama, hysterical accusations, tears, embarrassment and estrangement for the time being at least. It would have done so – the embarrassment was most certainly there for Toby – had his wife not possessed quick wits and a cool head. In her hard and somewhat devious way Letty also had, when necessary, a warm heart; and, besides, whatever had happened or when, there was clearly no need to regard this dreary breast-feeding creature as a rival. Also, Letty was aware of Toby himself, standing crestfallen and confused behind her: he was after all her husband, and she loved him. Had he not been so attractive to other women, he would not have caught the attention of herself; so she reasoned, commendably and within instants. She contrived to smile, saying brightly 'What a fine little fellow. Have you eaten, my dear? You must be weary after the journey. I will have them bring you a tray upstairs, and after that you and the baby can sleep.' One supposed their direction here had been obtained somehow; the little fool had evidently known where to come.

Later, after Amy, more like a rag doll than anything else, had been manipulated upstairs, Letty ordered dinner to be served for herself and Toby as usual. She had meantime dressed for it, as she always did whether or not there were guests; civilisation was maintained at Aberaniog, with the silver laid out, the lamps lit, and conversation held on general topics. Letty even pointed out, for something to say and because it had recently been hung, the real value and usefulness of the new Dutch chandelier. 'See how it adds to the light!' she remarked, surveying the added balls of reflective glass disposed here and there among the candles. It was a fairly new invention; they had been fortunate to obtain one unbroken by the carrier.

Toby stared at his own reflection, diminished to a dwarf's by the spherical glass: no doubt that was what he was by now, a shrunken creature. Letty was being most generous. It made him feel more than ever small. It had in fact been a mortification to see Amy again. Something would have to be thought of: she and the new child couldn't stay on here with them.

Afterwards, in their room, Letty sat at her dressing-table, brushing out her dark hair with strong regular strokes. Since their marriage she had given up curlpapers and tongs, and dressed it by day simply, with a heavy knot at the back of her head and a light fringe left straight on the forehead. It added serenity to her strong face, and became her: she tied it nightly with a strand of wool. He watched; some husbands brushed out their wives' hair on such occasions with a hundred strokes, but he was uncertain whether Letty would like him to do this or not; she was so extremely competent, and at the moment he himself felt like an apologetic schoolboy. If only she would refer to the matter! Toby went into his dressing-room, and with trembling fingers untied his stock; in the country he did not employ a valet.

'Do you think, dear,' he heard Letty call through the open door, 'that you could contrive to give me a little son of my own? It would make me feel superior: at present, I find myself somewhat at a loss.'

She had laid down the brush, and was smiling. He hastened in, and gratefully kissed her hands.

Later, as they lay together in bed, she said by way of idle enquiry, 'By the way, my own dear love, what did that creature mean about *this time*? Were there others? I confess I would find a family of adopted children somewhat difficult to endure.'

He told her, gallantly, that she had best obtain the story from Amy herself. He hesitated to tell tales about the number of men with whom the poor girl had in fact slept: nothing was as it seemed, and anyway Letty had endured enough. It had been, if so, he assured her, before he met her: he himself could not recall by now if this was precisely the case.

Letty moved against him comfortably, warm and fulfilled. 'But, my darling, that little Henry is quite young. There are others, are there not? You may safely tell me; I will not scold you.'

'Ask Amy,' he said again. He could think of nothing else to say. 'Dear fool,' said Letty at last. 'Never mind it: I have a plan.'

The plan was that Amy and her son should remain at Aberaniog; it was a roof over their heads, well away from scandal in town. 'That is for *your* sake,' she told him. 'I want you to take your place in the Cabinet one day. Remember what poor Lord Melbourne endured by way of that Norton woman's claims: luckily the charge was thrown out of court, but mud clings. You must never, never give rise to cause for further gossip of such a kind.' She kissed him. 'I love you, you see, great imbecile. I will tell everyone here that Amy is a relative; that will account for the child's red hair, and her name after all is Croom: they need know no more. You must be thought of as a family man for prospective candidate. The other situation was in order in Fox's day, but not now, in the dear Queen's and the way things are.'

She persuaded him then that he must go to London and stay at his club meantime while she herself settled matters about Amy, and later, in a day or two, she and Victoria would travel to town, they would all find somewhere to stay, and the pace of life would thereafter quicken. 'Of course,' Letty said soothingly, 'you shall come here again when things have blown over a little, to see to your garden, and I will be with you, never fear. I feel, you know, that young women everywhere you go are waiting to snap you up, like a choice morsel, the moment I take my eyes off you, great rogue. Can you behave yourself alone for a few days in London?'

She had another plan, which she began to put into execution almost as soon as Toby had gone. The first thing was to get the full story out of Amy, and this proved not at all difficult, with an initial show of sympathy: but the end of it was that Letty felt the young woman was like some bitch that had littered to every dog that had visited her, and would certainly do so again if given the opportunity; there must be none, therefore, or at least none as regarded her own husband; the only thing to do was to provide what was evidently required in the way of nature. St. David's

Fair happened to be in a day or two; she would find somebody suitable there, without doubt. Meantime she saw that Amy had proper food, that she rested after her journey and the birth, which must surely have taken place only just before it; and that she would be strong enough, in a day or two, to come on little carriage-jaunts while red-haired Henry – one thought of the baby already with ease – was left, quite safely, with Victoria and her nurse.

Amy didn't want to get out of the carriage to go and walk about the fair, as Toby's wife had suggested; she still felt languid even after several days in bed: the General had ordered her to be bundled out of Fortune's Field too soon after Henry's arrival. He hadn't even said goodbye.

She stared out of the window, pink mouth drooping: watching Letty go off, followed closely by the maidservant who had come, to the further end of the crowded field with its evocative smell of trodden grass. The coachman still waited with the horses. Nearby were gingerbread stalls, pedlars selling ribbons, a fortune-teller. There were other stalls selling farm produce; butter and eggs and great cheeses and fat hams, and still another stall with oranges. Amy regarded them idly. In the part of the field one could just see, where Letty had gone, there stood men and women waiting to be hired as servants for the coming year: that was evidently why they themselves had come today, Letty said, to hire a footman, as the Griffins couldn't do everything needed about the house; they were getting old.

Amy's mind flew back again to Fortune's Field, to which she'd been told she must never go back. Arrangements were being made to pay her money. The General had been so angry he'd even kept Ma from waving her off in the departing carriage: and as for himself and Anstey, they hadn't shown themselves. It was difficult to realise that that part of her life was finished, and to know what to do with the rest of it. She supposed there was Henry. The General had sent word that he wasn't to be sent to Tobias this time, but to go with her, everyone had had enough: what did he mean about sending to Mr Tobias? She hadn't ever sent anything to that end of the house.

The General. He'd come to her bed, those last few times,

the first conveniently only two days after she and Toby had made love again together, on the sofa. It had been advisable to put up with it, in case. After that she couldn't very well say anything about future visits, and he himself hadn't spoken much, only saying that she should leave everything to him and not say a word, and she hadn't; and then, as a rule, 'Good girl, good girl' in the middle of it, then getting up afterwards and going away in silence. It was all very well, then leaving her alone again as soon as it was known a baby was coming: she herself hadn't been sure whether it was his or Toby's: now, with the red hair, everyone knew in any case.

The General, in fact, thinking of it from the beginning, would realise that he'd never yet fathered a child on her certainly; Delahaye wasn't his, she herself knew as much: and she hadn't ever seen the girl twin who died. That was never mentioned by anybody.

Letty returned some time later, in company with a solid beady-eyed man in rolled-up shirt sleeves that revealed the powerful muscles on his sunburnt arms. He'd been showing them off, no doubt, to attract the best offer of money. His last job, he'd in fact told Letty on enquiry, had been heaving barrels down a manhole to a pub cellar; he'd had enough of that, it didn't pay well: it wasn't hard work that he minded. He was also a heavyweight champion at local wrestling matches. 'He will make a good bodyguard,' Letty said to Amy. 'Aberaniog is remote, and you want to be protected against thieves.'

It had already been mentioned to Amy that she herself would be left alone at Aberaniog for a little while, while Letty and Toby were in London. Meantime, the man who was to be her bodyguard – and footman, Letty said – stared in a familiar way Amy didn't much like, but she couldn't say anything; Letty was paying for everything, after all, as her own money had not yet arrived. There was nowhere else to go, in any case, but Aberaniog. She'd get used to it, she dared say; but it was lonely, among the enclosing hills, with nobody calling.

The man, whose name was Dai Johnson, looked Amy over: he knew, though Mrs Letty hadn't of course said as much openly, what was expected of him. A scrawny piece, no more than a mouthful to her: he knew the sort already, and it generally had knock knees. (In this, as he was soon to discover, he had misjudged Amy). They started with a fuss and squawk, that kind, as if you was raping them, then they settled down and, by the end, wanted it twice a day. He'd do it, as long as they paid him. It was an easy job, with nothing much else to do except help keep the garden tidy and – this was evidently the main point – keep this little lady from being able to stand up for too long at any time, let alone go away. Serving madam at Aberaniog was the way it had been put; well, he, Dai, knew how to do that well enough.

Driving home, with a few purchases including a great Caerphilly cheese to take on to London, Letty felt quiet triumph. Amy would be kept, contented enough by the end, at Aberaniog; she herself would have to interest Toby in gardens somewhere else, and why not Fortune's Field, his own home, to which he could take her down safely now and again, with that little bitch no longer there to raise her tail and trap him every time he crossed the grass to the further end? It was something to look forward to; and in the meantime, she'd had, only yesterday, a letter from Lord John Russell to say there might be a by-election soon at a constituency in East Anglia where he himself had some influence. This time, she'd have enough leisure to coach Toby more exactly in what he ought to say; he needed more confidence, more certainty; it didn't do to be kind-hearted in politics and promise only what you meant to perform. As for Victoria, the child would enjoy coming down with them to Fortune's Field when they visited there; it was time she met her boy cousins. There seemed no prospect yet of a brother for her; even the other night had proved fruitless, as Letty had happened to discover shortly afterwards. As a politician's wife it was perhaps not the best thing to be lumbered with a large family in any case: there was a great deal else to which to look forward, *après tout*. Perhaps she would even send for young Henry when he was a little older, by which time nobody any longer would ask questions.

Part Three

I

'Amanda Shearwater's been caned again, te-he-he. She'll have to take breakfast standing again, te-he-he.'

She heard them, from where she was standing with her pretty face stained with tears, hands behind her back as prescribed by beastly old Ludd. They, in their blue regulation school gowns which had cost money, and were used for day wear (muslin for evenings and satin for occasions, with the frilled pantalettes which needed careful ironing in the laundry) mocked at her anyway for having to wear an ugly grey stuff gown winter and summer, because she was to be made a pupil-teacher at sixteen.

As for the caning, that, as usual, had hurt. It had been for what Mrs Ludd called impertinence. She, Amanda, seemed to be impertinent every time she said what she really thought, so she didn't say anything very often although, having been very well educated, she could say things in French, German and Italian, not to mention the use of the globes. Earlier, before Great-Aunt Shearwater, who was after all very old, took her stroke last year, things had been pleasanter; but by now Great-Aunt was helpless all down one side of herself and could hardly speak out of her lopsided mouth. Ludd, accordingly, had it all her own way; and she'd never liked Amanda, who she said was becoming like her mother, bad little Amy Killigrew. Ludd knew everything of that kind since she'd taken over the running of the school and had direct dealings with some old man in the south who owned it, but she hadn't told Amanda anything more and, by now, Great-Aunt of course couldn't. Perhaps she didn't even know. In any case, Ludd having everything her own way, she, Amanda, was to be caned into submission, into a colourless creature despite her hair.

She flung her head up suddenly, proudly. In spite of the ugly gown she knew she was the prettiest girl present. Signor Silvestro had told her so, and it wasn't only because she could talk Italian with him and keep him from feeling homesick. The rest all knew it too, and that no amount of forced pulling straight by old Ludd could subdue the glorious red-gold curls which clustered, never growing very long, on Amanda's milk-white neck. Her eyelashes, she knew, were darker than the hair, and had gold tips. Signor Silvestro had told her that as well; and that her eyes were *opalino*, many-coloured, dappled green and brown and hazel like a moss agate. Her mouth, he had also told her, was delicious. All of that – it was a comfort to think of it now, while the others ate breakfast – had been when she was being officially instructed in extra Italian to become more proficient, but instead, of course, they'd waltzed together: secretly, humming the tunes in low voices so old Ludd wouldn't hear. Heavens! To have to become like Ludd, like Great-Aunt Shearwater, and worse because the girls already knew her as one of themselves, walking up and down between mocking rows, keeping a supposed eye and, later, correcting their work and having her corrections corrected by Mrs Ludd, again in front of everybody; having the mistakes she'd made publicly pointed out, to give her, she'd been told, a sense of humility.

This caning was one more humiliation, not that she wasn't used to it. Today, however, whether or not because it was the day of the secret waltzes with the Signor, the pain itself seemed to give Amanda's whole body a sense of tingling expectation, a kind of power, a glow; it made her blood beat fast, thick and warm. Presently, Signor Silvestro – he was married, with a sick wife in Milan – would be waiting up the half-stairs, with his musical box which played three tunes when wound. His sick wife was called

Giuditta and he could just afford to visit her in the holidays, in summer; that was all.

'You may take your porridge now, Miss Amanda,' called out old Ludd, in a voice everybody could hear. The rest had already had theirs, and Amanda, in disgrace, was allowed to go and scrape out the last of what remained in the great pot, pouring on what they'd left of the milk, which wasn't much. She spooned the mess down, without appetite. Last night, in the cubicle in the room she had to share with Mrs Ludd, she'd laid herself on her stomach on the pallet but still couldn't sleep. The cubicle was the most private place there was, except for the Signor's half-staircase. It was Friday today, and he was paid to give her extra lessons, although Amanda wasn't allowed to learn the pianoforte, which he taught the others; Mrs Ludd said a teacher didn't need accomplishments like a governess did. The Signor was glad of the extra money for teaching the piano. They didn't, he admitted, with his melancholy dark eyes rolling in their sockets, pay him much as a rule at all. They didn't pay her, Amanda, anything; there might be a small salary when she was sixteen, but Mrs Ludd said she'd had her board and lodging since anyone could remember, and all of that had to be paid back. It was true; she was kept here in the holidays as well. There must be a life beyond school, but she didn't know how to reach it.

'You may go in now and supervise the English class,' said Mrs Ludd coldly, having watched Amanda consume her porridge. 'I shall follow shortly; there must be no gossiping.'

One couldn't stop them, of course; they jeered as usual when she went in, until the good lady's presence swept majestically in, upon which there was a sudden hush. 'I can see that Miss Amanda has not kept you in order,' remarked Mrs Ludd, who never missed an opportunity. 'Young ladies, we will now turn to page 47 of the Lexicon and intone together. Amanda, you will join us. It is time you learned a little more if you are to teach classes unaided. An ignorant mistress is worse than none.'

The smirking class bent to its books, heads together in pairs as the young ladies continued their resented education. They knew more about Mandy Shearwater than Mandy knew about herself, and, somehow, it had come out that old Miss Shearwater had meant to leave her great-niece a half-share in the school in her will, but that she'd taken the seizure just in time for old Ludd to prevent its being signed. Ludd would probably be the next head; she was more or less that now, with the old lady never seen any more, lying in bed and fed twice daily from a porcelain spouted cup. Well, there it was. Three generations of female gentility had carved surreptitious initials in the wooden desks and rubbed them in afterwards with ink. The Shearwater Academy was known to accept only pupils of a certain social status, but they behaved in such ways exactly like any other.

Later, Amanda crept up the half-stairs for her beloved waltzing session. Not even governesses learned to dance; accomplishments might be required, but never frivolity. However it was the time of day old Ludd went over to the cottage to report to Great-Aunt Shearwater, and the other young ladies were playing cards. Outside, on the paths where one supervised the crocodile on a fine day, it was raining softly, pattering down on the raked gravel.

Signor Silvestro was waiting, but not quite as usual with a smile of dazzling welcome; instead, he had his head in his hands. An open letter lay on the table. Amanda went to him to ask what was wrong, but before she got the words out he seized her hands in his thin yellow ones; his face was yellow too, long and thin, with dyed whiskers. He was forty-two and had told her so, and was fond of reciting Dante. Something must have happened.

'My Giuditta is very ill indeed,' he said. 'They think that she may die. It may be that she is already dead. I cannot go to her. When I saw her in the summer she was like a little skeleton leaf, lying in the hospital in Milano where I can just, only just, pay for her to be looked after, as you already know, *signorina* Amanda. They send me word from time to time that I ought to be with her, but there is no money, no money at all after one has paid the fare. Alas that I must stay here in this place, except for yourself! Once Giuditta was beautiful, as you are beautiful now; but even she did not have your hair. It is like a flame, and you are like a young white blossom, a *camelia*; you spell it differently in English, is it not so? Words are different, but beauty in all languages is the same. We will not waltz today, as I am sad.'

He suddenly laid his head on her shoulder and began to sob. Amanda felt compassion rise: poor man, so far from his dying wife! 'I am glad that I can comfort you,' she said softly.

She knew nothing about how this might be done; she knew nothing about men, except already that to be with one was different from being with the girls, or Mrs Ludd or Great-Aunt Shearwater. She sensed the smell of macassar oil from the Signor's hair. It would stain her dress at the shoulder, and old Ludd would notice and ask questions. His hands weren't in hers any more; they were –

It was like a flood, a stream; this rush of pity, this desire to give; to give him her body, a gift she hadn't even known could be so given; to comfort and be comforted, like the time not long ago when he'd unbuttoned her ugly grey dress at the neck to make it easier to waltz, then said her throat was soft, like a long white lily; and below was what Mrs Ludd had always said must never be shown or mentioned. Now –

It was strange what was happening. There was a little pain, different from being caned; sharper, swifter, soon gone. Then, there was bliss; a long bliss, in a part of herself she hadn't known was there. It was beautiful. This was living; perhaps it was what happened to other girls when they married, which she of course would never be, because she never met anybody. This, this –

'*Graziosa, piacentà, amorina, bella donna mìa, Amanda, Amanda. Bellezza. Carità.* This is better than the waltz, no? You are so beautiful, so beautiful, like a little figure in ivory, in *porcellana*, but softer, softer always, always –'

'*Miss Amanda!*'

It was Ludd in the doorway, suspicious, triumphant, prying and vengeful Ludd; striding over, tearing them apart *in flagrante*, slapping, imprecating, screaming. Her china teeth rattled; through it all, Amanda noticed that. She even heard what was said.

'You wicked and abandoned girl, adjust your drawers, get downstairs at once and then go straight up to your room. I will have more to say to you. As for you, signor, you will go from the place now, without notice, without a reference, and with such salary as is owed you and not a penny more. To think of it! To *think* – and you were trusted – a *married man* –'

'Mrs Ludd, please, please give him the fare home. He can't get to his wife who is very ill. It wasn't his fault.' Amanda wasn't sure how she was so certain of what she was saying. Jemima Ludd turned her mask of cold fury back again, swinging towards one from the corseted waist.

'You heard me. You will pack your things, and go also, tomorrow; it is too late tonight. You will be permitted to say goodbye to your great-aunt before leaving. Not a word more, if you please; we have done with you here; out of the room. Signor Silvestro, I have more to say.'

She stood holding the door for Amanda to go out having tied her drawers, and not looking back at poor Signor Silvestro. There wasn't anything, after all, that she could do for him: she'd tried, and look what had happened. What did Mrs Judd mean about going? Where could she go? She'd never lived anywhere but here, at school. She didn't know anything except how to become a teacher, and wasn't even very good at that.

' – and so, my dear Ellen, I have written by means of a letter put in charge of Parsons the laundrymaid, who will have to go with her, to Mr Croom himself to tell him the *full extent* of Amanda's wickedness, and to explain that we cannot be expected to continue to house her. I have permitted her to say goodbye to you, and no doubt to express some regret at her behaviour after all your kindness. Here she is, the abandoned little creature.'

Miss Shearwater, whose mind had remained as clear as a bell although her body had become half useless and she could no longer utter with certainty, felt some resentment from where she lay, as always now, in bed. After all, it was she who had saved up enough to acquire rights in half the school, not Jemima Ludd; Jemima was an employee, albeit by now indispensable. The indignities of a spouted feed-cup and a bedpan reduced one to impotence, and although she herself had always been fond of little Amanda – the arrival of a very small baby fifteen years ago, and the subsequent finding of a second wet-nurse after the first went back, had fortunately happened out of term-time – and knew that Jemima had been perhaps too strict with the child, there was nothing else she could do except agree. One hadn't, of course, had direct dealing with Tobias Croom even when one understood he was actually outside in the carriage with an Italian woman on that occasion; on all others, one had dealt by way of the lawyers or else through dear Jemima. That Amy Killigrew was involved in some way had been made clear later on by the latter personage, but one had never asked questions or, for that matter, encouraged them to be asked. The status of great-aunt was convenient. Jemima, having been married in her time (it was difficult to imagine the late Mr Ludd in any fleshly sense) was more than competent now to assess the situation. Amanda must go: and it was a mercy, perhaps, in a way, that she herself had been just too late to sign her own will; disaster would have been the outcome, almost certainly. Fondness of any kind was imprudent, recalling the humiliations of Scarborough.

She was aware of the bright-haired little figure standing by her bed. Once she herself had had almost such hair, although of course it had always been kept permanently concealed under a cap. She felt her good hand taken; the other lay as usual lately flaccid; and, for the last time, heard Amanda speak.

'Aunt Shearwater, I must say goodbye. Thank you for all your goodness to me.' It was said in a rather flat voice, because although the old days had been better than lately, it was chiefly lately that one remembered; and Great-Aunt hadn't ever let her know where she came from or who her parents were. However she gave the hand a squeeze, and felt a little pressure back, as though there might be some affection left between them. Then Mrs Ludd intervened.

'Come, that will do now: the carriage is waiting. On the journey, you may reflect on the situation to which your abandoned wickedness has brought you, and the future which might otherwise have been yours.' That last statement was a trifle risky; Ellen might after all still send for the lawyers, and alter her will by power of attorney. It was as well in any case that the young person was going elsewhere.

She bundled Amanda, who had not been allowed to see the other girls again, with her few belongings in a hamper, out to the carriage, where a grim-faced Parsons already waited. She had been instructed not to speak to her charge on the journey, but to deliver her without further incident to Fortune's Field, likewise Mr Croom's letter, and then return at once to resume her duties, after one night necessarily spent at an inn.

The inn held no adventures, and Amanda was sent in silence straight up to her room, with Parsons sleeping on the pallet in rather less silence as she snored: and the bed was lumpy. Amanda tried to sleep but couldn't help wondering about poor Signor Silvestro, left alone to find the fare home with nothing but the remains of his salary, a musical box and, probably, his razor. Mrs Ludd had remarked that he could pawn both the latter and that foreigners were better out of the country in any case.

In company with the silent Parsons at last she downed some breakfast, saw Parsons count out the exact money from a cloth bag to pay the inn-bill – it would be put on Mr Croom's expenses and deducted from profits at the half-year's end – and they then entered the arriving post-coach. It jogged southwards without many occupants, because most people nowadays travelled by the new railways. Finally it stopped outside a gate, a lodge, and a long drive lined with shrubs.

'Fortune's Field,' said the driver. He helped Amanda lift down her hamper containing a hairbrush, night-things, two clean chemises and two pairs of extra drawers. She walked, followed by Parsons carrying her own bundle and also the letter for Mr Tobias Croom, and in the end came upon a sprawling house of grey-pink stone with wings and turrets on either side, office buildings, servants' quarters and a stable-block. On the lawn in front, three boys and a girl were playing cricket. Amanda turned her head; one of the boys was very handsome. She began to feel more cheerful. 'This door,' remarked Parsons, speaking for the first time; she had been precisely instructed, and it was anyway the first they reached.

'I say, what an awfully pretty girl,' had remarked Delahaye, thereafter continuing to bowl overarm like a god with Stephen batting uncertainly, young Henry catching the ball meantime as best he could, and Victoria recovering from running last, with difficulty as she'd grown, as dearest Mama put it, a trifle plump lately and was always short of breath, not to mention red in the face with the exercise.

Tobias in the last few years, especially since the death of his brother the General (considerable scandal having been caused at the time by the expressed last wish of the deceased, which was to be buried outside the churchyard wall next to dear little Mary Tregown) had become, by reason of his advanced age, the nominal head of the household at Fortune's Field. This had accordingly lost its earlier rigour as regarded east versus west and, meantime at least, everyone spoke to everybody else. Delahaye, who one supposed was now Lord Croom – Tobias was pleased, the boy was after all his grandson, and half the aristocracy of England were in the same predicament without admitting or, probably, knowing it – was still very young, and Clara Killigrew had stayed on in the rôle of general comforter and supervisor of the maids, who had become much easier to obtain since the General's funeral. Clara had too much tact to interfere with Paola, who continued in her own way and place as she always had.

Paola herself had happened to be out of the room seeing to the linen when Amanda arrived, and so entered it just in time to witness Tobias, in what was in fact a purely grandfatherly gesture, stroke the pretty creature's arm with affection and pleasure and pour her a glass of wine. He had not yet read the letter handed him by the sour-faced maidservant who had come with the girl, but having a wide experience of human nature guessed what it might well contain. It amused him also that nobody, except himself and doubtfully Paola, knew in any case for certain who Amanda really was.

In this he had, being a man, underrated the law of the jungle. Paola, on entry, at once recognised the small baby with red snail-shells of curls whom she had mistakenly nourished, till a wet-nurse was found on the way north, by means of a clean cloth dipped in diluted cow's milk at the corner. Now, the helpless baby had grown up into a beautiful, irresistible and potentially dangerous young girl. Granddaughter or no granddaughter, Paola was not going to have such an opening rose about the place for long. However to say so aloud would be to court opposition. She therefore said nothing, and meantime took Parsons – who would certainly need sustaining before the return coach passed by the gate in an hour's time – down to the kitchens. There, as Parsons had after all not been sworn to silence as regarded anybody but the erring Amanda herself, Paola was regaled with the whole disgraceful tale. It was exactly as she'd known; the girl was a little minx, like her mother. The thing to do was to tell Mrs Letty when she next came down. It wasn't that Paola liked Letty Croom: she didn't, and since Mr Toby had been got into Parliament his wife was far too full of herself and increasingly managing in her ways at the Field. It was also an open secret that she had earmarked young Delahaye for that fat puffing daughter of hers, Victoria.

Amanda meantime had been pleasantly impressed by the slim and urbane old gentleman in the armchair, who regarded her from beneath his drooping eyelids with appreciation and amusement. She felt at once that they had a great deal in common in some fashion. Of course Mrs Ludd had written him a letter; that might spoil everything, but one would have to wait and see. Meantime, Mr Croom poured her a glass of wine, to which beverage Amanda was not accustomed. She sipped it slowly, while he asked her permission to be excused while he opened the letter Parsons had silently handed him before being shepherded away.

Having read the letter, he tore it into little fragments with his long elegant fingers and cast it aside. Amanda felt extremely relieved, and waited for whatever might happen next. All that happened was that Tobias poured her, in the intervals of courteous talk, a second glass of wine, told her at what hour dinner would be and suggested that she might like to be shown her room before going out to meet the other young people.

In fact, Tobias himself, who by now seldom took part in anything at all and never these days went up to town, was diverted by the whole situation. He would certainly let this pretty and, evidently, abandoned young person stay on at Fortune's Field, which had grown distinctly dull since the General's death. Life was, after all, a game of chess: one took everything slowly. When that managing wife of Toby's came down to retrieve her fat daughter, or at least supposedly to see how everyone fared, he himself would consult her as a formality, no more. She might be down this week or next, depending on how and when the House was sitting. Tobias had always suspected that she, and not his son Toby, who had been far happier in Coutts's, was the real Member of Parliament.

Letty was travelling down to Fortune's Field by herself in the carriage. Toby would follow when this discussion about the future of the colonies resolved itself. Her own maid Letty had sent down some weeks before with Victoria, to make the poor child look her best, especially her hair; oneself had contrived in London with a substitute woman. Letty allowed her mind to rove briefly over the mild success of Toby since his election some years ago now: he was popular with the constituents though he would never be brilliant as a speaker, and his reliability had made its mark at a time when Lord John Russell himself appeared to be changing his mind over several issues. This had not gone without notice, and there was a whisper – no more so far – that Toby's reliability, as opposed to the shifting of others, would soon have its visible reward by way of the Birthday Honours: but one must not anticipate unduly, and for the present it was a question of walking on eggs.

She thought of Toby with affection; he remained an excellent husband and father. If only there could have been a son! It was by reason of that very lack that she, Letty, had rescued young Henry some years ago from

Aberaniog and sent him to share a tutor with poor little
Stephen at the Field. In any case Henry's mother was not a
fit guardian: by now, she was completely infatuated with
that muscular footman in Wales. One had had in fact to
appeal to the Griffin couple's sense of loyalty to the family
to induce them to stay on in the circumstances. Toby
didn't know, of course, about that part of it; he had been
persuaded that his Parliamentary duties required him to
take an interest in a garden rather nearer at hand, namely
that at the Field itself: he had dug flower-beds there and
by degrees had clipped the long overgrown and neglected
maze, the final acquisition of which delighted the children.
The man Johnson could no doubt clip the hedge at
Aberaniog when Amy left him time. He'd asked for more
money lately: the whole thing was in Letty's account-book.

Her mind flitted briefly back to London, where she was
planning a dinner shortly to include, of course, the
Palmerstons; then forward again to Fortune's, where there
had been a number of changes, naturally, since the
General's death. Henry had settled in there as easily as
little boys always did, and Toby thought, of course, that it
was generous on her own part to accept him; such things
were of benefit. Also, poor Stephen needed stimulating
company; he resembled his father Anstey rather too
closely, poor Anstey's ghost being said by now to haunt the
orchard since his death in the stone cell he latterly
frequented in life. Perhaps, at last, the pollen had ceased
to trouble him in the spiritual state.

The carriage bowled in past the lodge. There were the
trees, Toby's flowerbeds, the maze beyond, the folly
before that, and the lawn. On the latter, the young people
were playing cricket as usual in the fine weather; one could
see Victoria's plump little form. There was somebody else
there; a red-haired girl, very active. Drawing nearer, one
saw that she was wearing a dress made up, no doubt by
Clara, from light material set aside some time ago by Letty
for summer curtains. She was running at speed,
gracefully, round and round the pitch, red hair flying.
Red hair.

'Victoria, go up to your room, if you please. You are not to remain in the garden with the others at present.'

Victoria, having run to kiss dear Mama on her arrival, was unwilling to leave Del with that girl Amanda, who ran much faster than she did. He was taking too much notice of Amanda as it was. She went, however, sullenly up, to find the maid already unpacking Mama's things. Victoria went to the window, to look out at what was happening now. Why had she been told not to stay in the garden? The cricket was finished and it wasn't yet time for dinner.

It wasn't ladylike to be seen at a window either, Mama had told her, so Victoria stood back obediently. However she could see and hear what was happening now. There was the sound of laughter; then presently, across the grass, Amanda herself came running, with Del pursuing her. They went into the maze, into which one could see quite easily from up here. He couldn't catch Amanda at first, and Victoria heard him call 'Amanda! Amanda! Wait, you'll get lost!' but Amanda ran on, laughing, showing her little white teeth like a kitten's, curls tossing over her teasingly turned shoulder. She didn't seem to care about propriety one jot. Del caught her up, of course, having longer legs and knowing the maze much better. He seized her round the waist and they kissed and kissed. It was improper, disgusting. She'd tell Mama.

Letty was, meantime, closeted with Tobias.

'Who is she? Is she one more bastard of Toby's? I must know. His career may be ruined if this is permitted to leak out at the moment. I trust you have not taken her to church? That hair is unmistakeable.'

'You have answered your own question,' he said, smiling. 'Truth lives at the bottom of a well, my dear Letty. It would have remained there, but for a recent unforeseen circumstance.' He did not mention Jemima Ludd's letter or the incident it contained; Paola by now had swept away the torn-up fragments. Young Amanda seemed happy here. He himself enjoyed her company. She had been well educated, as he had hoped. He regretted to hear of Miss Shearwater's helpless state; so far, he himself had avoided such a contingency, but it might happen.

He became aware that Letty was still very angry.

'Something about the way she moves, and the shape of her arms and legs, remind me of Amy,' she said in a bitter voice. 'In *that* case –'

'Well, well, as you have guessed it, there is no point in disguising it; yes, my dear, Amanda and Delahaye were twins. The girl was delivered to me at birth and I had her educated elsewhere. Amy believes she died. It will do you very little harm in fact if she stays; this is some way from London, and with Henry here also it is already evident that red hair is, for some reason, in the family. It will not be immediately obvious that all the children who possess it are necessarily Toby's own.'

Letty was not comforted; the truth had dawned on her. 'Then Delahaye is also Toby's son,' she said slowly. He was moreover, at that rate, as she did not add, Victoria's half-brother. The planned marriage was, therefore, impossible. Victoria – so swiftly did Letty's arrangements modify themselves in her active brain – Victoria must marry Stephen instead, as the title must after all be clearly Stephen's. She herself would do everything to set legal recognition in motion, even if it meant digging dates and shameful memories out of wretched little Amy in Wales. One need have no mercy where one's only daughter was involved. As for that girl, she could go to her mother. Whatever this old man said, it was *not* advisable to have her continuing here. Red hair! She would send Amanda to Wales, no doubt to Amy's immense surprise. As for young Delahaye, perhaps a European tour while the case was being heard; and afterwards, some occupation or other when he had lost his title. No doubt Claud Croom would help, from Hamburg. She had heard in fact that he was coming to London shortly, to see about the sale of those works of art which had belonged to the late nabob. Gerald Whittinghame's had been yet another death, hardly noted.

Tobias, thinking he had soothed the formidable Laetitia, poured her wine. Wine was, after all, an answer to most things.

Letty might, after all, have relented in some way: she was not entirely heartless, and she was well aware that conditions at Aberaniog by now were unsuitable for a young girl: there would only be the Griffins to protect her. Moreover, what Tobias had said about red hair in the family might well be accepted, by now, as general; Letty acknowledged this to herself somewhat drily. However as she went thoughtfully upstairs to where Victoria obediently waited, she was met by Paola. The woman stood on the landing, a letter in her hand. It had been torn up, and carefully stitched together again with black thread. Paola held it out.

'This came for him,' she said. 'I heard what you were saying. He had torn it up. I found the pieces. Read it for yourself. She should go.'

The unfathomable eyes surveyed Letty as she scanned the pages, at first in some bewilderment at the necessity; then, having taken in Jemima Ludd's expressed view of what had actually happened at the Academy for Young Ladies, was shocked as well as convinced. Amanda was evidently depraved as well as inconvenient; totally unfit company for Victoria, who of course must certainly continue her visits down here; Stephen, not Delahaye, being now the quarry, who might after all – Letty was under no illusions about the waywardness of handsome young men regarding matrimony to plain young women – be easier to spear. It would of course not happen for a year or two, but meantime that little seductress might as well be at Aberaniog as anywhere else; what happened to her there was not one's affair. Del's twin sister! A mercy the truth had come out. Stephen also would, of course, grow up to be a man; temptation must therefore be put out of his way at once. He would, after all, make an excellent husband for Victoria. It was merely a question of altering one's perspective. Clara Killigrew, who was, when one thought of it, Amanda's grandmother on the maternal side, should escort her to Aberaniog and then return.

Clara however did not immediately conform to pattern. 'Why can't the pretty dear stay on with us? She's doing no harm, and that dress I made her suits her down to the ground. It's time she had a bit of happiness; that school was horrible strict.' Clara had had many little talks with Amanda herself while the intended summer curtains were being fitted, although the dress hadn't taken long to make. That ugly grey thing had been put away for the winter, and watching Amanda in the other had been like watching a bud open to a flower.

Letty explained, gently, the situation. Also with gentleness, she reminded Clara that her allowance was still being paid her despite the fact that she had broken the conditions of old Abe Killigrew's will by seeing her daughter Amy. Letty had found out about all this in the way she always did find out about things; Clara's plump face set obstinately.

'That there will said I wasn't to go near Amy, and now you're telling me to go to her,' she pointed out with logic. Toby's wife had given herself airs from the beginning; who did she think she was? If the General had been still alive, Mrs Letty wouldn't dare. However Letty then stated that she herself would be the last person to betray Clara in that or any other way provided Clara now did exactly as she was asked, returning, for her own sake, from Aberaniog immediately. There was obviously no choice about it, and Clara unwillingly agreed to go and pack her night-things for one inn-stay there and another back. It wouldn't do, no doubt, to have the little thing stay on here after what had been made known to one or two of them: it wasn't like the old days, when people minded less. She herself wasn't in a position to answer back, never herself having been married to the General. His wife, they said, was still alive in Tunbridge Wells, playing cribbage with her sister. No doubt it kept both of them young, or as young as could be managed.

'Amanda. It means she-who-must-be-loved; they told us that at Harrow. Amanda. It's pretty, like you, Amanda Shearwater. A shearwater's a bird, a funny little bird on the sand, dipping its tail and then raising it. Let's go to the swing now, and I'll make you raise and dip yours.'

Delahaye laughed, throwing back his handsome head so that the light wind ruffled the fair hair which later would darken slightly. Further off, Henry, although younger, was vainly teaching Stephen how to fight: the two boys rolled over and over on the grass. Del and Amanda

wandered off hand-in-hand, making their way to the
orchard where the blossom was still white and thick. It
clustered lately on the boughs leaning over Anstey's
former cell: there was no sign today of his ghost. Del had
told Amanda about the ghost and that nobody bothered
about it; it had been seen by one or two of the housemaids.
Everyone knew, in any case, that he himself was really the
old General's son. His mother, whom he remembered, had
gone away. 'It comes to the same thing,' said Del. 'Here, let
me lift you up, Amanda, Amanda. I like to say your name.
Kiss me before we start, and then I'll swing you high, high,
higher so that you'll fly off, and then I shall catch you, and
kiss you again. You liked that, didn't you? So did I.'

Delahaye was not in fact quite sure what had happened to
him; he wasn't in the habit of saying such things, let alone
kissing girls: as a rule they looked like Victoria, pale wax
dolls. This one was a fairy, the Fairy Queen; he had never
met anyone as beautiful, he felt he'd known Amanda all
his life and the time before they were born. He had loved
her at once. It was impossible not to love her. When he
went back to Harrow for two more terms, he'd still think
constantly of Amanda; after that, he wanted to marry her.
Meantime, here was the swing; of silvery wood, put up in
his childhood by somebody, probably Aunt Letty for fat
dumpy Victoria.

Amanda let him lift her up, then swing her gently at
first, then wildly; she loved it. Being with Del was like
being by herself; they were somehow one person. It was
extraordinary, as before that she herself hadn't known any
boys. It wasn't the same with Henry and Stephen, only Del.
Flying high up in the air now among the branches,
glimpsing the blue sky above where heaven was, she knew
this very moment itself was heaven: and from now it would
go on and on, now she'd known this, this. Swing, swing;
back and forth, higher and higher, skirts flying, hair
tossing wild; she hadn't known, when she came here, who
she was or why, in an old grey gown, but now Clara had
made her a pretty one, and she and Del loved each other,
and soon they would be together always, he'd said so once,
in a confident voice like a man. He was after all almost a
man, dear Del. There would be no more school, no more

canings and being turned into a pupil-teacher in an ugly grey gown. Grey gowns, a ghost. They said the one here wore a monk's habit. Swing, swing. Who cared about a ghost? If it came this minute, nobody would bother about it at all. Higher, higher ...

There was somebody else in the orchard; Clara, who'd made her new dress. She was standing in her cloak and bonnet, looking grave. What was wrong? 'Let me down,' Amanda called to Delahaye, who hadn't noticed, he was too busy manipulating the swing. Clara came over, held the ropes and made them still. There was silence; everything had grown different now in some way. Amanda got down, feeling herself again on firm ground. Heaven had receded. Clara was saying something or other; what was it?

'Come with me, dear.' That was all; but why? She heard herself ask, and Clara replying that she'd tell her all about it later, but now she must come.

'Come back again,' called Delahaye after them. Amanda turned her head and smiled, and blew him a kiss. Of course she'd be back, and she'd get on the swing again, or else they'd play cricket, or run together inside the maze, and anyway kiss each other. She liked the kissing best. Del stood there with the sun on his hair, making it golden. She would remember it like that, till the next time she saw him; it wouldn't be long, not long.

It was only when Clara got her inside the house that she was told they were going to see her mother, and to get her cloak on at once. There wasn't time to say goodbye to anybody. How had they found her mother? She'd never in her life been allowed to ask about her, or who she was, except that old Ludd had said her name was Amy Killigrew.

The journey seemed longer than expected; evidently her mother didn't live round the corner. Clara had said very little. Amanda at last asked where they were going.

'Wales, dear.'

Amanda's heart sank. 'That's a long way, isn't it? When are we coming back?' She yearned already to be again with Del; he couldn't have known she was going as far in the carriage.

'It depends, dear,' said Clara prudently. She hadn't the

heart to tell the little creature she wouldn't be coming back. They'd looked so happy, that pair with the swing. She began, to pass the time and avoid further questions while they travelled on, to tell Amanda what she could about her mother; it wasn't, of course, possible to say everything.

'She was my little girl, you see. I'm your grandma, you know. Amy was taken away from me when she was a little thing. Her grandfather had her sent to school.' Clara was not in fact aware that it was the same school from which Amanda herself had come; she lumped all such institutions together as nasty strict places. 'Amy lives now,' she said, 'in a lovely old house with a garden, and she'll be pleased to see you.' Poor Mr Toby, Clara knew, had used to work in the garden in Wales, but lately hadn't been allowed to: that was how she'd heard about it.

'Why didn't she send for me before?' The dreary years, the canings, Mrs Ludd, had been allowed to happen instead: why?

'Because she thought you were dead, dear. Don't go asking any more questions. It'll be a surprise for her to see you at last, won't it, and you so pretty?'

Del had said she was pretty too. It was pleasant to be told such things, and no longer to have to try to straighten her hair. There was no help for it meantime but to go where she was taken; she hadn't any money.

By now it was almost dark, with strange hills closing in about them. 'Where is the house?' Amanda asked; Mrs Ludd would have said she was asking too much, becoming impertinent; but she was in fact beginning to be uneasy. Clara replied that they weren't there quite yet, they would have to stay at an inn for one night, then travel on next day. She began talking brightly again about Aberaniog. 'You didn't meet Mrs Letty Croom for more than a minute,' she said. 'It's her house, really.' It was as well to mention that, in case the bitch came later on some visit to Wales; but that wasn't at all likely. No doubt she'd been glad to get rid of a pretty girl like Amanda to push her own wax-faced pudding of a daughter, apart from what had happened.

Amanda submitted to whatever else was going to

happen next. After all it would be pleasant, as Clara said, to meet her mother, who'd evidently thought she was dead.

At the inn, lying awake beside Clara's already sleeping bulk, Amanda again remembered Delahaye, and the bliss of the swing, only that morning. She must have slept then, and presently had a dream. In the dream, it wasn't Del swinging her up and down to untold bliss, it was Signor Silvestro, till now almost forgotten. She knew he wanted to get home to Milan; evidently he hadn't. Where was Del? Why wasn't he swinging her instead? It was pleasant to see the Signor again, but she wanted Del. Where had he gone? When would they let her return to him?

She was awakened by Clara shaking her shoulder. It was morning, and time to get up; the coach came early. Very soon now, she was told, she would meet her mother.

II

'A guinea, like I said. Otherwise nothing doing.'

Amy, lying on the bed, whimpered with deprivation. The sight of Dai Johnson, straddled above her, filled her at the same time with expectancy and fear. He was so strong, and did everything of the kind so well, that by now she couldn't do without it. It was like drink with some. She couldn't deny him, and knew it, but there had after all been a guinea paid yesterday. Amy knew where the money went: other women. By now, she'd stopped resenting that or anything else Dai did, or didn't do. He knew she'd give him the moon if he asked for it. All she herself asked in return was one thing, only this.

She fished in her reticule, which lay beside the bed. Johnson took the money, spat on it by habit, then came and lay down with her as usual. He had no feeling for her and had never had, used rag as she was now; but the money, added to what Mrs Letty still sent him for keeping this creature mostly on her back here, was useful. Later on he would visit jolly little Marion down at the inn, and drink beer afterwards in a companionable silence, looking down Marion's dress.

He used Amy's small avid body, finally subduing its writhings. As he rose from her he heard a carriage. 'There is someone coming,' he said. 'You had better dress yourself.'

Amy watched him, her sated flesh already beginning to stir again. He'd made her like she was now, having cared nothing from the beginning; oh Dai, Dai. All he wanted from her, demanding it always in the short sharp upward lilt of Powys, was money; and she was running out of it. Letty Croom paid him something to stay on here; he shouldn't need to ruin her, Amy, as well.

'It won't be the county calling,' she heard him remark with contempt now from the window. 'I do not know who it is; an old woman and a young one.' His eye brightened: the young one was pretty. 'Get your wrapper on, at any rate,' he jerked back at Amy. 'You will have to go down.'

She obeyed listlessly, thrusting her feet into slippers. Whoever had come, they could go away again. Nobody much ever visited here.

Amanda was tired after the jogging coach-journey; the railway hadn't yet come to these parts. After the gate had been opened she saw the long box hedges with a feeling of being at home; they reminded her of the maze at Fortune's Field, and somebody kept them clipped, though the rest of the garden had run to weeds. The house sprawled beyond, like Fortune's but older, faced with timber and plaster. Amanda had hardly more time to take in anything before they came to the door, she and Clara, carrying their own baggage; inside hers was the old grey gown, she'd come on it at the inn while getting her night-things. The sight had chilled her; its inclusion meant a long stay, it wasn't winter yet. When would she see Delahaye again? Perhaps she could write from here; yes, she'd write. Then, soon, he would answer. That would be something.

This must be her mother, coming downstairs. She didn't look pleased to see them. Clara had come forward, her arms outstretched. It was clear what they'd let happen to Amy over the years. A faded sloven in a wrapper, with hair that needed a comb through it; this wasn't her little girl, this was a listless stranger. Clara kept the tears from rising in her eyes: after all, they'd been separated early; it wasn't poor Amy's fault. 'Amy, dearie,' she said, 'it's your Ma.'

Amy dutifully allowed herself to be kissed, then allowed her vague uninterested gaze to wander to the young girl who had come. 'Who's that?' she asked resentfully. A pretty girl here wasn't safe, she knew already.

'That's your own daughter, dearie. Your own little girl Amanda. Tell her she's a love.' Clara had a kind heart, but not much perception; and perhaps did not know that a puppy taken early from the litter no longer interests its dam on later return. Amy scanned her daughter, then said 'I always had an idea that that one might have lived after all. I heard it cry. They took away Henry when he was six.' She'd been getting fond of Henry, he reminded her of his father. This girl had Toby's hair.

'Make yourselves at home,' she said then, without greeting Amanda. 'Griffin will show you your rooms. There's a mutton bone for supper, I dare say. I'll go up and dress.'

She went, and Mrs Griffin, old, bustling and still competent, who had greeted them at the door, now showed them their rooms in silence. She then announced in flat Welsh tones that she would have hot water sent up to wash, and that supper would be at seven. They didn't call it dinner here, Amanda noticed; Mrs Ludd would have said it showed they didn't belong to the upper classes. She no longer cared: she would be glad of the mutton bone whatever they called it. Her mother hadn't seemed interested in her. What had she meant about "that one"? Had there been another? Probably it was Henry, whom she'd spoken of. It was difficult to work everything out. Perhaps Clara – that was, grandmother – would tell her more before she went back. It didn't look as if it would be of much use to ask her mother anything.

Clara herself remained depressed after the renewed sight of Amy. It must be with staying on alone in this place. She looked out at the bare hills, the darkly enclosed neglected garden with its unending hedge, the sky heavy with rain about to fall. She herself would have to go back in it, beating against the windows of the post-coach: that bitch didn't want Paola left alone in charge of Fortune's. A pity poor Amy couldn't come back herself to Fortune's, even for a little while; who was Mrs Letty, after all? Amy had been poor Anstey's wife, and had as much right to visit Fortune's Field as anyone.

But Amy, approached next day, refused to leave Aberaniog. She was happy enough, she said. Asked about Amanda, she said she supposed she might as well stay; it didn't matter. The remark seemed strange. 'She's out now,' said Clara, 'looking at the garden.'

Amy said nothing, and later that morning Clara caught the coach after kissing both women goodbye. It seemed a shame to leave pretty Amanda here alone, without company except for her mother, who didn't, if you faced it, seem to care much for her either way.

Amanda had already walked in the garden, and later crossed the bridge with its posturing stone figures so old now as to be covered with lichen, seeing the deep brown pools and currents of the river beneath. At the further side, beyond the path, were thick trees. At the bridge's end she suddenly came on a curious stone hand, thrusting up out of the ground. It was so extraordinary that she touched it. She was still staring at it when she became aware of being watched. A muscular man in working clothes was standing there, regarding her fixedly out of eyes like dark glistening beads. She didn't like the look of them. He came closer.

'That is the giant's hand,' Dai told her, adding 'I can show you a better part of him if you were to come with me. It is in the woods.'

A certain part of his anatomy was already stirring favourably. The wind was ruffling her red-gold curls; her bodice fitted nicely, revealing the little breasts she had. He wanted to handle them, and her hair, and the rest of her.

Something warned Amanda to say politely that she must go back to the house: her mother was expecting her. 'Your mother, is it?' he said. Amanda picked up her skirts – she was wearing the grey gown today, as it was damp weather – and saw him try to move and bar her way. She evaded him, and fled. If only Clara – Grandmama – hadn't gone away! She was alone here, with her strange uncaring mother and that man. The housekeeper, Mrs Griffin, however met her presently in the hall, saw that she had been running, and was distressed: and had an idea why.

'Keep yourself to yourself, miss, and don't go too far from the house,' she said. 'There's all sorts about.' That Dai Johnson, she knew, was working up at the bridge. He helped in the garden, when the mood took him; otherwise, everyone knew what went on. It wasn't right for this young girl to have been left here, without anyone.

Amanda herself was beginning to feel very much alone.

* * *

'She is pretty. I will have her, I tell you. Until it happens, I will not come to you again.'

'Dai, Dai –'

Amy wept and protested, knowing it was in vain; knowing he was anyway as unfaithful as a tomcat, couldn't see a young woman without taking her. She herself hadn't asked for Amanda to come. It wasn't like a daughter one had ever known.

In the end she gave in; she would give Dai anything. 'You will guard the bedroom door,' he said to her, 'and if that old woman Griffin comes, or her husband, you will tell them to go away.'

'They won't listen – and I can't stay outside the room while you and she –'

'You will do as I say,' he told her, and Amy knew it was true; she'd do anything rather than lose him. 'You must promise to come to me afterwards,' she said. 'Promise.'

Dai Johnson gave his rare, closed smile. 'Maybe,' he told her, 'if there is anything left in me.'

Amanda found supper alone with her mother, while Mrs Griffin silently removed the plates, dull and almost worthless; but so after all had been meals at school, with the young ladies talking to one another, never to herself. Fortune's Field had been different; oh, to be back there soon, with Del, before he went back to Harrow!

She said very little, therefore, till the end, when she ventured to ask Mama a little about what had happened when she herself was born.

'I don't know what they did, I'm sure,' said Amy vaguely. 'I wasn't in a state to care. Ma tells me they took you up, after all, to old Miss Shearwater, of all people. She and Mrs Ludd never liked me when I was there myself at that school. I dare say it's still much the same.' She added that in her day, they'd worn dresses that were too short, to save money on the laundry.

Amanda, not knowing (she never did know) what Great-Aunt Shearwater had to do with it, explained that nowadays the parlour-boarders wore blue stuff gowns with ruched decoration and starched and ironed pantalettes. 'They're pretty, but they take a great deal of ironing,' she added politely. She was about to add also that she herself had always been made to wear this old grey, and to speak bitterly about the prospect of being almost, but not quite, made into a teacher; but Amy seemed no longer to be attending to her, and to be looking about as if somebody else ought to be coming in. She yawned then, and said she was going to bed and that Amanda might as well go too. She gave a sudden furtive look sideways, as if there was something she didn't want noticed. 'It's set in for a storm, by the sound of it,' she explained. Rain had begun beating against the old plaster and timber walls; it made a softer sound than at Fortune's, against the hard classical stone front. Amanda made a resolve to talk some more to Mama tomorrow about Fortune's; she seemed, at any rate, to know who lived there. That Amy was the widow of the orchard ghost was never made apparent to Amanda. There seemed nothing else but to do as she was bidden, and go to bed.

She went upstairs, undressed, brushed out her hair – one thing she was glad of, it never needed curling-rags like some of the others' had – washed, put on her chemise, and was about to climb into bed when she decided to look out at the storm-tossed moon. It was beset by scudding clouds, and lit the room fitfully now she'd blown out the candle.

She turned back to the bed behind, square-set and dark behind its undrawn curtains. Then she realised that there was somebody else in the room, had been from the beginning; somebody moving stealthily towards her now, like an animal. It was the man she'd met yesterday in the garden. What was he doing here? He must – she blushed a little – have watched her undress, seen her wash herself. She heard herself gasp; she tried to reach the door, but Johnson barred her way, as he'd almost done earlier at the bridge. This time, it wasn't so easy to escape. She tried to reach the door, crying out, but nobody came; the sound of the storm drowned everything, and Mama and Mrs Griffin mightn't hear. If she'd got straight into bed without going to look out at the moon, he'd have got in with her, and she wouldn't have been able to kick out. Now, she could; something told her to, and where.

He'd come closer meantime. 'Don't be afraid, my pretty,' he said. 'I will not hurt you at all, a pretty thing like you. Come and lie down, like I said in the wood. Lie down, I say. Nobody will come in.'

His hands were upon her, about her, fumbling in the way Signor Silvestro's had, but differently. Amanda struggled, fought, bit – his hand tasted nastily of sweat – then did a thing nobody had ever had to learn at the Shearwater Academy for Young Ladies: she brought up her knee hard. Dai gave a yell, let her go to clap both hands to his outraged parts, and stood doubled up, screaming. Amanda ran to the door and found it jammed. She hammered on it, hurting her fists. Behind her, the man was cursing, perhaps already beginning to recover.

'Mama! Mama! Mrs Griffin! Come, help me. Help me. There's a man here. I can't open the door.'

He was still cursing and sobbing behind her; she'd kick him again if she had to, if he laid hands on her a second time. Suddenly the door opened and Amy stood there in her nightgown, her mouth slack with terror. She'd heard Dai scream, not Amanda. He'd been hurt. She turned to Amanda and clawed at her face, beating at her within the frame of the opened doorway.

'You little bitch, you've hurt him. Get out of here, get out; leave me with Dai. I didn't ask them to bring you, did I? Oh Dai, Dai, you're hurt, she's hurt you; let me –'

Dai spat, and thrust her savagely aside. 'Let me get at her now,' he said. 'Let me get at her, I say; I'll show her something.'

But Amanda had fled; in thin chemise and bare feet, down the cold flagged corridors, not knowing anything except that she must escape from horror and loathing. Her face was bleeding from Mama's late scratches; she could feel the blood trickle down on her cheeks. She heard her own sobbing breaths; supposing he found her, having followed already? Where was she to go, in all the house? She didn't know where anything was. There would be nobody in the kitchen, or anywhere.

She found a door downstairs, and it was open. Beyond was a glasshouse, with, even at this hour of night, the damp smell of ferns. Amanda huddled in among these, cowering down among the filled shelves and empty pots. If he came after her, he might not notice her in here. There hadn't been any bolt on the door: he could open it, and find her.

It began to grow cold, and the rain beat on the glass roof for a time and then died. There were no footsteps pursuing. She would stay here till morning, then, as soon as she could, go to wake Mrs Griffin. Could such an old woman help her? Could anyone? The man had been strong. A memory of the acrid smell of his body as he came at her returned, and made Amanda feel sick. She mustn't stay any longer at Aberaniog. There must be other places, people who would help her to get back to Del. There must be neighbours, somewhere among the hills. She couldn't go back for her clothes, however, and to appear in chemise and bare feet wouldn't, as Mrs Ludd would have put it, be at all ladylike. The thought made Amanda giggle nervously. Something would have to happen, one way or the other: she couldn't stay here without being found by someone, once daylight came.

Time passed. It had grown increasingly cold. Long before dawn, Amanda was shivering uncontrollably. She tried to subdue the sound of her chattering teeth, but couldn't; suppose they heard! Mama was on the man's side, not hers; it was useless to ask for help from her. She herself had never been as wet and cold in her whole life; at least, at school, there had never been anything to endure like this. She thought with intense longing, as the hours passed, of Delahaye; that already seemed another world. If he had any idea what was happening to her, Amanda-who-must-be-loved, he'd come and rescue her at once. He was almost as strong as that man. Del could not, however, possibly know; she hadn't yet been able even to write to him. There was nobody to help her now except herself.

The rain, quieter for having spent itself in the storm, began again and soon drummed down on the roof of the conservatory. There was a leak somewhere and the drip, drip invaded the silence as Amanda crouched there shivering among the ferns. Soon now it would be day, and perhaps after that the Griffins would help her; but – the thought brought added terror – perhaps not; Mama after all hadn't, and the Griffins were servants, paid to do as they were told.

Amanda began to cry, the salt tears scalding the recent scratches Mama had made on her cheeks. They ran down and dripped on her already wet chemise; she could see it happen in what was, after all, increasing daylight. Perhaps – the fancy grew in her – perhaps she would catch a chill and die in here, in the end, in this cold damp place, among the ferns. They'd find her dead body at some time or other, and nobody would be sorry, except Del.

Griffin the groundsman, aged eighty, had gone out early from the cottage he and his wife shared and made his way, now the rain had finally stopped, to see to the weeds before they sprouted uncontrollably. It was always the same after a wet day, they grew. Nobody much cared except himself, though that Dai was supposed to help in the garden and occasionally, when he felt like it, clipped the hedge; but it wasn't as if Mrs Letty ever came here nowadays, or her husband who'd taken an interest in the place before she put him in Parliament. Certainly that Mrs Amy cared for nothing except Dai; easy to size *her* up from the beginning, he and Gladys had both said so at the time. He, Joe Griffin, himself had been here man and boy, since Mrs Letty's mother's day when the house had been full of guests who liked to walk in the grounds whenever it was fine. It grieved Griffin now to see the place going to rot, and nobody calling now it was known everywhere about Dai Johnson and Mrs Amy. What couldn't be cured must be endured, however, as Gladys was always saying; and by now, the pair of them were too old in any case for anybody else to employ them. At least Mrs Letty paid them regular, from London. If their son had lived it would have been different, no doubt; but Huw had been killed in the Crimea, only twenty-four he'd been. It was hard to think of, an only son.

The old man went, moving with difficulty, to fetch his hoe, which was kept in the shed next the greenhouse nobody had time to look after now. As he did so Griffin heard, or thought he heard, a knocking against the glass.

Who could be in there? It was maybe a thief. Griffin grasped his hoe firmly as a weapon; the fork would be better, but he hadn't time to get it out. However when he looked, it was nobody but a small shivering figure in a chemise, red hair darkened with the wet. He let her out, as the door was fastened from the outside. It was Mrs Amy's daughter who had come lately. That Dai must have been at her already. She was soaked: must have been out here all night.

'Please – please – help me, I'm so cold. Take me somewhere to get warm.' It was all she said. Joe Griffin took off his old working coat and put it round her shoulders. It was the best he could do. The ache in his bones wouldn't allow him to carry her, in her little bare feet, across the wet grass to Gladys. He tried to explain. 'Quick, quick,' she said, 'or they'll know where I am. Hide me, please. I'm so cold.'

She had begun to cry again, and the sight reminded him of Gladys that time the news had come about their son. Gladys didn't often cry, she wasn't that kind of a woman. He and she would see that this poor little creature had her rights, whatever they were. Meantime, a pair of slippers, and the cottage fire was ready lit; he himself always cleaned it out for Gladys last thing at night, and lit it in the morning, and the wood had begun to crackle before he left. The kettle would be boiling by this time.

'Don't trouble any more, miss,' he said. 'You come with me, quickly. The best thing now is a good hot cup of tea.'

The Griffins had savings they kept in a teapot. It was as good a thing to do, they decided, conferring together in low voices while Amanda sipped her tea by the fire, as anything else to spend them on the fare for two to London, as Mrs Amy would be no help in the matter any more than any other person. 'After all there is nothing else for the money to be spent on now,' remarked Mrs Griffin with calm: the grief for Huw was there, always would be, but one didn't mention it. 'It is likely,' she added, 'that Mrs Letty will pay for some of it. She cannot have meant such a thing to happen. The young lady must not stay here, and I will tell her myself, in London.'

Griffin offered to go and collect Amanda's things at the house. 'You will do nothing of the kind,' replied his wife with spirit. 'That Dai would go for you; he will not go for me. I will tell Mrs Amy, if she is alone, what is happening, and if she is not you must tell her afterwards when she is.' She had heard Amanda's story, and that was enough. One could only hope that the child had not caught her death later on in the greenhouse, all night in a thin shift like that, and with the rain.

She told Mrs Amy, making few bones about it. 'Mrs Letty will know what to do,' the housekeeper ended. Amy heard her without interest: the Griffins always did as they liked: she didn't care what they did now with Amanda, except that it was better that she should go away.

Letty, to celebrate Toby's knighthood as a result of his work on the Conspiracy Bill, was preparing for a distinguished dinner-party to include everybody of note, and had already been disturbed by two unexpected visitors in the afternoon. One was Claud Croom, in London seeing to the sale, at last, of the old nabob's valuable art collection, taking some of his by now almost equally valuable time from the Hamburg branch of Crowbetter's to come over to do so. With him was the agent formerly employed, a stout middle-aged Flemish personage named Van Hakluyt. At any other time Letty would have found both visitors interesting, especially as the agent spoke reasonable English; but on this particular day she was a trifle impatient, gave them tea, made courteous talk – Toby was of course at the House – and showed them out into the hall shortly with what she hoped was not impolite haste. The day was already darkening, but one understood the two men were only returning to the Piccadilly mansion, and could walk there from Albemarle Street.

They were all three in time to glimpse, therefore, from the opened door, the inconvenient arrival of a shabby hack, whose emerging occupants were of an appearance which would, had Letty herself not been present in the hall, have caused her footman to say that she was not at home. Letty

uneasily recognised the first: a militant Welshwoman in a
pork-pie hat and enveloping cape, with the indefinable air
of being in service despite her air of assumed authority.
The second was, of course, to Letty's increased unease,
Amanda.

Letty would not have been human had she not permitted
her anger to show. The exigencies of having become Lady
Croom were already profound: dinner for twenty guests
in three hours' time, her own toilet to make after ensuring
that the new cook knew exactly what to do; also, nagging at
the back of her mind, the recollection of having seen old
Miss Shearwater's death in the papers quite lately. In any
case, they wouldn't take the girl back there, and in the
presence of visitors she couldn't put her out on the street.
'Go upstairs to the attics, and someone will come to see to
you,' she instructed Mrs Griffin in a cold voice; there was
no time to ask the woman why she had left Aberaniog
without instructions to do so. Everything, including one's
own careful planning, seemed to be getting out of hand.
Letty was also aware of the connoisseur's stare of the
Flemish art dealer as he surveyed Amanda. Before
obeying the order to take her charges upstairs, however,
Mrs Griffin spoke out in independent Welsh fashion; you
couldn't keep that nation quiet; it had been the same from
the beginning.
     'I have brought Miss Amanda to you, Mrs Letty –'
Gladys was unaware of the new distinction and had she
known, it would have made no difference – 'because she
shouldn't be left with that mother of hers, and that's the
truth. I can tell you much more, ma'am, when these
gentlemen have gone, but meantime the little creature
may have caught her death, and I'd be glad if she could be
put to bed with a hot brick, and maybe hot toddy and
lemon as well.'
     It was all of it said in the lilt of Powys, and Mr Van
Hakluyt looked on with interest. The spectacle of the
white-faced young girl, red-gold curls escaping delight-
fully from under her bonnet, and livid scratch-marks still
on her cheeks, unmanned him; it was like seeing a marred
Greuze. The scratches would heal, however. Mr Van

Hakluyt remained silent meantime, watching the pair go up the grand staircase. He must learn much more from Claud Croom.

Claud himself, while recognising the inherited colour of his half-brother's hair, had also, in the instant's gaze allotted him, perceived in the drooping and exhausted young woman a trace of the formerly much too available Amy, whom until now he had permitted himself to forget. He also watched the pair go up, then bowed over Letty's hand, congratulating her once again on Toby's knighthood. Unacknowledged between them was the memory of Flora, and how Letty had done him a certain favour neither acknowledged by now: but she knew, Claud had no doubt, that he was at her disposal for that reason. There was likewise no reason for objection to her acquaintance now poor Flora was dead.

The men left, and the distracted Letty returned to her duties as hostess: in fact, the dinner was a moderate success and it was not till the last distinguished guest had gone that she remembered about the hot toddy for Amanda. By then, the girl was tossing in bed with fever, cheeks flushed, with Mrs Griffin beside her, sleepless and distracted: she herself must, she said, return to Griffin at once, he couldn't manage by himself any longer, but the young lady was certainly ill. She then related the sequence of events to Letty, who was not without sympathy, but was by then herself quite exhausted. She promised to have an eye to Amanda; Mrs Griffin might return on tomorrow's coach: there was no need for anyone to trouble themselves further.

By next day, a letter was brought round from Piccadilly addressed to Lady Croom. The superscription, the first of its kind to be delivered by hand, restored Letty's equanimity no little.

My dear Letty,

As you know, I was a witness with my friend Van Hakluyt to the arrival yesterday, which I think took you unawares. We discussed the matter on our return. Van Hakluyt has offered, on hearing her story, to take Amanda with him to Hamburg to be a companion to his eldest daughter. Until then, she may stay here, as he has

brought his housekeeper and is at present in residence on the second floor until the paintings are auctioned. I trust that this arrangement will suit you, as I am aware that it will be difficult for you to know what to do with the young woman. If you are agreeable to this arrangement, perhaps you will send the young lady here at your own convenience and hers. Mr Van Hakluyt is not leaving London for a day or two. I remain, my dear Letty,
Your affectionate brother-in-law,
Claud Croom.

Letty's eyes narrowed on reading the letter. She was well aware that, had the girl in question been her own daughter Victoria, she would not have agreed for one moment to such an arrangement. As it was, matters had been taken out of her hands, or at any rate one could always say so if asked: not that anyone would ask. In either case, it solved the problem of what was to become of Amanda. There was no need to consult Toby in the matter in any detail. The sight of the young woman in Albemarle Street for any length of time could, after all, still ruin his career.

As it turned out, Amanda was unable to be moved for a day or two, and in the meantime Claud Croom returned to Hamburg. Mr Van Hakluyt sent anxious enquiries daily as to the invalid's progress, edifying in a father acquiring a companion for his absent daughter. Amanda, who had taken a very bad chill in the greenhouse, lay however still flushed and coughing, and it was Letty's task to see that the condition did not turn to pneumonia, Mrs Griffin having departed safely to Wales. Although it would have solved everything had Amanda succumbed totally, Letty was a woman of too much principle to allow this to happen, and she nursed the girl adequately enough without calling in a doctor. At the end of a week Amanda was able to leave her bed for the first time, still shaky; thereafter she was despatched as promptly as possible to Piccadilly.

In the carriage for the short journey, she recalled Letty's last words to her, delivered majestically when that lady was already dressed to go out to dinner elsewhere, her hair fashionably looped over her ears. 'It might have been hoped,' she said, 'that your great-aunt, Miss Shearwater, would have left you a little money; but that has not happened.' (They would have heard, she knew, by now). Amanda tried to recall what the old lady had looked like, and remembered only a lopsided face beneath a night-cap. Long ago, Great-Aunt had been kind; one ought perhaps to be sorry she had died. Amanda tried to look grave. Letty was still speaking.

'That being unfortunately the case, it would have been suitable instead for you to become a governess, as you seem to have been well educated; but the reported impropriety at your school makes that out of the question; no respectable household would employ you without a character from your headmistress, or else a former employer. Marriage for you is unlikely, as you are penniless. What then is to become of you?'

She paused, and Amanda said she didn't know. Del would marry her, but he mustn't be mentioned now, as something certainly told her; the only thing to do was to listen. Lady Croom didn't want her to stay on here, that was evident.

'Fortunately, Mr Van Hakluyt – you may have seen him the other evening – has offered to take you to Hamburg as a companion for his daughter,' Letty said, 'You are most fortunate to have been offered this situation, and you will be able to teach the young lady English.' She smiled, showing her still unimpaired teeth. 'You would do well to obey Mr Van Hakluyt in every particular,' she said. 'He has offered to take charge of you as soon as you are fit to travel. Meantime, you will go to my brother-in-law's house in Piccadilly, in which he lives when he visits London. There used to be a famous art collection there, but it is to be sold. You may however be able to see a few pictures before they are taken away.'

'When am I to go?' Amanda had asked. She seemed to have been travelling for ever: from the north to Fortune's Field, from the Field to Wales, all with inn-stops; then back here to London from Aberaniog, and now Piccadilly, then Hamburg. Hamburg, she remembered from school, was a port. They would have to sail there. Once she was there, or perhaps even from Piccadilly if it could be done, she would write to Del. She recalled Mr Van Hakluyt briefly; he had been a stout man in half-moon spectacles, standing in the hall. Amanda supposed his daughter would be about her own age: it was perhaps something to look forward to.

'Get ready to leave at once, please,' Letty then said coldly, and stated that the carriage would be waiting outside at half-past four o'clock. She herself was, if Amanda had known, preparing to break the news of the whole thing to Toby lest he hear that his daughter had been in the house and nobody had told him. She would say merely that Amanda was passing through on her way to employment in Hamburg. There was no need to let dear Toby suspect anything else.

Amanda, already in travelling-clothes, was therefore able to meet, very briefly, a tall dark-clad distinguished man with silvering hair which had once been red. He regarded her from the opened door rather sadly, then came and kissed her. He smelt agreeably of lavender-water.

'I hear that you are on the way to become a companion to a young lady in Hamburg, Amanda,' he said. 'Perhaps you will meet my half-brother Claud, who is the manager of Crowbetter's Bank there. Farewell, my dear; your name suits you very well. I chose it myself.'

He went, and left Amanda staring after him. At least she'd learnt one thing more about her birth. At that rate, she was Del's cousin. Del himself had told her he was really the old General's son; everyone knew about it. One day, perhaps soon, they would be together again. She would certainly write from Hamburg. Meantime, it was useful to know about Mr Claud Croom at Crowbetter's Bank there; it made one feel a little less helpless.

Mr Van Hakluyt himself had meantime spent his days in increasing anticipation, sending faithfully each morning for hopeful news of Amanda's continuing recovery. In the intervals of transacting business from the office he still kept on in Vine Street, he made ready for her arrival in the rooms he leased meantime from Claud Croom, and in which Claud and his young first wife had once lived, one understood happily. Van Hakluyt's own housekeeper, a native of Alsace who had been with him for some years and who remained in whatever premises he chose to occupy on business visits to London, was fully instructed as to what to do with Amanda; she was, of course, not to be permitted to go out unaccompanied, and for the sake of Lady Croom – he did not explain this to Zélie – she must always wear a bonnet with a veil. At the same time, while waiting, Mr Van Hakluyt pictured in his own mind the clothes in which he would dress, and undress, Amanda. They must be kept simple and girlish; he himself preferred young girls. In Hamburg these were of course readily obtainable, but Mr Van Hakluyt in Hamburg was a family man, and known; it was only in London that he permitted himself a little delectation. As regarded that, he had never yet possessed any young mistress to compare with Amanda; he had only seen her briefly, but was convinced that a closer survey would be more than rewarding. He had already found a negligée of simple flowered muslin, and little mules for her feet. The rest of her – he smiled – would need no adorning, except, naturally, when she went out for walks, escorted always by Zélie. The thought that this might be somewhat like taking out a dog on a lead did not occur to Mr Van Hakluyt; he only recalled that Lady Croom had indicated, in one of her return notes, that it would be inconvenient for the young lady to be allowed to show herself about London but that, of course, they would shortly be departing abroad. As Mr Van Hakluyt did not intend Amanda to go abroad quite yet, the veil was meantime necessary for all reasons. It would soon be winter in any case.

He was grateful also to Claud Croom, who might have objected to the arrangement but had not done so. Croom was responsive, after all, to the opportunity of a reduced percentage on the sales of the various pictures the late Gerald Whittinghame had acquired in his time and which Claud, for lack of anyone else, had inherited; several by Metsu, a couple of Dutch interiors, pastorals, landscapes, a Fragonard, as well as the primitives, especially the Masaccio one was glad to see again, its value having increased greatly. It was to be regretted that they had now gone to auction; he would have liked to instruct Amanda in such ways in detail. He understood that she had been taught several languages; she had intelligence, that was evident, as well as delicious and tangible beauty. Ah, how slow the time was to pass!

At this point a sentimental longing for Hamburg, where his wife and children were, overcame Mr Van Hakluyt quite irrationally. He would of course travel back and forth as usual with regularity, leaving Amanda in the competent charge of Zélie.

Amanda duly arrived at the door, emerged from Letty's carriage and was shown in by Zélie herself, Mr Van Hakluyt not yet having returned from his office. She was ushered upstairs and told to wait. The room to which she was taken held a large pianoforte, open, with sheets of music ready to play; a pity she couldn't. Beside it lay a white marble model of a young woman's hand, with a stiff narrow frilled cuff and a wedding ring. Amanda stared at it and at the objects in the room; the rest of the house seemed empty, with pale patches on the staircase walls where, evidently, pictures had lately hung. It was depressing, and one's ascending foot-steps had echoed in the empty silence. The housekeeper had gone away now and Amanda didn't mind; she seemed dragon-like, rather like Mrs Ludd, and had said very little. Amanda sat down, and spread her skirts; she was wearing the old grey dress again for travelling to Hamburg, as summer was over. She wondered what a lady-companion was supposed to do, other than teach English to a young German. A great many people now spoke German; the Prince Consort had made it fashionable even before the fairly recent wedding, while she herself had been still at school, of his daughter the Princess Royal to the Crown Prince of Prussia. Mrs Ludd had given them all a talk on the subject. Why think of Mrs Ludd so much here? She had, after all, gone thankfully out of one's life.

Mr Van Hakluyt then entered it, coming in smiling and enquiring for her health. 'But you must take off your bonnet and cloak, my dear,' he said, and helped Amanda to divest herself. This being done, he bade her sit down again, and Amanda ventured to ask him about the white marble hand to be seen beside the pianoforte. It was something to say.

'Ah, that is the model of the hand of Mr Croom's young wife, who is dead,' he told her. 'For a long time Mr Croom would not allow this room to be used or disturbed, even leaving her music open as it was on the instrument, as she had left it that day. Now, however, that he is oftener in Hamburg than in London, and has married again, he has decided to sell the house, and the hand and other things will go to him there, although the pictures, which were his first wife's father's, are to be sold. I regret that I am unable to show them to you. You would like a little wine, mademoiselle? Supper will be brought up shortly; until then, let us perhaps drink to one another?'

He got up and poured the wine, which was in a decanter on a table, with glasses. She remembered last drinking it with old Mr Tobias Croom, but she still wasn't used to it. Presently the housekeeper appeared with cold supper on a tray.

They ate together, and Amanda drank some more wine; it was interesting to talk to Mr Van Hakluyt, who told her about places to which he travelled abroad on business; Paris, Italy, Vienna. 'It is excellent that you speak several languages,' he told her approvingly. Amanda was no longer by then listening intently; she had glimpsed a curtained bed through the open door of the further room, and longed to go there. Since being ill she tired easily. However it wouldn't be polite to say so.

She smiled on, pretending to listen but feeling increasingly sleepy. The room wasn't cold; there was a stove lit, she'd noticed, although it was still quite early autumn. This time yesterday, she'd been in the attic bed in Albemarle Street. When would they leave for Hamburg? It couldn't now be till tomorrow. She heard herself asking, but Mr Van Hakluyt didn't seem to give any reply. He offered her, instead, a little schnapps, as he said, to finish with.

Amanda hadn't been sure what schnapps was; it burnt all the way down, and made her feel giddy. Presently the world was whirling, and Mr Van Hakluyt with it, so that his figure seemed to loom ever closer, but unsteadily; or was the unsteadiness in herself? He seemed by now to envelop her, like a large pervading cloak; she wished she hadn't taken the schnapps after quite so much wine. She didn't know, really, any longer what was happening, except that Mr Van Hakluyt seemed to be unfastening her dress.

He himself proceeded, predictably, to ecstasy. Amanda's naked body was more delicious than anyone could have dreamed; a little perfect porcelain nymph, like those to be seen at Munich; to be handled delicately, enjoyed with perception like any other work of art; so, he enjoyed her at leisure. He caressed every part of her, his hands probing into secret places while she lay unconscious on the bed, to which he had by then carried her; clefts, curves, little orifices, every one as it should be: ah, delightful! He bit gently at her small shapely breasts, still almost a child's, but he himself would in due course cause them to ripen; meantime, the nipples were pink buds, a little virgin's. No; there was after all some imperfection: at this point Mr Van Hakluyt grew faintly irritated. He himself would greatly have preferred to remove the *pucelage*, and somebody had done so already. For instants, remembering the reduced art sale percentage and also an offer he had made to Claud Croom of preferred railways shares in France issued by a certain Morny, Mr Van Hakluyt felt cheated; then the delight of the remaining bargain overcame him and he forgot his chagrin, remembering on the second occasion to peel down Amanda's garters and stockings as a final gesture. Ah, the little bare high-arched feet, with nails like tiny shells! He kissed them, then again all the other parts in turn; her mouth, with its delicious natural pout, was for the present unresisting, like the rest. Her long lashes lay on her cheeks; mercifully, during the brief illness, the scratches had healed on these: who could have violated such a work of art? Perhaps the same brutal assailant had removed her virginity: there was certainly some mystery there. He himself would not enquire further, except perhaps to reproach her, at first, a little; thereafter he would cherish her and improve her education. She would make a most desirable mistress of a kind he would not soon relinquish. Travelling regularly between here and Hamburg would mean pleasure at both ends of the journey. Mr Van Hakluyt began to give vent to little chuckling sounds, evidence of his late physical satisfaction. The bed had trembled, but by now was again still. Outside, the carriages had ceased in Piccadilly. London itself was quiet. He would sleep, then waken again to renewed pleasure. How satisfactory life had become!

It was almost dawn when Amanda came to herself with a splitting head, wakened at last by Mr Van Hakluyt's softly squealing renewed transports. He was within her by then for the third time.

'You are awake,' she heard him say. 'I have to scold you a little; you have been a bad little girl, is it not? There has been a small adventure, perhaps, already. We will not however mention it again.'

He pinched her thigh, playfully. From below in the street, there came the sound of a passing milk-cart.

Piccadilly, October 16th.

Dearest Del,

    This is the first time I have been able to get hold of pen and paper. I am sending this to Fortune's Field in the hope that you will receive it. Please, please rescue me from this place. I do not know how long I will stay in it; they speak of moving to another part of London. I am watched all day and am writing this in haste. I did not know, believe me, when I came here what was to happen. You know I love you more than anybody else in the world, and always will. If they say I came here of purpose, it is not true; they told me I was to become a companion to Mr Van Hakluyt's daughter in Hamburg. I must stop as someone is coming. My love for ever and ever and ever.

Your Amanda

Zélie, the housekeeper from Alsace, had been instructed to destroy any correspondence arriving for Amanda or leaving the house. When she found the letter on the tray – the young lady couldn't take it out herself, or of course do anything else unaccompanied – she took it to the stove and put it straight in, not being adept at reading English in any case. Then she got out her knitting, with which she passed the time when her housekeeping duties were done. She had been with Mr Van Hakluyt now for many years, and had no complaints. It would be possible soon, as he had said he was going to France shortly with this young lady, to pay a visit to her relations near Nancy. Before then, there was to be a brief removal to a flat near Park Lane, as the Piccadilly house had meantime been sold. There were to be walks then, and occasional drives, in Hyde Park, but not at the fashionable hour and always in a veil. One understood one's instructions as usual.

Amanda waited in desperate hope that Delahaye would have received her letter and that she would, in some way or other, hear from him. After she had been taken in a closed carriage to the new flat, and thereafter went to Hyde Park often, she once saw Lady Croom pass by in her carriage, for some reason at the unfashionable hour: and, breaking away from Zélie, ran after her, calling out her name.

'Lady Croom! Lady Croom! It's Amanda. Please help me.'

It was useless; whether Lady Croom heard or not she stared stonily ahead, and the carriage drove on. There hadn't, by then, been any word from Delahaye either. There was a scolding from Zélie in her broken English when she caught up: that must not happen again, or the walks would be stopped.

Mr Van Hakluyt, now that winter was here, had arranged for Amanda to learn painting on velvet to pass the time between his visits. The result was ugly, as ugly as what kept happening with him in bed. It had happened so often that by now, it didn't matter any more. London was lately in black for the Prince Consort, and she herself had wept as many tears for Delahaye as the Queen, Zélie said, had for Albert. Del might as well be dead; he'd forgotten her, he hadn't either answered her letter or come to her. She must endure what her life had become. After all, as Mrs Ludd had used to tell her, she was fed and clothed, and ought to be grateful. Mr Van Hakluyt came and went; sometimes he was there and at other times he wasn't. It was probably no worse than being a governess. The thought occurred to Amanda that if she hadn't troubled to escape that time from the man at Aberaniog, things would have become much the same as they were now. She supposed she'd get used to it: only, there was a part of her Mr Van Hakluyt wouldn't reach, however hard he tried.

Part Four

I

Delahaye, no longer these days Lord Croom by legal arrangement, sat at his counter in the London branch of Crowbetter's, to which, by virtue of a favour to his uncle Claud at the request of Letty, old Nick had admitted him as a junior teller some months previously. The experience of having his title stripped from him by proceedings at law had naturally left Del less carefree than he had been, and a good deal less godlike. His fair hair had darkened but not yet thinned, he was still bewildered at the treachery of the world's reasoning, but he was, after all, still extremely handsome and still young; moreover, by now, of age.

Aunt Letty's machinations – it was becoming difficult to know who *was* his aunt, though it was now evident, by way of depositions obtained from the wretched Amy, that he himself was not the son of the late Anstey or even, as he himself had always quietly assumed, of the late General, which would have made the odds even – had taken some years, but in the end, like everything else Letty decided on, had been successful. Stephen, not Delahaye, was now Lord Croom. Stephen also, rather than Del himself, was engaged to Victoria, gratitude having manifested itself in such a way under persuasion. Letty meantime, out of her immense fortune, had made a settlement of money on Delahaye to console him for the above proceedings. As he had had no intention of marrying Victoria in any case, he regarded this as net profit and felt no gratitude whatever: the money had been invested meantime. Del remained coldly furious at the loss of his title, angry with the Lord Chancellor and everybody else concerned, and totally uncomforted concerning the whereabouts of Amanda. Nobody seemed able to tell him where she had gone.

He had made such enquiries as he might. Amy in Wales didn't answer, though the last Del knew was that Amanda had been taken there from Fortune's Field without even time to say goodbye. Del himself had thought of enquiring, in the end, by way of the old coachman at Aunt Letty's, with whom he shared an interest in the prowess of certain horses. In this way he had learned that a pretty young lady had arrived from Aberaniog and had shortly been driven in the coach to Mr Claud's former residence in Piccadilly. That, by now, was sold: but a footman who had been kept on there remembered – it was certainly easier to obtain information from the lower orders – that, for a time before the sale, one floor had been occupied by a Mr Van Hakluyt who kept an art dealer's office in London. Del had located the office in Vine Street, but had obtained no further information except that Mr Van Hakluyt dealt mainly from Hamburg at an address which was not forthcoming. Del would have written to his uncle Claud for information at this point, but the crisis had meantime broken in the Lords about his own unsuitability to maintain the Croom title, and the humiliation of the whole thing had almost caused him to forget even Amanda for the time. It meant, in fact, that despite Letty's *solatium* it would be necessary for him to earn his living, apart from being looked down on by most of the fellows who had once looked, as expected, up.

He would of course go on searching for Amanda; it had begun to resemble the quest for the Holy Grail. Meantime, banking hours restricted one's activities no little, and there was work to be done after the doors were closed. Now, however, it was half past ten in the morning, and the early rush of customers had subsided. Del continued to serve sporadic arrivals with some expertise; one counted out the sovereigns into a provided net bag before handing them over, recording the results in the ledger provided. One also, naturally, inspected the client.

It so happened that a well-fed stomach in black

broadcloth approached. On it reposed a gold watch-chain, and from the chain hung a miniature of a young woman's face, painted on ivory. Del's eyes fixed themselves upon this in a kind of incredulity that was nevertheless immediate certainty. There was no doubt about it; the red-gold curls, the exquisite heart-shaped face, the great long-lashed hazel eyes with their remembered wistful expression, the mouth with its pout as if waiting to be kissed, could belong to nobody but Amanda. Amanda! Amanda painted expensively, hung on the stomach of – the young man looked up then – a middle-aged man of obvious prosperity whose cheque revealed the sinister name Van Hakluyt. Everything fitted into place, unspeakably.

Del rose to his feet behind the teller's place. He was no longer a clerk, but a scion of the best blood, more or less, in England. This foreigner knew where Amanda was. He had – he had – one could no longer think for rage; one could only act. 'Sir,' Delahaye heard himself asking, 'how did you come by the portrait on your watch-chain, and where is the young lady now?' He meantime squared his not inexpert fists.

There had fallen a silence in the bank. It was as if all work were suspended, and heads raised themselves from other counters. The floor itself was relatively empty of custom, and Mr Crowbetter's door remained, as usual, shut. Del saw none of this: he was only aware of the reddening of the face, with its half-moon spectacles and sparse contemptible goatee, of the villain who wore Amanda's portrait on his watch-chain, and who answered in a thick accent by no means English.

'By what right do you ask, young man? These are not the manners of a clerk. I will report you, I think, to your employer. The money, if you please.'

Del's fist shot out, in a straight left to the jaw. The art dealer jerked backwards and collapsed on the elegant marble inlaid floor of Crowbetter's, followed by a scatter of already counted gold coins. It was the first time such a thing had happened on these premises since the long-ago subsidence of old Nick's elder niece Athene on the discovery that she had married a fortune-hunter. All the clerks present rose to their feet: the chief accountant stepped forward with a threatening aspect, but did nothing more; and, with the prescience which had after all made his fortune in the first place, old Nick himself opened the door of his inner sanctum and stood watching, his golden eyes speculative but not surprised, as this they never were. He came forward, moving stiffly as was nowadays his wont. He was in fact at least eighty, but still spry.

'Assist Mr Van Hakluyt to his feet,' he said to another clerk, ignoring Delahaye meantime. Van Hakluyt was raised, spluttering, and led into the office to be resuscitated with Napoleon brandy. Del stood with fists still clenched, aware that his means of earning a living had without doubt ceased for the time. It didn't greatly matter; the first sign had come, however unwelcome, to point him in the direction of Amanda. He would rescue her if it took the remainder of his life, as well as all Aunt Letty's money. That filthy fat lecher! The thought made one vomit. Del was glad he'd swiped him.

Delahaye and his employer Nicholas Crowbetter faced one another after Van Hakluyt had been found a hackney and tenderly despatched with his due withdrawal of sovereigns. Del's chief annoyance was that he himself had been prevented from hearing the address given, having by then been unavoidably sent for. The expression in the old man's golden eyes was not entirely unsympathetic; however, as Del expected, it was made clear that he must go. Such incidents were, as Crowbetter reasonably stated, bad for business; and Mr Van Hakluyt was an important client, with an account also in the branch in Hamburg.

'Sir, my uncle Claud Croom –'

'Certainly not,' said Crowbetter kindly but firmly. 'Your conduct this morning rules out employment by any of our branches, or, I may mention, branches of any other bank, such is the strictness imposed in general by banking as a profession. You might, in any case, attack Mr Van Hakluyt in Hamburg as you have done here, and for the same reason. I would then be blamed for having recommended you.' He smiled. 'It is possible that the young lady in question is to be found over there; I do not recall having set eyes on her in London.' He reflected on the beauty of the miniature he had studied on Van Hakluyt's stomach while the latter was composing himself after his ordeal. It was unlikely that he himself would have forgotten the original if met. 'Do not, I beg you, refer to any information as having come from me,' remarked the old banker somewhat engagingly.

'I will not, sir, and I regret the disturbance,' said Delahaye, adding manfully 'I am not without private means, and I will spend every penny of it to find Amanda.'

'Amanda,' mused Nicholas Crowbetter. 'It is a pretty name. I wish you all luck in your search, young man. The balance of your salary will be paid you on application at the cashier's desk. I do not expect to see you here again. Farewell, Mr Croom, and good fortune. I wish that I myself was young again.'

He did not, in fact, himself greatly take to Van Hakluyt and never had. He watched the boy go out. Young love! The results of it had plagued Nicholas Crowbetter all his life.

Mr Van Hakluyt was meantime conveyed to just behind Park Lane, his jaw swelling rapidly and making it difficult to return to the office that afternoon. He was aware of anger at his own lack of prudence in wearing the miniature of Amanda on his watch-chain; he liked, however to finger it, and it was never worn in Hamburg, where acquaintances of his wife's family might take note of its presence. Meantime, the reality, awaiting him as a rule in evenings, would console him for everything were it not that the effects of that young puppy's blow had rendered him, Hans Van Hakluyt, a trifle shaky; he could confirm his habitual possession of Amanda again perhaps tomorrow, before the journey commenced. As it was, he let himself into the flat behind the famous thoroughfare with a gait that had continued a little uncertain as he mounted the stairs. He crossly instructed Zélie, who opened the door as usual, to prepare a cold poultice, and then, because he could not help himself, went in merely to behold Amanda. She was seated by the fire wearing a striped dress he had lately bought her, and reading a novel. Van Hakluyt allowed his finger to stray on her bent white neck, where a curl shone brightly, having strayed from the confined knot above. She had betrayed no surprise at his visit at such an early hour in the day; she hadn't, now he thought of it, even turned her head.

'And what have you been doing with yourself today, my pretty? Have you walked in the Park?' It occurred to him, unbearably, that that young man might perhaps have visited her; was Zélie as trustworthy as she seemed? They must, one way and another, leave London for a time. He would not risk another such encounter; that young brute had been in good condition: his own jaw hurt remarkably.

'No,' replied Amanda without interest, adding that they might go for a walk later as far as she knew. She did not ask the reason for his early visit; nor, as he realised with added injury, had she so much as noticed his swollen face. It was perhaps as well.

He surveyed her as usual with open possessiveness. With his continued instruction, she had become by now no longer a nymphet but a young goddess; perhaps Psyche after initiation, and admission by the gods. Van Hakluyt had no intention of letting his ownership lapse in any respect, despite the discouraging results of a recent visit to Paris in course of which, unveiling Amanda for once, he had taken her to the opera. 'How your young daughter is beautiful, a *rousse* like our Empress!' had been the general response, and Van Hakluyt had hurried Amanda away from the too open admiration of French gentlemen and had then most decidedly shown her, back in the hotel, that he was not, after all, her father. Now, following today's unpleasant episode, he would again take her with him, this time on a planned business trip to Venice, travelling by land and visiting certain notable places on the way. It would be as well to be out of London for some considerable time, as he had already told himself: he would instruct Zélie accordingly.

Meantime, he detached the miniature from his watch-chain and put it in a drawer. One could not be too prudent. It had been foolish to wear it openly, as the Duke of Wellington had still done, one remembered, in old age with the miniature of Mrs Arbuthnot, making himself slightly ridiculous thereby, even though his distinguished stomach was enviably flat.

Another portrait decorated the walls of the inner office of the Hamburg branch of Crowbetter's; that of Flora Croom, painted posthumously. It idealised her slightly. The long blue eyes stared down in an intent, almost witchlike way they had never done in life, when Flora had at last become the obedient wife of Claud Croom in Piccadilly. She had become his icon, his inspiration especially since his anaemic second marriage. The rest of the furnishing was Biedermeier, having been chosen by Claud's predecessor in the management, Hugo Loriot. Poor Loriot had died suddenly: the circumstances of his death were still strange enough to recall now, especially in view of Crowbetter's telegram from London, which lay open on Claud Croom's desk. The telegram outlined the circumstances of young Delahaye's dismissal. It was unlike Crowbetter to take so much trouble over a junior clerk. IS ON WAY TO YOU, the message finished. LEAVE INFORMATION ON VAN HAKLUYT TO YOUR DISCRETION.

Claud thrust the yellow paper from him, thinking not of the pending visitor but, curiously, of Loriot. Loriot had also been, long ago, involved with a young woman; Crowbetter's pretty niece Sal. Claud himself had probably caused the manager's death. It had happened before his own remarriage to Loriot's only daughter Lise, that arrangement having become convenient on Claud's own promotion to manager in Hugo's stead; an unmarried candidate would not have been considered, and Lise at that time had a sentimental adoration of Claud which had not survived the facts of marriage. Only last year, and with difficulty, he had contrived to get a son on her; she was nursing young Hugo now, at home in the house at Altona where Claud himself had at first lived as her parents' lodger. Loriot's German widow, Agnes, kept house there still, being more adept than her daughter. Claud himself had installed a placid and greedy German mistress long ago in the centre of town. That would not have been advisable in Loriot's lifetime, but caused nobody any trouble now: he himself visited Ilse as a rule in evenings.

At first when Claud had come to Hamburg, Hugo Loriot had been reserved at home, though helpful in the bank; he did not speak about his own past life. One already knew, however, that he had started as a clerk at the London branch, and having fallen in love with old Nick's niece who was already reserved for the nobility, and likewise having his love returned, had been sent smartly over here. Sarah Crowbetter's marriage had been advertised in the English gazettes immediately, or almost so. One evening, in the smoking-room over cigars at Altona, the two men had been discussing faithfulness in general, and Loriot, his lined face bitter, had made some sudden remark about never trusting any woman. 'Why so?' had asked Claud, thinking of stout devoted Agnes and the dinner she had cooked for them both. It was a pity perhaps that she and Loriot had only one daughter, who was delicate; was that perhaps what was wrong? Probably not.

'Long ago I trusted a young woman, and was betrayed. I do not refer to it,' said Loriot.

Claud then made the one generous action of his life. 'I have heard,' he said, 'that Miss Sarah Crowbetter was starved into submission, that letters were withheld, and that she married Lord Witham at last under intolerable compulsion. The marriage proved most unhappy. As you know, she is dead.' He knew all this from the London clerks' gossip after hours: the tale by now was a generation old.

Loriot had risen: his worn face was again that of an eager boy. 'Sal,' he said. 'Sal, was it indeed so? Then I have wronged you, my heart.'

His face changed then and he dropped in his chair. It was as though he had seen someone come in at the door and let his spirit go out to meet them.

The doctors gave a verdict of heart failure, although there had been no previous complaints about Loriot's health. The funeral was well attended, as the English manager had been greatly respected in the town. Agnes and young Lise were left desolate; and so, with as much speed as allowed the decencies to be preserved, he, Claud, had duly married Lise. She had become, as Flora had, an obedient and submissive wife, even tolerating his own frequent references to Flora as such, as if Lise herself did not exist. Young Hugo, however, now most certainly existed; and there was no doubt about Hugo's paternity such as afflicted the young man about to call today, except that Delahaye was late. Claud frowned, and glanced at the ornate inlaid clock on the mantel: punctuality was a fetish with him, and it was as well that young Del expected no permanent appointment at the branch. What the devil did he want? He was Toby's son, and Toby, like Loriot, was dead. There had been a short illness during which Letty had ruthlessly obtained her husband's sworn statement that he, and no other, was the father of Augustus Delahaye Croom. Letty hadn't much heart, and schemed constantly. She'd get what she intended, no doubt, with the marriage in due course of young Stephen and Victoria: Stephen hadn't much will of his own. Nothing of the kind would have happened, naturally, with poor Toby left alive, as it would have ruined his prospects in the Cabinet. Amy, meantime, had evidently married a working man in Wales named David Johnson. One followed events from here with remote amusement: the man would no doubt spend Amy's remaining money on beer and women. It seemed a very long time since he, Claud, had briefly enjoyed her body.

As for young Henry, Letty had said he preferred to enter the Navy: his temperament was apparently too mercurial for work in a bank. That settled one matter, at any rate.

The door of the office opened then and a German clerk, eyes popping, announced Mr Augustus Delahaye Croom.

Del set down his hat and cane with an air of nonchalance, resembling the well-tailored English aristocrat he no longer was. His grey direct eyes, however, were still the General's; this fact had no doubt helped, in its time, to prolong the prevailing confusion. Claud found himself trying to work out ifs and buts in a manner foreign to him; meantime, he invited the young man to be seated.

Delahaye wasted no time except to explain his lateness; he had mistaken the way, he said, and had had to take a *droschke*. Claud reflected on almost the last person to arrive here in a *droschke*, but penniless; a young woman, who had run into the bank and accosted him as he was crossing the floor, flinging back her veil to reveal red hair and a face of trembling unmistakeable beauty. It was the young woman he had seen briefly in the hall at Piccadilly, in company with Van Hakluyt that time; later, Claud knew well enough what had happened.

'Mr Croom! Mr Croom! Help me, help me!' She had come here without money, she said; she had seen the Crowbetter's sign. She wanted to return to Fortune's Field; he must help her. At that point a servant, a woman, breathless from the chase, had hurried in; Claud himself had stared coldly at the anguished girl, denying any knowledge of her. Van Hakluyt was a valued customer. One must not offend him. Now, this puppy seated before him was asking for his address. It was unlikely the girl Amanda was kept there; she had been taken away firmly by the servant after he himself had called for a carriage for them both. It was probable that any witness had thought the young woman was deranged.

'I must find this man,' said Delahaye now. 'I know that he has an account with you; you can tell me his direction.' He spoke sternly; it was almost as if the old General sat there. Was there confusion, after all, about the parentage? It no longer mattered: the title was settled on Stephen.

Claud was still thinking swiftly. Van Hakluyt's residence had two drawbacks; the first was that, to reach it, one of necessity passed the apartments wherein Claud himself kept Ilse Schnee, his mistress, and it would be unfortunate to be met with entering or emerging. Secondly, he knew well enough that if young Delahaye were to find the house in any case, as he would almost certainly do whether or not informed now, Van Hakluyt's wife, or more likely still the Van Hakluyt daughters, would tell the handsome stranger that the good Vater was at present in Venice on business. It was simpler to tell the boy so himself. Claud did so, accordingly, and Delahaye rose to his feet.

'Thank you, uncle. I am grateful for the information. I

will make my way there at once and will not rest till I have found Amanda. I intend, now that I am of age, to marry her.'

That, thought Claud, would be awkward, in the event; he had lost the threads now, but remembered his mother Paola telling him of the red-haired girl twin who had been born to Amy alongside Delahaye himself, and promptly removed to the north. A marriage between brother and sister would be a disaster, and void; but it was after all not his concern. The less one appeared to know about anything of that kind, the better; and nothing about the births was in any case certain. He bowed young Delahaye out, not escorting him as far as the front door; one had to preserve one's position. Claud spared a glance shortly for the view of the Elbe from his window, and the vessels rising on it at high water. He had no idea which way the young man had gone. It was no longer his business: and business was of the first importance now. He had glanced, on return, at the portrait of Flora, as though for inspiration or advice: but the blue eyes today were made of opaque paint, and told him nothing.

Amanda was meantime travelling south in a carriage between Mr Van Hakluyt and Zélie. She had been scolded for trying to reach the Hamburg manager in his bank. It would have been different if she'd had any money; as it was, she couldn't pay the driver, who had afterwards made a scene. It had perhaps been foolish, but she'd glimpsed the Crowbetter's sign as they came in, and slipped out of the Posthof in the old Hanseatic region somehow alone, hailing the carriage for herself. One had to risk something. She'd of course heard, while at Fortune's, that Claud Croom was in the Hamburg bank: it was at least a link with Del. Claud had pretended, however, not to know her, in the same way as Letty Croom had done that time when encountered in the Park. it was evident they wanted nothing to do with her; the present situation must be endured, wherever she was being taken now. Paris had been diverting, with the gentlemen raising their glasses to survey her at the opera; but, afterwards, it had of course been as usual.

By now, Amanda loathed Van Hakluyt; his intimate nocturnal pryings and eventual squeals of triumph, his general smug inadequacies, his meanness, her own lack of freedom. He had never allowed her a penny of her own; Zélie handled the money, counting it out carefully from a brown leather purse. They were to part with Zélie meantime at Nancy, where her people were. After that, one would perhaps be watched less; there might therefore be some chance to escape, but where and to what? The immensity of the world, and one's own lack of knowledge of it, was terrifying. At least, as things were, day followed day securely enough. Amanda looked dispiritedly out of the window, beyond Zélie's black-clad form and Van Hakluyt's stout one. They were coming to some lavender-coloured fields. Van Hakluyt explained instructively that these contained flax. 'Presently they will harvest it, then put the stems in pits to rot, then next year take them out, beat them and make good linen to be bleached,' he said pleasantly.

If Amanda had known, Delahaye was following them, not too many miles back; but he would go straight to Venice, while they, meantime, turned east.

II

Mr Van Hukluyt remained complacent to a certain degree, but no more. He told himself he had firmly put the little disobedience of Amanda at Hamburg in its place; moreover, he carried with him a large and precious folio of irreplaceable drawings. They had been got by good fortune, of the kind which often attended him, from a riverside atelier rented by a young artist in Chelsea. Turner had died there nine years previously, leaving his works to a shy executor named John Ruskin, himself under the excessive influence of a prudish and interfering father. It was known that Ruskin had rummaged among the crowded stocks of papers shoved in cupboards, in drawers, under dirty cups and long-piled plates; some had lain undisturbed for so many years that mice had nested in them, others were half destroyed by damp. Many more had been destroyed by the orders of Ruskin *père*, being considered by him thoroughly shocking. However the young artist in question, taking up loose floorboards, had found still more; enough, had he known, to make a connoisseur's dream, but like many artists he had no strong commercial awareness. He had brought them to Van Hakluyt in Vine Street in the hope of turning a penny or two, no more; it was not that Turner was unknown, but that the items were in lamentable condition, ragged, chewed and mouldy. It had taken Van Hakluyt himself, with the infinite care he bestowed on precious objects, two years to repair them to a state where they might be considered by some discerning private buyer. The unspeakable Ruskin had done one good turn; what remained after the orgy of destruction was even more valuable than would otherwise have been the case. Van Hakluyt, through certain discreet makings known, had at last found a client in Zürich rich enough to

pay the price he asked; it was unlikely the drawings themselves would see the light of day again. They were on the
way there now, in slow stages as he himself went. Meantime
he, Van Hakluyt, had had the immense benefit, and perhaps even instruction, of surveying the themes at leisure:
such varied, such diverting detail! Only a man who had
been a genius both at architectural drawing, perspective,
and the finer aspects of human flesh portrayed in pencil
could have evolved them. One in particular had struck Van
Hakluyt so forcibly he had almost, but not quite, kept it for
himself: a sketch of a sprawling woman entitled, in a
scribbled word across the corner in the dead man's writing,
Paola. He himself would be sorry to part with Paola, and
with the folio as a whole; but money was money, and he
after all possessed Amanda.

He had decided to keep a strict eye on her in Zürich, in
case there were further attempts to escape by way of
bankers or similar hoped-for allies. Thereafter there
would be a little holiday together in the Bernese Oberland,
following Vienna and, finally, Venice, where Van Hakluyt
had word of a convent-hung Bellini. Amanda's continued
listlessness, not to mention the episode at Hamburg,
however disturbed his self-satisfaction a trifle: did she lack
anything he could provide? She should be thankful for so
generous a protector, one moreover who valued her
beauty as equalling that of great sculpture, great and
delicate painting, exquisite carving; his handling of her
remained as knowledgeable as when he handled other
such items. She had never on any single occasion
manifested gratitude for all of this care, and Van Hakluyt
admittedly began to feel a little petulant by this time.
However, the money about to be paid for the Turners was
nearing daily; after that, he would regain full confidence
in himself.

He was perturbed also to know what to do lacking Zélie
as a watchdog. She had not seen her family for seven
years, and it was permissible to allow her meantime to
leave them at Nancy; but no hired maid would be as
efficient, and it would be necessary to keep Amanda
permanently on his own arm, even during business visits;
otherwise, the possibilities troubled him. Ghosts of
music-masters, bankers, and ogling Frenchmen continued

to disturb the good dealer's habitual calm of mind on the journey. However in Paris that time, when they had watched the red-haired Empress pass, lolling in her carriage – it had formerly been the practice of whores, but had been taken up by the élite, and nobody could describe Eugénie as other than virtuous – he had taken Amanda to a couturier and had purchased, among other things, a white satin encrusted dress to be worn with bare shoulders like the Empress: Amanda should wear it to promenade at the Staatsoper in Vienna, in what had become the fashionable marriage-market at the interval, but always, naturally, on his arm.

There, however, so lamentable an adventure befell that Mr Van Hakluyt considered serious action on the day following. At the hotel, which was in the centre of the capital near the Hofburg, he had ensured that there should be provided a bed to eclipse all beds; baroque, curtained, broad as a river and spread with snowy silk. There was however no time to use it before attending the performance at the Staatsoper and, afterwards, as a little treat for Amanda, the purchase of tickets for a reception at which an archduke would be present in the flesh. It would, he told her, be good for her to see the great world at a slight distance. Meantime, as he acted for the present as her personal maid, he laced Amanda into the white décolletée gown. It was said that the Emperor of the French constantly caressed his wife's swanlike shoulders, and Mr Van Hakluyt did the same now with Amanda's. She looked superbly beautiful; it would be a pleasure to be seen with her. The impertinence of the French would not be repeated here, where manners were respected by the subjects of a distinctly more ancient dynasty.

Having sat through half the opera – Mr Van Hakluyt, not being musical, was unable afterwards to recall which one it had been – everyone went, as ordained, to promenade up and down the foyer with the rest of polite Viennese society. Young ladies came here with their mothers in order to be seen, but tonight everybody looked instead at Amanda, resplendent in the white encrusted dress, her revealed hair bright beneath the sparkling chandeliers: and in particular there stared a Hungarian hussar, gorgeous in his green uniform with its fur half-cape. His virile moustaches bristled; his slim figure, which Mr Van Hakluyt already envied, was enhanced by tight trousers, frogging and epaulettes. Van Hakluyt guided Amanda again upstairs to their red velvet box for the second half, thankfully.

At the reception, however, at the Hofburg, the hussar was there again; moreover there was an orchestra and presently, it was evident, dancing would follow. The archduke sat stupidly in his white coat and medals representing the Emperor, who was with his family at Ischl. The orchestra struck up. 'We will sit quietly at our table,' remarked Van Hakluyt firmly, while crinolines began to whirl past like balloons. Amanda's little foot in its white satin slipper tapped hungrily to the music. Along, without delay, came the hussar.

'You will not accept,' hissed Van Hakluyt. 'I forbid it.' It was useless; the fellow had seized Amanda by the wrist with great impertinence. They waltzed off together, leaving an infuriated Van Hakluyt alone at his table. The young pair – he had to admit that both were young – waltzed like a dream, without instruction. Who had taught Amanda to do so in such a fashion, as if she were borne on air? The music-master, naturally; and now, a hussar.

Amanda herself was for some moments in fairyland. The violins lilted in a way she had always known they would do: she had been born for this. If only she could speak Hungarian! The hussar made eyes, deliciously, above his moustache which occasionally brushed her cheek. His gloved hand held hers, his arm encircled her slender waist, everything was delicious. If only the waltz would never come to an end! But it did; and there was Mr Van Hakluyt, wading across the floor to repossess her, insisting that they go back at once to the hotel. He always spoilt everything.

On return to the bedroom, he was still very cross. He stripped the dress from Amanda as if it had done wrong, casting it aside on an upholstered chair and finally undressing her till she stood quite naked. He then ran his hands briefly over her, telling her to get into bed: the sheets were cool and silken, and by that time she could have slept, with an unsullied memory of the waltz and the hussar. But Mr Van Hakluyt was there as usual in his nightshirt, climbed in beside her and proceeded to ensure his claim, with prudence in all the circumstances, but with emphasis. It had been the same that time she ran away to the Hamburg bank, and at other times. Amanda tried to remember the hussar, and his moustache brushing her cheek; it was all of it less far away than Del by now, and anyway Del hadn't answered her letter that time. She stared now over Van Hakluyt's jerking head to the bluish gaslight below in the street. The rest of Vienna was dancing till dawn.

Next day, Mr Van Hakluyt took her with him to an apothecary's in the Fürichsgasse. He placed Amanda in a chair while he purchased, in a low voice, certain little powders over the counter. It had become necessary; he was convinced, more so than ever since watching the waltz yesterday evening, that the fires of Aphrodite lurked somewhere within that delectable exterior, but as usual he had found himself unable to light them. He had left the folio of drawings in safe custody downstairs in the hotel; after parting with them in Zürich, perhaps during the little holiday in the Bernese Oberland, he would apply himself with greater firmness to the question of Amanda's responsiveness to his embraces. That she should continue to elude him in this way was impertinent, almost after the manner of the hussar.

In fact, he caused her to take the first of the powders at Zürich, following the sale of the drawings to a satisfied customer: but Amanda, left downstairs meantime to drink coffee with the customer's wife, who thought she was the visitor's niece, had been guilty already of further disobedience. Madame, who like all Swiss wives was subservient and devoted to her duties, had come upstairs at last in some perturbation to say that the young lady had denied being Mr Van Hakluyt's relation as he had stated, and had moreover asked if she, Madame Grünewald, could possibly find her a situation, as she said she spoke several languages. It had not been advisable to remain in the room. Van Hakluyt, having completed his sale, smoothed the offended lady over, said that his niece took these turns, which was why he had to guard her closely; and called for a carriage at once. In it, he made her own position clear to Amanda.

'You are of the half-world; understand that it will never be possible for you to obtain any situation except the kind you already occupy. As you have everything provided for you, it is unreasonable that you should not be content. Kindly do not embarrass me in future in such a way; it is not often that you are compelled to mingle with respectable women. Hold your tongue, and remember what I have said.'

That night he induced her to take one powder in water, telling her it was for her health. Amanda swallowed the drink obediently; she had been bewildered when the prosperous Swiss lady rose and went stiffly out of the room, leaving her alone with the coffee-things and little almond biscuits. It was evident that she could not yet escape from Mr Van Hakluyt, and must continue to do everything he told her. Fortunately, at that point the powder took effect and Amanda remembered nothing more.

On the following day, wearing a pleased smile like a tomcat, Van Hakluyt took her to the shops and bought her a small enamelled watch to pin on her dress. The colours were turquoise and white on gold, with tiny daisies, and if one turned the watch round it was possible to see the inside parts ticking. She was unable to be certain why Van Hakluyt was so particularly pleased with her, but had the feeling that it was better not to ask. The bed-linen had seemed unusually crumpled, her head ached and her mouth felt dry and swollen. She didn't want to take the mysterious powder again.

The little holiday in the Bernese Oberland followed, but Mr Van Hakluyt did not again administer powders. It was not that the particular one had failed of success: on the contrary, so flame-like and ardent a creature had manifested herself for the first time beneath him that he had, in process of events, finally forgotten caution. This must on no account happen again; as it was, the recollection troubled Van Hakluyt notably. To get a mistress pregnant made a laughing-stock of anyone: but perhaps after all it had not happened. He employed prudence thereafter as hitherto, writing regular letters to his wife and daughters in Hamburg while Amanda waited obediently for him beneath the feathered Swiss quilt. Thereafter, the dry air kept Van Hakluyt in fettle, and he was able to console himself with the certainty that fire lay below and that perhaps, with accustoming, it would again emerge in some more controllable fashion than before. Meantime he continued to examine Amanda's body anxiously for signs; it was true that her little breasts had grown plump, but that was as anticipated, with his constant caresses; it had happened gradually from the first. Altogether she was like a young soft rose; he was unable to keep himself from plunging into her, but never – he admitted this to himself with sentimental sadness – in such a way as to reach her heart.

'Of what do you think?' he would ask, lying within her, and she would answer in no way that satisfied: when he tried to kiss her mouth, Amanda turned her head away.

'I gave you the watch,' he said this time, aggrieved. 'I have been good to you, have I not?' But she made no reply.

There was also the matter of the English family who visited the inn.

They themselves had walked together from the low wooden-eaved house to view the waterfall, and admire the towering Jungfrau in the distance. Amanda now wore a cheap wedding ring Van Hakluyt had purchased in Zürich; it had been necessary to sign themselves in as Monsieur and Madame Hanse. So far there had been few other visitors, and they had taken meals in the inn-parlour, even the delicious little pastries one consumed at English tea-time; Van Hakluyt had watched Amanda eat these with some relief, remembering how his wife, on certain notable occasions, had found it impossible to enjoy pastry at the beginning for some time. It was increasingly evident that there was nothing to worry about. He forgot his vigilance sufficiently to go in, alone, to the inn on their return, while Amanda lingered to gaze once more at the incredible mountain. There was always snow up there, and a village. At night, the lights from other villages were strung along the heights like stars.

A bouncing ball disturbed her; a little boy was throwing it, playing by himself. He wore nankeen trousers and a frilled shirt, had fair hair and looked about six years old. Amanda laughed and tossed the ball back to him. 'Thanks,' he called, to her delight; she ran to him at once.

'You are English? So am I. What is your name?'

The child said it was Bobby. Bobby and Amanda played for some moments with the ball, tossing it back and forth, and then a voice called from the inn door; Bobby's mother. The family had arrived yesterday; there were several of them, a husband, two little girls and an older boy. Bobby was taken inside, one supposed to play with his brothers and sisters, and Amanda prepared to mount the stairs, smiling at the Englishwoman. The latter stared coldly, and drew aside her skirts.

When Amanda rejoined Van Hakluyt it was to find him in a state of fury. The English bitch had already complained to the management; they themselves would have to go. It was useless to ask questions and Amanda didn't; by now, she knew enough to know that the unedifying sounds Van Hakluyt constantly made while in bed with her could be heard through the wooden wall, and last night it had happened again. Nobody could ever mistake them for husband and wife. She belonged to the half-world, not respectable enough to play with anyone's children. Bobby had been taken away at once. The management regretted. Six customers were no doubt of importance, and there was one's name to consider as a reputable inn.

They moved back to Interlaken, where there was a large impersonal hotel and meals could be sent up to the room. Amanda missed the sound of zithers there had been in the eaved inn, and the peasants' singing downstairs to them in the late evenings. Here, there was no music. Soon, however, they would be in Venice. She was beginning to feel languid, as if they had been travelling on and on, all her life; and there was nothing for her but the foreseeable heavy embraces of Mr Van Hakluyt, beneath more and more feathered quilts in inns and hotels. He couldn't seem to leave her alone.

III

The fashionable hour for promenading in the Piazza San Marco was before sunset. Crowds gathered there following the siesta and prior to supper, mostly eaten at home. Meantime the spread skirts of the women vied with the lithe narrow forms of pickpockets, vendors whose shops were closed by now, hurrying forms of priests in black shovel hats, the great bulk of San Marco itself, the bronze horses, the immense shining water running out to the harbours and islands. Inevitable loafers with nothing else to do called out at the beauty of young women passing by with their cavaliers: there was one such in particular, seen now for several nights, a young bright-haired goddess on the arm of a stout man in spectacles who ought to have been her father but probably was not. *'Bellezza! Bellissima!'* came, also *'Bruto! Volgare!'* The latter epithets hurt Mr Van Hakluyt, who that very day had completed, satisfactorily from the accredited convent, what had turned out to be indeed a genuine Bellini for a most interested client in Amsterdam.

He had taken Amanda with him to the convent, causing her to sit waiting in the grille-parlour while he completed his orders for crating and conveying the picture. The parlour had been cold and damp; she had no wish to become a nun, and being of the half-world as he had said could have no hope of rescue by the silent preoccupied sisters with their hushing robes making the only sound: so she did not speak, merely taking Van Hakluyt's arm again afterwards to be escorted back to the hired palazzo. He would usually transact business there in the mornings; this one had been an exception. The house itself was on the canal, next door but one to the Palazzo Mocenigo, where,

as Van Hakluyt informed Amanda, the great Lord Byron
had lived for a year and had never been forgotten in
Venice. Amanda, who knew very little about Byron – they
hadn't been allowed to read him at school – listened
politely. It was more interesting to hear the stories of
Bianchina, the maid, who was married to a gondolier and
lived with him in a dark little house near the *traghetto*; she
came in daily. Outside, the gondolas themselves waited,
tied to their red-and-white striped poles. Mr Van Hakluyt
hadn't hired a gondola, saying it was cheaper to walk.
Bianchina had however told her that if one did hire for
any length of time, the gondolier would decorate himself
in ribbons of one's chosen colour. 'Yours, *signorina*, would
be *fiamma*, the colour of fire.' Bianchina also said that if
Venice did not like anybody, they were bound to see a
dead cat in the canal: perhaps the *signor* would soon see
one if he hadn't already. She made no bones about
disliking Van Hakluyt; it was iniquitous that he should
possess so beautiful a young girl, but as he paid one
regularly there was nothing to be done. However Amanda
felt, for the first time, that she had a friend.

Bianchina would come in mornings, fill Amanda's
hip-bath, dry her after it, and brush out her hair till it
shone. She would then put the girl in a wrapper, as there
was as a rule no point in dressing till the evening stroll.
The apartment on the first floor could not be left without
going down through Mr Van Hakluyt's office or else by
way of the kitchens, so Amanda idled away the time
looking out at the canal, the passing boats and gondolas,
seeing the tricks of light from the water below play on the
ceiling, which was painted with some scene or other whose
figures had long since faded with the damp. Mr Van
Hakluyt, having dealt with any clients, would come up
then to share a light collation brought up by Bianchina
from the kitchen, following which the latter went home.
Afterwards there was the siesta, during which nobody in
Venice did anything; even the cries of the gondoliers on
the water were stilled. Amanda, divested of her wrapper,
was expected to lie naked on the bed, while Mr Van
Hakluyt removed his shoes, coat, spectacles and trousers
in proper course: what followed was hot, weighty and

uncomfortable, not differing otherwise in any way from what had happened interminably on this side the Alps and beyond. Amanda would watch the ceiling again during the process and think of everything of the kind as having taken place with someone who was not herself: the tricks of light played over a girl's body which was not hers, emphasising the fair clarity of the invaded flesh. Her mind was elsewhere; and her mind, no doubt, did not interest Mr Van Hakluyt as greatly as what presently occupied him.

Afterwards, he himself would dress Amanda for the evening stroll, taking pleasure in it as though a child dressed a doll, tying the laces of her stays with little sated chucklings, slipping on her garters, her shoes. Then they would go out together to the promenade, where they now were. He had taken her at the beginning into San Marco. It was, she decided, a place of dusty skulls and ancient gilding; she liked the shops best. Once or twice Van Hakluyt had taken her down side streets he already knew; there was a small shop which sold masks, only those and nothing else: black velvet, gold and scarlet for the festival, white with long noses, others. She had stared so long that Van Hakluyt had asked if she would like a mask.

'Then you will perhaps be kind to me, eh?' He squeezed her arm, and she moved away, to the shop next door which sold coral jewellery.

'I don't want anything,' she said. However he took her back inside and bought her a mask: black velvet, such as were still used by women who went out at night. Amanda put it in her deep cloak pocket. It was still there; it was quite small. She hadn't yet worn it.

She felt languid in the warm air now, walking and hearing the cries of *Bellezza*. She was used to them and it didn't matter. However Van Hakluyt seemed irritated, and for once, when they had left the main square, called a gondola. He was tired of the cries of *volgare* following him: Venice was full of red-haired young women; here, they showed their hair by custom. Amanda was attracting too much notice, as had already happened in Paris and Vienna.

The dark shape slid towards the jetty, the gondolier

balancing his long pole. They stepped in, Van Hakluyt's hand possessively under Amanda's elbow. Evening was already coming down and the rear of the *barca* was in shadow. He guided her into it and they moved off. The cries from the piazza had died away.

With the sensation of the gliding water beneath her, Amanda realised that Mr Van Hakluyt was about to make love again in the protection of the covered hood. She was not to know that Byron had compared this part of a gondola to a coffin, but was stifled by the stale smell of the frequently used black cloth. She felt confused and ashamed: it was almost as if what Van Hakluyt was as usual about to do was, this time, happening in public. The gondolier's broad back was turned and he poled on towards the islands; no doubt he was beyond surprise. Lights began to reveal themselves across the darkening canal. The ancient city rose as in a dream, and San Marco had disappeared in mist. Amanda turned her head aside, and was sick on the black upholstery. At the same time, Van Hakluyt glimpsed a dead cat floating in the canal, seen clearly in the lantern from the *barca*.

Van Hakluyt, though cross with Amanda, was of course unable to blame anybody but himself. It had, after all, been the night of the administering of the little powder purchased in Vienna. Had he not been moved by a similar emotion now, it might have been too late to discover the situation; as well, perhaps, that it had happened as it had. He paid the fare angrily: they had returned to the *traghetto* near the house. Next day, he sent for a certain doctor, who examined Amanda with slim expert hands. There was no doubt that she was pregnant. It was not, however, too late, the doctor stated, to reverse matters.

Mr Van Hakluyt, perceiving a kindred spirit in such ways, confessed that he was afraid the same thing might happen again. He feared as a rule to rouse his young mistress to full passion, likewise himself. The Italian doctor was again reassuring; something could be achieved. 'Such operations are not uncommon in these circumstances,' he said, explaining that what was needed, after curettage, was a small circular cut, only a little inward trimming, as it were; and a few stitches inserted for the time. Thereafter, there could be no possibility of conception. It had been done, they said, to the Empress Josephine, who in all circumstances had later regretted it.

He named a fee, the size of which made Van Hakluyt purse his mouth for moments; it was in fact blackmail. However he reflected how delicious it would be to enjoy Amanda fully and without stint, occasionally, if needed, to adminster again the little powders which had so transformed her; ah, the prospect of such joy was well worth paying for! One understood that such things had been arranged since the time of the ancient Greeks; certain women were left as they were to perpetuate the race, others duly prepared for sexual pleasure. It was sensible to consider such things. He agreed to the doctor's swollen fee. The latter likewise agreed to visit the *signorina* on the following evening; the sooner the better, after his surgery hours, naturally. He would bring the required instruments. There must then be a short time allowed for recuperation; it was to be understood.

As all this happened in the morning, Bianchina had been listening at the door. Mr Van Hakluyt's faulty Italian had made the conversation slow and easy to follow. She went in to Amanda afterwards, her mouth grim. The girl was lying on the bed, white-faced. It was doubtful how much she had understood beyond the examination: the men had talked together afterwards elsewhere.

'Listen, little one,' Bianchina said, and told her everything that was to happen. Amanda began to cry. She didn't want the baby, but she didn't want an operation: certainly not two. '*Ché farò*, what shall I do?' she asked Bianchina. 'I have nowhere to go and no money.' She was still crying.

'It is to be tomorrow,' the woman said. 'You must go, therefore, tonight. After the siesta, when he will come to you as usual, excuse yourself from the promenade later on: say you do not feel well. He will perhaps by then hope that he has given you a miscarriage: he is a devil, and if so it would mean that he need pay less.' Bianchina spat; she had no illusions about Van Hakluyt, and like all Venetians knew everything that went on. 'When he has left you, dress yourself and put on your cloak,' she told Amanda. 'I will be waiting at the end of the passage that leads to the kitchens. I will then take you, quickly, to my husband Beppo at our house, and he in turn will take you to someone who will look after you, an English lady. Beppo will convey you to her garden door by water, and you will be let in only when you knock in a certain way. I will arrange it. Next day I will come here as usual and pretend I do not know anything about what has happened, or where you have gone. That *porco* will search Venice for some time, but he will never find you. You will be safe.'

Amanda found herself trembling. There was after all nothing to do but what she was told. The siesta was endured as usual. Van Hakluyt came in, and used her more savagely than was his custom: there might be something in what Bianchina had said about his trying to bring on an *aborto*, a miscarriage. He bit at her breasts, hurting her; it was different from the beginning, when he'd told her she was a little figure carved in ivory, in porcelain, other such things. The thought of being rid of him, that this was the last time it would have to happen, sustained Amanda through it: otherwise, he seemed to have become an animal. After he had finished she said what Bianca had told her to say and which was by then the truth, that she felt unwell. She saw the small shrewd eyes regard her behind their already replaced spectacles.

'You may remain in bed,' Van Hakluyt told her. 'This evening, the doctor will visit you.' He explained nothing more, and went out. She heard the door of his downstairs office close; he wasn't, evidently, going for the stroll, no doubt unwilling to bear the cries of *volgare* by himself. He would probably spend the evening sorting through accounts.

Amanda swung her legs down from the bed; Van Hakluyt's late treatment had made them unsteady. She dressed herself quietly, careful to make no noise that would be heard below, and put on her cloak as instructed. The mask Van Hakluyt had bought her was still in the pocket: her fingers closed on it and she brought it out, holding it by its string. Perhaps Bianchina would advise putting it on, though it was not yet dark. She herself could not, she realised, even decide as much; she was, had always been, in the hands of others. What was to happen to her now she did not know.

She tiptoed down the passage, still finding it necessary to support herself now and again by balancing against the wall. Supposing Bianchina had been unable to come? That was the main terror; however it was not yet dark, not yet time for the doctor with his knife.

But Bianchina was there, waiting in the shadows of the kitchen passage. When she saw the mask the woman nodded favourably. 'Put it on, *cara*, and draw the cloak over your hair,' she whispered. 'Now you might be anyone. Hurry; take my arm.'

They hastened out somehow towards the back region, to a part of the city Amanda did not know although it was not far off from the palazzos; dark little houses clustered alongside narrow canals. On the green water of one there waited a boat with oranges. 'In here, in here,' muttered Bianchina, and drew aside a cloth curtain into one waterside hovel; it was no more, there was a wooden table inside, chairs and a bed. 'Lie down if you will,' said Bianchina. 'When it is dark, we will go together to the *traghetto*.'

It seemed a long time till dark. By now, Van Hakluyt might know she had gone, might already be searching. Presently, though, a man's voice was raised outside in song: a verse of Tasso: Beppo the gondolier.

'It is my husband,' whispered Bianchina. 'I will guide you to the boat, but I cannot come with you further; I must not be seen with you, or *he* may be told of it. In Venice, most things are known by everyone. Farewell, little one.'

Her eyes were dark and pleading; if one judged by the furnishing of the house, they must be poor. 'What can I give you?' Amanda asked. 'I have no money.' She unpinned the enamelled watch from Zürich. 'Take this,' she said. 'Sell it later, when he has stopped searching.' The woman's dry hand closed about it and she murmured a blessing. Amanda wrapped the cloak about herself, put on the mask once more, and stepped into the darkly waiting gondola a few feet ahead. Beppo was there, a dark shape also, pole poised. He had stopped singing. The boat shot away, with herself seated alone in it. It was as though the whole thing was still happening to somebody else. The daylight had gone and lamps were already lit along the canals and islands.

Beppo, like every gondolier, seemed to know where he was going in the dark. If Amanda had guessed, he was remembering the talk he had had with his wife earlier in the day. They both knew the Englishwoman, the Marchesa, as she was called without any right to such a title. Everyone knew her. However her girls themselves were kept secluded.

'She looks after them, and the food is good,' had said Bianchina. 'She is particular about who comes: some of them have married well as a result. What else is to be done with the poor little creature? Left on the streets she would be worse off, or *he* would find her. There is no English consul in Venice. That is the only house in which she will be safe.'

'The House of the Live Cat,' said Beppo. Not being devout, he remarked that the Marchesa would rid Amanda of her child in any case. That could not be helped, Bianchina admitted; but at least it would not be done with instruments, the *rimedio*, but with herbs. 'Perhaps one day she will be free, having found a better protector,' the woman added. 'The world is hard for her, poor little one.'

'We are doing what we may,' Beppo said. It would have been inadvisable to place the *signorina* in the care of good nuns in a convent. There was no doubt the Marchesa was the answer, though he would not have allowed it to happen to his daughter had he had one. Bianchina, most certainly, would pray regarding the whole situation. No doubt it was necessary.

The gondola stopped beside a high wall over which oleanders clustered, pale against the night. A lamp stood above the gateway, illumining the stone figure of a seated cat. Amanda climbed out and stood uncertainly on the narrow edge by the water. 'Give three sharp knocks, then pause, then knock again,' the man said. 'The Marchesa knows that you will come; I told her myself, this afternoon. Farewell, *signorina*, and good fortune. I will tell no one; it is better so.'

He watched till the gate opened safely, and saw Amanda's cloaked figure go in. The gate closed firmly, with a little click. Beppo, unusually, crossed himself and said a prayer for the young lady. It seemed hard, but as Bianchina had said there was nothing else to be done; they themselves were poor, and the rich man could cause trouble if they were suspected. He took his pole then and plied it, making his way back to the *traghetto* from which his own patrons would call him tomorrow morning; he wore their colour, emerald green. His father had been a gondolier also, and his before that; those had been the days when Tasso's verses were flung alternately from side to side of the canals as the boats came home, but times were changing; hardly anyone knew all the verses now except himself.

IV

Peg Whittinghame had caused herself to become known as the Marchesa partly because she fancied the title, partly because she wanted to conceal her origins although the deserted nabob, her husband, had continued to pay her an allowance till his death. Before that, he had preferred her to stay away from Piccadilly. She had left him after three years of marriage because he caused her *ennui*, she had no affection for their only child Flora, and she was moreover in love with her seducer for the time. The latter had abandoned her in Paris after four months, leaving her pregnant. Peg had had this matter corrected and in various ways, had become acquainted with the half-world, which she found diverting and, now that she was too old to sustain further personal passion, rewarding. Her present brothel was the most exclusive in Venice. Both her girls and her clients had to undergo careful scrutiny before admission; the latter were, on the whole, noblemen. Riches were prevalent, but not essential; Peg took as much interest in the history of her preferred gentlemen, as she called them, as any physician in those of his patients. As for the girls, that had begun with the two Dalmatian maidservants Peg had off the wine-boats; by now, there were several nationalities as well as various languages spoken. The girls' health was regularly preserved.

The Marchesa had at first listened to Bianchina's story with some scepticism; one would inspect this young woman for oneself, and if necessary get rid of her tomorrow. However having received Amanda by lamp-light and seen what was revealed when the mask and heavy cloak were removed, the Marchesa was entranced. This was not only the most beautiful girl she had ever interviewed, but there was the added quality of desirability without which a good whore enjoys no career worth mentioning. 'Be seated, my dear,' said the Marchesa, and Amanda sank thankfully into a chair upholstered in red velvet; the entire room was decorated in red, and one had entered through a dark narrow garden after leaving the outer gate. She was too tired to take any great interest in the questions asked by this stout lady in a black wig with rouged wrinkled cheeks, or to take in much of what she was told. 'You will sleep tonight in a comfortable bed,' said the Marchesa, 'and I will bring you a *tisane.*' It was ridiculous that the child had been got pregnant; the woman Bianchina had been explicit about that.

She took a lamp and, without more words, led Amanda up to a bedchamber, not large but with a carved ceiling round which cherubs cavorted. She was told that the house had once belonged to the Giovanelli princes, which meant very little to her. She was however thankful to undress and to lie down in the delicious bed, with its crimson brocade curtains. The Marchesa reappeared presently carrying a tall glass with a twisted stem, such as they fashioned on one of the islands; Amanda regarded it incuriously while she drank down the hot *tisane.* This was bitter, and black in colour. 'Now you will sleep,' said the Marchesa, smoothed the covers, ran a hand over Amanda's forehead and wished her a good night. Amanda was grateful for being here, for being safe; she asked no questions.

She slept at first, then woke to pain and coldness in her hands and feet. There were cramps; she could feel herself bleeding. She began to cry out, and the Marchesa, by this time in a quilled nightcap and robe, came in again, carrying a basin and towel. In the midst of the pains, Amanda noticed that the older woman had removed the rouge from her face: in it, her eyes looked dead.

'It is nothing,' she told the girl, and stripping down the bedclothes applied cloths wrung out in cold water. 'You will recover in a day. There will be no further trouble. Such things do not happen again here.'

'The baby –' For the first time she thought of Van Hakluyt's unborn baby. She hadn't wanted it, but it had received rough treatment, first this afternoon and now tonight. Where was she? What sort of house was this? Who was this woman? There were a great many things she ought to ask, but was afraid; it was like being in the power of a witch, in exchange for the power of Van Hakluyt.

'It was not yet anything worth mentioning,' said the Marchesa. 'Do not think of it any more. Sleep, as I have told you. In the morning, coffee will be brought to you; there is a bell if you should wish to summon anyone, but you will not bleed further now and there is no need to disturb the house unnecessarily. We all need our rest, even myself.' She smiled mirthlessly, and went out.

Who were the others? What was to happen now? Amanda felt tired, drained, old; almost as old as that witchlike woman. Tomorrow, perhaps, some of the others, whoever they were, would tell her more. It seemed as if she was safe from Van Hakluyt, at least for the time; and Bianchina must after all have known where she was sending her.

Next morning, the coffee was brought, again by the Marchesa, who told Amanda the rich man was hunting in vain for her all over Venice. 'You are safe here,' she said again. 'There is one thing I demand, which is obedience to orders. They are not unreasonable; today, you will stay in bed. Tomorrow or the day after you will meet the others; meantime, there will in any case be the dressmaker.'

The dressmaker came on the following evening; by that time Amanda was feeling better, and able to stand. Her clothes, including the cloak, had been taken away; she could not escape now if she would, and there was nowhere else to go. Later still, to the sound of coming and going in the house, the Marchesa entered again, this time with a length between her hands of gorgeous red and gold brocade, the *fiamma* of which Bianchina had spoken.

'This is to be your dress,' the Marchesa said. 'It will not disagree with your hair, as there is a high ruff. The design is taken from a painting by Tintoretto.'

The dress was made very quickly; it was ready in a further day. It had full sweeping folds; Amanda had never worn anything as beautiful even when Van Hakluyt excelled himself that time in Paris. What disturbed her, however, was that the dress had a fitted bodice which revealed the naked breasts provocatively. Amanda protested at this when it was finally put on.

'Nonsense,' said the Marchesa. 'All the others wear a similar dress. You are ready to meet them now; come down to the salon.'

In the salon several young ladies sat about, though some were evidently absent on business. They wore similar dresses to Amanda's, some red, others green. Behind them on the wall was a fresco, copied no doubt from the original painting but with its colours still bright. Masked ladies portrayed in it, with their hair dressed in twin horns, wore exactly such indiscreet and inviting garb; Amanda began on the whole to feel a little less conspicuous. The Marchesa made her known to the other *signorine*, one of whom was black. Her name was Sophie, and her rich dark beauty set off the magnificent gown. All the young women had artificially bright red nipples. The Marchesa reappeared with a little pot and a wool-wrapped stick, and carefully painted Amanda's, saying nothing. Then she went away.

'You will be sent for soon,' said a fair girl enviously; she wore the green brocade, which set off her skin and hair. Her breasts were large, like twin melons. She appeared ready to converse in German. Her name was Kaatje. She was amused by Amanda's questioning.

'You must be innocent, or you would have guessed by now,' she said. 'We are watched all the time; she is watching us now, and perhaps so are the arriving gentlemen.' She indicated the frieze of golden *putti* which was again carved near the ceiling. 'If you look carefully, you will see a little shutter of glass in a certain place between two cherubs' bottoms. That is where the gentlemen are brought and where we are selected, and where *Madama* keeps an eye.' They continued in German, though Kaatje said she herself had come from The Hague. 'The House of the Live Cat is well known,' she added. 'Conditions here are good; there are many worse places. You are fortunate to be accepted. It is not a good idea to ask questions. We receive gifts sometimes, sweetmeats and flowers, and there is the food. It is not a bad life. Some leave to marry if enough is paid to the Marchesa. Maria, who has just had this done, has left the place you will fill. She has gone with her new husband to Trieste.' Kaatje sounded envious. Amanda, perceiving the situation at last, was stubborn. Next time she saw the Marchesa she would ask to be lent the fare back to England; she could be repaid from there; Del would surely pay. Desperation claimed Amanda at the thought of Del. He couldn't refuse to take pity on her in such a way, even though he hadn't answered that time she wrote. He surely wouldn't want her to be left in a place like this. It was however better than being found by Van Hakluyt, and having the horrible second operation Bianchina had told her of. It sounded as if they didn't perhaps have to do that here.

'You will accustom yourself,' said Sophie in Italian, smiling and showing her magnificent teeth. She seldom in fact spoke, and was shortly taken away to a client.

Amanda's own initial client was produced next day. She had meantime found that it was not easy to see the Marchesa unless the Marchesa wished to be seen. She came in person to lead Amanda for the first time out of the salon, which was an unusual favour. Amanda trespassed by asking for the fare back to England. 'That is ridiculous,' replied Peg Whittinghame coldly. 'You already owe me money for food and the dress. You are not, after all, an innocent. Here is your young man; he is more frightened than you are. His name is the Chevalier de St Genêt; remember it.'

The Chevalier's terrified china-blue eyes stared out of a face like a girl's; at the sight of Amanda he began to weep and say he was full of sin. She felt sorry for him, in the way that long ago she had been sorry for Signor Silvestro, and it proved easy to comfort this young man in the same way; it was after all a great deal pleasanter than enduring Van Hakluyt and his squealings. During the process the Chevalier told her about himself; he was a member of a famous and exclusive celibate lay order, but at certain times found the demands too much. He copulated quickly and often, like a sparrow, and afterwards would lament his sins and say he must do penance. Suddenly he said in

French 'How beautiful you are, how gloriously beautiful! If it were not sinful I would come back often.' However he was in any case about to leave Italy for a septennial chapter of his order, which sounded a severe experience. On the following day gifts from him arrived for Amanda; flowers, wine and a little note to say he had gone, but would never forget her. Amanda shared the wine with the other girls and felt a little more cheerful; it hadn't been so bad.

'She eased you in, naturally,' said Kaatje sourly.

After that it was certainly less trouble than anticipated. Amanda was always told the names of the clients who came, but could not remember them all. She ate her food and did as she was told; she endured the daily painting of her nipples with vermilion and the deliberate provocation of the brocade dress; it unfastened with a single button as required. She would have thought that she was giving satisfaction in general, and seemed popular, being often asked for; but one day the Marchesa sent for her. She was frowning.

'You must remember that our clients come here for pleasure, not duty. You are not generous enough with them. You must do better, and exhibit passion whether or not you feel it. It is not enough to lie there like a wax image or a corpse. There have been complaints.'

Who had complained Amanda never knew; it might not have happened. Kaatje, and another girl from the north Italian towns, told her what would be the next stage. 'You will be turned over to Count Fornjôt,' they said. 'He knows what to do with prudes. He is from Finland, and ungracious; do not talk to him, it's a waste of time.' She found out later that Kaatje at least was jealous, as Fornjôt was her special client; after that the Dutch girl was less friendly than at first. Fornjôt appeared, and Amanda soon learned what it was that he could do with prudes and, no doubt, all women: he had the gift of prolongation equal to none, and never having met it before she felt the tide of sweetness rise in natural course, while the Finn's cold light eyes stared down impersonally; she meant nothing to him, he had been designated to her today by the Marchesa, but himself much preferred Kaatje's full breasts and hearty acceptance. Amanda's body had almost however curved upwards into the arc; she was about to cry out, when a small sound above disturbed her; the faint sliding open of a shutter. The Marchesa, here as well as in the salon, evidently kept an eye. Amanda bit her lip and somehow controlled the uncontrollable; that woman wasn't going to obtain satisfaction by watching her writhe. She lay primly, while the Finn rose at last, not pleased, and went out, still saying nothing. It was perhaps his first failure.

'You are a little fool,' said the northern Italian girl, who heard. 'She will give you to Il Vecchio next. He pays extra to whip us, and that brings it on.'

Being whipped by Il Vecchio – he was a thin melancholy creature – was like being back in the days of Jemima Ludd, except that what he used was a long-handled thong of plaited leather, pitilessly till the tears ran down Amanda's face. This seemed to enliven him and he leapt upon her; she felt the ardour rise, but less strongly than before; however, there it was. She tried to make herself remember Delahaye, far away now, further than ever; she herself was being changed, turned into a person she hadn't been before and didn't want to become.

'Perhaps you will do better now,' said the Marchesa afterwards: and sent Amanda down to Izmir.

Izmir was, in his way, one of the less pleasant aspects at the House of the Live Cat: although pain and pleasure became so inextricably mixed there that it was at times hard to tell which was which. The food continued delicious; it was sometimes served in the garden when there was no business, at the hour for luncheon. Beyond the high walls and the oleanders lay the canal; none of them went out, as though, in its way, this were an enclosed nunnery. Nor did they, as Amanda was slow to realise as she had never had any in her life, handle money. The gifts they received were, by order of the Marchesa, not to be of value, only pleasure: flowers, sweetmeats, wine; no jewellery, as that might have been turned into cash, and with that a girl could escape and, perhaps, set up in business on her own, or at least report to everyone what went on behind the walls of the Live Cat. Peg put her customers' money in the bank, but used much of it to see that the girls wanted for nothing. Izmir was there to cater for certain needs, and the first sight of him greatly frightened Amanda. He was an enormous creature in a round white cap and a loincloth, otherwise naked, his limbs shining with oil. He was rumoured to oblige lady clients by special arrangement. He laid Amanda down on a sofa and began, wordlessly, to pummel her painfully on her stomach, hips and thighs, later reversing her to do the same to her lately whipped bottom. She cried out and begged him to stop, but he might have been deaf. Bruised all over, or feeling like it, she pled later on with the Marchesa not to let it happen to her again. Peg Whittinghame smiled mirthlessly.

'Love, as you are beginning to find, is a pleasure, but it brings debts which have to be paid,' she said. 'The demand for your services is such that if this were not done, by the end of six months you would be as fat as a little pig and custom would diminish, though many men like a plump girl, certainly. Izmir is from Russia. I pay him to remain deaf.'

Amanda therefore had, like all the rest, to endure Izmir's pummellings; and after Il Vecchio's visits, which happened more than once, he would massage her buttocks back to the peach-bloom perfection which even Mrs Ludd's frequent canings had been unable permanently to mar. Amanda somehow learned to accept the situation. There was the decided compensation, by then, of El Duque.

'He is in a sad situation, as his entire family are insane,' Peg Whittinghame had told her. 'His parents were first cousins, which was imprudent in the circumstances, but in Castile they do not consider such things.' She went on to explain that the marriage had been arranged when both parties were children, because of the estates. 'His mother raves in a tower on one of them, and his wife in another, the poor El Duque,' remarked the Marchesa with unusual charity. She shrugged her ample shoulders. 'There will be no children, as he decided, all things considered, to have a vasectomy. It used to be the fashion in ancient Rome, and he himself is a scholar; you will find his talk cultivated, and he can please a mistress without inconveniencing either her or himself. You are in fact fortunate.'

El Duque lived in a house behind the Accademia, and knew everybody but said little of it. He preserved, at first, a grave Castilian silence, then succumbed to Amanda's still innocent charm. He was of darkly distinguished appearance and ancient descent, which was apparent also in his perfect habitual courtesy; he used her from the beginning like a duchess, and she thought more than once what a pity it was about his wife. El Duque had beautiful hands and a classic profile; his shoulders and thigh muscles were powerful, a horseman's. Amanda's education had not included Spanish and he proceeded to teach her, finding her quick at picking it up; thereafter, though she never managed the clickings and rolled r's of true Castilian, they conversed together in it often. Despite the vasectomy operation, or perhaps because of it, El Duque was an expert lover. Once, feeling the inward sweetness rise, Amanda also felt her eyes fill with tears. El Duque put up a long finger and gently removed one from her cheek.

'What do I do to you that makes you cry?' he asked. Like everyone else he was entranced by her appearance and, having become acquainted further with her, her nature and intelligence. How in the world had she come here? By degrees, she told him; always mindful of the Marchesa, occasionally listening behind her shutter to make sure all continued well. It began with a mention of Delahaye, the first time she had been able to speak of him to anyone.

'He does not know where I am and I cannot write to him. Will you do so for me? If he knew where I was, he would come at once and take me away.'

She was like a child, he thought; why should he trouble to retrieve this unknown lover? Englishmen were not accomplished in such ways. To soothe her, he promised to write, at the same time stroking her arms and breasts knowledgeably. He had never lain with a woman who satisfied him so completely; he knew pity for her, also, probably, love despite his self-induced condition. As a rule this made him uncaring, able to take women impersonally. With Amanda, it was different; he asked for her increasingly in the intervals of sailing beyond the islands in his yacht.

In the end he paid a great deal of money to hire the Marchesa's *balconata*, which looked out on the canal, and at the same time hired Amanda for his exclusive use at the Live Cat. Kaatje, who had formerly received his attentions oftener than anybody else, was again openly jealous.

One day, when they were alone on the balcony, Amanda asked El Duque if he would take her away. He gave her a deep look. 'If I do that,' he said, 'I will fall most truly in love with you and will kill myself if you leave. You will also have to see how, when I am at home, I must live.'

'I do not mind that. I should like in any case to leave here.' It was almost a year since she had come to the House of the Live Cat; Van Hakluyt must have given up his search and quitted Venice long ago. Del would never find her if she stayed on where she was. Perhaps he had forgotten her, in which case she would stay with El Duque. She had grown very fond of him, and liked to see his sad face lighten into a sudden unexpected smile. It didn't matter about meeting the mad wife; by now she could face anything, and there would no longer be the Marchesa peering through her small glass screen between the cherubs' bottoms to see what was happening below. It occurred to Amanda that El Duque might have to pay a great deal of money to be allowed to take her away. Fortunately, she never knew how much.

'Now that I have you with me always, I hope to induce you to love me instead of this Englishman. The English are bad lovers. Last time I was at sea, I thought how pleasant it would be to have you there with me, watching the Aegean, like the goddess Aphrodite who sprang there from the foam. I will take you to her island, to other places where there is white sand and the sea. I will take you to my castle in Aragon, my house in Seville, my farms in Galicia. As my mistress you will be held in honour. If you express a wish, it shall be granted. This I promise you. In time, perhaps, you will come to love me.'

She was glad they were leaving Venice. She was still unreasonably fearful of meeting Van Hakluyt in its streets, searching for her, though she knew he must have gone long ago. El Duque shepherded her for the last time out through the garden gate of the Live Cat, and took her by gondola to his yacht which was moored at the Malamocco. It was a relief when it began to move, with the water gliding darkly under.

They stayed five months in Spain, after a short idyllic cruise to the Greek islands. It was at last the season when oranges are ripe enough to fall off the trees and their flavour is unlike that to be experienced anywhere else. She saw the gardens of the Generalife which are also like no other, and which El Duque nevertheless said he was trying to copy on one of his estates: he was interested in gardens, with much else. She had by now learned his old and complex name, but continued to call him as she always had. She found herself growing satisfied with the roving life, accompanied as they always were by the cook he had had in Venice and who had been brought with him from Seville. The food at first seemed strange, chicken with sausage with fish, but Amanda learned to like it. She saw the dry brown rocks of Aragon and the cool grey-green of Galicia, riding side-saddle on a mule except when they were in towns, where El Duque conveyed her everywhere by antique carriage. He bought her the clothes worn by custom in the country; flounced skirts with petticoats starched by his servants and ironed to stand out by the yard; a Moorish bodice threaded with silver, beneath which El Duque would slide his hands to caress her breasts. 'I am growing fat with your food,' she told him one day, and he smiled, saying that in Spain they preferred plump women.

He liked to make love twice a day. At times it happened in the enclosed garden in Seville, where they stayed for some time and where pink roses climbed everywhere and smothered one's senses with their scent. At other times it took place in his castles, where the beds had been made two centuries or more back and were immense, hard to lie on, but with embroidered silks flung grandly over and El Duque's arms, a great lion rampant with argent claws, rearing always on the tester. He was considerate, tender;

she began to feel that she could love him. Once they went
to church, and while he remained downstairs Amanda was
escorted to sit behind an upper balcony lattice by herself,
unseen like a Moorish woman, looking across at statues
with spectacles and silver lace. She herself was wearing a
white mantilla he had bought her, draped over a low comb
which was all her short hair would hold. Its folds fell
forward as she leant over to watch El Duque during Mass;
at the Elevation she saw tears run down his cheeks. He did
not go out to receive Communion.

Later on she asked him concerning it. 'You often tell me
I am crying when we make love,' she said to him. 'Why
were you crying in church?' She said it timidly; it was
perhaps improper to ask, and she respected him. El
Duque turned his head away.

'It is because I am unworthy to receive the Sacrament,
having had myself rendered infertile,' he replied. 'You
know of that already. They will not give me absolution, but
it had to be done because of my family's madness; it would
not have been right to have children.'

He turned to look at Amanda again. 'If I could have
caused you to bear me a child, I would have been the
happiest of men,' he said. 'As it is, I may possess your
glorious little body, but never your soul. We make love of a
kind, perhaps, without hindrance.' His tone was sad.

'I am content,' she said. On an impulse she reached up
and kissed him on the mouth. His melancholy eyes lighted
up, and they began to make love together with satisfaction.
Drowsing afterwards, Amanda found that she had almost,
for the time, forgotten Del; and yet, she recalled now that
it would be summer by now at Fortune's Field, and the
apple blossom would be giving out its last faint scent
before blowing away unheeded on the grass, and the swing
would be hanging quite still. Del would never, she was
convinced, push any other girl in the swing.

'Now you are the one who is crying,' remarked El
Duque. Next day he bought her a pair of silver filigree
earrings. They swung like Mrs Letty's had used to do, but
with a gleam instead of a glitter. Amanda wore them
grandly with the mantilla until they both changed into
travelling-things to visit one of El Duque's castles; of

course he owned more than one.

This one was a pinkish tower on a high rock, and seeing it Amanda felt afraid, but said nothing. At night, however, El Duque did not come to her as usual, and on an impulse she went to look for him. She followed a narrow passage towards a door studded with iron; beyond was silence, and Amanda turned the door-ring carefully. Inside was a woman seated in a chair by lamplight, rocking herself to and fro. She turned a white mad face at the sound of the open door, and at sight of Amanda flung herself on her like a fury, scratching her on both cheeks. It was like the same time long ago in Wales with Amy, her own mother. Amanda flung an arm across her eyes to protect them and ran back again, shutting the door fast behind her: in the morning there were weals across her face.

'You should not have gone into that room,' said El Duque. 'That was my wife. I will not take you to see my mother. I should have locked the door.'

They left next day, like nomads; and travelled instead towards one of his farms.

It was autumn by then, and the pigs were farrowing. El Duque had the unusual certainty that if a pig was left free to roam it would be happier and would in the end make better sausage. His sows knew him and would come grunting towards him trustfully to have their backs scratched with his stick. He would walk between the thatched huts in rough shooting-clothes and wearing a broad old straw hat frayed at the edges. He was welcomed by the peasants, who had worked on the soil for generations and knew they were fortunate to do so, as El Duque cared for them in a way few landowners did and moreover recognised all their children. The babies were brought to him to be blessed after christening, as though that by itself would not be quite enough; he was almost worshipped among the *paisanos*. Amanda herself was received by them with a respect which would not have been accorded her in England. Nevertheless she did not meet the visiting nobility, merely regarding their occasional arrival from a high window, as she had done

that time in church. They would come in great creaking
carriages made last century or the one before, manned by
postilions standing stiffly behind in powder and livery.
The occupants of the carriages were themselves like
pictures Amanda had seen long ago in the history books at
Shearwater's; ancient marquesas in filth-encrusted diamonds, with their hair piled beneath the mantillas in a
crow's mysterious nest; their husbands, toothless and
dignified, wore powder like the postilions. 'They are like
Goyas,' said El Duque to her afterwards. She asked him
what that meant, having herself seen no great paintings
except for the remembered Bellini in the convent that
time with Van Hakluyt.

'What, you have never seen a Goya?' El Duque
remarked. 'Your education has been lacking, my child. I
will take you to a famous house in Madrid, where many of
his paintings are.' He added that there was also a collection
of sixteenth-century swords there in which he was
interested. He seemed restless and anxious to leave the
farm; he could never remain in one place for long. She was
sorry, as they had been happy there together.

The house in Madrid was not open to the public, but they
were admitted as privileged guests: the owner, a grandee,
was absent. Amanda was led into a wide dark hall where
the view of bright paintings could be seen beyond in a
further room. While El Duque talked to the custodian she
herself ventured towards a polished table on which lay an
open folio of drawings. These were evidently also by Goya.
One was horrifying, of a great black goat as Satan. Witches
surrounded him carrying dead children, and something
unspeakable was about to happen to a living child; its
buttocks were bared ready. She shivered a little, recalling
how she had lost her own baby on the first night at the
Marchesa's, with bleeding and coldness in her hands and
feet. That had given her the same feeling as now, of
present evil. She looked up for the comfort of El Duque's
presence; and, instead, beheld Van Hakluyt.

'So this is where you are,' he said, and took hold of her
wrist. El Duque was elsewhere, having no doubt gone to
look at the collection of swords.

*   *   *

'What are you doing here? Who is with you? You will return with me at once. I am in Madrid to make a purchase for a client. I am admitted to this house accordingly.' It was as though, while expressing his anger, he had to explain himself. He evidently considered that he owned her, body and soul.

What was she to do? If she screamed, somebody would no doubt come; but she knew enough by now to know that it wasn't the right thing to scream, here in the house of an aristocrat. She struggled a little instead. 'Let me go,' she said. 'You are hurting my wrist.' Last time, she recalled, he had hurt her breasts, that day in Venice, over a year ago now.

'You will come with me,' he told her again. 'We will leave at once. Later you will explain this situation fully. Where did you go? I hunted for you for some time, to the detriment of my business. You had no right whatever to abscond in such a way.'

The half-moon glasses surveyed her, by a trick of the sparse light making Van Hakluyt seem blind. She remembered the operation he had tried to make her undergo, and screamed at last. 'Be silent,' said Van Hakluyt. He still held her wrist in a hard grip. He started to make with her towards the door.

'Wait,' said El Duque, behind them. He was standing in the inner doorway, a sixteenth-century sword in his hand. He withdrew it from its ornate scabbard with a little swish.

'You are molesting this lady,' he remarked quietly. 'Leave the house at once, and cease to cause trouble now or later.' He had remembered to speak in Italian: his voice was cool.

'I am her guardian. She is under age.' In this Van Hakluyt was, by now, incorrect. 'I will complain to Lady Croom,' he squeaked; it was like the voice which had used to emerge from him during transports. 'She disappeared unaccountably in Venice; it is I who can have trouble made for you, signor, not the other way round. I am not without influence, and she is a minor.' He seized Amanda's other wrist; it was evident that he was not going to let her go by persuasion of words.

'So,' said El Duque, and with a deft movement thrust the naked sword into Van Hakluyt's stomach. He might have been sticking a pig. The dealer gasped, and collapsed to the floor, in the process freeing Amanda. His guts had already begun to extrude. There was a smell. He writhed and died. El Duque wiped the sword fastidiously on a curtain, replaced it in its scabbard and handed it to one of the servants who had come. The man received it impassively.

'There is something on the floor which should be removed,' said El Duque then. He tucked Amanda's arm into his own and prepared to leave. 'You did not see the Goyas,' he remarked to her. 'It is a pity.'

She never knew what had happened to Van Hakluyt's body. Only in Spain could there have failed to be questions asked. Had this been Venice, El Duque would have been under arrest at once: here, he was one grandee in the house of another. Etiquette had been observed. There would no doubt, she thought, be enquiries from Hamburg in due course, but it was a long way off and there would be no satisfaction given. She found that she herself was completely devoid of feeling about the matter.

Next day, El Duque said to her 'Now that you are free of fear, let us return to Venice. I love it more than any place in the world, and like to go there at least once a year. We will live in my house behind the Accademia that you know already.' He spoke calmly, smiling; it was as if all his sadness had gone. Amanda was pleased, though still incredulous at what had been allowed to happen. 'How did you know I was afraid?' she asked him.

'Because I love you, and therefore know your every mood and feeling: nothing escapes me. That is tedious for you, I admit. However perhaps I have done you a little service: that pig was unfit to live.'

She readily agreed to return to Venice with him. They would be free there now, and he would take her to the glass-working islands and to ridottos. She looked forward particularly to the latter. There would be dancing at them, perhaps even a waltz. She hadn't waltzed since the time long ago with the hussar, in Vienna.

V

Venice when one was free was quite different from Venice when one was a prisoner, either with Van Hakluyt or at the House of the Live Cat. Amanda had money to spend that El Duque gave her, for the first time in all her life; they went together to the little shops that sold coral, other shops, the water-markets; through narrow streets and beneath old graceful arches, sitting at last, when the light failed, to drink green mint and seltzer together in some inner square bright with risen moonlight, then at last wandering home. They found the place on another day where fishermen dried their nets behind San Nicolò, and there were dried pumpkin seeds for sale if, as El Duque said, anyone ever realized how delicious dried pumpkin seeds were: hitherto, one had not. He had hired a *gondola di lusso* and when they felt like it they would lie in there at ease, visiting Murano of the fantastic twisting glass the making of whose secret had been kept for centuries, and the gardens and monastery. The *laguna morta* in the last rays of the setting sun brightened on Amanda's chosen colours, red-gold, *fiamma*, on the ribbons the gondolier wore for them, and on her hair.

The gondolier was not Beppo. Beppo was dead, and someone else now lived in the little dark hovel; as soon as it could be done, she had gone there to enquire. No one knew what had happened to Bianchina except that she had gone away. Everyone came and went here. The *gondoliere di lusso*, Francesco, was deferential, as El Duque was known to be rich. Francesco would bow and convey letters on the brim of his hat, a signal favour. El Duque, Amanda found, was in fact known and respected by everyone; the poor loved him and he was generous to

them. Each day, when they went out, he would scatter
sequins right and left to the beggars clustering round the
house-door; beggars brought luck, he said. He gave large
sums yearly to the hospitals, especially those which looked
after the mad. She said nothing of this to him after
hearing of it; she remembered the woman in the Spanish
tower, and his mother whom she had never been allowed
to see. El Duque himself seemed to have fewer moments of
deep sadness than when she had first known him. He
often told her she made him happy. She was glad in her
turn. This, she supposed, was her own happiness: she
knew she was fortunate compared with other women.

She discovered he had talents she had not before noted;
among these was drawing. One of the rooms in his house
faced on to the canal, and had already been made into a
studio with a light window let into the roof. There was a
sofa on which they would make love often by day. She
laughed at El Duque, saying he was not an artist at all. 'You
only have a studio.'

'*Chi va piano va sano*, as the Venetians have it,' he replied,
and came to her to carry it out; and for the first time with
him Amanda felt the full, incomparable arc of passion rise.
She found herself grappling with El Duque, kissing him
smiling again and again, her limbs entwined with his while
she babbled heedlessly aloud. His sad eyes lightened as
they would often do these days. 'Can I say at last,' he asked
her at the end, 'that you love me?'

'You may say it. I think perhaps that I do.' She was
confused, sweating, happy. She turned and gave his
shoulder a little bite.

'That illumines my life,' he said. 'Without you, it would
be finished.'

'I am here with you,' she assured him. They made love
again more gently, and then he rose and, with strong
certain strokes, made a chalk drawing of her as she lay
naked and fulfilled. At the end he showed it to her.
Amanda blushed. 'I don't want anyone to see it,' she told
him uncertainly.

'There is still something of the little English prude left in
you, *querida*. As you dislike the drawing, I will tear it up.'
He did so, tearing the paper across and across with elegant

fingers. 'It is,' he told her, 'in any case inspired by another, which I saw some years ago in Switzerland, in private hands. It was signed, I recall, by Turner, with the name Paola.'

Paola. She recalled the woman at Fortune's Field, who seldom left the side of old Tobias Croom. It brought back a memory of England, and of Del. Amanda suddenly rose from the sofa.

'It's time to dress for the ridotto, is it not?' she asked, turning to look out at the canal.

'You are weary of me, then, after all. We will go and dress.'

When she thought of it, she was astonished that he had destroyed the drawing at her request, making no difficulty. It had been done with as much ease as he had earlier destroyed Van Hakluyt. He brought the same accustomed ease to everything, even destruction.

For the ridotto, Amanda wore a lilac dress with silver lace he had bought her, and her filigree earrings. The mask was the one of black velvet in which she had escaped from the dead art dealer. The domino matched the dress; they had found both together in a shop beneath the arches near the Bridge of Sighs. A black lace veil disguised Amanda's chin and she wore the customary black tricorne. She told herself again that she was growing fat; the sketch had revealed the body of a plump sated goddess she herself hardly recognised. She must take some exercise; dancing at the ridotto would help. One remained anonymous until midnight, when everybody would unmask. The lilac colour would show off her hair after that: for now, it was hidden by the perched tricorne hat and veil.

El Duque wore maroon, the long domino's folds outlining his tall figure as they walked together to the Sala, Amanda's hand on his arm. As usual, it was a public ball; anybody could come. Inside the building, Amanda heard German spoken a great deal, as expected; many of that nation came here for the honeymoon, it was almost *de rigueur*. El Duque had told her of a couple from Berlin who were so much in love, or at any rate the husband was, that he was seen to bite his bride's nails as they lay in their gondola. 'At least I have not done that to you,' said El Duque.

He himself would not dance with her yet, saying he preferred to watch her instead. 'You will keep the final waltz for me, perhaps.' He stood back while she was demanded by one partner after another, as it was perceived that she was a good dancer: from time to time she would remember to look for El Duque, tall and smiling beneath his mask among the watchers, but generally she lost herself in the renewed joy of dancing. Waltzes were everywhere by now, even in Venice; nobody any more danced anything else. The Germans were particularly at home when waltzing.

Nearing midnight Amanda was swept off her feet by a dancer who however spoke English. He danced correctly, but without her innate dedication. He wore a green domino, and sounded young but sad. Amanda, in the midst of the dance, remembered suddenly that long, long ago Great-Aunt Shearwater had told her green was unlucky and never to wear it, but not why: when asked, she had fallen primly silent. Great-Aunt Shearwater had been dead now for a long time; one seldom thought of her.

'I should be interested to see what you look like,' said the Englishman politely. It was growing near the time for the unmasking. Amanda moved towards where El Duque waited; she'd promised him the last waltz, after all. She undid the string of her mask and the Englishman did the same.

'Delahaye!'

'Amanda! At last, at last! I have searched for you everywhere. I kept coming back to Venice, because it is the place where I heard you would be. I was going to leave at last tomorrow. Now, you will come with me.' Del sounded confident; his grey eyes shone. She should have known who it was in the green domino: something should have told her. As it was –

They had however fallen into one another's arms at once, laughing and crying. Everyone watched, amused and sympathetic; here were two young lovers, reunited; one could tell from the joy on their faces. Ah, to be young!

Amanda then remembered about El Duque. It would be

courteous to inform him. When she turned to look, however, he had gone. Later, she would take Del along to the house to explain. The situation could not be helped. This was after all her lost English lover, the true love of her life, who had pushed her long ago back and forth in the swing at Fortune's Field among the apple blossom. El Duque would understand. He understood everything. Meantime, she and Del must talk together. There was so much to say.

'Of course I never received your letter. Do you suppose that I would not have answered?' She could not afterwards remember where they had gone after leaving the dance, or how they had got where they by now were: only that they were wandering in a strange part of the city, hand in hand. Dawn had already broken over the streets and canals of Venice, showing the prows of the gondolas rising dark at first against the ripple of everlasting water, the tide that rose and fell daily to keep the city clean. Del had begun to talk, with the firm confidence of a young upper-class Englishman who knew what he wanted and had obtained it. They must be married, he said; but it would mean delay to linger in Venice. 'I have a great deal to tell you, but there is an important appointment waiting which may bring me recognition in the Diplomatic Service; I must go to Valletta, and the Governor's yacht leaves with the tide at half past eight o'clock. We must go there quickly. I had not realised the time.' He seemed in no doubt that she would come unquestioningly with him to the anchorage. It occurred to her to remember the things she'd left at El Duque's; she couldn't take all of them, but they must certainly call in there before leaving. She explained, then blushed. 'There are things I must say as well,' she told him, then suddenly began to cry, saying she wasn't fit to marry him now. Del took her in his arms and kissed her. 'I know about that brute Van Hakluyt,' he said. 'You were defenceless. I was elsewhere at the time. It is to be forgotten, you hear? I will not have you mention it again. From now on, Amanda, you are my affianced wife.'

He did not, however, as others would have done, make love immediately. It was apparently necessary to wait till after the ceremony. This, she realised, was the English way of thinking. It was difficult to explain further about the Marchesa and then El Duque. She thought she would say, which was the truth, merely that the latter had been kind to her and that she must certainly say farewell.

Light had come, and by then Amanda had persuaded Delahaye to return with her briefly to the familiar house behind the Accademia. 'We will still be in time for the boat,' she told him. She could remember similar occasions among the Greek islands, wasting time as they had done on the white sands with shells between her toes, then hastening together into small boats that waited. The fact of having found Delahaye again made her strangely heady, as if she couldn't think or remember clearly about things in proper order. They hurried towards the Accademia; Del knew the way, which was as well: it was easy to get lost in Venice.

Once there, they found that a small crowd had gathered already outside the house, early as it still was in the day. The crowd was murmuring; some of the women were weeping. The beggars were there as always. Something had happened; something had gone wrong.

'It was the cook,' she heard someone say. 'The cook told us. He found him, and ran out of the house to fetch the doctors, but it was too late.'

'What happened?' Amanda heard herself ask sharply. 'What has happened in the house?'

'Why, the poor El Duque has cut his throat. He is dead. That is why the women are weeping. He was much loved by everyone.'

Amanda turned sobbing into Delahaye's arms. She felt the tears run heedlessly down her face. There hadn't, after all, been any need to explain to El Duque that she'd found her lover. He'd known at once, last night. *Without you, my life would be finished.* He'd destroyed himself, therefore, as readily as he'd destroyed the sketch that didn't please her: as readily as he'd destroyed Van Hakluyt for her sake. In fact, she'd killed him.

'It is dreadful for you, my darling. I can understand your distress, but now you have me with you; this dead man was kind to you, you say, and you will remember him with kindness. Our life now is to be together, always.' Del probably thought of El Duque as a benevolent old man he had never seen. Amanda realised that she herself had never known his actual age.

They sat on the deck of the Governor of Malta's yacht, and it was making out to sea. Amanda still couldn't help crying for El Duque, but it was as well Del had got her away in time; otherwise, she might have been held for questioning in Venice by the city authorities. It wasn't like Spain. Amanda shivered against the day, and Del again comforted her, wiping away the tears in time-honoured fashion with a clean white British handkerchief.

Part Five

I

Mrs Brownleigh was the widow of a naval officer who had elected, after her late husband's demise, to stay on with the British colony on Malta, where she had made friends over the years. Being without children of her own and, of course. respectably connected, she was considered a suitable person to chaperone young brides coming out from England. Delahaye had heard of her through his Maltese friend Count Inguanez, whom he had encountered on his travels and with whom he was at present engaged on a mysterious assignment for the purpose of mending his fortunes. Amanda was, therefore, lodged meantime with the British naval widow in Sliema.

From the first – the banns were, naturally, called in dear Queen Adelaide's new English church as soon as satisfactory proof of residence had been established – certain aspects of the situation, on which she could not quite put a finger, bewildered the good lady. For one thing, the little creature – she was exceedingly pretty, of course, with that red-gold hair, and had lost weight since she came, so that the lilac and silver dress, which was in any case rather unsuitable, had had to be taken in – seemed very sad, not in the least like a bride-to-be, although Mr Croom visited often from where he lodged in Mdina. Moreover no trousseau had been brought by the bride-to-be, and hardly any belongings. One understood of course that the departure had been made in some haste from Venice; but Mr Croom, who after all was very well

connected himself, had assured Mrs Brownleigh that there
was no question of an elopement. *That*, of course, she
would not have countenanced. However it was a little
unexpected to have to go shopping in Valletta for such
things as ordinary female underwear, even a nightgown,
for the young woman in question.

Amanda – what a pretty name, and such a taking little
thing if she could only be more cheerful! – was wearing a
pair of silver filigree earrings which must be of great
value, not to mention the dress itself and a domino, both
of which could be described as decidedly frivolous. Young
Croom admitted that he himself had not enough money
left to consider a special licence, which was why everyone
had to wait for the banns; but Amanda had refused, with
some obstinacy, Mrs Brownleigh's own practical suggestion that the earrings would surely sell for enough
money to purchase a modest trousseau. Tears had risen in
the girl's extraordinary eyes – what colour were they? One
could not determine – and she had persisted in her
refusal. That being the case, there was nothing to be done
but for Mrs Brownleigh herself to purchase what was
needed, so there was no call for excess. Two pairs of
drawers, a chemise for when the other was at the laundry,
and two plain nightgowns would surely do. Resisting all
blandishments and temptations – the lace handmade in
the shops from Gozo was certainly very beautiful – Mrs
Brownleigh, accompanied by Amanda, made the purchases carefully, still vaguely aware that there was
something unusual about the whole business. Going home
with the parcels, she thankfully put on the kettle for tea.

Amanda still spent her nights quietly weeping for El
Duque. It was not only that she had failed fully to realise,
till after his death, what she must have meant to him, but,
lacking his twice-daily lovemaking, she was beginning to
realise what he had meant, physically, as well as in every
other way, to her. If only Del were less correct, they could
have made love on the ship; or even now, somehow,
though Mrs Brownleigh of course made a point of
accompanying them everywhere out of propriety. Propriety! On the high places where prickly cactus grew, and

strange goat-like sheep wandered with bags of fat in their tails, and hardly anyone came up, they could have made love together long ago. The halycon hours when Del came down from high-walled Mdina, where he was to take her to live for a little while after they were married, were accordingly spoilt and dull; it was almost like being back in the days of Mrs Ludd. It was ridiculous to have to behave so after the carefree times in Spain; but one had best say nothing, only weep for El Duque in the night and, now and again, writhe with deprivation when alone. If only the time would pass quickly till the wedding! It was dull among the British naval wives, who talked about nothing except each other and what happened down here, which was nothing much at all except when the Fleet was in, and at the moment it wasn't. Ah, El Duque!

'Did you have a bad dream in the night, dear?' ásked Mrs Brownleigh kindly one morning. 'I thought I heard you tossing through the wall.'

Mrs Brownleigh was fortunately not present at the *dénouement* which took place shortly at the Co-Cathedral in Valletta, which Del was anxious to show to his betrothed: the reason was that the good lady would not set foot in Roman Catholic churches. A less particular chaperone was therefore found, a Mrs Babbage, whose husband, a naval lieutenant, had liberal ideas his wife obeyed conscientiously even in his absence. They drove there together. Del was happy; the temporary diplomatic arrangement by way of Inguanez, though not precisely official, was already financed and would take place shortly, but even yet he would not mention their destination to Amanda: it was a secret. 'Let us go to see the tapestries,' he said, smiling. 'They are famous.'

They were ushered through to these, and from among the distinguished hangings, with their memorials of embroidered pears, a sudden exclamation came; a slim young figure darted across to seize Amanda's hands and cover them with kisses. It was the Chevalier de St Genêt, her very first customer at the House of the Live Cat, recovered from his septennial chapter but still, apparently, to be found on the island.

'*Madamina! Amorina!* What a pleasure to see you again! I have never, you see, forgotten.'

His innocent Dresden-shepherd's face was flushed with delight, Amanda's with embarrassment. It was difficult to explain everything in present company. She introduced Mrs Babbage and Del; the latter bowed stiffly, while the Englishwoman merely gaped. The Chevalier, sensing that he was not entirely welcome, took his leave and vanished from Amanda's life.

Afterwards Del said gently 'My dearest Amanda, I trust that such persons will not be encountered in Mdina; there, the aristocrats despise them as upstart newcomers. How did you meet him?' It was important, he was thinking, not to offend Count Inguanez; he hardly listened to Amanda's explanation that she had met the young Frenchman briefly in Venice. It must, he thought, have been at the house of the elderly philanthropist who had been so kind to her and for whose death she had wept so bitterly on the voyage here. Delahaye had, in fact, never set eyes on El Duque except masked at the ridotto, certainly without noticing him in particular. He continued to cherish his dreams.

Mrs Babbage did not. She said afterwards privately to Mrs Brownleigh that to her way of thinking that little red-headed creature was no better than she should be. Mrs Brownleigh, however, from her increased experience of the world, pointed out that Frenchmen were as a rule very forward in their manners. In any case the banns had been called for the third time. It was really too late to do anything; one could only hope that dear Mrs Babbage was *wrong*.

Amanda was relieved that the episode appeared to have passed off. It wasn't that she wanted to be dishonest with Del, but he himself had forbidden her to mention the past, so she hadn't. She would always try to do exactly as he told her.

Delahaye was in fact that rare phenomenon in any age or country, a male virgin of the school of Galahad. Not even at Harrow had this state been lost, partly because his physical strength was as the strength of ten and those who took habitual advantage of innocence nevertheless respected muscle. Since then, devoted to the memory of Amanda and his search for her (in course of which he had spent nearly all Letty's compensation money) she had remained in his mind, both helpless and innocent, although the unspeakable Van Hakluyt had almost certainly taken advantage of both aspects. That was in the past; the past was not to be spoken of; and soon, in Queen Adelaide's church, with only a few witnesses – the Count and his wife, being strict Catholics, would not be present, but would receive them afterwards – soon, soon now, Amanda would be his, and the unblemished future would be theirs together. The pending visit to St Petersburg was most important; it could set him, Delahaye, on the ladder to fame and fortune. He pictured Amanda already in furs, in a sledge, beside him in the snow; how refreshing it was to think of snow in this pleasant, but certainly humid island! Soon they would be gone; and redeeming the loss of his title and the resulting humiliations must be foremost in his mind, not that one could obtain the same title back again: but for services rendered there could well be others, as had happened to Talleyrand. Those who had looked down their noses after he himself became plain Mr Croom could do otherwise when he was of admitted importance to the Foreign Office. Also, they themselves could go home, in holidays, to Fortune's Field again. Like Amanda, Del remembered with nostalgia the apple-blossom and the swing. He had kept himself pure till they should meet once more, though many young women on his travels had given him the chance to be otherwise. He was glad of the English upbringing which had enabled him to keep a stiff upper lip, to master his natural desires, and keep them, till they were actually man and wife, even from his expectant bride. She, dear little thing, had seemed, at times, almost unbecomingly eager in embracing him. That was of course her innocence, and the relief of finding him again. It was as well that the good British matrons had always, hitherto, been present; but all would be well on the wedding night, in old, elevated, and extremely private Mdina.

All was not well, or not quite. Amanda Shearwater,

spinster, and Augustus Delahaye Croom were married in the Protestant church endowed, for the improvement of unenlightened persons, in her time by the late Queen Adelaide, who had visited the island for her health some years before and had found it unbecomingly Papist. The bride wore, at the last minute, a concealing muslin fichu discovered by Mrs Brownleigh in a trunk and which, imposed on the lilac dress from which the silver lace had long been unpicked, had the effect of making Amanda look almost mousy. After the ceremony, which had been attended by very few, cake and wine were served in Mrs Brownleigh's apartments at Sliema, overlooking the beach and the tideless ancient sea. Amanda found herself remembering other water; the active canals of Venice, where each day the rise and fall of tides swept away the dirt and rubble, leaving the narrow mysterious streets clean by dawn; and the blue running power of the Adriatic, where she had cried for El Duque all down the channel so hard she failed even to see the distant mountains of Albania. However this was her wedding day and she was married at last to dearest Del; there was no need to continue to feel depressed.

He drove her himself in a small mule-carriage up the steep way to Mdina, sent off with good wishes from such of the English colony as had attended – many had been put off by the whispers of Mrs Babbage – and somebody flung old slippers as the carriage departed. 'I am uncertain what that particular custom means, but they always do it at weddings in England,' remarked Delahaye, who had at one time briefly considered entering the Church instead of Crowbetter's. However the Diplomatic Service beckoned now instead. Happy and confident, with his bride seated beside him, he looked back briefly, as though he were a stranger, at the tense young man who had called on Claud Croom long ago in Hamburg. All memories of Crowbetter's, British and foreign, were now forever laid aside; travel, adversity, and the finding of Amanda at last, had given him, Delahaye Croom, assurance. He told himself that he was certainly capable of handling the Russian visit to advantage. It was time also to instruct Amanda, now that they were alone on the uphill road and nobody could overhear; the yells of passing drivers came briefly as always; the Maltese yelled all the time when on wheels.

'Recently, my dear,' he began, 'following the war in the Crimea, a goodwill embassy was at last sent from France to St Petersburg in the person of the Comte de Morny, the Emperor's half-brother. They say he has immense charm. At any rate, he won over the Russians who as a result are no longer the enemies of France. It is considered time that England follows suit, but as always our statesmen are slow to make such moves, and in any case an official embassy is not always successful. In Malta, the British presence is much respected since the time of Napoleon and Nelson, and it was considered by many here that something informal ought to be set on foot on behalf of England without delay. My friend Inguanez, whom you are about to meet, is particularly involved, as his father was so in the days of the late Tsar Paul's attempted annexation of this island in the name of the Knights, whose official head Paul had meantime illegally constituted himself. He was, of course, said to be mad. The action was greatly resented by the Maltese aristocracy, who as I have already said regard the island in any case as theirs. Altogether, Inguanez and certain of his friends have arranged that I, with you beside me, will represent Britain informally for a time at the Russian Imperial Court with a view to ensuring international friendship. I myself am fully instructed as to what to do. It only remains to buy you suitable clothes on the way.'

He eased the reins; they were approaching the old walled town, and the carriage would have to be left at the outer gate. Del reflected that he had once seen a portrait of Tsar Paul and that he had had sad eyes and, apparently, no nose to speak of. He was dead long ago, they said murdered: by now, his grandson had succeeded; that had of course happened during the late war. It wouldn't have been as easy to do all this during the reign of old Tsar Nicholas, Paul's son who was said to have been a martinet. Now, matters were more hopeful under Alexander II.

'Here we are, my darling,' he said, seeing Amanda's enchanting profile intent on the walls of the high and secret town. She would certainly impress the Russians. They walked arm-in-arm the short distance to the Inguanez house, narrow and silent behind its shutters. The silence was everywhere.

'The aristocracy here keeps itself close,' Del told her. 'We are fortunate to be invited to stay. You will be interested in the house, with its old interior tiles; there are hens on the roof.' He did not know why he had added this humble fact, which intrigued Amanda; she had understood very little else of what Del was talking about except that they were going to Russia and, thankfully, she was to have some new clothes. So many had been wastefully left at El Duque's house in Venice; but the Moorish bodices wouldn't have done here or, no doubt, in Russia.

They were greeted by the Count, a tall saturnine individual who said little except to kiss Amanda's hand formally and to invite them inside for a collation. His wife, a mature beauty with blue-black hair and a skin the colour of apricots, smiled and welcomed them lazily from where she sat. She proved to be the least mobile creature Amanda had ever encountered; after the bustle of Mrs Brownleigh, however, and her Sliema acquaintances, it was restful.

Amanda ate sparingly, and soon it was evident that she was expected to go upstairs. There were interesting coloured tiles everywhere, as Del had stated; and a stone staircase in the Italian fashion, but older: its carvings were worn with time. The bed in their room was without curtains, no doubt for coolness; and was covered with a local pattern woven in white and blue. Amanda undressed, brushed her hair, put on the respectable nightgown Mrs Brownleigh had purchased for her in Valletta, and climbed in between the sheets. Later, when she was half asleep, Delahaye came; they had been talking downstairs for a long time.

'Del darling. Del darling, darling, darling Del. At last, at last.'

It was not a success, however. Not only was he unaccustomed and therefore a trifle clumsy; that she could have expected; but it was as if his ardour must, at all costs, be tinged with propriety. *Englishmen make bad lovers.* She could remember who had said that, and, looking out afterwards at a single star seen shining in the Mediterranean night, she wondered if El Duque's soul was up there, watching. Del was asleep; the whole thing had been over much too quickly. Had she known, he had found himself shocked at his bride's unabated leaping eagerness; it wasn't the manner in which she ought properly to behave, the vile Van Hakluyt had no doubt taught her such ways. Gentle firmness would discourage the habit; he must maintain the upper hand, reform his young wife till she became, again, the girl who had sat innocently on the swing.

Amanda however looked across at his sleeping form with tenderness. How handsome he was! Perhaps, with time and accustoming, he would get better at it. After all, they loved each other; that was the important thing.

On the following day, Amanda was invited by the wife of Inguanez to accompany her to Mdina Cathedral. The Count had stirred his consort into activity for once, as he had already heard – he kept an eye on everything that happened on the island – that the Croom wedding had been sparsely attended by the British naval wives down in Valletta. He himself already considered Amanda's manners too free-and-easy for full acceptance at the Imperial Court of St Petersburg; a timely word in her ear by his wife would be of value. Meantime, after eating the small eggs laid by the unseen hens who scratched decorously on the roof, Amanda found herself being led by her hostess through the narrow mediaeval streets of the ancient capital; Valletta, the new one, was not considered here.

In the Cathedral, which was mostly empty, two cardinals sat on elevated thrones by themselves, in purple and lace, while an unseen choir sang very beautifully. Monica Inguanez explained that the whole thing was in memory of King Roger of Sicily, who had died in 1154. Women in black *faldettas*, looking like walking coffins, came furtively in and out. When they emerged Amanda asked Inguanez' wife why these monstrosities were worn. The latter answered coldly. She was of old and impeccable island stock, and resented any criticism.

'There is a stupid legend among certain persons that the women here were put into the *faldettas* to preserve their chastity against the French, but that quality has never been in doubt among us. It is true that when the French held our island for a year against your Nelson they took away the silver gates and other things from the church in Valletta, but that is not our business. We live up here as we have always done, except that we know that discretion is of value, especially among women. When you go to St Petersburg, be careful; they may appear at ease, but nevertheless have their etiquette.'

Amanda, aware of this Maltese lady's idle but shrewd gaze upon her, promised to do her best. 'Your husband is personable,' Monica said. 'He will make an excellent impression. You must support him. A palace has been arranged, not of the splendour of that allotted to Morny, it is true; but comfortable enough. The owner, Princess Bagration, an acquaintance of my husband's, will visit you and, no doubt, introduce you to society. You will by then, of course, have other gowns.' She glanced with disfavour at the well-worn lilac. 'See what you can do to make friends with the Russians,' she said more amiably. 'I am told you speak French and German; that is useful. A personal visit is worth many letters and treaties. The rest may follow by way of London if it is known that you have both been a success.'

Amanda was torn between resentment – it was evident that they were expected to be grateful to the Count for financing the expedition – and determination to help Del in his task. He had said very little about no longer being Lord Croom, but had merely told her the title had been given to Stephen instead and that he didn't want the matter discussed. There seemed to be a great deal she wasn't allowed to discuss or mention. However it would be diverting to buy new clothes in Paris, and after that to go up by sea. They were to set off from Hamburg; that didn't matter now, Van Hakluyt would trouble nobody any more. What a great deal there was to say, if only she could have been allowed to say it! Silence, however, or what this woman called discretion, was evidently the order of the day. She would be, on the whole, glad to leave Malta. It was possible that, in other places, a wife's situation might be a little more interesting than to do always as one was told, keep quiet and, above all, lie still.

Paris was altering; everywhere there was building, widening of roads, completion of boulevards lined by young trees, erection near the Seine of imposing buildings and hotels. The one to which they were driven was not one of the richest, being situated in the old part where the houses still jumbled one on top of another. Next day, a Mrs O'Grady called. She was evidently a trained dressmaker, employed by a couturier who would accommodate Amanda's custom at a lesser price than that demanded of other ladies. 'It is a favour,' explained Mrs O'Grady, who was talkative. The whole thing had been arranged by Inguanez. Mrs O'Grady measured Amanda and said that as her size was suitable, certain items already in their stock would do. Del excused himself, evidently having business to attend, and Amanda and the Irish lady took a *fiacre* together to the dress-shop. It was less grand than that which Van Hakluyt had formerly taken her to buy the white satin gown worn once, and memorably, in Vienna; but those she was shown were pretty and becoming enough, and Amanda chose several which fitted her. In course of talk – Mrs O'Grady hardly ever stopped talking, different from the reserved Englishwomen on Malta – she explained that M. Bosquet, the proprietor, was already becoming known among those ladies who were in the company of the Empress, and who came here because he was cheaper than M. Doucet, who had already let fame go to his head. 'There is one who will arrive at any moment for an appointment, Lady Bly, she is; her husband works at the Embassy: she has bought several things here to wear at the Tuileries,' said Mrs O'Grady proudly. At the same time she questioned Amanda's choice of a black ruched velvet pelisse and bonnet; that velvet was very warm, she said. Amanda explained, without thinking, that she was going to wear it in Russia. The indiscreet Irishwoman exclaimed aloud.

'Russia, now! That is a long way. I will tell Lady Bly, surely, for she is a friend, naturally, of young Madame de Morny, who came back from there as the Comte's bride after his grand embassy there. He designs all her clothes, they say; some of them are wonderful, indeed; the stripes and little half-boots, and the hats with ostrich feathers! She is a beautiful little creature, full of fire, they tell me; about the same size as yourself; but her hair is fair, like silk. I have seen her with him driving to his new racecourse, Chantilly being too far from town. We see everyone who passes by, late or soon.'

Amanda hoped that the woman had forgotten any mention of Russia; it had been foolish to speak of it. Del was right in asking her to be discreet; Morny and his wife must be the last to hear of their own pending journey, no doubt, and she herself might well have betrayed it already. She bit her lip, and was in time to see a fashionably dressed personage ushered into the shop. Amanda herself was still in the fitting-room, but Mrs O'Grady flung open the curtains.

'There, now, this is the young lady who is to go with her husband to Russia. You will mention it to the Comtesse, will you not, Lady Bly? She will be glad to hear, no doubt; they say she surrounds herself with things from home, and smokes cigarettes constantly.'

Lady Bly was meantime staring fully at Amanda. She – her name before marriage had been Etheredge – had been, long ago, one of the parlour-boarders at Shearwater's Academy; one of those young ladies who had tittered by habit so cruelly when they knew Amanda had been caned. It was certain, gossip being what it was, that she knew why Amanda had left school so suddenly. She averted her eyes almost at once, and said coldly 'You are going a long way away, madame. If I may say so, you have also come far.'

She turned away, and gave her orders, whatever they were. Amanda, on her lower rate of custom, was kept waiting meantime; there seemed no other assistants in the shop. She jerked the curtain shut angrily. There was one comfort; she herself, in chemise and stays, looked better by far than that other had in her fashionable gown and furs.

When Mrs O'Grady returned at last, chattering on and having noticed nothing amiss, Amanda had already dressed herself and ordered such things as she had chosen to be delivered to their hotel. She found that she was trembling; the encounter had been unpleasant. She hoped it hadn't, or wouldn't, do harm to Del's forthcoming mission to St Petersburg even before it started. If she herself was gossiped about to any extent in the circles of the Comtesse de Morny, it might; but it was too late now to alter anything.

Del was still disappointing her as a lover, but when they reached Hamburg he delighted her by making her a present of sables. There was a little dark toque and matching muff, with a set of skins to drape about her shoulders. 'You will not be cold in the snow,' he said. They drove past Crowbetter's bank but did not call in: when asked if he didn't want to visit Claud Croom, he replied that he didn't care if he never saw him again. They set sail; the Baltic proved as smooth as a lake, and at last, with Petersburg seen glimmering among its ethereal golden spires, the snow had come. They really were in Russia. Amanda snuggled into her furs and kept her hands in her muff, close against Del. She was charmed with everything she saw; the episode at the dressmaker's was probably unimportant.

II

The streets of St Petersburg seemed to be composed entirely of palaces. Their own allotted residence was one such, not the grandest or nearest to town: but interesting and comfortable enough, painted green with yellow shutters, and with necessary stoves lit inside each room. The building seemed to Amanda to wobble slightly. She assumed that she was queasy after the journey, but on mentioning the matter to Delahaye he laughed.

'Peter the Great founded this entire city on a marsh. He was determined to have what he called a window on the West, by the sea. They say thousands of workmen died of fever while digging the foundations; the whole city still quakes now and again.'

Peter the Great had evidently also deserted Moscow, the old capital, with its long tradition and its famed onion domes and bearded boyars; he had made these last, said Del, who seemed to know everything, pay a tax for their beards and wear a receipt pinned on them in the form of a medal. Nevertheless even here, though in many ways it was like Paris and the women dressed fashionably in the western manner, there was an air of a remote, alien and pervading world. Once they ventured into a church, watching the processing round and round of yellow-robed priests and listening to the deep inspired singing. There was a wedding taking place at one of the altars and the bride and groom had jewelled crowns held briefly over their heads. 'We should have been married in Russia,' said Amanda.

Princess Bagration had called early on after their arrival at the green-and-yellow palace. She was a middle-aged woman with worldly eyelids, who dressed well. She regaled

Amanda with half the gossip of St Petersburg, especially about the Mornys; Russian society was not yet forgotten the half-brother of the Emperor of the French.

'He is bald, a pity, but has charm, as they say; and how he could waltz! The little Sophie is enchanting, but I doubt if Morny will be faithful. She was a Troubetskoi, or so they suppose; but, in fact, everyone knows she was the daughter, of course by the Princess, of the late Tsar Nicholas himself. Morny is aware of it. He says, "My mother was a queen, my brother is an emperor, my wife is the daughter of the Tsar, *et tout cela est naturel*." Is not that charming?'

Amanda agreed that it was charming, but wondered what the worldly Princess would have to relate concerning herself as soon as she was out of earshot. She resolved to behave exactly as everyone else here did and to give no cause whatever for scandal: on a return visit to the Princess, she watched the latter presiding over a samovar, and on reaching home again practised the same thing. It made the tea taste pleasant, in tall glasses taken with lemon. Otherwise, one smoked long cigarettes, and everyone talked and talked into the night. In Amanda's presence, to show their manners, they spoke in French: it was not necessary to state to anyone that she knew German. As it was, in this way she heard one or two things about herself. It was stated that her presentation would take a little time to arrange. The English were not yet in fact entirely welcome; in some circles there was strong feeling remaining against them, remembering the battles of Sebastopol and Inkerman. 'Those whose relations fell have long memories,' said Princess Bagration.

Del had already made himself known at Court, and was liked. However his wife's presentation to the Tsarina at the Winter Palace continued to be delayed, then was arranged somehow, but failed to take place for a pedestrian reason: Amanda had caught a snuffling and severe cold. She stayed in bed, with a number of handkerchiefs, while Del, kissing her despite the risk, went off by himself. He returned in triumph; the Tsar had spoken with him personally, and they had dealt together very well. 'I might almost have been the British Ambassador,' he told Amanda. Whether or not this meant lasting success for the mission she had learned, by then, not to ask. The Tsar, they said, was interested in everybody. His German wedding had been the acme of splendour. As it was, everything sounded very splendid; Amanda was sorry that she'd missed her presentation.

'Very soon an informal card will be sent you instead, my darling,' remarked Del comfortingly; one of the aides had told him of it. 'There will be dancing in one of the smaller salons, as they call them here; they are large enough, however, and as usual full of blazing chandeliers.'

After this somewhat banal statement, he went off to sleep in his dressing-room. Much as he loved Amanda, he did not want to catch her cold.

He caught it, nevertheless, and was therefore unable to accompany her to the little informal dance, the invitation for which came within a few days as promised. Laced into the low-cut satin gown she had chosen in Paris, Amanda fitted on her swinging filigree earrings herself without the help of the hired Georgian maid. The earrings never ceased to remind her of El Duque, and she hoped he was watching over her. He would have been at ease in this world of diplomacy, and would always have said and done the right things. She herself was naturally a little uncertain, especially lacking Del's company.

She had been conveyed by droshky, and was ushered in at last at a side door of the immense palace: music sounded already from the requisite salon. Princes Bagration appeared at once. 'I will make you known,' she pronounced, and proceeded to guide Amanda round the company. Presently the orchestra struck up a polonaise. Amanda's hand was asked for immediately, and although she felt strange in this particular dance and said so, she was assured, in French, that there would be no difficulty; every gentleman saw his partner through it safely, at all costs.

Amanda was a natural dancer, and having watched what all the others did contrived it herself well enough. She found herself however growing hot-cheeked and heady with the wild music and energetic figures; the room smelt of violets, jewels of vast value glittered on most of the women, the uniforms the men wore were brilliant and glittered likewise with numerous orders. One danced on, up and down the line, earrings swinging; a small slim officer with a brown moustache picked Amanda presently up by the waist, whirled her about and set her down again. She was glad she had lost weight since her marriage; fat ladies surely did not venture to dance the polonaise.

The music stopped and Amanda perceived that two men had entered the salon. One was a handsome bearded man in a white uniform coat, with orders. The other was Count Fornjöt, the Finn whom the Marchesa had sent to her, once only, at the House of the Live Cat.

She found herself standing frozen, not at first aware that every other lady in the room had already sunk to the floor in a deep curtsey. She felt herself do so, too late. The Finn's light contemptuous eyes had fastened on her; so, with the lateness of the obeisance, had the Tsar's. She had certainly been recognised: it wasn't only her hair. There was no possibility that she had not ruined Del's mission unless, as was unlikely, Fornjöt kept quiet.

Alexander II, Tsar of All the Russias, exchanged a few polite words with those to whom he had already been presented, then went out, followed closely by the Finn. No movement had been made by Princess Bagration or anybody else to present Amanda: her *gaffe* had been noticed, as such things are, and worse was certainly to come. It was unlikely now that, in this closed community where gossip was rife, she would after all be considered suitable for presentation, at a later date, to the Tsarina. The alteration in her status was already evident in the expression in the narrowed eyes of the slim officer who'd picked her up in the recent whirling movement in the polonaise. His name was Count Alexei Cantemir.

She went out at last to the returning droshky, aware of the intense cold of the street after the warmth of the salon. Nothing here was far from the river Neva, which was nearly frozen over. The thought strayed through her mind that Del had told her that when the waters thawed again in spring, there would be a ceremony to bless them. It was unlikely they would be still here for that.

She drove home miserably, to find Del slightly better of his cold. He asked her about the evening and she told him she had seen the Tsar. 'Were you presented?' he asked eagerly. He seemed disappointed by her answer, saying that Alexander was usually interested in any new face, especially a lady's. 'We must jog the old Princess into action,' he said cheerfully, and went to sleep. Amanda herself lay awake till dawn.

It wasn't only that after that episode, Princess Bagration and other ladies ceased to call: she ceased to be invited to anything. The Finn must have talked at once. If she had known, the net of espionage established by the late Tsar Nicholas still operated to such effect that not only were Count Fornjôt's disclosures now superfluous, but a letter's contents had already been made known while being conveyed by post from the young Comtesse de Morny to her mother in Petersburg, Princess Troubetskoi, relating certain gossip the Comtesse had heard from her English friend Lady Bly about the young wife of the English milord – evidently he was no longer even that – who was trying to eclipse Morny in Petersburg, although that would of course never be possible. The whispers of Mrs Babbage in Malta would themselves be gathered in due course, and the sparseness remembered of the English presence at young Croom's very wedding: also, a certain death in Venice, even the fragments of a torn-up drawing there. Young Croom himself was a pleasant fellow, and would be sent off with every appearance of hospitality; but his wife was unsuitable, and they must go.

All of this was not immediately made manifest, though their reception had never been anything in the least like Morny's. Amanda sat alone with her samovar, drinking glass after glass of tea with lemons; she didn't feel like smoking any more cigarettes. There was snow lying outside, earlier in the year than usual. Del was out, at one of the conferences still held at the Winter Palace. The curtain by the doorway slid open silently and a servant in his embroidered tunic came in with a letter. It was a pale grey wafer, with a sealed crest. Amanda slit it open, and did not at first recognise the name Cantemir; then she remembered. He was the officer with the brown moustache and blue eyes she'd met in the polonaise. He wrote now that it had been a delight to dance with her, and to hope that, as he understood she and her husband were leaving Russia shortly, she herself would care to join him and a party of friends for an expedition, on the following Tuesday, to Petrodvorets. 'The fountains will be frozen if the weather continues as at present so early, but there is still much to see, and my fast sledge will transport us there and back in daylight if we leave early,' the Count wrote. He added that, unless he heard to the contrary, he would have the honour of calling on her at nine.

It seemed odd that he hadn't included Del, but Del, when asked, said that was usual enough here and that in any case he himself was to meet a further important delegation on that day. Asked about Cantemir's statement that they were leaving Russia shortly, he frowned a little. 'It is possible that goodwill has been established,' he said stiffly.

He recovered his equanimity then and pointed out that a sledge could only hold so many, a party of friends made the whole thing perfectly proper, and that Amanda was to enjoy herself. 'That place has, I believe, been made as like Versailles as possible, with canals cut through to the sea,' he said. He appeared preoccupied and Amanda did not trouble him further. Everything seemed to have fallen a little flat. She would wear, of course, her sables for the drive to Petrodvorets. It was a good thing she had brought warm clothing.

On the day in question, Del had already departed early for his conference, kissing her absently and again wishing her an enjoyable visit to the famous summer palace. Amanda watched him go off, his erect well-tailored back expressing confidence still, although he must know by now that England was still far less popular in St Petersburg than France. She supposed that she ought to be proud that he was beginning at least to resemble a diplomat, but her own unwilling part in proceedings depressed her; the past kept catching up in ways one hadn't foreseen. However the Georgian maid dressed her in a wine-coloured wool gown, and Amanda herself arranged her own sables, adjusting the dark toque softly over her bright hair and sliding her gloved hands thankfully into the muff. It had been snowing again outside, but had stopped. Winter had evidently come. Count Cantemir's sledge would have a smooth run on the early roads, no doubt, before they grew rutted.

She heard him draw up promptly as arranged, and went out. To her amazement there was a long double team of black-and-white dogs, only one with a brown coat, tongues lolling pinkly, breaths congealing visibly in the cold air. The Count, who had emerged from his place behind the driver's back, bowed, handed Amanda a great bunch of hothouse violets to pin on her muff, and helped her in with ceremony. Where were his friends? The low sledge was quite empty except for herself and him, with the driver at the ready. Del might perhaps think it wasn't altogether proper. She asked the Count about the rest of his party.

'Why, we will pick them up on the way,' Cantemir answered cheerfully. His face was bright with the sudden cold beneath the fur hat he wore with flaps; the oblique blue eyes roved over her attire approvingly. Fornjöt had warned him this little piece was difficult to arouse, and they had made a wager on it. She looked, however, delicious, as always. He was glad the snow had come.

The driver flourished his whip and the dogs pulled away, gathering a speed which became almost breathless as they passed the outskirts of town. Amanda soon lost her nervousness at travelling so fast so near the ground – it seemed even faster than it really was – and buried her face in the cool violets. Hothouse flowers didn't have much scent, but it had been a thoughtful gesture. She turned and smiled at Cantemir. He was a handsome young man, evidently very proud of the moustache; she wondered, but of course didn't ask, if he wore, in private, one of the machines somebody had invented to ensure such appendages curled upwards for the time being. She'd heard, it must have been at Shearwater's, of a man who never took his machine off till he was on the steps of church, where he removed it to take the collection.

'Of what are you thinking?' enquired the Count; the white road whirled past, like the polonaise. 'These dogs are from Alaska,' he added. 'I find them more convenient than horses; if one falls ill it can speedily be replaced by another. They are hardy brutes.'

She wondered if that was why one had a brown coat, but merely asked again when they would collect his friends; there was no sign of stopping at any of the houses they passed by. They weren't palaces any longer; they were made of wood, with low eaves, reminding one of Switzerland.

'They will meet us presently,' he said reassuringly, and asked how she liked Russia. Amanda began to feel a trifle of disquiet; it wasn't at all what he had implied in the first place: he'd said they were picking the friends up. Del certainly wouldn't have liked her to drive all this way with the Count alone.

They turned into woods, and then at last into the grounds of what was apparently Petrodvorets. It had been about an hour's ride and she herself was far from any help. However he ordered the sledge to stop, and the dogs to be uncoupled to run at ease among the trees. There was still no sign of any friends. 'They are late, no doubt,' remarked the Count with unconcern. 'Let me take you to see the fountains and the great artificial canals. One cannot leave this country without having witnessed them. In summer, the play of water is supreme.'

She walked on his arm while he conversed agreeably about Peter the Great's daughter the Empress Elisabeth, who had liked to come here and had built much of the palace after her father. 'She had many lovers, but the favourite was a man of no birth named Razoum. She made him into Count Razumovsky, and he had after all great chivalry. After her death someone had the impertinence to ask if he had ever married the Empress. The Count took down a scroll of parchment from his shelves and flung it on the fire, making no answer.'

The sky was still grey with snow although it did not fall.

The great summer retreat had frozen fountains and closed shutters. 'They called the Empress the North Star,' he told her. 'She was very beautiful, with appetites like her father's. I will tell you how I came to be a descendant of Peter the Great.' He sounded like a boasting boy. 'They will relate how his wife, the Empress Catherine, caused the death of an unborn baby of the Tsar's by Maria Cantemir, daughter to the Hospodar of Moldavia. That child did not die.' He winked, and squeezed her arm a little. 'I too have my ancestor's appetites,' he said, smiling.

'Take me to your friends,' Amanda said coldly. 'Let us go back if they have not come.'

'But, madame, we have brought a picnic. At least allow me to give you a little wine against the cold. Then, if you wish it, we will return.'

They walked back to the shelter of the trees and the nearby pergolas, skeletons bare of roses at this season. The driver, evidently knowing what to do, had spread out the fur rug ready on the snow and, beside it, a bucket of ice containing bottles, likewise tall glasses and a bowl of preserved black cherries. There were also cushions, taken from the sledge. It waited some way off and the dogs were still roaming free. No doubt they would come when called. Amanda was tired after the walk, and there seemed no choice but to sit down on the cushions, also to accept the proffered champagne. Nothing stirred in her blood to tell her of an earlier occasion, long before she was born, in a wood full of bluebells, when champagne had been the downfall of Miss Ellen Shearwater. Now, as then, it was welcome, but heady.

'A little more, madame. It will lose its bubbles if not consumed.' He had taken her glass.

She tried to refuse, hearing herself say that they must keep some for his friends. However she was increasingly certain that something was not as it should be about the friends: they would have come by now. It was inconceivable that he had played a trick on her with deliberate insolence; Del would be furious. One couldn't, however, say anything more or, in fact, do anything much except swallow more champagne; she watched the Count fill her glass a third time. 'Let us drink,' she heard him say, 'to the success of the British mission.' His face, as he said it, suddenly wore an ugly look. She was beginning to be afraid. She couldn't refuse to drink to Del, however; dear Del. If the mission wasn't a success it wasn't his fault, but her own. She felt tears rise to her eyes and knew it was the champagne having its way with her; she shouldn't have taken as much.

The Count was coming closer; much closer. He was holding the bowl of preserved cherries and made as if to offer it to her, then said 'No, you must not sticky your pretty fingers. Let me put one in your mouth.' He didn't stop at one; he popped in one after another, and she found, to her alarm except that it was by then too late, that they were steeped in brandy. *A little schnapps.* It was the same thing, after all. The two kinds together were fatal. After that, nobody would have known if they were cherries or kisses, or the Count's tongue. His moustache was brushing her cheek; and his hands, his hands, no longer concerned with cherries at all but with untying, expertly, what turned out to be the tapes of her drawers. The driver was meantime prudently out of sight.

Afterwards, she tried to tell herself that if Del, dear Del, had given her fulfilment in their marriage it wouldn't have happened; but as things were, it would in any case have been impossible to avoid. As it was, it was almost as it had at certain times been with El Duque; she felt ecstasy rise, and then her own crying out at last with savage achievement, beneath the empty pergolas in the flattened snow, miles from anywhere, with a man who wasn't her husband.

'You have exquisite legs. I have had a little look by now, no? Now that we are together under the rug again, I can no longer see them, but I can feel, ah, yes. Many things can continue to happen under a fur rug, while one travels safely on.'

They happened, more than once. She couldn't prevent it, and, by now, didn't try. There was, in addition, no other way of getting home. It was in fact astonishing what could happen under a fur rug in the company of Count Cantemir. She had no memory of again entering the sledge, of seeing the dogs attached once more, or even of moving off. The driver's broad back was turned impassively. The snow had begun to fall and they were, by now, again nearing the wooden houses; soon they would reach the little palace itself. 'Please, please let me go,' she heard herself beseeching; but he remained firmly within her. She had never known anyone to do so for as long, not even Count Fornjöt. Cantemir must certainly know him. How much did men tell one another? Oh – oh, oh –

'Please, please. We will be noticed.' The wooden houses were long passed, the city on the Neva, built on a marsh by his boasted ancestor, was approaching; soon people would be met with on the streets, hurrying home through the snow. Perhaps there would be carriages. They wouldn't, or one hoped not, be able to see or guess what was going on; the fur rug was copious; but to have to sit here, with his member still erect in her, knowing oneself what was happening even if no one else did – ah, ah, there it came again, she had to bite her lips, this wasn't even private like Petrodvorets – there it came, she hadn't known anything like it since – since – since Seville, since Venice, Venice.

'Count, that is my house,' she had reminded him uselessly as they sped past the little palace. It looked helpless, squat and almost reproachful, telling her she had let Britain down. What would everyone think, British, Russians, French, as they skidded on through Petersburg in such a position? People were after all on the streets; here was the long ornate bulk of the Winter Palace, and he still didn't stop: they veered round the corner at last, past St Nicholas' Church, and somebody on the pavement raised his hat; Amanda made herself bow in acknowledgment.

'Well done, well done,' said the Count. 'You are developing *savoir faire*, madame. It is a useful quality at any time.'

'Take me home at once. I will call out if you do not.' It did not sound convincing even to her own ears. He smiled.

'I do not think that you will, my dear. I will decide when to return.'

She would never forget such an experience; it was worse than anything that had ever happened at the Live Cat.

Worse still, she'd been unfaithful to Del, several times over. She felt her face grow red as fire with the cold, the heat, her constant blushing. To think of what had happened as pleasure was certainly wickedness, but, but – Del loved her and she loved him, oh, Del – what a wicked man the Count was to go on so, in view of half the town, if they were to guess – it didn't bear thinking of –

'Here is your little house again now, madame. It has been a pleasure. I regret that you are leaving Petersburg, otherwise we might have savoured other such expeditions.'

Amanda climbed out shakily, feeling her legs betray her. It had never in her life been as bad as this. She felt like a wrung rag. Next time he called, she would certainly send word that she wasn't receiving. To have behaved like that, and make her behave likewise!

Count Cantemir bowed formally over her hand, having aided her courteously out of the sledge. He then handed her a small tidily folded white oblong: her drawers. Amanda stowed them, incredulously, in her muff, on which the violets had understandably wilted. She still felt as if the world was reeling. Perhaps it was the marshy foundations Del had told her about. Del. She wouldn't ever mention this to Del, or to anyone.

The Count, still bowing her hand, was meantime speaking in Russian. 'You are a willing little English flower-bed, in which I have today planted much good Moldavian seed,' he remarked in a low voice. He then stood smartly to attention as she regained the palace. A charming little bourgeoise: Fornjöt had underrated her responsiveness. No doubt the seed would ripen into fruit, far away in England. She had been consoled, at least, for the evident dullness of the English husband. Also, he himself had avenged the death of his brother in the Crimea. He drove away with mouth pursed, beyond the criss-crossed tracks of the day's snow. It would soon be dark already.

Delahaye came home some hours later after what had proved to be his farewell *Zacouska*: the news had been broken to him during it that the unofficial mission was at an end. Nevertheless there had been much friendship expressed and a letter given him to take to the Comte de Morny in Paris. He was feeling, as a result, somewhat less correct than usual; flowing vodka and caviar in rich black gleaming piles had inflamed his Anglo-Saxon sensibilities to an extent which led him to take Amanda at once as a matter of course, where she lay in their bed evidently asleep. For once, he was pleased with her awakened docility; that was the way a wife should be, passive and obedient. He turned over to sleep at last himself with a sense of total well-being, which had merged by next day into a shocking headache, almost like the chaps who played Russian roulette. A bullet in one's brain could hardly feel worse. Del was, in many ways, glad they were leaving Russia. It had been an experience, however, and would no doubt mean advancement of some kind somewhere. He would write to Inguanez when his head was better.

By the time they reached Paris, Amanda knew without doubt that she was pregnant. She was not certain, and never would be, whether the child was Del's or the Count's from Moldavia. Either way it was best to say nothing more than necessary: life had at least taught her as much. She informed Delahaye of her state and he was predictably pleased, and kissed her.

'You must take great care of yourself,' he told her. 'We will go out very little. I am waiting for word from the Comte de Morny; he has promised to do something for me. The Tsar wrote to him personally.' It was the second time he had told her.

III

Amanda lay on the sofa in the Paris apartment, regarding her distended body. She had been Morny's mistress now for five months. This was Thursday afternoon and as usual at such a day and time, she expected him to arrive, Del being safely at the office. One of the remarks Morny had made early on was that as she herself was already *enceinte*, there was no need for unnecessary prudence. It was the kind of saying which made all women dote on this upstart Comte, by now a Duc: in accord with *tout cela est naturel*.

She was particularly looking forward to his visit today; she had not seen him for some time, as he had been away with his wife and children, on whom he doted, at Nades, their resort in the country. She herself had, of course, remained in town, where Del was employed through Morny's influence in some connection or other with selling railway shares. He came home in the evenings. He was increasingly enchanted with the prospect of the baby and continually urged Amanda to take every care of herself: he hadn't touched her as a husband since her condition had been made known to him, and their journey across Europe, owing to her wretched lassitude and sickness then, had necessarily been slow. Del had shown great kindness and patience. He thought of her, it was evident, already as a contented wife and mother. She herself, on the other hand, didn't care about the baby; if it was Cantemir's it might as well be lost, and if it was Del's they could make another. Morny's visits were the only gleam of contentment she knew. Otherwise the days passed slowly; they themselves never went anywhere.

There had been one exception, near the beginning,

when they were still living in a cheap hotel awaiting word about the pending employment. A card had come for Amanda from the new Duchesse de Morny, to attend a soirée held at the Petit-Bourbon, the Paris residence, in a few days' time. Amanda had gone in a fiacre to find half the world there. The young Duchesse had been idling at one end of the long crowded room, surrounded by Russian cronies and smoking her long cigarettes as predicted: it was said she had even smoked one with impunity in the Empress's carriage. Her dark glance swept over Amanda briefly and without evident interest, then she turned her blonde head to talk again to whoever was beside her. She had no manners and had been known to remark that the French had small minds. Amanda had moved about the salon afterwards and had stared at the portrait of the late Queen Hortense, Napoleon's step-daughter and Morny's mother, which hung on one wall in a prominent position, though the Emperor himself had not wanted the situation known. Morny's father was the diplomat Charles de Flahault, himself an illegitimate son of Talleyrand by a blue-stocking lady said to be a bastard of Louis XV. It was all of it complicated, and the Empress herself, being strait-laced, had demanded angrily that the portrait be taken down; but it was still there, and Morny himself already had an illegitimate daughter by a former mistress who resembled Queen Hortense exactly. His children by Sophie Troubetskoi were still very young. He had brought her as a bride, trailing clouds of glory from the successful Russian embassy a few years back, and Sophie had brought Russia with her rather than adapting in any way to Paris. In another part of the house were screaming monkeys in cages, and everywhere one tripped over incontinent Pekingese puppies. Everyone talked to everyone else; Lady Bly, thankfully, was not here today, and neither were Lady Keith and her daughters; that Scots lady had married Charles de Flahault in the end and had been a kind stepmother to Morny all his youth, as his own mother dared not recognise him openly before she died. One heard all this among the gossip of fashionably assembled Paris.

However Amanda made no lasting acquaintances; the wife of a seller of railway shares was not important, and she had no doubt only been invited in recognition of the fact that Del had been put in his recent employment by the Duc. There was no sign of the latter at the soirée, but on her way out, Amanda was approached by a flunkey. M. de Morny would like a word with her before she went.

It was evident that she had been watched and recognised, perhaps on entry. It was possible, of course, that she had already been seen and remarked walking on Del's arm about Paris; his handsome English looks and her beauty had caused poignant comment of the kind remembered from the early days in Venice with Van Hakluyt, but differently. Moreover, if Lady Bly's tongue had been busy it would be known that she, Amanda, was not considered entirely virtuous after the English fashion. Amanda herself felt as if she had grown a hard shell; anything was to be expected. Lacing and the crinoline in any case disguised her state.

The flunkey had escorted her past the cages of screaming apes; the smell was abominable, but beyond, behind a door which opened, a tall man with a bald head and prosperous moustaches, closely resembling the Emperor himself, waited; and taking her hand in his own turned it over to kiss the palm with devotion. The eyes that surveyed her coolly beneath their hooded lids were those of a lecher. They said Morny could never pass by a business enterprise or a woman. He had immense charm, as they had related in Petersburg; she could feel it already. He led her to a chair. Amanda said, for something to say, that she had seen the animals. Morny smiled.

'All of the apes answer to the same name, Glaize-Besoin. He is a member of the Opposition. I myself am a representative in the Assembly, madame, as you know. I should like to hear a little more about the state of things in St Petersburg. It is some time since I left it. I had, however, a letter lately not only from the Tsar, who begs me to do what I can for your husband in the matter of some employment; that is most necessary. I heard also, about the same time, from a particular friend of mine, a Moldavian, Count Alexei Cantemir. He desires to be remembered to you, also that I should behold you for myself.'

* * *

That had been the beginning of it. There was no doubt that he knew everything. The end had been the little apartment Morny had found for them both, more expensive than Del could otherwise have afforded; and a middle-aged maid, whom Amanda disliked, called Sidonie. Sidonie admitted the Duc on Thursday afternoons, vanished then discreetly, and showed him out again at the end. Hints from her now and again showed that she knew a good deal about Morny himself. He and the Emperor had once mistaken the days for visiting a well-known actress privately, had encountered one another in her waiting-room, had raised their hats simultaneously and burst out laughing. Then there was Cora Pearl, who appeared on stage in knickers. There was also a high-born lady about Court Morny was pursuing, so far unsuccessfully 'but he will draw the net close in the end'. Her name was Lalage Beeding-de Lezay; she was half English. 'At the same time he adores his wife,' remarked Sidonie. 'Do not flatter yourself that you have the whole of his attention.'

It was an impertinent remark from a maid, and Amanda flushed. Unfortunately it was not Del who paid the woman's wages, whether he knew it or not, but Morny; there was nothing therefore, to be said. However Amanda resented the sly insinuations and the occasional side-glance from the snakelike eyes, implying that Sidonie knew a good deal she would not mention, at least for the present. As for the neighbours, they must be well aware of Morny's carriage, waiting down in the street on Thursday afternoons; the Emperor had recently given him the right to display his father's coat of arms, with its device of Flahault blackbirds, and this was evident on the carriage doors. It was better, no doubt, than Morny's earlier habit of wearing a hortensia in his buttonhole everywhere he went. Amanda awaited his coming with amusement and growing eagerness; in no time now, the points of his prickly moustache would be progressing up her inner arm from the wrist to the elbow. It was only one of the aspects of Morny's expert lovemaking. Without him, life would be intolerably dull: and they were doing no harm to anyone, after all. He was late; she wished he would arrive.

The door opened presently, and it was not Morny but Del, his face grave. 'There is bad news,' he said. 'We have just received it at the office. The Duc de Morny is dead, after a few days' illness. Nobody expected him to die; he was not an old man. They say the Emperor is heartbroken, and his wife – why, my darling, have I alarmed you too greatly?'

The tears were running down her face. He came over at once and tried to comfort her. He should have broken such news more gently; women were fragile creatures. Amanda turned her face into his shoulder, sobbing; then presently tried to explain her behaviour in a way he would perhaps understand.

'It will mean the end of your employment,' she wailed. 'Take me back to England. The child can be born there. Something else will surely be found for you. Take me back; I cannot endure it any longer in Paris.'

He promised, but said they must at least wait for the funeral; it would be a State one, fit for the brother of the Emperor and the man who had brought so much goodwill to France by the exercise of sheer charm.

Amanda had made the mistake of dismissing the maid Sidonie at once. She knew at the time that it was unwise; the woman knew too much, but she herself could no longer endure the constantly sensed but unseen prying, the innuendoes, the frequent open insolence. She handed the creature enough money to last for enough time to find more work, and was angered to be asked for more, also for a character in writing.

'I won't be able to get much otherwise, not with him gone.' It was well known that Morny's death had caused chaos among his dependents, great and small; the cause of his death was said to be some failure of the pancreas, not fully understood by the doctors. Amanda firmed her lips and said to Sidonie that she could not recommend her with any honesty. 'You have references from former employers, have you not?' she asked. 'Go now, if you please; there is no more money for you here.'

'And no more work, I dare say.' The sneer was unfeigned. In the end Sidonie bundled her few black clothes together and went, mouth pursed ominously. Amanda should have known that that would not be the end of it. On the day of Morny's funeral – the service was to be at the Madeleine, but the church itself would be packed with notables, and they themselves must stand with many hundred others to watch the procession wind afterwards through the streets on its way to Père Lachaise – on the day, Amanda had dressed herself, and was ready to go down with Del when he should come in; his office was closed for the day, but he had looked in there briefly to see to certain papers which had piled up. His key sounded in the lock and presently he came in, wearing a black arm-band. His face was grey. He handed her an opened envelope; inside was a grubby piece of paper, unsigned.

Your wife has been Morny's little Thursday cocotte for months. Ask the neighbours. How do you suppose you kept your own situation, and who paid the rent? It was beyond your pocket, you fool.

'Is this true?' he asked Amanda. It was needless to try to blame Sidonie; she had, after all, told no lies in the letter.

Amanda stood there for instants, hands hanging at her sides. If it was the end between her and Del, there was nothing left. Morny had been a diversion; she had been fond of him and he had given her what Del had refused from the beginning; an understanding of mutual physical accord. She clenched her fists suddenly and began to shout at the young man standing there grim-faced.

'Do you suppose that if you had ever let me love you as I could, this would have been necessary? Do you suppose that I do *not* love you, that it should not be between us as if we were conceived together before the beginning of the world, of life itself? Yet you, you have always denied that I was anything but a vessel, to be kept still beneath you, something without feeling, without response. Love me now, as you could have loved me always; let us truly love, the way it was meant to be between us.'

She had drawn down her idle hands meantime over her belly, outlining the child where it lay. Del must be allowed to go on thinking that it was his; that was, after all, possible; it was one hold she still had on him. Otherwise –

She flung herself at him suddenly, kissing him passionately, not only on the mouth but round it; also on his face, his eyes, his lips again at last. Her arms were about him. She felt him respond. It was as though the wild blood within them both had begun to beat in him also with her urging; his eyes blazed suddenly. 'Come, then,' he said at last, and laid her down on the sofa where she had so often lain with Morny. Was it the memory of Morny that spurred Delahaye, as the coffin passed by to sombre music and drums below in the streets? It was for as long as that that they lay together, as long as it took for the service itself to be concluded in the Madeleine and the candles extinguished: as long as it took for the widow, the Emperor, the great of the land to pass by, back to the Tuileries. They themselves heard nothing, not even the clattering horses: nothing but one another's sighs.

'I have never loved you before,' murmured Delahaye, forgetting Harrow, forgetting England and who he was or might be, or else might become; it no longer mattered. 'I have never loved you before.' Nothing was of importance now except the magic creature beneath him; how could he have been so blind, so heedless of Amanda?

Delahaye again felt himself a god, as much so as when he had used to bowl overarm cricket. He was confident by now that he could achieve anything. It wasn't the early, inborn confidence that had been his without thinking about it; then there had been the certainty of the title, the best tutors, the foremost school; the constant superiority over wretched Stephen at games and all other prowess, and, most of all, the unspoken belief that he himself was not Anstey's son but secretly the General's. As one had always assumed, it came to the same thing in the end: and was a more glorious assumption by far.

At a blow, all that had been lost, as it were cut from under him. There had been the shame of his mother's admission – he'd never really known her – that she had taken several lovers, and had not cohabited with her husband at the time of his, Delahaye's, conception; Letty

had got all that out of Amy in a document at the place
where the latter lived in Wales. All of it had been so
shameful that Del had since then refused to allow himself
to think either of his mother or his father, even of who the
latter might have been one way or another. He was, after
all, nobody: Letty had won, it had all come out into the
open, and from being one of the lords of creation he, Del,
had had to accept a clerk's place in a bank, calling himself,
and being called, not only commoner but bastard. It had
reduced his estimation of himself to a marked degree
which the altered behaviour of others did not help: and, by
then, as well, he had lost Amanda.

Soon, however, there had been the consolation of the
straight left to the jaw he had given to the late unlamented
Van Hakluyt. That had begun to make Del his own man
again; he had cast off the shackles of Crowbetter's (he told
himself this rather than admit that it was they who had
done the casting). Then, however, ill-equipped as he was
to be anything but an aristocrat, it had meant living on
Letty's money, accepting money later on from Inguanez
and, still later, from Morny. That last still hurt. Now,
however, with an incomparable wife beside him, he,
Delahaye Croom, could conquer worlds. They would, he
had decided, after the child was safely born, go perhaps to
the United States, Canada or even Australia. Others had
carved a fortune out of all those places from nothing, and
so could he. He was strong; he would work, if needed, with
his hands as well as his head. Amanda! Delight and beauty,
personified by her presence, would be with him always;
her body now, heavy as it was with their child, seemed in
some way lovelier than ever. It was still a few weeks till the
birth; they would go to Fortune's for that, and thereafter
please themselves. He, Delahaye, was a husband and
father, also of late a most manfully disposed lover. The last
few nights in France had convinced him that there was
nobody more to be envied than himself as he had now,
with full instruction from Amanda, become.

What a fool he had been to cling for so long to
propriety, to convention! Now she had taught him to cast
off such chains they would love and love together. It
would go on into old age while they remained, in such

ways, always young. Del was in fact drunk with loving, no longer Galahad but Lancelot, at the beginning of the affair.

On the Channel crossing, which for once was smooth, he found he couldn't leave hold of Amanda's hand; they had to touch one another constantly in some way, surely, lovingly. At the Lord Warden Hotel – Del was feeling expansive, the money was almost finished, but more would be made somehow or other – they stayed overnight, and after dinner made love again, his hands caressing Amanda's pregnant belly considerately in the soft bed. The child had moved once or twice. 'It won't be long now,' he told her. 'Tomorrow night we'll be at Fortune's, then you shall rest.'

'I won't fit into the swing,' said Amanda.

'Afterwards. After it's over. By then it will be apple-blossom time again, Amanda-who-must-be-loved, Amanda, Amanda.'

She smiled against him; he hadn't forgotten, after all. She was drowsy with contentment and relief. It didn't matter about anything that had happened in the past: one could forget it, and start again. She would make it up to Del about Cantemir, one way or the other. He must never, never know. It was probable that he didn't even recall what the Moldavian looked like, together as they must have been at *Zacouska* and all the rest of it. If the baby resembled somebody Del didn't remember, that was all right; and she'd give him others. This one might, after all, in any case be his.

Next day they hired a coach to Fortune's, seeing their baggage strapped on the roof. They journeyed on, still hand in hand inside, her head on his shoulder; and at some point noted that it was spring, an English spring at last. 'Soon there will be bluebells in the Nether Wood,' said Del. He remembered them from his childhood, a carpet like the sky, and blackbirds had left blue-green eggs in nests in the forks of the beeches.

The laurel drive came presently, and the sight of the lawn. It was a fine day, and four people were walking on it: Letty, her daughter Victoria, Stephen, and, surprisingly, Claud Croom. 'Let's get out here and meet them,' said Amanda. Del told the driver to take the baggage on to the stables, where he would be paid and the horses watered before return.

They got out, and still with clasped hands walked together towards the lawn.

Letty Croom had for some uncertain time had reasons for being discontented with life, both in political circles and family ones. In the former, it was not of course possible for the widow of a politician to wield as much influence as a wife had: and although in her day Letty had been considered a hostess second to none, it was noteworthy that she was no longer bidden on every occasion to the Palmerstons', though Em still regaled her with gossip from Paris correspondents and they had, only lately, shrugged off together the memory of young Del's ridiculous and unnecessary mission to St Petersburg; an insult, as both had agreed, to the existing government, and anyway bound to fail. Ruling a nation rather than a party was, likewise, Palmerston's expressed intent, and Letty disagreed with it; the rub of opposition had spiced her own life in its day, but the day was evidently over. That was one thing; and the news of the Duc de Morny's death, and the indignation of his wife when she discovered his manifold letters from other women, was no more than a passing matter on this side of the Channel. At home, here at Fortune's Field, Letty however had made herself mistress as before: Victoria had always done as she was told, and so in the event did Stephen; not that there seemed any hope at all of an heir. This troubled Letty, who suspected, quite rightly, that Victoria had never quite got over her early *tendresse* for Delahaye. However that young man was evidently married, it hardly mattered to whom. Also, an obedient housekeeper had been installed after Clara died; Letty's word at Fortune's Field, except of course for the part where Paola and Tobias still reigned, was law.

She progressed up and down the lawn on Stephen's arm, reflecting that if poor Anstey's ghost was indeed said to haunt the orchard, his single accredited son was no more than the ghost of a ghost. Stephen had all his life been known to say very little, except, at the time, necessarily and under compulsion, his marriage vows.

Letty steeled herself to ask more questions. There *must* be an heir; there was certainly nothing wrong with Victoria. All her own efforts to secure the title in that direction would prove vain, and Henry being by sheer physical proof, and his mother's affidavit, out of the picture, the name of Lord Croom would eventually revert to Tobias if no more came of the young people's marriage. The thought of that possibility infuriated Letty; she was about to turn away from Stephen and seek advice from Claud Croom, who was over on one of his visits to the London branch of the bank, when two figures approached, hand in hand, happy and smiling; a tall young man, with the sun shining on his hair, and an extremely pregnant young woman: Amanda. Her remembered hair flamed even more brightly in the sun, beneath her bonnet.

Had they both been less openly transfigured, less radiant, it was possible that Letty would have held her peace; after all, no harm was done to the title, Del's illegitimacy having been well established. As it was, however, the sight of Amanda's triumphant condition, the barrenness of Victoria, and the imperviousness of the couple to the disgace of the whole thing, was too much. Incest! It was not a word to be used in any kind of society, even the lowest. Letty drew herself up. Del was approaching, smiling, bringing forward Amanda.

'Aunt Letty, you must meet my wife. Victoria, my wife Amanda; you've met. Uncle Claud, my –'

'That trollop is not your wife. She is your twin sister. Your *sister*. You were separated at the births. Is that not so, Claud?' Claud nodded curtly. 'How dare you bring her here?' continued Letty. 'How dare you? She must leave at once.'

'Aunt! You do not know what you are saying. Amanda and I are married. We were married in Malta.' The young man's voice was suddenly loud, as if to drive away echoes, shadows; a deep, hidden doubt. He had turned white, and so had Amanda; she swayed as if about to fall. Stephen, for once moving on his own initiative, came and steadied her, standing behind. 'I say –' he began uncertainly. Letty's harsh metallic voice screeched on, without mercy now; having started, she would by no means stop.

'She is a trollop, I say. Even if it were not incest it would be a disgrace to call her your wife. In St Petersburg, to which I suppose it was she you took, she was noted by several – I have a letter – in a compromising position with some nobleman in his sledge. Before that her history has been that of a harlot from the time she was sent away from school for immoral behaviour with some Italian man who evidently taught there.' Letty no longer remembered who had told her all of that; it had accrued over the years in letters, gossip from everyone everywhere; one moved in the same circles and sooner or later heard everything by way of Paris that was to be learnt.

'Mama,' said Victoria. Nobody else said anything. They watched the couple fly apart, like two jarring planets which have made disastrous contact once in a million million years and will travel thereafter in entirely separate orbits till the end of time. Delahaye turned his back and blundered off towards the house. 'Del,' called Amanda. 'Del.' He did not turn. She struggled out of Stephen's grasp and tried to follow. The tall figure of Claud Croom moved inexorably to bar the way.

'Leave him,' he told Amanda. 'You can do nothing to remedy the situation.' In the back of his cold mind was the reasoning that, one way or another, the state of affairs, if allowed to continue, would reflect adversely, sooner or later, on Crowbetter's bank.

'She will not enter the house,' said Letty. 'Order the other carriage, and my valise. Her baggage can be sent on later to where we are going.'

Victoria had begun to cry: the whole thing was monstrous, and poor Del's face had been that of a dead man already. 'Where are you going, Mama? Where are you taking her?' She didn't like Amanda, but it was like punishing a wax doll; after all, the doll hadn't meant any harm.

'There is only one place for her to go now, and I am taking her there myself,' replied Letty. 'We are going to Aberaniog, to leave her with her mother.'

Only one thing delayed the immediate departure of the carriage; an explosion from the gun-room. The men hastened there and found Delahaye lying dead, a gun in his hand and his brains scattered pinkly over the carpet.

It was Victoria who forced her way in, although they said it was no place for a woman. She knelt down and tried to revive Del, uselessly; how could anyone live without half his head? The bright hair was dark with blood. It was strange to see the actual brains of somebody you'd known, somebody you'd loved. If Del had married *her*, this wouldn't have happened. It was Mama's fault for making her marry Stephen. Mama had killed Del.

Victoria began to bawl. Letty was conveniently elsewhere, having been told before entering the carriage. No doubt she would break the news to Amanda. A servant was sent for the police after the carriage had gone off; Claud Croom would see to everything. It could be said, no doubt, that poor young Delahaye Croom had never recovered his stability since losing the title. The rest of the affair could probably be hushed up.

'Where are we going?'

It was the first time she'd spoken; before that, she had been like someone who has died. As it was, memory had already begun to return in fragments; the clearest was that Del had dropped her hand from his as though it burnt him, and had turned away, gone away. He wasn't here any more. Instead, a hard-faced woman sat opposite, and it seemed that they had been travelling always. It was like last time; they were going away from Del, going away from life: where to?

'To Wales, to your mother,' replied Letty Croom, aloud. She turned her head to look out at the passing country; she had no more to say than necessary to this creature. She would deliver her, and then return. The journey was faster these days, with the improved roads. They should reach Aberaniog by night.

Her brother. Her twin brother. That was why she, Amanda, felt they'd known one another since the beginning, in the womb. Evidently to love in such a way was wicked. Mrs Ludd at school had often told her she was wicked, like her mother. She was going to her mother now.

Back to the womb; but it would mean enduring the man
Johnson she remembered. This time, there would be no
escape. She could recall that more clearly than the things
that had happened lately: those still seemed to lie behind a
veil. Perhaps this had after all been meant for her from the
beginning, and she shouldn't have hidden that time in the
conservatory. It wouldn't be any worse, after all, than Van
Hakluyt, or the House of the Live Cat: except for dear El
Duque. He'd killed himself because of her. Perhaps she
must, in such a way, expiate that sin: but she hadn't meant
any harm. She hadn't meant harm to anybody, from the
beginning: certainly no harm to Del. Del. What was to
become of Del now? She couldn't ask this woman sitting
opposite; it was better not to look or speak. Perhaps she
herself would die at the birth, then Del would at least be
sorry: even though he had been made to feel joy in what
was sinful, the oldest sin of all except murder, a sin all
society shunned. It was whispered that that was why Lord
Byron had been forced to leave England, because he had
loved his sister. They hadn't been allowed to read Byron at
school. School. Why did she keep going back to that? The
whole of life was a school; except that she herself felt there
was nothing more to be learnt, and could feel nothing
now, nothing. That was the strange thing; after
everything, and knowing well enough what was about to
happen, she, Amanda, still felt nothing at all.

The rain had begun to patter against the carriage windows
and continued after it grew dark. The driver had lit his
lamps; evidently they weren't stopping anywhere after
having once got out at an inn to relieve themselves. The
roads grew rougher as they neared Aberaniog and
Amanda felt discomfort at the jogging. Then at last they
stopped at the gate. Letty signalled to her to get out alone.
The driver climbed down with Amanda's valise and
guided her with his lanthorn as far as the house, where a
light shone; somebody was at home. The rain beat against
them on the way to the door. 'I'm to leave you here,' said
the man compassionately. The garden was overgrown;
nobody for some time had trimmed Toby's hedges, and
they had struggled past them in the fitfully lit dark. 'I will

be looked after,' said Amanda strangely. She watched the man go and leant meantime against the door-post. Her cloak was already wet through. It didn't matter; nothing mattered any more. She heard the carriage turn and drive off.

Letty Croom, leaning back against the cushions, considered duty done; the rest was Amy's business. It hadn't seemed wise to tell Amanda in her present state about the death of Delahaye; the news might after all have brought on premature labour while in one's charge. She would no doubt hear in proper course, in the care of her mother. Meanwhile, one must get back to deal with police enquiries, and, no doubt, an inquest: that prospect was distasteful. Claud would, one hoped, remain meantime to assist. It was curious how he and she had established a kind of unwitting alliance over the years, despite everything. She was glad of him now: Stephen would be no help, nor, probably, would Tobias or Paola. As for Victoria, she was out of her mind for the time.

There was a chink of light beneath the door, yellow against the dark now the driver's lanthorn had vanished. The rain beat on. It occurred to Amanda that, last time, she had caught a severe chill and almost died in Piccadilly: perhaps it would happen again. The child was moving in her a little, no doubt disturbed by the movement of the coach. It wasn't quite time for it to be born. The whole thing was happening to somebody else, not herself. That was the best way to look at it, from outside; from beyond, as she'd done at first in Venice.

The door creaked open and the man Johnson stood there, his bulk solid against the light from the hall. She could smell drink on his breath. Behind him she saw the remains of a cold meal on the table. She wasn't hungry, but became suddenly and sharply aware of fear, cold and pain. The man's brutish eyes roved over her; her cloak concealed her condition. He remembered her, it was evident; and how she'd got away last time after kicking him.

'So you are back. Come in, then, and I will take my belt to your bottom. After that we will go to bed.' She had, he remembered, hurt him badly in a certain place; that shouldn't happen again.

'I am going to have a baby,' said Amanda. 'Don't beat me. I will do as you say.'

'You will do as I say in any case.' She felt him pull her into the hall. 'A baby, is it?' he said, feeling her. 'Then you are no better than you should be, as I knew well enough when I saw you beside the giant's stone.'

There was a fire in the hall. She went thankfully towards it and he threw on a log. Then he came and felt her body again. 'It is near, but not yet,' he said. 'You can eat something, and then we will go to bed.'

He poured beer, and Amanda sipped it; she didn't want any food. Dai drank what she set aside. She watched him, already feeling heady with the small amount of beer she had taken. Van Hakluyt had made her drink a powder in water, and before that schnapps; Cantemir the Moldavian had given her champagne and then brandied cherries. It was the same thing now. She felt Johnson pick her up and carry her into what had been, in former days, the dais-chamber; evidently he slept in there. He took off her cloak. Amanda wondered idly where her mother was. She felt Johnson fumble among her clothes, and was aware of pain increasing. 'I think the baby's coming,' she said. Dai was unbuttoning his trousers. The thought came to her dully that she was glad she had relieved herself with Letty at the inn.

'It is not yet, I tell you. I know about such things. Lie quiet.' But she had begun despite herself to sob and cry. She felt him enter her; but there was force already within her, thrusting downward. Her body had become a battlefield; she heard herself screaming. The pain became worse than any she had ever known, than any that could be imagined; and, in the end, the inner force won. There is one thing stronger than a thrusting male member; a child's emerging head. Dai swore, and withdrew. She heard him call out, at last fully aware of the situation.

'Amy! Amy! Come down, it is your little bitch back again with a baby coming.'

Amanda did not see her mother creep fearfully downstairs, and would hardly have recognised the thin defeated shadow she had become: these days, Dai Johnson blacked her eyes if she refused him money since their marriage. In the end Amy stood uselessly watching, wringing her hands and making small terrified noises. Johnson strode over and slapped her across the mouth.

'Get back to your own place, then, for all the good you are doing. I know what to do. I am one of nine of a family.' He rolled up his sleeves. In the rough way which was all he knew, he tried to do his best for Amanda, crying out as she was by now in labour on his bed; he would have done the same for any woman. No doubt he'd brought it on early: she hadn't been ready when she came. After the birth, in a day or two, he'd have her again.

In the end the child came out. Dai wiped its mouth and nose; he remembered doing the same when two of his sisters had been born, down in Newtown back street. He didn't need to slap the baby, it cried of itself. It was a boy, premature and small, no doubt with all the trouble. Dai wrapped it in a sheet, laid it aside and returned to Amanda. There were other things to be done; he remembered them through the accustomed haze of beer. Her lips were parted over her little white teeth, and she'd stopped yelling; that was something. That mother of hers was no manner of use. Dai pummelled knowledgeably, then realised that Amanda's eyes were partly open between the long lashes. Suddenly they widened and a look of gladness came into them the like of which he'd never seen; she raised a hand as if to welcome somebody at the door.

'Del,' she said, and then her eyes glazed over. Dai was touched: she'd said his name, after all, or what sounded like it. He could not believe at first, when he realised it, that she was dead; the birth had gone off all right; if a woman was going to die it was during the labour, or else in a day or two, of fever afterwards. There had been nothing wrong, he'd seen to everything he should: what had happened? A pretty thing, she'd been. It was a pity.

He turned away from her, and back to the new baby. What was any man to do, left with so small a creature? It would need feeding tomorrow. He had better send down to Marion at the inn. There was no need to explain anything to Marion; she'd take the whole matter in hand, including no doubt himself. The baby had red hair.

Letty Croom, on being informed some time later, refused to have the child at Fortune's Field, and nobody now questioned her authority in such matters. It was Amy's business, she said: but apart from having insisted that the boy be christened Augustus Tobias, Amy seemed beyond anything, completely subservient to her drunken and unsuitable Welsh husband. Nobody knew, or greatly cared, what happened over the next six or seven years, but by that time it was clear that Stephen was wholly inept and never likely to produce an heir by any wife. Victoria, having been properly brought up and with her mother's eye upon her, gave herself over to good works in the village. Old Tobias, whose wits were still as in former days, then took a hand. He had the urchin rescued from wherever he might be in Wales and brought at last before him. Augustus Tobias, still in process of losing his milk-teeth, had curly red hair, which identified him. His eyes were bright blue, an unusual circumstance: there had never been blue eyes in the family, and their oblique cast was almost foreign. However young Gus, small as he would always be, seemed able already to square his fists to defend himself, and knew a good deal of vituperative Welsh if little else. Tobias, diverted, hired him a tutor and put him down for Harrow; it was like backing a small spirited horse. The boy learned English rapidly and appeared apt at most things. Tobias then made a fresh will, the details of which likewise diverted him notably in their preparation. It was, almost, a case of history repeating itself, an interesting experiment at any time even if one cannot reasonably expect to live to see its results.

Tobias left the house at Fortune's Field, inasmuch as it would become his heritable property on Stephen's death, between Augustus Tobias, who was to inhabit the east end, and Henry, who was so often away at sea that nobody knew him very well. However two red-headed males, despite the slight disparity in ages, would in due course no doubt become like two rutting stags in season; a great pity oneself would in all probability no longer be there to watch. As regarded the considerable fortune he had meantime accrued by means of investments in Crowbetter's and elsewhere, Tobias left it to the first of the two young men who would contrive, before witnesses, to seduce the existing schoolmistress at Fortune's End. It would exercise both young men's ingenuity enough to enable whoever inherited the money to value it in a proper manner. Having signed the will and had it witnessed, Tobias closed his eyes, half remembering his own long-ago adventure among the bluebells and its manifold results. Gus was already acquainted with the Nether Wood: that was at least a beginning.

Paola, who had been left an annuity, came in then, and passed a hand over the still smooth forehead beneath the thick white hair. 'You are tired,' she said predictably. Tobias did not answer. It was not only that he had heard the remark already numberless times, but that he had happened, some moments before, to have died comfortably in his sleep. It was a pity – this was his last waking thought – that he had never after all become Lord Croom; in a little while, it might have happened, but Stephen was lasting longer than anyone expected. Paola drew the hooded lids now over the dead eyes. She then crossed herself, and went to inform Letty. That bitch could make arrangements for the funeral; she liked to interfere and could have the blinds drawn down and all the rest of it. Oneself was going home, as soon as possible, to Italy again after all these years, to the sun and laughter, and the trodden grape harvests.

Newport Borough Libraries

CENTRAL 12/94 .

Z023489